S.A.COSBY

BLACKTOP WASTELAND

HEADLINE

First published in the USA in 2020 by
Flatiron Books

First published in Great Britain in 2020 by
HEADLINE PUBLISHING GROUP

1

Cataloguing in Publication Data is available from the British Library

Hardback ISBN 978 1 4722 7371 0
Trade paperback ISBN 978 1 4722 7374 1

Offset in Sabon MT Std by Jouve (UK), Milton Keynes

Printed and bound in Great Britain by Clays Ltd, Elcograf S.p.A.

Headline's policy is to use papers that are natural, renewable and recyclable
products and made from wood grown in well-managed forests and other
controlled sources. The logging and manufacturing processes are expected
to conform to the environmental regulations of the country of origin.

HEADLINE PUBLISHING GROUP
An Hachette UK Company
Carmelite House
50 Victoria Embankment
London EC4Y 0DZ

www.headline.co.uk
www.hachette.co.uk

For my father, Roy Cosby

*Your reach sometimes exceeded your
grasp, but once you got a hold of that
steering wheel, you drove it like you stole it.*

Ride on, wild man. Ride on.

*A father is a man who expects his son
to be as good a man as he was meant
to be.*

FRANK A. CLARK

BLACKTOP
WASTELAND

ONE

Beauregard thought the night sky looked like a painting.

Laughter filled the air only to be drowned out by a cacophony of revving engines as the moon slid from behind the clouds. The bass from the sound system in a nearby Chevelle was hitting him in his chest so hard, it felt like someone was performing CPR on him. There were about a dozen other late-model cars parked haphazardly in front of the old convenience store. In addition to the Chevelle, there was a Maverick, two Impalas, a few Camaros and five or six more examples of the heyday of American muscle. The air was cool and filled with the scent of gas and oil. The rich, acrid smell of exhaust fumes and burnt rubber. A choir of crickets and whippoorwills tried in vain to be heard. Beauregard closed his eyes and strained his ears. He could hear them but just barely. They were screaming for love. He thought a lot of people spent a large part of their life doing the same thing.

The wind caught the sign hanging above his head from the arm of a pole that extended twenty feet into the air. It creaked as the breeze moved it back and forth.

CARTER SPEEDE MART the sign proclaimed in big black letters set against a white background. The sign was beginning to yellow with age. The letters were worn and chipped. The cheap paint flaking away like dried skin. The second "E" had disappeared from the word

"SPEEDEE." Beauregard wondered what had happened to Carter. He wondered if he had disappeared too.

"Ain't none of y'all motherfuckers ready for the legendary Olds! Y'all might as well go on back home to your ugly wives and try and get some Tuesday night pussy. For real though, y'all ain't got nothing for the legendary Olds! She does 60 in second. Five hundred dollars line to line. Huh? Y'all mighty quiet. Come on, the Olds done sent many a boy home with his pockets lighter. I done outrun more cops than the Duke boys in the Olds! You ain't just beating the Olds, home-boy!" a guy named Warren Crocker crowed. He was strutting around his '76 Oldsmobile Cutlass. It was a beautiful car. A dark green body with chrome Mag rims and chrome trim that ran across its surface like liquid lightning. Smoked-out glass and LED lights emitted an ethereal bluish glow like some bioluminescent sea creature.

Beauregard leaned against his Duster as Warren pontificated about the invincibility of the Oldsmobile. Beauregard let him talk. Talk didn't mean anything. Talk didn't drive the car. Talk was just noise. He had $1,000 in his pocket. It was all the profits from the last two weeks at the garage after most of the bills had been paid. He was $800 short on the rent for the building that housed his business. It had come down to a choice between the rent or glasses for his young-est. Which wasn't really a choice at all. So, he had reached out to his cousin Kelvin and asked him to find out where the nearest street race was being held. Kelvin still knew some guys who knew some guys who knew where the money races could be found.

That was how they found themselves just outside of Dinwiddie County ten miles from the fairgrounds where legally sanctioned drag races were held. Beauregard closed his eyes again. He listened to Warren's car idle. Under the sound of the boasting and dick swing-ing, Beau heard an unmistakable ticking.

Warren had a bad valve in his engine. That left two possibilities. He knew about it but thought it was an acceptable defect that could be overcome by the sheer power of his motor. Maybe he had a nitrous boost on it and didn't care about one funky valve. Or he didn't know it was bad and was just talking a lot of shit.

Beau nodded at Kelvin. His cousin had been milling through the crowd, trying to drum up a big money race. There had already been four contests, but no one was willing to put up more than $200. That wasn't gonna cut it. Beau needed at least a $1,000 bet. He needed someone who would look at the Duster and see an easy payday. Look at its stripped-down exterior and assume it was a pushover.

He needed an asshole like Warren Crocker.

Crocker had already won one race, but that had taken place before Beauregard and Kelvin arrived. Ideally, he would have liked to watch the man drive before he made the bet. See how he handled the wheel. How he navigated the cracked asphalt on this stretch of Route 83. But beggars can't be choosers. It had taken them an hour and a half to get out here, but they had come because Beauregard knew no one in Red Hill County would race him. Not in the Duster.

Kelvin moved in front of Warren as he was preening around his car. "My man over there got ten friends that say he can be doing 70 in second while you still trying to drag your ass out of first," he said. He let his booming voice fill the night. All the chatter ceased. The crickets and the whippoorwills were working themselves into a frenzy.

"Or is all you do is talk?" Beauregard asked.

"Oooooh shit," someone from the crowd that had gathered said. Warren stopped strutting and leaned on the roof of his car. He was tall and thin. His dark skin appeared blue in the glow of the moonlight.

"Well, that's a bold statement, motherfucker. You got the paper to back it up?" he said.

Beauregard pulled his wallet out and fanned ten $100 bills out like a deck of cards in his large hands.

"The question is, do you have the balls to back it up?" Kelvin said. He sounded like a Quiet Storm DJ. He grinned like a lunatic at Warren Crocker. Crocker tucked his tongue into the inside of his cheek.

Seconds ticked by and Beauregard felt a hollow opening blossom in his chest. He could see the gears working in Warren's head and for a moment he thought he was gonna pass. But Beauregard knew he wouldn't. How could he? He had talked himself into a corner and his pride wouldn't let him back down. Besides, the Duster didn't look that impressive. It was clean, and the body was free of rust, but the red candy apple paint was not showroom ready and the leather seats had a few rips and cracks.

"Alright. From here to the oak tree that's split down the middle. Sherm can hold the money. Unless you want to go for pinks?" Warren said.

"No. Let him hold the money. Who you want to call it?" Beauregard asked.

Sherm nodded at another guy. "Me and Jaymie will call it. You want your boy to go too?" he said. He squeaked when he talked.

"Yeah," Beauregard said. Kelvin, Sherm and Jaymie hopped in Sherm's car. A primer-covered Nova. They took off for the split tree a quarter mile down the road. Beauregard hadn't seen any other drivers since they arrived. Most people avoided this stretch and used the four-lane highway that snaked its way from the interstate up through Shepherd's Corner proper. Progress had left this part of town behind. It was abandoned just like the store. A blacktop wasteland haunted by the phantoms of the past.

He turned and got in the Duster. When he started the car, the engine sounded like a pride of angry lions. Vibrations traveled up from the motor through the steering wheel. He tapped the gas a few times. The lions became dragons. He flicked on the headlights. The double yellow line down the middle of the road came alive. He grabbed the gearshift and put it into first. Warren pulled out of the parking lot and Beauregard took a position next to him. One of the other guys that was in the crowd walked up and stood between them. He held his arm up and reached for the sky. Beauregard glanced at the stars and the moon again. Out of the corner of his eye, he saw Warren put on a seat belt. The Duster didn't have seat belts. His father used to say if they ever wrecked the only thing seat belts would do was make it hard for the undertaker to get them out the car.

"You ready?" the guy standing between them yelled.

Warren gave him a thumbs-up.

Beauregard nodded.

"ONE, TWO . . . THREE!" the guy screamed.

The secret ain't about the motor. That's part of it, yeah, but that ain't the main thing. The real thing, the thing most people don't want to talk about, is how you drive. If you drive like you scared, you gonna lose. If you drive like you don't want to have to rebuild the whole engine, you gonna lose. You gotta drive like don't nothing else matter except getting to that line. Drive like you fucking stole it.

Beauregard heard his Daddy's voice every time he drove the Duster. Sometimes he heard it when he was driving for crews. In those moments, it offered him bitter pearls of wisdom. Nonsensical chatter that reminded him not to end up like his Daddy. A ghost without a grave.

Beauregard slammed the gas pedal to the floor. Wheels spun, and white smoke plumed up from the rear of the Duster. G-forces pressed against his chest, crushing his sternum. Warren's car jumped off the line and the front two wheels left the road. Beauregard jammed the car into second as the Duster's front wheels grabbed the road like a pair of eagle's talons.

The trees on both sides of the road were shimmering blurs as he tore down through the night. He glanced at the speedometer. 70 mph.

Beauregard hit the clutch and shifted into third. There were no numbers on the gearshift knob. It was an old 8-ball his Daddy had fixed to fit on top of the shifter. He didn't need numbers. He knew what gear he was in by feel. By sound. The car shivered like a wolf shaking its pelt.

90 mph.

The leather-covered steering wheel crackled in his grip. He could see Sherm's car up ahead idling on the side of the road. He shifted into fourth gear. The motor went from a roar to the war cry of a god. The duals were the trumpets that heralded his arrival. He had the pedal flat against the floorboard. The car seemed to contort itself and leap forward like a snake about to strike. The speedometer hit 105 mph.

The Duster had passed Warren like he was mired in glue. The old bisected oak tree was rapidly receding in his side mirror. He could see Kelvin pumping both his fists in the rearview mirror. Beauregard popped the clutch and downshifted until he was back in first. He slowed down even more, executed a three-point turn and headed back to the old convenience store.

Beauregard pulled back into the parking lot with Warren right on his heels. A few minutes behind him were Sherm, Kelvin and Jaymie. Beauregard got out, walked around to the front of the car and leaned back against the hood.

"That old Duster got some get-up-and-go!" said a heavyset brother with a wide nose and beads of sweat gathering on his forehead. He was leaning against a black and white Maverick, Ford's answer to the Duster.

"Thanks," Beauregard said.

Sherm, Jaymie and Kelvin got out of the Nova. Kelvin trotted over to the Duster and held out his left hand. Beauregard slapped the palm without looking.

"You whupped his ass like a runaway slave," Kelvin said. A deep laugh erupted from his chest.

"That bad valve fucked him up. Look at that exhaust. He's burning oil," Beauregard said. A plume of black smoke was trailing from the exhaust of the Olds. Sherm came over and handed Beauregard two wads of money. His original thousand and Warren's roll.

"What you got under the hood on that thing?" Sherm asked.

"Two rockets and a comet," Kelvin said. Sherm chuckled.

Warren finally got out of the Oldsmobile. He stood by the car with his arms crossed. His face was twisted into a snarl. "You giving him my money after he jumped off the line?" he asked.

The boisterous crowd became deathly quiet. Beauregard didn't move off the hood, didn't look at Warren. His voice cut through the night like a razor.

"You saying I cheated?"

Warren uncrossed his arms, then crossed them again. He swiveled his large head on his thin neck.

"I'm just saying you was two lengths ahead before he got to three. That's all I'm saying," Warren said. He put his hands in the pockets of his baggy jeans. Then he took them out again. He didn't seem to know where to put them. His initial bravado was evaporating.

"I ain't gotta cheat to beat you. By the sound of that leaky valve, your motor gonna seize up tighter than virgin pussy any day now. Your driveshaft and rear end too heavy. That's why you pop up when you take off," Beauregard said. He pushed off the hood and turned to face Warren. Warren was peering at the night sky. He was studying his feet. He was doing everything except looking at Beauregard.

"Yo, man, you lost. Just take the L and admit the Olds ain't as legendary as you thought," Kelvin said. This elicited a few guffaws from the crowd. Warren shifted on the balls of his feet. Beauregard closed the distance between them in three strides.

"So why don't you tell me how I cheated again," he said.

Warren licked his lips. Beauregard wasn't as tall as he was, but he was twice as wide. All broad shoulders and wiry muscle. Warren took a step back. "I'm just saying," he said. His voice was as thin as crepe paper.

"You just saying. You just saying but you ain't saying shit," Beauregard said. Kelvin got between them.

"Come on, Bug, let's go. We got our money," he said.

"Not until he takes it back," Beauregard said. A few other drivers had crowded around them. Kelvin thought they were two seconds away from chanting "Fight! Fight!" like they were back in school.

"Yo, man, take it back," Kelvin said.

Warren twisted his head left and right. He wouldn't look directly at Beauregard or the crowd gathering around them. "Look, maybe I was wrong. I'm just saying—" he started to say but Beauregard held up his hand. Warren's mouth closed with an audible plop.

"Don't say 'you just saying' again. And don't say you was wrong. Take. It. Back," Beauregard said.

"Don't let him punk you, man!" someone yelled from the crowd.

Kelvin turned and faced Warren. He spoke in low tones. "Don't let these boys get your face fucked up. My cousin takes this shit seriously. Take it back and you can go home with all your teeth."

Beauregard had his hands down by his sides. He clenched and unclenched them at steady intervals. He watched Warren's eyes. They kept peering around like he was looking for a way out that didn't entail taking back what he said. Beauregard knew he wasn't going to take it back. He couldn't. Guys like Warren fed off their own arrogance. It was like oxygen for them. They couldn't back down any more than they could stop breathing.

Headlights lit up the parking lot. Then blue lights flashed off the weathered exterior of the SpeeDee Mart.

"Ah shit, it's the sex lights," Kelvin said. Beauregard saw a red unmarked cop car parking diagonally across the SpeeDee Mart exit. A few guys were walking slowly toward their cars. Most of them were just standing still.

"Sex lights?" the sweaty brother said.

"Yeah, cuz when you see them, you're fucked," Kelvin said. Two deputies got out of the car and pulled out their flashlights. Beauregard held up his hand to shield his eyes.

"So, what we got here, fellas? A little night racing? But I don't see no NASCAR signs. You see any NASCAR signs, Deputy Hall?" the deputy that wasn't Hall said. He was a blondish white guy with a chin so square he probably had to study geometry to learn how to shave.

"Nah, Deputy Jones, I don't see no NASCAR signs. Why don't you boys get out your IDs and have a seat on the pavement here?" Deputy Hall said.

"We ain't doing nothing but parking here, officer," the sweaty brother said. Deputy Jones whirled around. He dropped his hand to his gun.

"Did I ask you a goddamn thing? Get your ass on the ground. All of you get out your IDs and get on the ground." There were about twenty of them in the crowd and about fifteen cars. But they were all black and the two cops were white, and had guns. Everyone pulled out their wallets and sat down on the pavement. Beauregard sat on a sprig of scrub grass that had broken through the concrete. He grabbed his driver's license out of his wallet. The cops started at opposite ends and worked their way to the middle of the group.

"Anybody got any warrants? Child support, assault, shoplifting?" Deputy Hall asked. Beauregard tried to see what county they were from, but they kept the light in his eyes. Deputy Jones stopped in front of him.

"You got any warrants?" he asked as he took Beauregard's license.
"No."

Deputy Jones shined the flashlight on Beauregard's license. There was a patch on the deputy's shoulder that said POLICE.

"What county you from?" Beauregard asked. Deputy Jones shone the flashlight's beam in Beauregard's face.

"Fuck You County, population of one," Deputy Jones said. He handed Beauregard his license. He turned and spoke into the radio on his shoulder. Deputy Hall was doing the same thing. The whip-poorwills and frogs and crickets had resumed their concert. Minutes ticked by as the two deputies conferred with whoever was on the other end of their radios.

"Alright, fellas, here's the deal. Some of you got warrants. Some of you don't. But that don't matter. We don't need y'all tearing up and down our roads here in Shepherd's Corner. So, we're gonna let you go on down the road. But to discourage you from coming back, we gonna get you to pay the racing tax," Deputy Hall said.

"What the hell is a racing tax?" the sweaty brother asked. Deputy Jones pulled out his gun and put the barrel against the sweaty brother's cheek. Beauregard felt his stomach tighten.

"Everything in your wallet, fat boy. Or do you want to be a victim of police brutality?" Deputy Jones asked.

"You heard the man. Empty your pockets, gents," Deputy Hall said. A soft breeze began to blow. The wind caressed Beauregard's face. The scent of honeysuckle traveled on that breeze. The deputies filed up and down the men sitting in a row and grabbed the money out of their hands. Deputy Jones came to Beauregard.

"Empty those pockets, son."

Beauregard looked up at him. "Take me in. Arrest me. But I ain't giving you my money."

Deputy Jones put his gun against Beauregard's cheek. The harsh smell of gun oil wafted up his nose and stuck to the back of his throat.

"Maybe you didn't hear what I said to your friend over there."

"He ain't my friend," Beauregard said.

"You want to catch a bullet? You trying to commit suicide by cop?" Deputy Jones said. His eyes glistened in the moonlight.

"No. I just ain't giving you my money," Beauregard said.

"Bug, let it go," Kelvin said. Deputy Jones shot him a glance. He pointed his gun at Kelvin.

"He's your friend, isn't he? You should listen, Bug," Deputy Jones said. He grinned, exposing a row of crooked brown teeth. Beauregard pulled out his roll of money and the one he had won from Warren. Deputy Jones snatched them out of his hands.

"Good boy," Deputy Jones said.

"Alright, fellas, go on and get out of here. And don't come back to

Shepherd's Corner," Deputy Hall said. Beauregard and Kelvin got up. The crowd dispersed amid a smattering of muffled complaints. The night was filled with the howl of Chargers and Chevelles and Mustangs and Impalas coming to life. Kelvin and Beauregard climbed into the Duster. The cops had moved, and cars were leaving as fast as they legally could. Warren was sitting in the Olds staring straight ahead.

"Move along, Warren," Deputy Hall said.

Warren rubbed his hands across his face. "It won't start," he mumbled.

"What?" Deputy Hall said.

Warren's hands flew away from his face. "It won't start!" he said. Kelvin laughed as he and Beauregard pulled out of the parking lot.

Beauregard turned left and headed down the narrow road.

"Interstate is that way," Kelvin said.

"Yeah. The town is this way. So are the bars," Beauregard said.

"How we getting a drink with no money?" Kelvin said.

Beauregard stopped and backed the Duster into the entrance of an old logging road. He killed the lights and let the car idle.

"Those weren't real cops. They didn't have no county insignia on their uniforms. And that gun was a .38. Cops haven't carried .38s for twenty fucking years. And they knew his name," Beauregard said.

"Motherfucker. We got played," Kelvin said. He punched the dashboard. Beauregard glared at him. Kelvin ran his hand over the dash, smoothing down the leather. "Shit, sorry, man. So, what we doing here?"

"Warren said his car wouldn't start. He the only one that stayed behind," Beauregard said.

"You think he was the snitch?"

"Ain't no snitch. He in with them. He stayed behind to get his cut. None of us was from here that was racing. I'm thinking somebody like Warren gonna want a drink to celebrate," Beauregard said.

"All that shit he was saying about you cheating was just a show."

Beauregard nodded. "Didn't want me to leave. Give his crew time to get there. He ran a few races to get people in. Probably was checking for how much money was on the table. Then when I dropped that grip, he texted them."

"Son of a bitch. Huh. Dr. King would be so proud. Whites and blacks working together," Kelvin said.

"Yeah," Beauregard said.

"You think he really coming this way? I mean he can't be that stupid, can he?" Kelvin asked.

Beauregard didn't speak. He drummed his fingers on the steering wheel. He figured not everything Warren had said and done was for show. He really was a conceited ass. Guys like that never think they can get caught. They always think they're one step ahead of everyone.

"I used to run into guys like him when I was driving for crews. He ain't from around here. He sounds like he from somewhere north of Richmond. Maybe Alexandria. Guys like that can't wait till they get home to celebrate. And he wants to celebrate. Cuz he thinks he won. He thinks he fooled us good. He wants to get to the nearest place that sells alcohol and get his drink on. He'll be by himself cuz his partners can't go walking around in their fake uniforms. He'll be in there talking big shit like he was before. He can't help himself."

"You really think so, don't you?" Kelvin said. Beauregard didn't answer. He couldn't go home without that money. A thousand wasn't enough to pay the rent but it beat a blank. His instincts told him that Warren was gonna go into town and get his drink on. He trusted his instincts. He had to.

Minutes ticked by and Kelvin checked his watch.

"Man, I don't think he—" Kelvin started to say. A car shot past them. A bright green paint job that sparkled in the moonlight.

"The legendary Olds," Beauregard said. He pulled out behind the Oldsmobile. They followed him through the flat plains and the gentle slopes of slight hills. The moonlight gave way to porch lamps and landscape lighting as they passed single-story houses and mobile homes. They sailed through a curve so sharp it could slice cheese and downtown Shepherd's Corner came into view. A collection of drab concrete and brick buildings illuminated by pale streetlamps. A library, a pharmacy and a restaurant lined the street. Near the end of the sidewalk was a wide brick building with a sign over the front door that said DINO'S BAR AND GRILL.

Warren turned right and drove around to the back of Dino's. Beauregard parked the Duster on the street. He reached into the back seat and grabbed a crescent wrench. No one was on the sidewalk or loitering outside Dino's front door. There were a few cars in front of the Duster. The deep tribal thump of a hip-hop beat seeped through Dino's walls.

"Stay here. You see anybody coming, hit the horn," Beauregard said.

"Don't kill him, man," Kelvin said. Beauregard didn't make any promises. He got out and hurried down the sidewalk and across Dino's parking lot. He stopped at the back corner of the building. Peeping around the corner he saw Warren standing next to the Oldsmobile. He was taking a piss. Beauregard ran across the parking lot. His footsteps were hidden by the music coming from the bar.

Warren started to turn just as Beauregard hit him with the wrench. He slammed the tool into Warren's trapezius muscle. Beauregard heard a wet crack like when his grandfather would snap chicken wings at the dinner table. Warren crumpled to the ground as piss sprayed across the side of the Oldsmobile. He rolled onto his side and Beauregard hit him again in his ribs. Warren rolled onto his back. A trickle of blood flowed out of his mouth and down his chin. Beauregard knelt beside him. He took the wrench and laid it across Warren's mouth like a gag. He gripped both ends of it and pressed down with all his weight. Warren's tongue squirmed around the handle of the wrench like a plump pink worm. Blood and spit ran from the sides of his mouth down his cheeks.

"I know you got my money. I know you and them rent-a-cops was working together. Y'all travel around setting up races and pop the fools who show up. None of that matters to me. I know you got my money. Now I'm going to move this wrench, and if you say anything about anything other than my money, I'm going to break your jaw in seven places," Beauregard said. He didn't yell, and he didn't scream. He straightened up and moved the wrench. Warren coughed and turned his head to the side. He spit a globule of pinkish saliva and it landed on his chin. He took a few deep gasps and more blood-spit flowed across his chin.

"My back pocket," he wheezed. Beauregard rolled him over and Warren wailed. It was a high animalistic moan. Beauregard thought he could hear the soft clicking of his shattered clavicle bones rubbing together. He pulled out a wad of cash. He flipped through it quickly.

"There's only 750. Where's my thousand? Where's yours? Where's the rest?" Beauregard asked.

"My . . . . mine was a dummy roll," Warren said.

"This is your cut," Beauregard said. Warren nodded weakly. Beauregard sucked his teeth. He stood and pocketed the money. Warren closed his eyes and swallowed hard.

Beauregard put the wrench in his back pocket and stomped on Warren's right ankle right at the joint. Warren screamed but there was no one around to hear except for Beauregard.

"Take it back," Beauregard said.

"What . . . what the fuck, man, you broke my fucking ankle."

"Take it back or I'll break the other one."

Warren rolled onto his back again. Beauregard saw dark patches that spread from his crotch to his knees. His dick was still hanging out of his pants like a bloodworm. The smell of piss wafted up Beauregard's nose.

"I take it back. You not a cheater, okay? Fuck, you not a cheater," he said. Beauregard saw tears slip from the corners of Warren's eyes.

"Alright then," Beauregard said. He nodded his head then turned and walked back to the Duster.

TWO

The motion-activated lights on the roof of the garage flicked on as Beauregard pulled up in front of the building. He stopped and let Kelvin hop out of the Duster to open one of the three roll-up doors. Beauregard swung the car around and backed it into the garage. Echoes from the motor reverberated through the cavernous interior. Beauregard shut off the car. He ran his wide, thick-fingered hands over his face. He twisted around in his seat and grabbed the wrench off the back seat. It still had Warren's blood and a bit of his skin on it. He'd have to soak it in water and bleach before putting it back in his toolbox.

He got out and headed for the office. A pale blue light flashed overhead from a flickering fluorescent fixture. He went to a mini-fridge behind his desk and grabbed two beers. He dropped the wrench on the desk. The sound of metal against metal clanged against his ears. Kelvin came in and sat down in a folding chair in front of the desk. Beauregard tossed him a beer. They opened them in unison and raised their bottles. Beauregard killed most of his beer in one loud gulp. Kelvin sipped his twice before putting it on the desk.

"Guess I'm gonna have to cuss Jerome the fuck out," Kelvin said. Beauregard finished his beer.

"Nah. It ain't his fault. Them boys probably go up and down the East Coast doing this shit," he said.

"It's still fucked up, though. I can ask around again. Maybe down in Raleigh? Or Charlotte?" Kelvin asked.

Beauregard shook his head. He finished his beer and tossed it in the trash can. "You know I can't go that far out. Not for some maybe money. Anyway, the rent is due by the twenty-third. I didn't really want to ask Phil for another extension. Not getting that contract with Davidson's construction company really put us in a bad spot," Beauregard said.

Kelvin sipped his beer. "You thought about talking to Boonie?" he asked.

Beauregard fell into his swivel chair. He put his boots up on the desk. "I've thought about it," he said.

Kelvin finished his beer. "All I'm saying is we been open three years and then Precision comes along and it's like people forgot we was here. Maybe Red Hill ain't big enough for two mechanic shops. Or at least not a black one," he said.

"I don't know. We was in the running for that Davidson's contract. Twenty years ago, we wouldn't even have been in the goddamn conversation. I just couldn't go as low as Precision," Beauregard said.

"That's why I'm saying you might want to talk to Boonie. Nothing too big. Just something to keep us afloat until . . . I don't know, until more people move to Red Hill who don't know how to change their oil," Kelvin said.

Beauregard picked up the wrench. He grabbed a rag from the pile sitting in a plastic bin next to his desk and began wiping the blood off it.

"I said I'm thinking about it."

"Alright, well, I'm gonna get up the road. Christy is off tonight and since Sasha is working I'm gonna go by and say heyyyyy," he said, singing the word "hey" until he hit a falsetto.

Beauregard smirked. "One of them girls is gonna cut your thing off and mail it to you," he said.

"Man, whatever. They gonna dip it in bronze and put that thing on a pedestal," Kelvin said as he rose from his chair. "Catch you in the morning?"

"Yeah," Beauregard said. He set the wrench down again. Kelvin gave him a two-finger salute and left through the office door. Beau-regard swung around and planted his feet on the floor. 750. That was worse than having a grand. That's not even considering the gas it took to get out to Shepherd's Corner. Phil Dormer had told him last month that he wouldn't be able to give him another extension.

"Beau, I know times are tight right now. I get it. But my boss has told me we can't extend you any more credit or time on this loan. Look, maybe we can refinance it—"

"I'm only one year away from paying it off," Beauregard said. Phil frowned.

"Well, that's true but you're also technically three months behind. And per your loan agreement once you're 120 days behind the loan becomes delinquent. I don't want that to happen, Beau. Refinance and you'll have more years, but you won't lose the building," Phil had said. Beauregard heard what he was saying. He saw the pained look on his face. And in a perfect world, he would have believed that Phil really was concerned about his livelihood. The world was far from perfect. Beauregard knew that Phil was saying all the right words. He also knew that the lot he sat on was right next to a devel-opment. They were building Red Hill's first fast food restaurant. The old Tastee Freez didn't count. They had closed ten years ago. They were never fast but they had made one hell of a milkshake.

Beauregard got up and put the keys to the Duster on the hook in the corkboard and grabbed the keys to his truck. He locked up the garage and headed home.

The sun was just peeking over the horizon as he backed into the street. Beauregard drove past the municipal offices of Red Hill County out to the wide-open fields. He always thought it was funny a county with "hill" in its name had a terrible paucity of actual hills. He passed Grove Lane. His daughter lived down there. The sky was streaked with gold and red as he turned down Market Drive. Two more turns down two more side roads and he was pulling down the dirt lane to his double-wide.

Beauregard parked next to Kia's little blue two-door Honda. He never drove the thing, he just kept it running. He was an American Muscle kind of guy. The house was quiet as he stepped up onto the porch. He made his way through the rectangular house, passing the room where his sons slept. The sun spilled through the blinds as rays of light filled the double-wide. His and Kia's room was at the end of the trailer. Beauregard slipped into the room and sat down on the foot of their bed. Kia was sprawled across it like a piece of origami art. Beauregard touched her soft, exposed thigh. Her caramel-colored leg twitched. She didn't turn over but spoke to him with her face still buried in her pillow.

"How'd it go?" she mumbled into the pillow.

"I won but the guy didn't want to pay. It got a little messy."

She turned over then. "What you mean he ain't wanna pay? What kind of shit is that?" she asked.

She was propped up on one elbow. The sheet that had barely covered her had fallen away. Her hair was sticking off her head in strange geometric patterns. Beauregard kneaded the flesh on her thigh.

"You didn't get arrested, did you?" she asked.

Yeah, by some fake-ass cops, he thought.

He took his hand off her leg. "No, but the guy, he didn't have all the money he said he had. The whole thing was messed up. I'm still 800 short," he said. He let it sit there between them for a while. Kia pulled the sheet up and drew her knees up to her chest.

"What about that contract to work on them trucks from the construction company?" she asked. Beauregard moved closer to her. His shoulder brushed against hers.

"We didn't get it. Precision got the contract. And then we had to get those glasses for Darren. And last month I had to give Janice money for Ariel's cap and gown. It's been a slow couple of months," Beauregard said. Actually, it had been a slow year. Kia knew this, but neither one of them liked saying it out loud.

"Can we get an extension?" she asked. Beauregard stretched out beside her. She didn't lie back but instead wrapped her arms around her knees and squeezed them. Beauregard stared up at the ceiling. The fan spun on a shaky axis. The globe on the light of the ceiling fan had the image of a Rottweiler.

They'd had that damn fan for five years and it never failed to give him the creeps. But Kia loved the damn thing. One thing he'd learned about marriage was that a novelty fan was not the hill you wanted to die on if you could help it.

"I don't know," he said. She ran a hand through her tousled hair. A few minutes went by and then she lay back against Beauregard. Her skin was cool to the touch and smelled like roses. She had showered before bed. He snaked one arm around her midsection and laid his hand on her belly.

"What if we can't get an extension?" Kia asked.

Beauregard stroked her belly. "I might have to sell something. Maybe the hydraulic lift. Or the second tire-changing machine. Which is why I got the damn loan in the first place," he said. He didn't mention going to talk to his Uncle Boonie.

Almost as if on cue, Kia turned on her side and touched his face.

"You thinking about it, ain't you?" she asked.

"Thinking about what?"

"Going to Boonie. Looking for a job. You know that's not an option, right? You were blessed. We all was. You never got caught and you got out and you opened the garage. That's a blessing, baby," she said. Her light eyes searched his dark ones. They'd been together since he was nineteen and she was eighteen. Married since they both were twenty-three. Almost fifteen years together. She knew him about as well as anyone did.

A lot of couples liked to say they couldn't lie to each other. That their partner could spot their falsehoods from a mile away. That line of thinking was a one-way street between him and Kia. He knew when she had gone out drinking with her girls. He knew when she had eaten the last chocolate chip cookie. Her face was an open book and he had read every page a long time ago. He hated lying to her, but the ease with which he could do it never failed to shock him. Then again, he did have a lot of practice with mendacity.

"No. I'm not thinking of it. Did it cross my mind? Yeah. Just like buying a lottery ticket crossed my mind," he said. He hugged her close to him and closed his eyes.

"It's gonna be alright. I'll figure out something," he said.

"I got a call from the dentist yesterday. Javon might need braces," she said. Beauregard squeezed her tight but didn't say anything.

"What are we gonna do, baby? I can try to pick up some extra shifts at the hotel," she said.

"That ain't gonna buy braces," he said. Silence enveloped them both. Then Kia cleared her throat.

"You know you could sell—" But Beauregard cut her off midsentence.

"The Duster ain't for sale," he said. Kia laid her head on his chest. He slipped his arm around her shoulders and watched the blades on the ceiling fan spin until he drifted off to sleep.

"Daddy. Daddy. Daddy."

Beauregard opened his eyes. It seemed like he had just closed them five seconds ago. Darren was standing by the bed. He was holding his favorite toy. A twelve-inch-tall Batman action figure. His tiny brown hand gripped the Caped Crusader in one hand and a rapidly disintegrating biscuit in the other.

"Hey, Stink," Beauregard said. His youngest got Kia's eyes and his complexion. Powerful green eyes that contrasted with his dark chocolate skin.

"Mama say come get your food before she gotta take us to Aunt Jean," Darren said. A smile flickered across his lips. Beauregard figured Kia had used colorful language when she had instructed Darren to wake him. Whenever anyone cursed, Darren was overcome with the giggles. They didn't subside quickly either. Judging by the slight grin on his son's face, Kia had probably cussed him out nearly an hour ago.

"I guess I better get my ass up then," Beauregard said. Darren exploded in a shower of giggles. Beauregard hopped out of bed and grabbed Darren around the waist. He hoisted the boy off the ground and headed for the kitchen, making airplane noises as he went.

"Bout time you get your ass up," Kia said, but there was no malice behind it. It was more for Darren's benefit than anything else. Darren howled with laughter again.

"Oooooh, you said bad words," Darren whimpered between deep breaths. "You going down there!" he exclaimed. Javon was sitting at the small table, lost in his ear buds. Beauregard thought Javon could have passed for his twin when he was that age. Slim and tall with sleepy eyes. He put Darren down and gently plucked Javon on the ear. Javon snapped his head up and pulled out his ear buds.

"Good morning to you too," Beauregard said.

"Y'all finish your biscuits so we can go to Aunt Jean's," Kia said. Beauregard grabbed a biscuit and dipped it in the gravy that was in a bowl on the table. He plopped the whole thing in his mouth.

"I knew I married you for some reason," he said through a mouthful of bread. Kia snorted.

"It wasn't the biscuits," she said as she slipped by him to put her plate in the sink. He saw her in his mind as the young girl she had been when they first met. She had been dancing on the hood of Kelvin's car to a funky go-go song. Her wild hair in braids and wearing a black jumper with a white T-shirt. They had all been hanging out at the basketball court in the park near the high school. He had been a teenage ex–juvenile detainee with a two-year-old daughter. She had been an eighteen-year-old high school senior. Three weeks later, they were exchanging promise rings. Four years later, they were married and expecting Javon.

"Can I go to the shop with you today?" Javon asked. Beauregard and Kia exchanged a glance.

"Not today," Beauregard said. A long time ago, when he had worked in a different industry, he had taken great pains to make sure his private and professional lives never shared the same space. He didn't want that world to touch his family. He didn't want it to sully them with its filth. He was three years removed from that place, but he knew it still had teeth. He didn't want it to reach out and bite his boys or Kia. He kept them away from the shop just in case someone from that world came knocking.

Javon popped in his ear buds and got up from the table. He went and stood by the door. Beauregard knew the boy wanted to hang out with him. He liked cars and he was good with his hands. He hoped Javon would still be interested in cars by the time it was safe enough for him to come by the garage.

"Come on, Darren, let's go," Kia said. She stood on her tiptoes and kissed Beauregard on the lips. He could taste peppermint on her breath. He slipped an arm around her waist and returned her kiss tenfold.

"Eww," Darren said. He stuck his tongue out and rolled his eyes.

"Watch your mouth, boy," Kia said after she had pulled away from Beauregard.

"I'll call you on your lunch break," Beauregard said.

"You better," she said. She and the boys left. School was out, and Kia worked the ten-to-six shift at the Comfort Inn over in Gloucester. Javon wasn't quite old enough to watch out for himself and his little brother, so while Beauregard and Kia were working, she took the boys to her sister's place. Jean Brooks ran a hair salon from the back of her house. The boys got to play with their cousins the way Beauregard used to play with Kelvin and his brother Kaden at his Aunt Mara's house. Kaden had been dead for seven years. He'd been murdered when he was just twenty-three years old in a motel robbery. Word on the street had been that it had been a setup. Kaden and his buddy had been lured to a motel in Church Hill by some party girls they had met in the club. Church Hill was one of the roughest neighborhoods in the city of Richmond. It was so bad the postal service had stopped delivering mail there. They had gone there expecting some casual sex and some bomb-ass weed. What they had gotten were two bullets to the head and a closed-casket funeral.

When Kelvin and Beauregard had found the two guys that had popped Kaden and his friend, they had tried to shift blame to the girls. Then they had blamed each other. Finally, they had cried for their mothers.

Beauregard slipped out of his underwear and padded down to the bathroom. He was going to take a shower and head to the garage after making a few stops. As he turned on the water, he heard a chirping coming from the bedroom. It was his cell phone. Kia had taken it out of his pants and put it on the nightstand. He ran to the room and picked it up off the nightstand's scarred surface. He recognized the number.

"Hello," he said.

"Hello, is this Mr. Beauregard Montage?" a slightly nasal voice asked.

"Yes, it is, Mrs. Talbot," he said.

"Hello, Mr. Montage. It's Gloria Talbot at Lake Castor Convalescent Home," she said.

"I know," Beauregard said.

"Oh yes, I'm sorry. Mr. Montage, I'm afraid we have a problem with your mother," Mrs. Talbot said.

"Has she verbally abused another aide?" he asked.

"No, it's—"

"Has she peed on someone on purpose again?" he asked.

"No, it's nothing like—"

"Did she call 10 On Your Side again and tell them the staff was beating her?" he asked.

"No, no, Mr. Montage, it's not her behavior . . . this time. It appears there is a problem with her Medicaid paperwork. We were hoping you could come by in the next few days to discuss it," Mrs. Talbot said.

"What kind of problem?"

"I think it's best if we discuss it face to face, Mr. Montage."

Beauregard closed his eyes and took a deep breath.

"Okay, I can come in a few hours," he said.

"That would be fine, Mr. Montage. We will see you then. Goodbye," Mrs. Talbot said. The line went dead.

After his shower, he put on fresh jeans and a button-down short-sleeve shirt with his name over the breast pocket and MONTAGE MOTORS over the other. He made himself a cup of coffee and stood in front of the sink taking quick sips. The house was as quiet as it ever got. Through the window over the sink he could see his backyard. A wooden shed to the right and a basketball hoop to the left. Their property went back into the woods for nearly two hundred yards. Two does were walking across the yard. They stopped every few moments to nibble at the grass. It was so quiet around the house this time of day that the does didn't seem skittish. They were taking their time, like shoppers at a flea market.

Beauregard finished his coffee. Once upon a time, he had dreamed of living in a house like this one. A house with running water and a roof that didn't leak like a sieve. A house where everyone had their own room and there wasn't a slop bucket in the corner. He put the coffee cup in the sink. He didn't know what was sadder. That his dreams had been so modest or that they had been so prophetic. That was in the days before his father had disappeared. Seeing him again had taken over the top spot on his wish list. But after all these years, he had learned to accept that some dreams don't come true.

He grabbed his keys and his phone and walked out of the house. It was only ten and it was already as hot as hell. When he stepped off the porch, he could feel the sun beating down on him like he owed it money. He hopped in his truck and revved up the engine to get the AC cranking. He backed up, turned around and drove down the driveway, leaving a cloud of dust in his wake.

He hit the main highway, but instead of turning left toward the garage, he turned right toward the outskirts of town. He cut through Trader Lane and drove past the desiccated husks of several deserted houses. A little bit farther up the road, he passed the abandoned Clover Hill Industrial Park. Years ago, the Powers That Be of Red Hill County tried to reinvent the former farming community as a mecca for manufacturing. They offered fat tax breaks to the corporations, and in turn the corporations offered the town hundreds of jobs. For a while it was a mutually beneficial relationship. Right up until the 2008 recession hit. This was right about the same time the corporations realized they could ship their plants overseas and cut expenses by half while doubling profits.

The empty buildings stood like forgotten monoliths to a lost civilization. The ice plant, the insulation plant, the flag factory and the elastic plant were hardly discernible anymore. Mother Nature was reclaiming her land with steady, implacable persistence. The pine trees and the dogwoods and the honeysuckle and the kudzu were slowly but surely enveloping the old buildings in an arboreal embrace. Beauregard's mother had worked at the elastic plant from the time it opened until its untimely demise. Which just happened to be two years before her retirement, but only a week after she had been diagnosed with breast cancer. A month later, he had taken his first job. Boonie had set him up with a crew out of Philly who needed a driver. Since he had been the new guy, his cut had only been five grand. That was the going rate, or so they had told him. He had only been seventeen so he didn't really question it. That was a mistake. He would learn that the going rate was a full share or nothing at all. He didn't really dwell on it too much. A mistake is a lesson, unless you make the same mistake twice.

As he got closer to the county line, fields of corn and beans began to dominate the landscape. Residential encroachment hadn't yet reached this part of town. Eventually some enterprising developer would drop a dozen or so narrow rectangular boxes out here and call it a trailer court.

He rolled through a narrow curve and spotted the sign. A five-foot-wide saw blade attached to a three-foot-tall metal pole. RED HILL METALS was spelled out on the sign with sections of rebar painted bright red. The saw blade had been painted white, but the paint was peeling like a bad sunburn. Beauregard turned down the gravel driveway. The driveway was buffeted on both sides by enormous blue and white hydrangeas. At the end of the driveway was a set of fifteen-foot-tall chain-link gates. As Beauregard approached, the gates began to roll on large metal caster wheels. Boonie had attached a motion sensor to the gate a few years ago. He'd gotten tired of having to stop working every time someone pulled up with their mama's old wood stove. Rusted razor wire topped the gate and the equally tall fence that was attached to it. Two dark-skinned men nodded at Beauregard as he drove past them. They were both wielding massive reciprocating saws. A mangled AMC Gremlin appeared to be their intended target.

Beauregard drove over the ten-foot-wide scale that was embedded in the ground, took a hard left and parked in front of the main office. He got out of the truck and immediately started sweating. The heat had gone from volcano to Hell in the span of twenty minutes. Metallic screams of agony filled the air as the two compactors crushed cars, trucks and the occasional washing machine. Cubes of steel and iron were stacked across the yard like giant dominoes. A graveyard of vehicles rose up from behind the office building as they waited their turn in the maw of Chompy Number One and Chompy Number Two. Kaden had named them on a summer day long ago.

Beauregard's Daddy had taken him, Kaden and Kelvin out riding in the Duster that day. "Gotta go see ya Uncle Boonie for a minute, then we can go to the Tastee Freez. Y'all want some whiskey with your milkshakes?" his father had asked with a wink.

"Yeah!" Kelvin had spoken up. Of course it was Kelvin. He had even raised his hand.

Beauregard's father had laughed so hard he had started coughing.

"Boy, your Mama would have both our asses in a sling. Maybe in a few years."

When they had pulled into the yard the three of them had leaned over the front seat to watch the belching, groaning claw crane drop a car into the crusher. It tumbled trunk over hood before slamming into the compactor.

"Chompy Number One, finish him!" Kaden had howled. Beauregard's Daddy had told Boonie and the names had stuck. They'd never had that shot of whiskey, though.

The word "OFFICE" was spelled out on the door using lengths of copper tubing. Beauregard knocked three times on the door in quick succession. You never knew what kind of business was being conducted in there, so it was best to knock.

"Come on in," a raspy voice said. Boonie was sitting behind his desk. A slab of iron on four wide metal cylinders. A ragged AC wheezed from the window over his shoulder. It was making more noise than cool air. A smattering of file cabinets and shelves ran along the walls. Boonie smiled.

"Bug! How the hell you doing? Boy, I ain't seen you in what? Six months? A year?" Boonie said.

"Ain't been that long. Just been busy at the shop."

"Aw, I'm just fucking with you, boy. I know you working your ass off over there. I ain't mad atcha. I just . . . just seems like you ain't around like you used to be," Boonie said. He took off his oil-stained baseball cap and fanned himself. His iron gray flattop contrasted with his coal black skin.

"I know. How things been around here?"

"Aw, ya know. Steady. People never run out of junk."

Beauregard sat down in a folding chair next to the desk. "Yeah, always got shit to throw away."

"How you been? How's Kia and the boys?"

"They alright. Darren had to get some glasses and now Javon

gotta have some special kind of braces. Kia doing alright. Coming up on five years at the hotel. Anything else going on?" he said.

Boonie replaced his hat and cocked his head at Beauregard. "You asking?" he said.

Beauregard nodded his head.

"Not that I ain't glad to see you cuz you know I am, but I thought you was done," Boonie said.

"I've just hit a rough patch. Things been kind of tough ever since Precision opened up," Beauregard said.

Boonie entwined his fingers and laid them on his prodigious belly.

"Well, I wish I had something, but things have really dried up these last few years. The Italians got pushed out by the Russians, and the Russians only using their own crews. Shit, Bug, it's been real quiet. Them Russians coming through sounding like Ivan Koloff trying to be all scary and shit," Boonie said. He made a face like he had bitten into a rotten apple.

Beauregard let his hands hang between his knees and lowered his head.

"You ever thought about going out West? I hear there's still some work out that way for a fella who know his way around a steering wheel."

Beauregard grunted. "My Daddy went out West and didn't never come back," he said.

Boonie sighed. "Your Daddy ... your Daddy was one of a kind. I only seen two other men who could handle a car under the hood or behind the wheel like Ant Montage. You one of them. The other one is locked up in Mecklenburg. Your Daddy was as good a driver as he was a friend. And he was a damn good driver," Boonie said. He pushed his baseball cap back on his head and stared at the aluminum beams in the ceiling.

Beauregard knew he was seeing it in his mind. Seeing him and his father flying down the road moving moonshine or speeding away from a bank robbery on the streets of Philadelphia, hooting and hollering all the way.

"You still think he might come back?" Beauregard said.

"Huh?"

"Daddy. You still think he might show up on my doorstep one day? Carrying a basketball and bottle of Jack so we can go catch up," Beauregard said.

Boonie blew some air between his full lips. "Men like your Daddy, like me, like you used to be, we don't die in hospital beds. Ant wasn't perfect. He loved driving, drinking, and women, in that order. He lived life at 100 miles per hour. Men like that, well, they go out on their own terms, usually with a bang. But I tell you what, if he did go out that way, you can bet your ass he took some boys with him. You look so much like him. It's like he spit you out. But you different. Your Daddy, he just won't the settling down type. That made things hard for him and your Mama. How is Ella these days?"

"She doing. She over at the nursing home. Her cancer done slowed down but she still smoking like she got a bad ring in her engine," Beauregard said.

"Damn. That cancer, boy, it just takes 'em down inch by inch. Louise went down so fast. Doctor told her she had it in March, she was gone by September. How long your Mama had it?" Boonie asked.

"Since '95." Beauregard said. He thought his mother was going to outlive them all. Unlike Mrs. Boonie, she was too mean to die.

"Ella was always tough as shoe leather," Boonie said. He smiled at his own joke.

"Well, I guess I should get on down the road, Boonie." Beauregard stood.

"Hey, hold up, let's have a drink real quick," Boonie said. He swiveled in his chair and grabbed a mason jar out of one of the drawers in the filing cabinet directly behind him.

"It's 11 o'clock."

Boonie unscrewed the lid. Two shot glasses had magically

appeared on the desk as well. "Hey, like Alan Jackson says, it's five o'clock somewhere. I'm sure glad we been able to catch up," Boonie said.

He filled both glasses. Beauregard picked up a glass and clinked it against the one Boonie was holding. The shine was smooth as the glass it was held in. A warm tingle wound its way down his throat.

"Alright. Well, keep me in mind if you hear anything," Beauregard said.

"You sure?" Boonie asked.

"What?"

Boonie put the mason jar back in the drawer.

"Just saying maybe it's a good thing I ain't got nothing. Like I said, you different from your Daddy. You don't live for this. It ain't all you got," he said.

Beauregard knew Boonie meant well. Nowadays he was a connect. A guy who could put you in touch with some other guys. He also hired out Chompy One and Two as garbage disposals. They disposed of the kind of garbage that bled and cried for its mama before it died. He was the guy who could help you move your loot without charging an exorbitant finder's fee. He was also Beauregard's de facto godfather. Boonie had helped him refurbish the Duster. He'd given Kia away at their wedding because her father was doing twenty to life in Coldwater for killing her mother. Boonie was the third person to hold Javon when he was born. Boonie did all the things Anthony Montage should have done. So Beauregard knew he meant well. But Boonie didn't have a daughter graduating from summer school next month. He didn't have two sons who seemed to grow six inches every night. Or a wife who wanted a house with a foundation before she died. Or a business that was one month from going under.

"Yeah, I'm sure," he said.

He left.

THREE

Kelvin rolled up to the shop around eleven. Bug wasn't there yet, so he went across the street to the 7-Eleven and got a chicken salad sandwich and a soda. He slipped into a weathered booth and ate his sandwich and sipped his soda. Most 7-Elevens didn't have a place to eat but this one had once been a diner. When the Egyptian family that owned the 7-Eleven bought the building they had kept the booths. It was a scorcher today. Not for the first time, he contemplated cutting off his braids. But he knew he had an odd-shaped head with a few too many indentations to rock the bald look. By the time he finished his food, Bug still hadn't arrived, so he walked back across the road and opened up the garage. They had a transmission to put in for Lulu Morris that was going to be a bitch. Shane Helton had dropped his truck off complaining of a shimmy in the steering column. Kelvin thought it might be the rack and pinion. Bug was of the opinion it was just the velocity boot on the driver side. Bug was probably right, but a velocity boot was only 300 bucks. A rack and pinion was at least 1500.

He hoped to God it was the rack and pinion.

Kelvin raised the three garage doors on the three repair bays and turned on the overhead air handler. Whistling, he drove Shane's truck onto the hydraulic lift. As he was hopping out, he saw a faded blue Toyota pull up to the first bay door. The car stopped and a short thin white man got out and walked into the garage. He stopped just in front of the tire changer. He had longish brown hair and a scraggly brown beard. His muddy brown eyes darted from side to side.

"Beauregard?" he asked with an inquisitive inflection at the end.

"Nah, I'm Kelvin. He ain't in yet. Can I help you with something?" The man licked his dry lips.

"I really need to talk to Beauregard," he said.

"Well, as he ain't here can I help you?" Kelvin asked.

The man ran his hand through his hair. He stepped a little closer to Kelvin. He smelled like cigarettes and old sweat.

"Just tell him my brother Ronnie is looking for him. Wants to talk to him, patch things up, maybe have some work for him," the man said.

"Ronnie who?" Kelvin asked.

"Ronnie Sessions. He know him. They used to work together," the man said.

Kelvin sighed. He knew who Ronnie Sessions was, or at least he had heard the name. Ronnie was a crazy-ass good ol' boy from Queen County down on the back heel of the state. Ronnie was known for two things: his twenty-three Elvis tattoos, and stealing anything that wasn't nailed down with titanium fasteners. Last Kelvin had heard, Ronnie was doing five years up in Coldwater on a burglary charge. Robbed a marina or something. This was after he screwed Beauregard over on a job.

Bug had not been pleased.

So Kelvin couldn't imagine why in the hell Ronnie wanted to be within one hundred feet of Bug. Let alone tell him he was back in town. Maybe he had a fetish for getting his teeth kicked down his throat.

"Alright, I'll tell him," Kelvin said. Ronnie's brother nodded his head up and down rapidly then turned and headed for his car. He stopped halfway and turned back around.

"Hey, you wouldn't be holding, would you?" he asked.

"Why would you think I'm holding? Because I'm black?" Kelvin asked.

The man frowned. "Nah. It's just most everybody in Red Hill be holding. I was just asking," he said. He got in his car and slammed the door. He tried to spin his tires on the gravel but the car stalled. He started it again and eased out of the parking lot.

Kelvin chuckled. He hit the "up" button on the lift and raised Shane's truck until he could walk under without ducking. "He gonna spin tires like I offended him. Motherfuckers will look high and low for a reason to feel disrespected," he muttered as he began inspecting the undercarriage of the truck.

The Lake Castor Convalescent Home took great pains to not look like a nursing home. The front of the building had an elaborate brick portico that covered the automatic doors at the entrance. Lush green boxwood shrubs that appeared to have been trimmed with lasers lined the sidewalk like verdant sentries. The brick carport had a pair of flying buttresses at each end. The whole campus seemed more like a small community college with a decent alumni organization than a nursing home. Beauregard stepped through the automatic doors and was smacked in the face by the pungent scent of urine. All that fancy architecture couldn't do anything about the smell of piss.

A blond receptionist smiled at him as he entered the building. He didn't return it.

"Hello, sir, can I help?" she asked.

"I'm going to see Mrs. Talbot," he said without breaking his stride. He was intimately familiar with the patient coordinator's office. He had hoped that putting his mother in the nursing home might make his life just a tiny bit easier. She could yell at the staff not putting her drink on a coaster or being too rough wiping her ass. The fact that she only had one coaster or that her hemorrhoids were inflamed never seemed to cross her mind. Instead putting her in the home made her meaner and in turn made his life harder. In the two years she had been in Lake Castor, he had been called in for corrective-action meetings at least thirty times.

Ella Montage was not a model patient.

In the beginning, he had smoothed things over with an extra payment here or donating a piece of equipment there. A few times he had even straight up handed the administrator an envelope. The money had been rolling in and he had still had some savings from the jobs he had worked. Those days were long over now. He wondered if this was the day they finally rolled his mother out to that lovely exposed aggregate sidewalk and told him to take her. He could see the administrator telling him she didn't have to go home but she had to get the hell out of there.

He knocked on Mrs. Talbot's door then checked his watch. Almost noon. Kelvin was probably already at work but it would take two of them to get Lulu's transmission out.

"Please come in," Mrs. Talbot said. Beauregard did as he was told. The slim and neat woman sat at a glass-top desk. She had her hair pulled back in a severe bun with a pair of decorative chopsticks jutting out of the back of her head. She stood and extended her hand.

"Mr. Montage."

Beauregard gripped her hand lightly and shook it.

"Mrs. Talbot."

She gestured toward the chair and Beauregard sat down. It struck him how many times his life had been changed by sitting across from someone at a desk.

"Mr. Montage, I am glad you could come in today to discuss this issue," Mrs. Talbot said.

"You didn't make it sound like I had much of a choice."

Mrs. Talbot pursed her lips. "Mr. Montage, I'll get right to the point. There is a discrepancy with your mother's Medicaid coverage."

"No, there isn't," he said.

Mrs. Talbot blinked a few times. "I'm sorry?" she said.

Beauregard shifted in his seat. "You said there's a discrepancy.

That makes it sound like some books ain't adding up. My Mama's Medicaid ain't got no discrepancy. Now is there something wrong with her coverage?" he asked.

Mrs. Talbot's face reddened and she leaned forward in her chair. Beauregard knew that he sounded like an asshole, but he didn't like the way she had framed the situation. Mrs. Talbot didn't like his mother and Beauregard couldn't really say he blamed her. At the same time, it was no need to make it sound like his mother was a thief. Cruel, insensitive, manipulative, yes. Thief, no. The Montage men held down the thievery crown in his family.

"I'm sorry, I used a poor choice of words. Let me phrase it this way. Your mother kept up a life insurance policy that she didn't declare when she entered the facility that now puts her over the asset limit for Medicaid assistance," Mrs. Talbot said.

Beauregard's mouth went dry. "Can't she just cancel it? Or cash it out?"

Mrs. Talbot pursed her lips again. "Well, she can cash it out but it's only fifteen thousand dollars. The discrep—um, the mistake was noted by Medicaid two months ago. They immediately ceased subsidizing her care. As it stands now, she has an outstanding balance of . . ." She touched a tablet sitting on her desk. "Forty-eight thousand three hundred and sixty dollars. She could cash out but that would leave her owing—"

"Thirty-three thousand three hundred and sixty," Beauregard said.

Mrs. Talbot blinked hard. "Yes. The facility is requesting that payment in full by the end of next month. If you and your family can't find the resources to pay the outstanding debt, Mrs. Montage will have to leave the facility. I'm sorry," she said. She didn't sound sorry to Beauregard. She sounded positively delighted.

"Do you know if my mother has agreed to cancel the policy?" he asked. His mouth was so dry he felt like he could spit sand.

"She has been made aware of the situation, but she insists this is an inheritance for her grandchildren," Mrs. Talbot said. The arch of her eyebrows told him she didn't believe that any more than he did. His mother tolerated her grandchildren. No, that policy was all about control. His mother reveled in being in control. Whether it was not allowing him to get his license unless he broke up with Ariel's mom or holding on to a life insurance policy, Ella Montage liked having leverage. She might quote the Bible from time to time but that was her religion.

"Let me go talk to her. Could you print me something with the date the money has to be paid on it and I'll pick it up on my way out," he said.

"Of course, Mr. Montage. If you like, I could also print you up a list of nearby facilities and their waiting lists."

"Yeah, sure," he said. He didn't need to see a list of other places. If his mother got kicked out of here, she would probably be dead before a bed opened up somewhere else.

Beauregard got up and headed for his mother's room. As he walked down the hallway, he thought about what Boonie had said. A quiet, dignified death in one of these dimly lit rooms didn't seem so bad. That is, until you realized that no death is dignified. It's a messy process. The Grim Reaper sneaks up behind you and squeezes you until shit fills your adult diaper and an artery bursts in your chest. He works his bony fingers in your guts and makes your own cells eat you alive from the inside. He skull fucks you until your brain retreats inside itself and you forget how to even breathe. He guides the hand of a man you've wronged and aims his gun at your face. There is no dignity in death. Beauregard had seen enough people die to realize that. There's only fear and confusion and pain.

The door to his mother's room was open wide. A CNA was standing next to the bed. He heard his mother's three-pack-a-day voice loud and clear. The CNA could too, and by the way her neck and shoulders were knotted up, she didn't like what she was hearing.

"I've been pushing that 'call' button for forty-five minutes. You girls up there with ya nose buried in a phone while I'm sitting in piss. I've pissed myself. Do you know how that feels? Do you understand that? I'm sitting here in a puddle of piss." She paused to take a deep hit of oxygen from her nasal cannula. "No, you don't, but don't worry, one day you will. You all cute and pretty now but one day you gonna be right here like I am and I hope somebody lets you sit in your own piss like your privates in a stew," she said.

"I'm sorry, Mrs. Montage. We just so short-staffed today," the CNA said. She sounded genuinely apologetic. That was a mistake. Ella was like a lioness on the Serengeti. She could sense weakness.

"Oh, I'm sorry, chile. You're short-staffed. I'll try to die more quietly," Ella said.

The CNA made a wet strangled noise and rushed out of the room. She brushed past Beauregard mumbling to herself. He caught the words "miserable" and "witch."

"Hey, Mama," Beauregard said. He stepped just inside the door.

Ella appraised him from top to bottom with a gentle flick of her eyes. "You getting skinny. I never thought that girl knew how to cook," she said.

"Kia cooks just fine, Mama. How you feeling?"

"Ha! I'm dying. Other than that, I'm feeling great," she said.

Beauregard inched farther into the room. "You ain't going nowhere," he said.

"Get my cigarettes out that drawer," she said.

"Mama, you don't need them cigarettes. Didn't you just say you was dying?"

"Yeah, so a cigarette ain't gonna hurt nothing," Ella said.

"Have you been smoking with your oxygen on? You know you could blow this place up, right?" Beauregard asked.

His mother shrugged. "I probably be doing most of the people here a favor," she said. Beauregard had to chuckle at that one. That was the thing about his mother. She could be emotionally manipulative one minute then making you laugh the next. It was like getting hit in the face with a pie that had a padlock in it. When he was a kid, she had combined that acerbic wit with her looks to pretty much get whatever she wanted. All children think their mother is beautiful, but Beauregard had noticed fairly early on that other people thought his mother was beautiful too. Long coal black hair like an oil slick ran down her back to her waist. Skin the color of coffee with too much cream told the story of her varied ancestry. Her light gray irises gave her almond-shaped eyes an otherworldly appearance.

Cashiers always seemed to have extra change if she was short at the grocery store. Cops always seemed to give her a warning even if she was doing the speed of light through a school zone. People always seemed to want to do what Ella Montage told them to do. Even if she was telling them to go fuck themselves. Everybody except his Daddy. She once told him that his father was the only man to ever put her in her place.

"I loved him for it. Hated him too," she would say between puffs on her omnipresent dark brown More cigarette. He could remember sitting on her lap as she told him over and over again how they met. He never got fairy tales as a kid. He got Sturm and Drang epics set against the backdrop of sultry country nights. Eventually he realized his mother considered it some kind of weird therapy. She had her very own captive eight-year-old psychologist.

The cancer and its subsequent treatments had taken her hair first. She wore a black scarf now. Then it withered her skin. The stoma in her throat stared at him like the mouth of some strange parasite. A lamprey eel that was trying to crawl out of her neck. Only the gray eyes remained untouched. So light they sometimes appeared blue. Smart eyes that never forgot anything they ever saw. And they never let you forget it either.

"Mama, why didn't you tell me about this policy?"

Ella fixed those cool eyes on him. "Because it wasn't none of your damn business."

Ella stretched her thin arm out to the drawer beside her bed and pulled out a pack of More cigarettes and a lighter. She lit one up and inhaled deeply. A thin trail of smoke leaked out of the hole in her throat and encircled her head like a dirty halo. Beauregard rubbed his hand over his face. A long sigh hissed out of his mouth.

"Mama, that policy counts as an asset. That asset counts against your Medicaid. Now you're behind on your payments to the nursing home. Do you hear what I'm saying? They talking about kicking you out of here," he said.

"And you and Little Miss Big Booty don't want me dirtying up your fancy double-wide, right? You know she never brings the boys up here to see me? I've seen Ariel more than I've seen Darren and Javon and her mama don't even like black people anymore," Ella said. Beauregard grabbed a metal chair from the corner and sat down close to his mother's bed.

"That ain't just on Kia. We've both been real busy and I'm sorry for that. Mama, look, you know I asked you when you first got sick to come live with us. You said no. You said you didn't want to live under my roof, under my rules. 'What it look like, a mother letting her child tell her what to do?' Remember saying that? Now it's just . . . you need a lot of help now. More than we can give you." He reached out and touched his mother's free hand. The skin felt like crepe paper. Ella took another drag on her cigarette and moved her hand to her lap.

"You said it but you didn't mean it," she said. Her voice was a low sharp rasp. Beauregard leaned back in the chair and stared up at the acoustical tiles in the ceiling. He'd gone down this particular road a thousand times over the years. He didn't need a map or a signpost to see where it was headed.

"Mama, we going to have to get rid of that policy. Ain't no way around that because you ain't got anywhere else to go," Beauregard said. Ella took another long deep drag off her cigarette.

"If your Daddy was here, I wouldn't need to be in no nursing home. If he hadn't walked out on me when I needed him the most I wouldn't be here sitting in my own piss. I'd be in my own house with my own husband. But when it came to handling his responsibilities we both know Anthony Montage was about as useful as a white crayon, don't we?" Ella asked. Beauregard let the question hang in the air between them.

"He left me too, Mama," he said. His deep baritone had dropped four octaves. The words seemed to emanate from his chest, not his mouth. If Ella heard him she wasn't in the mood to acknowledge it.

"He should have never walked out on me. Goddamn black bastard. He promised me he would always take care of me," Ella mumbled. Beauregard saw her eyes begin to glisten. He stood up and put the chair back.

"I gotta go, Mama," he said. Ella waved her cigarette toward the door.

Beauregard walked out of the room, down the hall and out of the nursing home. He would have to ask Mrs. Talbot how his mother was getting cigarettes. He couldn't stand watching her smoke. It didn't revolt him. He just couldn't stand watching her do that to herself. He was more disturbed by her eyes welling up with tears. He could count on one hand how many times he'd actually seen his mother cry. She gave up her tears as sparingly as she gave out compliments. If she was weeping, she was in terrible pain. Either spiritually or physically or both. Ella Montage was not an easy woman to love but seeing the reality of her fragility pierced him in places that were soft and frightened. It was like someone had shot him in the stomach then shoved their thumb in the hole.

By the time he got to the garage, it was lunchtime. Kelvin was sitting at his desk eating a cheeseburger with the radio turned up to eleven. A Stevie Wonder song was warbling through the busted speakers. Kelvin had his feet up on the desk as he bobbed his head in time with the music.

"Get your feet down," Beauregard said as he entered the office.

"Well, look what the cat dragged in. I figure I could put my feet up since I was the only employee who had actually done some work to-day," he said between bites. When Beauregard didn't laugh, he moved his feet and put the burger down. "Hey, you alright?" Kelvin said.

"Just got done talking to Mama," Beauregard said.

Kelvin sucked in a breath. "Aw man, Aunt Ella being her usual wonderful self?" Kelvin said.

Beauregard grabbed a beer out of the mini-fridge. Even though he had chided Boonie for day drinking, he needed something after dealing with his mother.

"There was some mix-up with her insurance and they might be kicking her out the home. Unless I can pay it off," Beauregard said. His head was beginning to throb.

"Did you, um, go see Boonie?" Kelvin asked.

"Yeah. He ain't got nothing. So I'm right where I started. Nah, actually it's worse cuz I gotta pay the nursing home," Beauregard said. He killed half the beer with one sip.

"That's one of the perks of having your own business. Beer for lunch," Kelvin said.

Beauregard chuckled. "I see you got Shane's truck up on the rack. What was it?" he said.

"Fucking velocity boot. I was hoping it was the rack and pinion. Don't worry, I already ordered it," Kelvin said.

Beauregard finished his beer. "Alright, let's get on this damn transmission," he said as he tossed his beer in the trash.

"Oh hey, a guy came by saying Ronnie Sessions was looking for you. I think it was Ronnie's brother. He never did get you straight about that thing with the horse, did he?" Kelvin asked. Beauregard sighed. He was sighing an awful lot these days.

"No, he didn't."

Ronnie Fucking Sessions. The mastermind behind what Bug liked to think of as the Fucking Horse Job.

Ronnie had approached him one night out at Wonderland. The way Ronnie had told it, some fancy-ass horse breeder out of Fairfax was selling a healthy young thoroughbred to some famous trainer in Kentucky.

One of the farmhands at the breeder's ranch was buying Oxy-Contin from Ronnie's cousin and had let the cat out of the proverbial bag while making small talk during a transaction. Ronnie had come sidling up to Beauregard to help him steal the horse and sell it to another trainer in South Carolina so he could put him out to stud. Beauregard had taken the job, then set about planning it out because, as Ronnie said, he was an idea man. Beauregard was the details guy. Beauregard had gone out to Fairfax and studied the breeder's farm, the horse trailer, the hitch on the trailer, the weight of the horse, everything. He ended up building an exact replica of the horse trailer, right down to the fist-sized dent on the right side. Put the equivalent of the horse's weight in sandbags in the trailer. When the boys towing the trailer stopped to get something to eat at the same diner they always stopped at when transporting a horse for the breeder, Beauregard and Ronnie were waiting. The fellas parked around the back of the diner and went inside. Beauregard and Ronnie parked next to them, towing their fake trailer covered in a tarp. Under the weak sodium arc lights in the parking lot of the diner Beauregard and Ronnie switched the trailers. It was just past midnight in the middle of nowhere in the Roanoke Valley when they pulled out of the parking lot and hopped on the interstate headed for South Carolina.

"Goddamn if that won't work just like a fucking magic trick!" Ronnie had said as they jumped on I-85.

Unfortunately, what Beauregard didn't know, what no one outside of the breeder and his vet knew, was that the horse had a fairly serious medical condition. A condition that required a certain type of medication. Medication that was in the pocket of one of the boys they had left behind at the diner. Rich Man's Folly was as dead as Dillinger when Ronnie and Beauregard had reached South Carolina.

Beauregard had not been pleased.

"I ain't got nothing to say to Ronnie Sessions," Beauregard said. It was a simple sentence but Kelvin felt the weight of the ominous intent that clung to it like a shadow.

By the time they got the transmission out, the heat in the shop had reached Saharan levels. They were both soaked in sweat despite the air running at full strength. The transmission had fought them every step of the way. Beauregard had busted one of the knuckles on his right hand after it slipped off of a socket wrench. Kelvin wiped his face with a red shop rag. Beauregard had the sickly sweet scent of transmission fluid so far up his nose it felt like it was infecting his brain. Kelvin looked at his watch.

"Shit, it's almost five. You want to call it for today? That torque converter is all the way fucked anyway," he said.

"Yeah. But we gotta get here early tomorrow. I wanna get both of them outta here so we can get paid. I owe Snap-on a grip and the light bill is two weeks past due," Beauregard said.

"Damn, do you ever feel like Jean Valjean?" Kelvin asked. Beauregard squinted at him. "Cynthia likes the movie. Anyway, I'm gonna get gone. See you in the morning," Kelvin said.

Beauregard grabbed his own rag and began to wipe his hands. He only succeeded in moving the dirt and grease to different locations. Kelvin headed for the door. Halfway there he stopped.

"Hey, Bug. We gonna be alright. You'll figure something out. You always do," Kelvin said.

"Yeah. See ya tomorrow," Beauregard said.

After Kelvin left, he started closing down the shop. He turned off all the lights except for the one in his office. He lowered the roll-up doors. Turned off the air compressor and the overhead air handler. On his way back to his office he stopped by the Duster. He ran his hand over the hood. The metal was warm to the touch. Like it was alive. His father had left the car at his own mother's house when he went West. It had sat in the backyard for five years while Beauregard was in juvenile detention. When he got out, his grandmother Dora Montage had handed him the keys and the title.

"Your Mama wanted to sell it to Bartholomew for scrap. I wouldn't let her do it. Her name might be on the title but this car belongs to you," she had said.

Beauregard remembered how strange it felt hearing Boonie's Christian name. He walked around the front of the car and got in the driver's seat. He ran his hands over the steering wheel.

His father was dead. He was sure of that now. Probably buried in a shallow grave or chopped up and tossed in a river by the same kind of men he had worked for as a driver. Just another job to killers who didn't care he had a son who loved his bad jokes. Anthony Montage always seemed so full of life it was difficult to accept the fact he was dead. Beauregard had no doubt that if his father was alive he would have come back by now. Most of the folks around here who wanted him dead were either in prison or the ground. When he hadn't shown up for Grandma Dora's funeral, Beauregard had finally believed he was gone. Kia wanted him to sell the Duster. He could probably get at least twenty-five grand for it if he spruced up the paint job. That was never going to happen. She didn't understand that the Duster was his father's tombstone. Beauregard let his head rest against the steering wheel. He sat that way for a long time.

Finally he got out, turned off the light in the office, and headed home. He had forgotten to call Kia. He called on his cell as he was pulling out of the parking lot. She answered on the first ring.

"Hey, I'm sorry I didn't call on your break. But we closed up a little early so I'm headed to get the boys," he said.

"They wouldn't let me work a double. They actually cut me a little early so I already got the boys. We at the house," she said. There was a pause. "Beau, there are guys here. They were waiting when we pulled up. They said they friends of yours. I told them to wait on the porch," she said.

Beauregard gripped the steering wheel so hard his hand ached. "What they look like?" he said. His tongue felt thick and unsuited to his mouth.

"They white. One got long brown hair. The other one got a bunch of Elvis tattoos running up and down his arm," she said.

Beauregard's vision got blurry for a second. He gripped the steering wheel even harder. "Alright. I'm a be there in like ten minutes."

"You want me to tell them you on your way? I told them you wouldn't be home till seven. They said they was gonna wait."

"No. I'll talk to them when I get there. Just give the boys something to eat and I'll be there in a minute," he said.

"Okay. Love ya."

"Love you too," he croaked. He hung the phone up and put it in the cup holder.

Beauregard stopped at the intersection of Town Road and John Byrd highway. He reached over and opened the glove box. There were no cars behind him and only a few passing him in the other lane at the stop sign. Lying there in the glove box mute as a stone was a Smith and Wesson .45 caliber semiautomatic. Beauregard rooted around in the glove box and found the clip. He took out the gun and the clip and slammed the clip home. He had gotten a concealed carry permit when he had opened the shop. Back then, a lot of people paid him in cash.

Beauregard thought about the clichéd scene in every crime movie where the main character who has gotten out of the "Life" buries his weapons under a hundred pounds of concrete only to have to dig them up when his enemies come knocking at his door.

He understood the appeal of the symbolism for filmmakers. It was just unrealistic. You were never out of the Life completely. You were always looking over your shoulder. You always kept a gun within reach, not buried under cement in your basement. Having a gun nearby was the only way you could pretend to relax. He had a gun in every room of the house. They were like good friends who were always down to do bad things.

Beauregard didn't know why Ronnie Sessions had come knocking at his door but he was going to have his friends Mr. Smith and Mr. Wesson ask him.

FOUR

Beauregard saw a faded blue Toyota sitting behind Kia's Honda as he parked his truck. He slipped the .45 into his waistband near the small of his back. He could feel the butt of the gun and the textured cross pattern on the grip against his skin. He got out and walked toward his house. Two men were sitting in the white plastic lawn chairs arranged on the porch. He didn't recognize the one with the long hair. He figured he was Ronnie's brother. They both stood when they saw him approaching. Ronnie stepped down off the porch first and extended his hand.

"Beau, how the hell are you, man? Long time no speak," he said. He was almost as tall as Beau so that put him around five eight or nine. He was thin but wiry. Veins pressed against the skin of his left forearm and bicep. He had a full sleeve on his right arm from his hands to his shoulder. The tattoo was a time line of the history of Elvis Presley. On his shoulder were images of gold-blazer-wearing Elvis. On his bicep and tricep were multiple Elvises from the sixties. The forearm was fat Elvises in the sequined white jumpsuit wearing Polynesian leis. The images continued until they reached the back of his hand. There in full color was an Elvis with a halo and wings. Angel Elvis. Ronnie was wearing a black T-shirt with cut-off sleeves. That was all Beauregard had ever seen him wear. It didn't matter if it was 100 degrees or 0. Beauregard wondered if he even owned a shirt with sleeves.

Beauregard grabbed Ronnie's left hand with his right. At the same time he reached behind him and slipped the .45 from his waistband. He put the barrel against Ronnie's stomach.

"Why are you at my house? My children in there. My wife. Why would you come here? We ain't got nothing to talk about. So now you gonna leave," he said. He spoke softly so that only Ronnie could hear him. His brother was standing on the second step on the porch just out of earshot.

"Hey, now hold on, Beau, I ain't mean no disrespect. Goddamn, man," Ronnie said. His blue eyes were open wide. His black goatee had more gray in it than Beauregard remembered. His temples had gone white too, giving him a redneck George Clooney look.

"Go, Ronnie. I don't want my family to see me splatter your guts all over the driveway. How did you even find my house?" Beauregard asked.

"Marshall Hanson told me where you stay. Look, man, I didn't know the goddamn thing had horse diabetes or whatever the hell it was," Ronnie said.

"But you should have known, Ronnie. That's the problem. Now leave."

"Beau, just wait a minute."

"My boys are here. My boys, Ronnie. What we did ain't got nothing to do with them. I don't bring that shit around my kids," Beauregard said.

"Come on now, Beau, just hear me out."

Beauregard pressed the barrel into Ronnie's stomach. Ronnie winced.

"I got a line on a job, Beau. A big one. One that can set us up for a long time. A long goddamn time," he said.

Beauregard eased up on the gun just a hair. Sweat dripped into his eyes. It was almost sundown and the heat hadn't slacked off at all. He felt like he was standing in an oven. Beauregard looked over Ronnie's shoulder and saw Kia peeking through the front window. The window of their house. He remembered the day the company brought the double-wide down. He and Kia had held hands as they watched the crew set the trailer on cinder blocks.

Beauregard pulled the gun away from Ronnie's stomach. He clicked the safety into place with his thumb. He let go of Ronnie's hand.

"What kind of job?" Beauregard said. The words tasted sour in his mouth. The fact that he was even entertaining this fool for one second told him how much his back really was against the wall.

"Can you put the gun away so we can talk? You gonna like what I have to say," Ronnie asked.

Beauregard eased up a little more.

"Come on, at least hear me out. Cuz I need ya, man. I need the Bug."

Beauregard put the gun back in his waistband. He looked over Ronnie's shoulder again. Kia was gone. "Meet me at my shop in thirty minutes," he said.

"Alright, alright, that's what's good, man. You won't regret it," Ronnie said. He motioned for his brother, who hustled over to the car and hopped inside. Ronnie got in the passenger side. Beauregard went to his window and squatted down on his haunches.

"I lost $3,800. That's the cost of retrofitting the trailer and my time. So what you got better replace that first. And Ronnie? Don't ever come to my house again. I'll shoot you next time. No questions asked, just a bullet in your guts," Beauregard said. He stood.

"I gotcha, bruh. Sorry, it's just I'm . . . uh, I'm just really hyped about this. You gonna get your money back and then some. I know I owe you, man," he said. Beauregard didn't say anything so Ronnie thumped his brother on the shoulder.

"Let's go, Reggie," he said.

The Toyota backed out of the yard and took off down the dirt lane like a bat out of hell.

Kia was pacing a hole in the floor. Beauregard went through the living room and sat at the kitchen table. Kia came and sat down across from him.

"What was all that about?" she asked.

"Just some guys with some work for me," he said.

"What kind of work?"

He took her hand and closed his fingers around it. "The nursing home called today. They say Mama owes them $48,000. Something went wrong with her Medicaid. With everything else going, I think I should just hear them out."

"No. NO. Why the hell does your Mama owe them that much? Bug, I don't mean to sound evil, but that's on your Mama. We got our own problems," Kia said.

"That's why I'm gonna hear them out," he said. Kia pulled her hand out of his grasp.

"No. I'm not gonna let you do this. I can't. Do you know what it's like laying in bed waiting for somebody to call and tell me to come identify your body because you got killed on a job? Yeah, the money was good, but I can't take you coming in here with a bullet in your shoulder and a head full of broken glass. Going up to Boonie's when you should be in a hospital."

Beauregard reached out to stroke her cheek. She flinched but did not pull away.

"We don't have any choice. We right behind it. If this is legit it might give us some breathing room," he said.

Kia inhaled, held it for a second, and let out a long breath. "Sell the Duster. It's worth at least twenty-five thousand. God knows you've put enough money in it."

"You know that's not an option." His voice was low. Dark.

"Why, because it belonged to your Daddy? I don't want you to end up like him. You holding on to that car like he was some kind of saint when everybody know he was a snitch," Kia said. Beauregard stopped stroking her cheek.

"Bug, I'm sorry. I shouldn't—"

Beauregard slammed his fist down on the table. Two jelly jars at the far end fell off and shattered on the floor.

"The Duster ain't for fucking sale," he said. He got up and stalked out the front door. The whole house shook when he slammed it.

Ronnie and Reggie were sitting in front of the garage when he got there. Beauregard didn't speak to them when he got out of the truck. He went to the door, unlocked it and stepped inside. They got the hint after a few minutes and followed him. He was sitting behind his desk by the time they got to the office. Ronnie sat and Reggie leaned against the door frame.

"Talk," Beauregard said.

"Damn, right to the point, huh? Alright. So I got this little piece I mess with. She lives over in Cutter County near Newport News. She works at a jewelry store. The manager is this big bull dyke who probably got a strap-on pecker bigger than yours and mine put together. Anyway, she been trying to get down Jenny's pants. That's her name, Jenny. So one night a couple of weeks ago, this carpet licker took Jenny out for drinks and let it drop they were getting in a shipment of diamonds. Diamonds that ain't on no manifest. Jenny said she was talking about giving her one of the diamonds. You know, because she all sweet on her and shit. Now this the part when you ask how much we talking about," Ronnie said.

Beauregard took the gun out of his waistband and put it on the desk between them.

"How much we talking about, Ronnie." His tone was flat as a pancake.

Ronnie ignored his apparent disinterest. He knew the next words out of his mouth would change that. "Five hundred thousand dollars' worth. I know a boy out of DC who says he will give us fifty cents on the dollar for them. That's $250,000 split three ways. Eighty grand, Beau. That can buy a lot of motor oil."

"It's \$83,333.33. My cut would be \$87,133.33. You owe me, re-member," Beauregard said.

Ronnie sniffed hard. "Yeah, I remember."

Beauregard leaned forward and put his elbows on the desk. "How many people know about this other than you, me, Jenny, your brother back there and the fence?" he asked.

Ronnie frowned. "Well, Quan knows," he said.

"Who is Quan?"

"He's the third guy. I met him upstate. He's good for this."

"When you trying to do this?" Beauregard asked.

"Next week," Ronnie said without hesitation.

Beauregard got up and grabbed a beer out of the mini-fridge, then sat down again. He popped the top off with the edge of the desk. "That ain't gonna work. Next week the Fourth of July. Traffic on the roads gonna be heavy as shit. Plus it's supposed to be nice. In the mid-eighties. Cops are out heavy in that kind of weather." He took a long swig and killed half the bottle. "Plus we would need to go check it out. Plan routes. Get the layout of the store. Things like that," Beau-regard said.

"So how long you thinking?" Ronnie asked. Beauregard hadn't offered him a beer, but he wanted one. Badly.

"At least a month. Depending on the route," Beauregard said. He finished his beer.

"A month? That's not gonna work. I need this like yesterday, man," Ronnie said.

Beauregard tossed his beer in the trash can in the corner. "See, that's why that damn horse died. You always in a rush," he said. Ronnie didn't say anything. He rubbed the palms of his hands over his thighs. He pushed the heels down into his thick-corded quadriceps.

"Look, man, can we split the difference and say two weeks?" he said.

"I didn't say I was in. I'm just saying what you would need to do," Beauregard said.

Ronnie leaned back in his chair until the front legs came off the floor. "Bug, I got a guy who is gonna be in DC on the twenty-sixth and gone by the end of the thirty-first. At the most, that gives us three weeks to get ready. And that's pushing it. This gotta move smooth and quick. Like I said, we can get paid. Real money. Not some pissy-ass stick-up money. Real dollars. But we gotta move fast. I need you on this, man. Not just cuz I owe you but because you the best. I ain't never seen nobody do what you can do with four wheels on the road," Ronnie said.

"I ain't some trailer park trick you trying to talk out of her panties, Ronnie. I'm listening to what you have to say. You lucky I'm doing that," he said.

"Alright, Bug. I hear you. I'm just trying to help you out. It looks like you need it," Ronnie said.

"What you mean by that?" Beauregard said.

The way he stared at him made Ronnie's balls climb up somewhere around his ears.

"I didn't mean nothing. Nothing. I noticed you only got the two cars on the lifts, that's all," Ronnie said. Beauregard studied Ronnie's face. His cheeks bloomed with red splotches that worked their way up from his neck. Ronnie's Adam's apple bobbed as he swallowed hard.

"I'll think about it," Beauregard said.

"Alright then. Look, let me leave you my brother's cell phone number. When you make up your mind, give me a call," Ronnie said.

"Go get a burner phone and call the shop tomorrow around noon," Beauregard said. Ronnie nodded his head up and down like he was in a lecture hall. He stood.

"Hey, man, don't think I don't understand what you are doing here. This is legal and ain't nothing wrong with that. I just figured I could give you a little help, that's all," Ronnie said. Beauregard didn't say anything. "Well, talk at you tomorrow, man," Ronnie said. He brushed past Reggie and headed for the door.

"Reggie, we leaving," he said. Reggie jumped like a demon had spoken to him.

"Oh yeah," he said. He slipped out of the office and ran after his brother.

Beauregard waited until he heard their car start, then he got up and cut the lights off for the second time that day. He locked up, hopped in his truck and headed back toward his house. He was passing the Long Street Mart when he saw a pink Ford Mustang idling by the gas pumps. He slammed on the brakes with his left foot while hitting the gas with his right. He swung the steering wheel to the right and the whole truck did a 180-degree turn. It slid into the parking lot sideways. He let it roll until he was behind the Mustang. He got out of the truck and walked up to the driver's side.

She wasn't in the car. That didn't mean the car was empty. A young black guy was in the passenger seat. He had frizzy braids sticking up all over his head like he had thumb-wrestled a light socket. A teardrop was drawn near his left eye. Beauregard thought the lines were too clean to be a jailhouse work of art. He had those small, thin features that teenaged girls loved and grown women avoided like the plague.

"What you want, old man?" the boy asked when he noticed Beauregard.

"Where's Ariel?" Beauregard asked in return.

"Why you asking about my girl, nigga?" the boy asked.

"Because I'm her daddy," Beauregard said. At first the words didn't seem to register. As they sank in, the boy's face broke into a wide platinum-toothed smile.

"Aw shit, man, I thought you was some old dude trying to holla at my girl. My bad, man. She in the store with her fine self," the boy said.

Beauregard thought he was entirely too comfortable talking about how fine Ariel was. "What's your name?" he asked the boy.

"Lil Rip," the boy said.

"No. Your name. What your mama calls you when she mad at you," Beauregard said.

The boy's smile faltered. "William," Lil Rip said.

"William. Nice to meet you. I'm Beauregard. You be nice to my girl, alright?" He squatted and extended his hand through the open car window. Lil Rip stared at it for a second before extending his own hand. Beauregard grabbed it and squeezed as hard as he could. Years of gripping pliers, stretching serpentine belts and pulling apart brake calipers ensured that was quite hard. Lil Rip winced. His lips parted slightly, and a few drops of spittle fell from his mouth.

"Cuz if you don't, if she ever tells me you giving her some problems, you and me are gonna have problems. And you don't want that do you . . . William?" Beauregard asked. He clamped down on Lil Rip's hand even tighter before finally letting it go. Then he straightened up and walked into the store without waiting for an answer. Lil Rip flexed his hand.

"Crazy motherfucker," he said when Beauregard was almost out of earshot.

Ariel was standing in front of the drink cooler. She was sporting a pair of cut-off denim shorts and a black tank top that Beauregard thought was at least one size too small. Her mop of brownish black curls was piled up on the top of her head in a loose bun. Beauregard's dark chocolate genes and her mother's French and Dutch genetic code had given her a light toffee complexion. Her light gray eyes were a gift from her grandmother.

"Hey," he said. She turned, gave him a once-over and then turned back to the drink cooler.

"Hey," she said.

"How's the Mustang holding up?" he asked.

"I'm driving it so it's doing alright, I guess," she said. She grabbed a fruit drink out of the cooler.

"I met your friend. Lil Rip. The one with the teardrop tattoo," Beauregard said.

"It's not a tattoo. He had me draw it for him with my makeup pen," she said. She pushed an errant lock of hair out of her face and then poked out her bottom lip and let out a gust of air. It was her tell when she was upset about something. He had watched her do the same thing in her car seat when he wouldn't let her have another piece of candy.

"What's wrong?"

Ariel shrugged her shoulders. "Nothing. Just getting ready for graduation. Me and the other five dummies who couldn't graduate with the rest of the class."

"You ain't no dummy. You had a lot going on," he said.

"Yeah. Like Mama getting her third DUI and wrecking my car. Of course, that ain't no excuse, according to her and grandma," Ariel said. She shook her bottle of juice lackadaisically in her left hand.

"Don't worry about them. You just concentrate on college and getting that accounting degree," Beauregard said.

Ariel blew air over her bottom lip.

"What?" Beauregard said.

"Since I won't be eighteen until January, Mama has to co-sign for my student loans. She says she don't want to put her name down on nothing like that. She says I should just take classes at J. Sargeant Reynolds and get a job until January," Ariel said.

"I could sign for you," Beauregard said.

"I don't think Kia would like that, do you?" Ariel asked. She put one hand on her hip and kept shaking the bottle of juice. "It's okay. I'll just get a job at the hospital or Walmart or something. Go to school in the spring," she said. Her body language said she was resigned to the fact that college was on hold for now.

But she didn't *sound* resigned to the idea. In fact, she sounded pissed. Beauregard thought she was about to blow up on him. He felt like their conversation was on the verge of devolving into a clichéd confrontation. She would start screaming at him about why he hadn't done more for her. She would ask why he hadn't taken her and raised her in his house. He would respond that he had only been seventeen and fresh out of juvie when he got her mother pregnant. He readied himself to take whatever came out of her mouth. He deserved it. Ariel deserved a better father and a better mother. She deserved a father who wasn't barely treading water. She deserved a mom who wasn't eating OxyContin like Tic Tacs and washing them down with vodka. She didn't deserve a grandmother who took one look at her tawny skin and cranked up Fox News as she tried to pretend her granddaughter wasn't half black.

Ariel didn't scream at him. She didn't ask him anything. She just shrugged her shoulders. "It is what it is, I guess. I gotta get Rip to work," she said.

Beauregard stepped aside. He wanted to ask for a hug. Wrap his arms around her and tell her he was sorry he hadn't been stronger. Apologize for not taking her from that viper's nest of a household. Tell her that every time he went on a job, he gave her mother half his earnings. Let her know he fought for her. Actually, fought her grandfather and her uncles and her mother for her. That he was the reason her Uncle Chad walked with a limp. Pull her close and whisper in her ear that her grandmother filed a restraining order to keep him away. Wouldn't even accept child support from him. That once he got married he filed for custody, but the judge took one look at him and threw the case out of court. Squeeze her tight and say he loved her just as much as he loved Darren and Javon. He wanted to say all those things. Had wanted to say them for a long time. But he didn't. Explanations were like assholes. Everyone has one and they are all full of shit.

"Alright then. Let me know if you have any problems with the Mustang," he said.

Ariel shook her head. "See ya," she said. He watched as she walked up to the counter, paid for her drink and her gas and strolled out of the store. As she stepped across the parking lot it was like he was watching a time-lapse movie in reverse. She was sixteen, then twelve, then five. By the time she got to the car, he could see her in his arms just after she had been born. Her little fists had been balled up like she was ready for a fight. A fight she was destined to lose because the game was rigged, and the points didn't matter.

Through the big picture window he saw her get in the Mustang and tear out of the parking lot spinning tires. Like grandfather, like father, like daughter.

He would tell himself later that he had slept on it. That he had mulled over the pros and cons and finally decided the benefits outweighed the risks. All that was true. However, in his heart he knew that when Ariel told him about skipping college, that was the moment he decided to take the job with Ronnie Sessions and hit the jewelry store.

FIVE

Ronnie rolled over on his back and stared up at the ceiling. The AC in the window of Reggie's trailer was as weak as a chicken. It pushed the heat around but didn't actually condition the air. A trickle of sweat was working its way down his forehead. He hadn't slept at all. He and Reggie had left Beauregard's and went over to Wonderland to score some Percs.

Reggie had $100 left from his disability check. Ronnie had nothing left from the $2,000 he had gotten for running some stolen eels up to Philly for Chuly Pettigrew. Eels were a delicacy in fancy restaurants all over New York and Chicago. Chuly's men had stolen a batch of eels from a fisherman in South Carolina who was now sleeping with the fishes. They weren't worth much in South Carolina, about $70 a pound. But take them up to Philly or New York and some pretentious celebrity chef would cream his linen pants for eel sushi. The guy in Philly had paid $1,000 per pound. There had been 125 pounds of eels in the trunk of the car he and Skunk Mitchell had driven to Philly.

That was $125,500 for some slimy sea worms. Skunk was one of Chuly's main men. Ronnie had done some of his time with one of Chuly's other main guys, Winston Chambers. He'd recommended Ronnie as a good ol' boy who could handle a gun and keep his mouth shut. Everything had gone smooth and less than a week after leaving prison Ronnie had a pocketful of money. Which he promptly blew up like the World Trade Center. That wasn't that surprising or that big of a deal. How he had blown it, however, was quite concerning. Ronnie swung his feet around and moved into a sitting position. He grabbed his T-shirt from the back of the couch he had crashed on and pulled it over his head. Reggie was in his room with a girl they had taken home from Wonderland. She was a big girl, but Ronnie didn't mind. She tried hard to please both of them, but Reggie couldn't get it up and Ronnie was quick on the draw. She didn't seem to mind that and curled up with Reggie after Ronnie had rolled off her.

Ronnie got up and went into the kitchenette and grabbed a beer from the fridge. When he had gotten back from Philly, he had gone down to North Carolina and celebrated a job well done at a strip club Chuly owned just outside of Fayetteville. A strip club that had poker games and craps in the back. Long story short, he had drunk away two hundred dollars, made it rain with a hundred dollars' worth of ones and gambled away the rest. Then he had done something so monumentally stupid he figured he should be the one getting a disability check. He had gotten a marker from Chuly's guy at the club. They let him play and play until Skunk had the guy cut him off. By that time, he was fifteen thousand dollars in the hole.

Skunk had called Chuly, and Chuly had said he had thirty days to get it to them.

"He gave you thirty days cuz he likes you," Skunk had said in that gravelly voice that made his skin crawl. He sounded like he gargled with battery acid.

"What happens if I don't have it in thirty days? You gonna kill me?" Ronnie had asked as they walked him out of the strip club.

Skunk had pushed him into the passenger seat of Reggie's car and closed the door.

"Nah, not at first. First, I'll come get you and take you out to the farm. Cut off a couple of your toes. Let you watch me feed them to the pigs," he said. He tapped the roof of the car and motioned for Reggie to leave.

"Jesus, Ronnie, what you gonna do? He was talking about cutting off your damn toes. I think that fucker would do it too. He got crazy eyes," Reggie said as they barreled out of the parking lot and onto the highway.

"Shut up, Reggie," Ronnie had said. His head had begun to spin and not from the all the alcohol he had drunk.

Ronnie took a sip from his beer. The sun was shining through the small window over the sink. The rays of light found every crack and crusty crevice in the trailer and highlighted them. Ronnie pulled a crumpled pack of cigarettes from his back pocket. He turned on the stove and lit his smoke from the blue flame of the front burner. He had gone to Wonderland last night to find another driver. He had fucked things up with Beauregard. That much was obvious. He might as well as gone to a chicken coop to count hen's teeth. There wasn't one decent driver among all the pill-popping, moonshine-swilling meth head patrons of Wonderland. At least not one he trusted with his life. And none of them had one ounce of the skill Beauregard had. Ronnie heard some noise from Reggie's room. Maybe they could do it without Beauregard. Him, Reggie and Quan. He pushed that thought away. He loved his brother but what little in the way of brains the good Lord had given him was being eaten away by pills and on occasion Mr. Brownstone. Technically Reggie could operate a motor vehicle. He just couldn't drive.

Reggie came stumbling out of the bedroom. He tripped, righted himself, then headed for the fridge.

"I gotta take Ann back up to Wonderland. You wanna go with?" Reggie said. He opened the fridge and pulled out a bottle of orange juice and took off the top.

"Don't drink that. That shit's rancid. I can smell it from here," Ronnie said. He took a drag off his cigarette.

"Might as well finish it. My EBT don't come until next week," Reggie said.

Ronnie took another hit of the beer. When you grew up poor you got used to waiting. Wait for a welfare check in the mail. Wait in line for the poor box from church. Wait for the parishioners to gaze at you with a sour look of pity on their faces. Wait for your brother to outgrow his no-name sneakers so you could take over gluing them back together. Wait, wait, wait. Wait to die so you can finally get out of debt. He was sick to death of waiting.

"So, you coming?" Reggie asked.

"Nah. I gotta find somebody to help me with this thing," Ronnie said.

"You gonna call Bug? He said to call him," Reggie asked.

"I don't think it's gonna happen. Anyway, I didn't get the burner," Ronnie said.

"I did. I got it from the 7-Eleven last night when we left Wonderland," Reggie said. He took a drink from the jug of orange juice.

Ronnie stubbed out his cigarette on the stove top. "When was that?" he asked. He didn't even remember stopping at a store last night. Maybe he was the one who needed to cut back on the moonshine.

"I just told you. When we left Wonderland. Ann wanted something to eat so I stopped," Reggie said.

"Well, that ain't no fucking shock," Ronnie said. Reggie grimaced.

"Hey, she might hear you," Reggie said in a hushed tone.

"And? What she gonna do? Sit on me?" Ronnie asked.

"Why you so mean, Ronnie?" Reggie asked. Ronnie finished his beer. He felt his gorge try to rise but he forced it back down through sheer will.

Hair of the dog my white ass, he thought.

"Where's the phone?"

Reggie jerked his thumb toward the door. "It's in the car. You gonna have to plug it into the charger," he said.

"Wow, thanks. I had no idea I'd have to plug a brand-new phone in to charge. I was only gone five years. I ain't Buck fucking Rogers. You and Big Bertha hang tight for a minute," Ronnie said. He walked out the door and down the rickety steps.

"Who?" Reggie asked as Ronnie went out the door.

Ronnie plugged the phone into the charger then called information and got the number for Montage Motors. He started the car and turned on the AC. The AC in the car was cooler than the one in the damn house.

"Montage Motors," a voice said.

"Hey, Beau? It's Ronnie."

"Yeah."

"So, um . . . that thing. We good to go or you ain't . . . ," Ronnie stammered. He didn't know how much he should say over a cell phone.

"You mean that car you want me to look at? Yeah, I'm good to go," Beauregard said. Ronnie had been slouching to his right. He sat up so fast he bumped his head on the roof.

"Yeah. Yeah, that's what's up. So, when you wanna get up and talk about it?" Ronnie said. His skin felt like he had sat too close to a wood stove. This was happening. He was gonna do it. He was going to be able to keep all his toes.

"I can come take a look at it later today. Where you got the car at?" Beauregard asked.

Ronnie didn't say anything. He was lost. "Um . . . I uh have it out at my brother's place. Over on Fox Hill Road," he said finally.

"Alright. I won't get done around here till seven. I'll see you then. If I call you back and can't get you, just sit tight. I know you been having trouble with that phone. Hope you don't have to trash it," Beauregard said.

Ronnie caught that one. He had to trash the phone. "Alright, alright, alright. See you then," he said. The line went dead. Ronnie got out of the car, threw the phone on the ground and crushed it beneath his black motorcycle boots. He gathered the pieces and carried them back into the trailer. He tossed the remains in the trash. Muffled grunts and groans were coming from Reggie's room. Ronnie flopped back on the couch and grabbed Reggie's cell phone off the coffee table. He called Quan.

"What up?" Quan said.

"The guy I was telling you about is in. We bout to do this. Can you get to my brother's place around seven thirty?" he asked.

"Man, I don't wanna come down to that country-ass, big-mosquito-having redneck town. Why can't y'all come up to Richmond?" Quan asked.

"Cuz I'm the one planning it. You in or you out? I mean if you don't want $80,000 I can always get somebody else," Ronnie said.

"Hold your horses, white boy, I'll be there. Shit. Goddamn mosquitoes driving trucks down there," he said.

"Don't worry, just put a Dixie flag in your back window, you be fine," Ronnie said.

"Fuck you, Ronnie," he said. The line went dead.

He dialed Jenny's number from memory.

"Yeah, what's up?" she asked in that honey-coated husky voice that drove him crazy.

"Hey, we on. You wanna come by tonight and celebrate?" he asked. All he heard was the hum of the open line.

"Celebrate what? Planning a robbery? I don't know, maybe we should call the whole thing off," Jenny said. He could see her in his mind. Sprawled out across her futon in that efficiency apartment over in Taylor's Corner. Her red hair fanning out around her head like a wreath made of fire.

"Come on now, baby girl. We done talked about this. Nobody gonna get hurt. Nobody is gonna get caught. I got it all planned out. Don't back out on me now. I need you. None of this works without you, baby girl," he cooed. He had known Jenny since high school. They'd been on-again off-again for decades. Whenever she got on her feet, they were off. Whenever she found herself adrift, they were back on. They usually made each other feel good for a few weeks. That was a better ratio than some supposedly monogamous couples.

"I only been working there for a few months, Ronnie. Don't you think they gonna be all up in my face if the place gets robbed?" she said.

"Not if you play it cool. Sit on your cut for a few months. Then slip away. We can go down South. Florida. Maybe even the Bahamas. If there's as much as you say, we can be farting through silk the rest of our lives," Ronnie said. He couldn't let her back out now. The thirty days were almost up. The guy in DC who was going to pay them for the stones was waiting. He had gotten Beauregard on board. He would sweet-talk her until she had Type 2 diabetes if he had to, but he couldn't let her back out.

More silence.

"This is what I do, Jenny. You know that. I been doing this since I had hair on my nuts. This is what I do, and I've only taken one fall and that was because of a fucking snitch," he said. That was partly true. He had gotten five years for robbery for stealing a gold-plated cupola from a vacation house out in Stingray Point. But he hadn't gotten caught because of a snitch. He had gotten caught because Reggie hadn't fixed the tail lights on his old truck. When the cops had pulled them over he had taken the whole fall. Reggie wasn't built for doing time. He couldn't be in tight spaces. He freaked out in elevators. He lost his shit in revolving doors. If you yelled at him, he would shut down like a robot who had gotten his plug pulled. So he took the weight. Those three years taught him two things. One: Prison food tasted like wet, piss-soaked cardboard. Two: He was never going back.

"I can't come down tonight. I gotta work today from noon till close. Then tomorrow I open," Jenny said.

Ronnie smiled. She was still in. He could hear her letting herself be talked into it.

"Alright, well, things gonna start moving fast," he said.

"I'll call you when I get off. Maybe you can come by," she said. Ronnie thought she was thinking about white sand beaches and margaritas the size of washtubs.

"No doubt," he said.

"Okay. I gotta go take a shower," she said.

"Thanks for that nice mental image. I'll be filing that away for later," he said.

"Nasty," she said. He could hear the smile on her face.

"Talk to you later, baby girl," he said. They hung up and Ronnie lay back down. He let his boots hang over the arm of the sofa. This was it. The big one. This was the one that you had wet dreams about. This wasn't some stupid-ass sickly horse or some roof trinket. This was the one that let you write your "fuck you" list. He'd told Beauregard there was five hundred thousand dollars' worth of diamonds.

That wasn't exactly true either. Lying in her bed after bumping uglies, Jenny told him it was three times that much. Even after taking a hit from the fence and giving Beauregard his cut plus his goddamn $3,800 and paying off Chuly, he would still be able to use ten-dollar bills for toilet paper. If everything worked out, people would be waiting on him from now on. If he was superstitious like his Mama had been, he might have worried about things falling into place so easily. Getting in the hole one week, then having this jewelry store drop in his lap the next. Things didn't usually work like that for the Sessions family. He didn't let it shake him. He didn't believe in superstitions or religion. His Mama had spent her life watching Sunday morning televangelists and throwing enough salt over her shoulder to season a full-grown hog. She still died broke and lonely on the bathroom floor of a bingo hall in Richmond. That wasn't how he was going out. Not now. He started humming "Money Honey." It was one of the King's lesser-known hits, but it was one of Ronnie's favorites. Because everyone knew in the end it always came down to money, honey.

SIX

Beauregard pulled down the first bay door and locked it while Kelvin shut off the air compressors and the overhead lights. The sun had finally set over Red Hill County, but the heat hadn't subsided at all. A few lightning bugs performed aerial acrobatics near the motion lights. They didn't have enough mass to set off the sensors. Beauregard paused and watched them for a second before closing the other two doors. They reminded him of summers gone by when he would sit on his grandparents' porch playing checkers with his granddad. The old man was a checkers savant. The day Beauregard finally beat him was the day he knew his grandfather was slipping away.

"You wanna go over to Danny's Bar and play some pool? I got a few hours to kill before Sandra gets off work," Kelvin asked.

Beauregard wiped his face with the least dirty rag in his pocket. "Who is Sandra? I thought you was seeing Cynthia and the other one," Beauregard said.

Kelvin grinned. "Met Sandra on Snapchat. She from Richmond. I'm riding up there when she gets off from her job at the tobacco plant," Kelvin said.

"Nah, I got something I gotta do," Beauregard said.

Kelvin raised his eyebrows. "That something got anything to do with Ronnie Sessions?" Kelvin asked.

"Something like that," Beauregard said.

"You want me to go with you?"

Beauregard shook his head. "No. I'm just getting more details. It still might be nothing," Beauregard said.

Kelvin shrugged. "Whatever, man. Let me know. I'll be at Danny's till about ten. If y'all get done. I might be down if it's something worth doing," Kelvin said.

"I'll let you know," Beauregard said. Kelvin walked toward Beauregard and held out his hand. Beauregard slapped it as Kelvin passed him and headed out the door. He heard Kelvin's Nova start up and tear out of the parking lot.

He went and sat in the Duster. The old leather on the seats smelled like tobacco that had been soaked in oil. He could see his Daddy sitting in the same seat he now occupied. He could see himself sitting in the passenger seat. Beauregard didn't dream of his Daddy. He didn't have dreams. He never had nightmares. At least none he could remember. He slipped into a quiet darkness when he slept and then emerged from that blackness when he awoke. Usually to the sounds of Darren and Javon fighting about any and everything.

When his father came to him, it was through memories. Waking dreams that grabbed him by the neck and pulled him into the past. He would see himself and his father as they had been. Sometimes he would see his grandparents or his mother. But mostly he saw his father. Smiling, laughing, sullen or sad. His father working on the Duster. His father coming up behind his mother and wrapping his tree trunk arms around her waist. His father storming out of the trailer and slamming the door so hard the whole structure rocked. His father beating down Solomon Gray with a bar stool. Him and his Daddy sitting on the hood of the Duster under a star-filled night sky looking for Orion's belt. He remembered how his five-year-old self had thought it would look like an actual belt. Whenever he went into these fugue states, he felt like Janus. Looking forward and backwards with equal amounts of trepidation.

Sitting there in the darkened garage, he was transported back to the last day he saw his father. It was hellishly hot that day too. He had waited on the steps of their trailer for his Daddy to come pick him up and go riding. He had known this visit would be a different one. His mother was more agitated than usual. He had overheard her talking to one of her friends about "Anthony done got himself in some shit he won't talk his way out of," but he didn't know what that meant. By the end of that day, he would learn.

His cell phone rang, breaking the spell. He pulled it out of his pocket. It was Kia.

"Hey," he said when he answered it.

"The boys want to spend the night at Jean's. Her neighbor's grandson got dropped off while they were there. I told them it was okay," she said.

"Hey, I'm sorry about yesterday," he said. When he had gotten home last night, she was in the bedroom pretending to be asleep. He had stayed in the living room playing with the boys. When he had finally put them to sleep and gone to lie down, she wasn't pretending anymore. He had left before breakfast. His temper could be like a lightning strike. Kia was like a smoldering forest fire. He knew he had to give her some space to let it burn itself out.

"Yeah, me too. I shouldn't have said what I said."

"I shouldn't have slammed the door like that. You know I'm just trying to do right by you and the boys. And Ariel," he said.

"You wanna do right by us, don't do nothing with them boys that came by yesterday. As far as Ariel goes, you been trying to do for that girl. Ain't your fault her mama a cracked-out bitch," she said.

Beauregard clucked his tongue against the roof of his mouth. "Knowing these boys, it probably ain't nothing too serious," he said.

Kia grunted. "Baby, nobody gets you to drive their aunty to the store. So, don't talk to me like I'm dumb. You wouldn't even be thinking about it if it wasn't something big. And that means it's dangerous," she said.

"I don't wanna argue with you, Kia," Beauregard said.

"And I don't wanna lose you, Bug," she said.

They both went quiet.

"I'll talk to you when I get home. I gotta go," he said.

"Yeah, you will. We need to do a lot of talking," she said. She hung up.

Beauregard put the phone in his pocket and got out of the Duster. The thing about loving someone was that they knew all your pressure points. They knew all the spots that were open and raw. You let them into your heart and they cased the place. They knew what made you feel weak and what ticked you off. Like somebody hanging up on you. He opened his mouth and closed it like a lion then shook his head violently side to side. He had to let that go.

He needed to have his head in the game. Getting ready for a job was like putting on a new coat. You had to make sure it fit. If everything didn't look right he would walk away. Leave that coat on the rack. No matter how much money was on the table. He glanced back at the Duster. The money was important. God knows they needed it. So many people were depending on him. Kia, his Mama, the boys, Ariel, Kelvin. He thought about what Boonie had said. About how he wasn't like his father. That's what he liked to believe. That they were completely different. In some respects that was true. No matter how intense the pressure got, he didn't run out on his family or his friends. He wasn't Anthony Montage. So why did he feel a flutter in his chest like a hornet was trapped in his ribs? If he wasn't like his Daddy, why did he miss the Life?

There were nights he would cruise around and find a race on his own without Kelvin. Mostly young kids with some aftermarket overseas windup toy of a car. Other times he took the Duster and blew it out on a backcountry road. Passing by the trees and the raccoons like a comet running on high-test. He'd get up to 160 before slamming on the brakes and drifting to a stop. No matter how fast he went or how many races he won it didn't compare to driving for a crew. Being behind the wheel with the cops behind you and the road in front of you while everyone around you was wishing they had worn brown pants. It was a high that couldn't be replicated with drugs or drinks. He'd tried both and they didn't come close.

They had never spoken about it, but he was sure if he could talk to his Daddy he would have felt the same way. The words "need for speed" should have been burned onto the Montage family crest. Along with a skull and crossbones.

He locked up the garage and hopped in the truck. As he drove away the sun cast elongated shadows against the front of the garage. Narrow black fingers squeezing the building in their grip.

SEVEN

Beauregard navigated his way down a pothole-filled dirt road that the county in their infinite wisdom had decided to name Chitlin Lane. When Virginia went to a statewide emergency GPS system, they required any road, lane or cul-de-sac with more than three residents to have an actual name. The county administrators decided to fully embrace the stereotypical Southern ethos and name all the side roads with names that sounded like rejected country song titles. They thought it might help tourism. The only problem with that was that Red Hill was no one's destination. It was a place you drove through, not to.

Wild blackberry bushes lined the lane, interspersed with the occasional pine tree or cypress. The black sky was moonless. The truck creaked and groaned as it rolled over the rough terrain. He passed a dilapidated one-story ranch and two newish double-wides similar to his own. Finally, the lane widened into a clearing with a rusty single-wide smack dab in the middle. The blue Toyota was parked near the door beside a tricked-out Bonneville with 24-inch rims and a matte black paint job. Beauregard parked behind the Bonneville, got out and knocked on the door of the trailer.

Ronnie Sessions opened the door and smiled at Beauregard. Beauregard didn't return the smile. Ronnie stepped aside and beckoned for Beauregard to come in.

"Quan just got here. We was about to have some beers. You want one?" Ronnie asked. Beauregard surveyed the living area of the trailer. A huge brown couch covered in threadbare suede uphol-stery dominated the room. It was too big and too ostentatious for the small structure. It had the feel of a yard sale find that was shoe-horned into the single-wide. A heavily scarred wooden coffee table composed of rough-hewn planks of timber sat in front of the couch. An easy chair sat at the head of the coffee table. Sitting in the chair was a chubby black guy with a forest of tiny braids protruding from his scalp. He was wearing a baggy T-shirt that was two sizes too big. On his feet were the latest incarnation of a washed-up basketball player's most enduring legacy. His jeans were so baggy they could have been pantaloons. He had a wide face that was slick with sweat. An unruly goatee covered the lower half of his face and threatened to envelop his mouth.

Across from the couch was a love seat. It was covered in a bright red and yellow floral print. Beauregard thought it looked like a clown had vomited on it. Reggie was sitting there next to a large white woman with a rat's nest of green and blue hair. Whoever had dyed her hair had missed a few places. Blond spots dotted her head like cheetah print. A wooden chair sat at the end of the coffee table nearest to Beauregard.

"No," Beauregard said. He sat down in the wooden chair. Ron-nie grabbed three beers out of the fridge and handed one to Reggie and one to the black man. Beauregard figured he was Quan. Ronnie plopped down on the couch and opened his beer.

"You got somewhere to be?" Beauregard said to the large woman sitting next to Reggie.

She scrunched up her face. "Uh . . . no. I mean not really," she said.

"Yeah, you do," Beauregard said.

The woman turned her head from Beauregard to Reggie then back to Beauregard.

"Huh?" she said.

"Reggie, go on and take her back to Wonderland," Ronnie said.

Reggie opened his mouth, closed it then opened it again. "Come on, girl, I'll take you back," he said finally.

"I thought I was spending the night again?" she whined. Her eyes pleaded with Reggie. Reggie stood.

"Let's go. I'll just crash up there with you," he said. The woman didn't seem like she was going to move at first. She crossed her legs at the ankles and her arms across her ample bosom.

"You deaf? Get the fuck up," Ronnie said. The woman flinched. Huffing and puffing she pulled herself off the love seat and got to her feet. Reggie shot Ronnie a dirty look, but Ronnie was studying the top of his can of beer.

"Let's go, Ann," Reggie said. He headed for the door. She followed him without saying a word.

"I bet people scream 'Godzilla!' when they see her walk into Walmart," Quan said. He tittered at his own joke, then sipped his beer. Beauregard caught his gaze. Neither one of them said anything for a few seconds. Beauregard turned to Ronnie.

"Three things. One: We don't talk to nobody about this but the five people that already know about it. Not no girl you might meet in the club. Not some homie you trying to impress. Not your mama or your daddy. Nobody. Two: When it's done, we stay away from each other. We don't go get drinks to celebrate. We don't go to Atlantic City as a group and hit the slots. We go our separate ways and we stay separate. Three: The day it goes down, we are all straight. Don't get high. Don't pop no Oxy. Don't smoke a blunt. Nothing. If y'all can get down with that, then I'm in. If not, I walk right now," Beauregard said.

Quan and Ronnie exchanged bemused glances.

"Alright, Ethan Hunt. I feel ya," Quan said.

"Hey, man, that works for me," Ronnie said.

Beauregard sat back in his chair and put his hands on his knees. "Then let's get to it," he said.

He listened to Ronnie talk about the job for twenty minutes before he held up his hand and stopped him midsentence.

"You haven't checked the place out, have you? Does your girl know the code to the alarm system? How far from the interstate is the store? How many ways are there other than the interstate to get away? Is there some construction going on down there? How often do the police patrol that part of town? Is there a lock-down system? Who knows the combination to the safe other than the manager?" Beauregard said.

This time it was Ronnie's turn to hold up his hand.

"I get it, okay? We need to do some recon on the place. Jenny can get the alarm code, but the way I figured it, nobody will have a chance to hit the alarm. We get in, we get the diamonds, we get out."

"You have to take more than the diamonds in the safe," Beauregard said. He flexed his left hand. His knuckles popped like knots of green wood in a fireplace.

"Why you say that?" Quan asked.

"Because if you only take the diamonds, the cops will know it was an inside job. And I bet there ain't more than five or six people that work at this store," Beauregard said.

Ronnie stared up at the ceiling.

"That's a good point," he mumbled.

"Man, fuck all this ying-yang. We go in there, blast the ceiling, them motherfuckers do what we say do. Or we ventilate they ass," Quan said.

He reached around to the small of his back and pulled out an enormous nickel-plated semiautomatic pistol. Beauregard thought it might be a Desert Eagle.

Quan held the gun near his face. "I got the gat, so I make the rules," he said. He punctuated each syllable by shaking the gun.

"Put that thing away," Beauregard said.

Quan smiled. "Don't worry, big man, I got the safety on. I know how to handle it," Quan said. He tucked the gun back in his waist-band. Beauregard figured it was a miracle of physics that the gun didn't fall to his feet every time he wore those baggy-ass jeans.

"We gonna need new guns too," Beauregard said.

Quan rolled his eyes. "Nigga, this my favorite gun."

"That's why we need new ones. How many bodies on that one? How many robberies? You think the cops don't keep them shell cas-ings?" Beauregard asked.

Quan seemed to ponder this for a moment. "Where we gonna get new pieces from?" Quan asked.

Beauregard rubbed his palms over his thighs. "I know somebody. We can get two pieces for five hundred. But before we get to that I need to go to check the place out."

"Damn, nigga, five hundred? I thought we was the ones doing the robbing," Quan said. Beauregard glared at him. The other man held his gaze. Eventually Quan looked away. Beauregard got up and went into the kitchen. He opened the fridge and grabbed a can of beer. He went back into the living room and sat at the end of the love seat near Quan's chair. He popped the tab and took a long sip. The beer was cold as ice and chilled him all the way to his belly.

"You know, I had this friend who had a Chihuahua. Little nasty ankle biter. Every time I came around, he would bark and bark and bark. Bare his teeth and shit. But if I stomped my feet at him, he would run and hide under the couch," Beauregard said. He set the beer on the coffee table close to the edge.

"Why the fuck you telling me about some dog, man?" Quan asked.

Beauregard didn't respond. Instead he tipped over the can with his right hand. Beer splashed over Quan's sneakers and pants. Curs-ing, he jumped up out of the chair. At the same time, Beauregard jumped up too. He grabbed Quan's gun from his waistband near the small of his back. Clicked off the safety and let the gun hang loosely by his side. Quan spun to his right until he was facing Beauregard.

Beauregard heard a strangled cough come from the couch as Ronnie choked on his beer.

"Because you remind me of that little dog. You yap and yap and talk a lot of shit, but I think at the first sign of trouble you might just piss your pants. Or run. Or both. Ronnie say you good people. He says he knows you. He trusts you. That's fine. But I don't. You talk like this a movie. It ain't. It's real life. My life. And I ain't putting it in your hands. So, I'm going to check the place out. I'm going to get the car. I'm going to take us to get the guns. You don't like that, then I walk. Cuz I ain't trying to wake up to three hots and a cot because you gonna ball up like a baby when the work goes down," Beauregard said.

He ejected the clip from the Desert Eagle and then racked the slide to eject the one in the chamber. It rolled across the vinyl-covered floor and came to rest against the far wall. He tossed the gun and clip onto the couch next to Ronnie.

"You got a problem with that, we can handle it. Or we can get this money. It's up to you," Beauregard asked. The AC wheezed as it struggled to cool the rectangular box. Quan scowled at Beauregard but didn't say a word for nearly a full minute. He glanced at Ronnie then turned his attention back to Beauregard.

"Oh, we gonna handle it, motherfucker. After. But for now, let's talk about making this money," he snarled. Beauregard sat back down. Quan waited for what he thought was an appropriate amount of time before he sat down as well.

"Alright then. Like I said, I'm gonna go check out the place tomorrow. Ronnie, can you talk to your girl and find out if she knows the alarm code and the combination to the safe? Once I scope the place out, we can go talk to my boy about getting strapped. The two of you should be able to come up with five bills for the pieces," Beauregard said.

"Sure, sure, I can talk to her. You need the address of the store, though," Ronnie said. He dug around in his pocket for a piece a paper. He pulled out an old receipt and grabbed a pen off the coffee table. Beauregard shook his head.

"Don't write nothing down. You said the store is in Cutter County. I think I can find it. We'll meet again in a week to get the guns. That will give me enough time to get some wheels and make some modifications. We'll only use burners from here on out. Keep your mouth shut and your head down," he said.

"What we do with the pieces after we done?" Quan said.

Beauregard tilted his head toward him. "If you don't have to use them, you can keep 'em. If you do, we break 'em down and toss them," he said.

Quan rolled his eyes. "Five hundred down the drain," he said.

"What, you want to make it a family heirloom?" Ronnie asked.

"Just a waste of money. That's all I'm saying," Quan said.

"I don't think you get what's going on here. Armed robbery in the state of Virginia is a Class 5 felony with a mandatory minimum of three years with a maximum of life. That's if no one gets hurt. The guns are just tools. Tools break. Tools get lost. Don't get attached to them," Beauregard said.

"Sound like you talking about people," Ronnie said.

"Same difference," Beauregard said. He stood. "I think that's all we gotta talk about right now."

"What kind of car you gonna get?" Ronnie asked.

"What difference do it make?" Beauregard said.

"It don't. I was just curious," Ronnie said.

"Can you get a BMW like in that movie with the motherfucker from England? The Transformer," Quan said. Beauregard closed his eyes.

"It won't be a BMW," he said. He ground his teeth together. "I'm out." Beauregard turned and headed for the door. He opened it and was just about to step out when he stopped. "You wanna see me after the job, that's fine. But if I see you coming and you ain't smiling and friendly, it ain't going to go well," he said.

He stepped through the door and into the night. A few moments passed, and they heard his truck start. The trailer was silent save for the shuddering AC and the slight hum of the overhead light fixture.

"Hey, man, he takes this shit seriously. I don't think he was trying to disrespect you," Ronnie said finally.

"Man, give me my fucking gun," Quan said.

Beauregard parked his truck next to Kia's car and got out. The air was still stifling hot. The house was dark save for the porch light. Beauregard unlocked the door and made his way through the shadowy interior toward the bedroom.

Kia was spread across the bed like a Botticelli painting. A thin white T-shirt and zebra-striped panties were her only accoutrements. Beauregard took off his boots and let his pants fall to the floor. He pulled his shirt up over his head and let it fall to the floor as well. He eased his body down to the bed, snaked his arm over Kia's stomach.

"That night you came home with that bullet wound, I asked you how much more of this we was supposed to take. You said the juice was worth the squeeze. Do you remember what I said?" she asked.

"You said that was the dumbest shit you had ever heard," Beauregard said. Kia grabbed his hand and pulled his arm tighter around her body. He could feel the warmth from the small of her back against the bottom of his belly.

"But you was right. It was worth it. We got the house. We got the garage. We got out, baby. We got out. And now you wanna go back, and I'm telling you this time the juice ain't worth it," she said. Her voice hitched a few times and Beauregard knew she was crying.

"If there was any other way, I would do it differently," he said. He spoke directly into her ear.

"Sell the garage. Take a job at the tire plant over in Parker County. Start selling vacuum cleaners," she said.

He moved closer to her and squeezed her tight. "It's gonna be alright. I promise," he said.

She squirmed against him and rolled over onto her back. "I shouldn't have said that about your Daddy. I'm sorry. But that's something he would tell your Mama. You can't promise that it's gonna be okay. You don't know that. What if it ain't? Then I have to tell your sons stories about you the way people told you stories about your Daddy. Because memories fade, Bug," she said.

Beauregard ran his index finger down the length of her face and under her chin. He tilted her head up and kissed her cheeks. The salt from her tears lingered in his mouth. He had no rebuttal to her argument. Things might go south. The job might fall apart. Anyone who was in the Life knew that was a possibility, but he didn't dwell on those kinds of thoughts. He had survived this long because he never envisioned himself behind bars. He refused to see that as an option. Five years in juvenile detention had given him focus. Sharpened his mind to a deadly edge. He would never be at the mercy of anyone who controlled his freedom again.

Beyond the vanities of his own ego, he could see that his wife was also right about memories. He thought about his father all the time and yet his Daddy's voice seemed to grow more and more faint. Did he sound the way Beauregard remembered or was there more vibrato in his speech? Did he have a scar on his right hand or left hand? His father's face was becoming blurred around the edges in his mind. Unless he was sitting in the Duster, Anthony Montage was a shade who spoke in whispers. Sitting in the car brought everything back into crystalline clarity. If he went through with this job, would his sons have to sit in the Duster to recall his face? Would they even want to?

"I promise you. We will be fine," he said. He leaned forward and kissed her on her mouth. At first her lips were set in a hard line but slowly they opened, and her tongue slipped into his. His hand slid up her thigh until he touched her in the center of her body. She shuddered and pulled away from him.

"You better keep your promises," she moaned. He crushed his lips against hers again, and they fell against each other in a tangle of arms and legs and groans and sighs.

EIGHT

Jenny awoke to a series of horns and trumpets going off like Judgment Day. Her text message tone echoed through her tiny apartment. The horns reached a crescendo then started at the top of the melody again.

She grabbed her phone off the nightstand. The contact name on the screen said Rock and Roll. Her first text message of the day was from Ronnie "Rock and Roll" Sessions.

Need the alarm codes, the message said.

Jenny stared at her phone and blinked her eyes. Hard.

I don't know what you are talking about. Call me. She typed. She hit send then grabbed her cigarettes and a lighter out of the nightstand. After her third drag off the smoke a set of bird chirps began to emanate from her phone. This was her ringtone. She touched the screen and answered the phone.

"Don't text me shit like that. Jesus."

"Well, good morning to you too," Ronnie said.

"I'm serious, Ronnie. Who do you think the police gonna be looking at with all the eyes they have if we pull this off? I don't need shit like that in my phone records."

"Damn, you woke on the wrong side of the crypt this morning. Sound like you need a good tuning up," Ronnie said.

"You know, your dick ain't the answer to everything," Jenny said.

"If my dick ain't the answer you ain't asking the right questions. But never mind all that. Can you get it?"

"Get what?" Jenny asked.

"The alarm code," Ronnie said. Jenny took a long drag off her cigarette.

"I already know it. Lou Ellen told me what it was the other day."

"How is your girlfriend doing? She get that call from the Cowboys yet about that starting offensive lineman position?" Ronnie asked.

"Not funny, Ronnie. She's nice."

"Don't tell me you're falling for her. She can't be that good at eating pussy."

"You so damn nasty. She's just nice to me. I don't want her to get hurt. I don't want anybody to get hurt. Not Lou Ellen, not you, not me. I just want to get out of here. Get out of Cutter County. Out of Virginia. I want to go somewhere and answer to a new name for the rest of my life. Try to start over. Maybe try not to make so many mistakes this time," Jenny said.

"And we will. All you got to do is exactly what I tell you to do. And before you know it we will be fucking on a bed full of hundred-dollar bills," Ronnie said. Jenny exhaled. A plume of smoke billowed from her nostrils.

"I just don't want to get fucked up behind this," Jenny said.

"Baby girl, you won't. All you got to do is trust me. Is that so hard? Now stop worrying about all that and let's get back to talking about more important things. What you getting into today? Maybe I can come over. I got some Percocets and a case of beer with your name all over them."

"Down, boy. I gotta go into work. You know, that thing people do instead of stealing."

"Well shit. Hey, tell your sugar mama I said hi."

"Bye, Ronnie."

"Wait, what time you get off?"

"About fifteen minutes after you roll off me and go to sleep," Jenny said and hung up the phone.

NINE

Beauregard got up at first light. Kia was curled up next to him like a cat. He slipped out of bed and put on a pair of jeans and a T-shirt. He grabbed a baseball cap out of the dresser drawer and pulled it down over his eyes. Then he kissed Kia on her cheek.

"You leaving early," she said without opening her eyes.

"Gotta get to the shop," he lied. He stroked her cheek with the back of his hand.

"I'm gonna need you to pick the boys up tonight. I'm going with Lakisha Berry to clean up some offices near the courthouse," Kia said.

Beauregard kissed her again. "That's good, boo. I'll get 'em when we close tonight. Love you," he said.

"Love you too," she said. The last part of the sentence disintegrated into a sigh. Beauregard left the house and got into his truck. He turned on the radio and scrolled through the stations until he hit one playing some old-school R&B. Rev. Al Green's trembling falsetto drifted out of the speakers like a cool mist. He headed out of Red Hill and onto Route 60 toward the interstate. Just before hitting the on-ramp he passed the abandoned Tastee Freez. The white aluminum carport that had covered the pick-up window had collapsed but the rest of the building appeared solid. A crowd of thistles and kudzu covered the eastern side of the building. Verdant green weeds had forced their way up between the seams of the pavement in the parking lot. Ellery and Emma Sheridan had run the Tastee Freez for fifty years before Ellery died in 2001. Emma had tried to soldier on without her husband, but Alzheimer's had snatched the remnants of her mind and tossed them to the four winds. The county had stepped in after some customers had pulled up and found Emma making milkshakes and burgers in her birthday suit.

When he had been a kid, Beauregard had loved the Tastee Freez double chocolate milkshake. It was a rare treat on a hot summer day like today. The kind of dessert that made you throw caution to the wind. His Daddy used to joke that if a van pulled up with no windows, Beauregard would jump in the back if they promised him they were taking him to the Tastee Freez. As they had ridden around on what would be the last day he would see his father, the Tastee Freez had been one of their stops. Years later, a legend spread through Red Hill that there were bloodstains on the pavement that no amount of water could wash away.

Beauregard turned the music up and merged onto the interstate. The sounds of Rev. Green did little to drown out the memories of that long-ago day.

Cutter County was seventy miles away from Red Hill County on the other side of the state. Through a combination of chance and design it had begrudgingly become a suburb of the city of Newport News. Most of the residents worked in the city at one of three large employers. The naval shipyard, the Canon manufacturing plant or Patrick Henry Mall. Beauregard could see the effect of those industries on Cutter County. It was like Red Hill's wealthier twin. He had only seen three mobile homes as he drove through town. There were more brick houses on one road than in all of Red Hill. He turned onto Main Street and passed two cleaners, a liquor store, three consignment shops and two medical offices. The traffic was light, but it was all BMWs and Mercedeses with a stray Lexus here and there. For a moment, he was afraid there would be five jewelry stores and he would have to call Ronnie from his personal cell and not a burner. Before he had to suffer that indignity, he spotted a sign for a shopping center that listed VALENTI JEWELERS as one of the tenants. Apparently, the residents of Cutter County needed a wide variety of choices for their dry cleaning, but when it came to jewelry, Valenti's had cornered the market.

Beauregard drove past the shopping center. He turned left at the next cross street and saw a blue sign that indicated the sheriff's office was 3.5 miles away. He followed the road until he passed a small brick building with the Cutter County seal emblazoned on its front door. Beauregard counted two cruisers parked in front of the building. They would have to move quick. The sheriff's office was much closer than he would have liked. He turned around at the end of the street and headed back to the shopping center.

Beauregard pulled in and drove through the empty parking lot. The shopping center was composed of one long L-shaped building divided into individual units. The jewelry store was the last unit at the bottom of the L. It was also closest to the entrance/exit. Beauregard rolled through the parking lot and out of the shopping center. He didn't need to go in the store. That was on Ronnie. His job was to drive. He committed the layout of the shopping center, Main Street and the road to the interstate exit to memory. He noted the one stoplight at the corner of Main and Lafayette. The speed bump at the exit of the parking lot. The coffee shop across the street with the big picture window, which would give any potential witnesses a bird's-eye view to the job. All these and dozens of other details filled his mind. It was like his brain was a sponge absorbing water. The counselor in juvie had told him he had an eidetic memory. Mr. Skorzeny had tried his best to get him to consider going back to school when he got out. Maybe college. Beauregard knew Mr. Skorzeny had meant well. Unlike a lot of the staff at Jefferson Davis Reformatory, he didn't view boys like him as lost causes. What Mr. Skorzeny didn't understand, what he couldn't understand, was that boys like Beauregard didn't have the luxury of options. No father. A mother who was one flat tire and a bad day away from a nervous breakdown, and grandparents who had lived and died in a constant state of abject poverty. For boys like Beauregard, college was the stuff of dreams. Mr. Skorzeny might as well have told him to go to Mars.

Beauregard turned onto Route 60 West and headed back to the interstate. He checked his watch. It was exactly thirteen minutes from the jewelry store to the exit with minimal traffic traveling at 55 mph. He would be going a lot faster than 55 when they left the parking lot. On his way into town, he had noticed the interstate was undergoing some extensive renovations. The road crested just before the exit to Cutter County and became an overpass for nearly a mile. Under that overpass was a single-lane highway that led to Cutter County through the back roads. The concrete median between the northbound and southbound lanes had been demolished. It seemed the state had finally decided to address the god-awful clusterfuck that was Interstate 64 and widen the road to six lanes. A silt fence encircled the gaping maw. Beauregard noticed that the distances between the overpass and the road couldn't have been over twenty feet.

Interesting.

Up ahead Beauregard saw brake lights flash like Christmas decorations. Traffic on Route 60 moved to the left lane then back to the right. Once the box truck in front of him had changed lanes, Beauregard could see what had caused everyone in front of him to hit the brakes. A small boxy car was sitting in the middle of the road with its hazard flashers on. A slim black man with a youngish face was next to the vehicle, frantically waving his arms. A diaphanous plume of steam was billowing from under the hood of the small car.

Vehicles zipped by the man like he was one of those tube men flapping in the air near the entrance to a car dealership. Beauregard started to pass by the man too. As he drove by, he noticed a woman was sitting in the passenger seat. A young white girl with blond hair too bright not to have come from a bottle. The blond hair was plastered to her head. She was panting like a hound dog and her eyes were closed tight.

"Shit," Beauregard breathed. He pulled over to the side of the road and hopped out of his truck. The man came running over before he had closed his door.

"Hey, man, I need help. My car just broke down and my wife is in labor. Piece of shit just died on me. No warning, no nothing. Fucking piece of shit," the man yelled.

"Why you ain't call a rescue squad?" Beauregard asked.

The man cast his eyes downward. "Our cell got cut off a few days ago. I got laid off last month from the shipyard. Look, man, I think the baby is about to come. Can you give us a ride to the hospital?" the man asked.

Beauregard took in the whole scene. The man was breathing hard. The girl in the car was moaning. He recognized that moan. He recognized the quivering lips of the man standing in front of him. They were terrified. The baby was coming, and they didn't know what in the hell they were doing. Fifteen minutes of fun was about to turn into a lifetime of responsibility. The weight of that responsibility was pressing down on them like an anvil on their chests. He was on his way home from casing the site of a job. He needed to get in and get out without being noticed.

The smart thing to do, the professional thing to do, was to get back in his truck and drive away. The girl moaned again. The moan became a scream that Beauregard could hear over the sound of traffic zipping by them on the lonely stretch of road. Ariel had been a breech baby. The doctors had a hell of time getting her out of Janice's uterus. They told him that if she hadn't been delivered in a hospital, she would have probably died.

"Let's get your car out of the road first," he said.

The two of them were able to push the car off to the side of the road without too much difficulty. Beauregard grabbed the young girl and half helped, half carried her to the truck. The man opened the door for her and together they helped her up into the cab. The man hopped in on the passenger side and Beauregard ran around to the driver's side.

"You think you can get us to the hospital before . . ." The man let the statement hang in the air. Beauregard almost smiled.

"Just hold on," he said as he hit the gas.

The nearest hospital was Reed General in Newport News. It was thirty-five minutes away. Beauregard pulled up to the emergency entrance eighteen minutes after picking up the couple. The man hopped out and ran into the emergency room. A few seconds later, a nurse was following him back out pushing a wheelchair. They helped the girl out of the truck and wheeled her into the hospital. The young guy lingered by the door. Beauregard got back into his truck. When he looked up, the guy was trotting over to the window.

"Hey, man, I don't know what to say. I wish I could give you something. I'm just so strapped right now, and Caitlin had to stop working because of the baby. We moved in with her mom and . . ." Without warning, tears began to trickle from the corners of his eyes.

"Hey. Hey. You don't owe me nothing. I just hope everything goes alright," Beauregard said.

The man wiped at his face. He had a close-cropped haircut and the beginnings of a moustache. Beauregard figured he was barely out of his teens.

"Yeah. Me too. Hey look, thanks, man. I don't know what would have happened if you hadn't stopped. Everybody else drove by us like we were shit that they didn't want to get on their shoes. I tell you what, you one driving mofo. I think we got here before we left," the man said. He held his hand out to Beauregard. Beauregard took it and shook it. The guy had a firm grip. A working man's grip.

"Hey, what's your name? If it's a boy, we might name it after you," the man said. Beauregard didn't say anything. He shook the man's hand again.

"Anthony," he said finally. His father's name tasted like a bitter pill that could save your life by almost killing you.

He let go of the man's hand and drove away.

Red Hill County
August 1991

Beauregard could feel the power of the Duster's engine rumbling up through the floorboards, through the seat and out the top of his head. A Buddy Guy cassette was playing in the tape deck. The warbling whine of Buddy's polka-dot guitar erupted from the radio speakers. His Daddy had one hand on the steering wheel while his other hand gripped a brown bag. He alternated between singing along with the cassette and taking swigs from the bottle. Beauregard glanced at the speedometer. They were approaching 90 miles an hour. The trees and the rolling fields looked like pieces of Technicolor taffy as the Duster flew by.

"You know why I wanted to have you come over this weekend, don't ya, Bug?" Anthony said.

Beauregard nodded. "Mama says you going away. For a long time," he said.

His Daddy took another long swig from his bottle. He switched it from his right hand to his left hand while holding the steering wheel steady with his knee. Then he launched it out the window. Beauregard heard it smash against a sign that stated the speed limit on Town Bridge Road was 45 mph.

"Your Mama say anything else?" Anthony asked. Beauregard turned his head and gazed out the window. "That's what I thought. Your Mama . . . your Mama is a good woman. She just can't stand herself for falling for my bullshit. She don't take it out on you, do she, Bug?" Anthony asked.

Beauregard shook his head. He hated lying to his Daddy. But he hated seeing his parents argue more.

"Well, I ain't going away for that long, Bug. A year, maybe two. Just until things cool down," Anthony said.

"Where are you going?" Beauregard asked. He already knew, but he wanted to hear his Daddy say it. Until he said where he was going, it wasn't real.

Anthony cut his eyes at Beauregard. "California. There's work out there for a man that can drive," he said. They slid through a curve without downshifting. Anthony pressed on the brake and the clutch with his feet and let the car drift into the turn then hit the gas before it could stall. Neither one of them spoke for a few minutes. The 340 did all the talking for them.

"Why you gotta go away, Daddy?" Beauregard asked.

Anthony didn't turn his head. He gripped the steering wheel so tight Beauregard could hear it creak. The muscles in Anthony's neck bulged under his dark obsidian skin. The Duster leaped forward as they descended a slight incline. Beauregard felt his stomach float up near his neck.

"Bug, I want you to listen to me here. Really listen. I'm gonna say two things and I don't want you to forget them, alright? Shit, what am I saying, you don't never forget nothing. First thing is I love ya. I done some fucked-up shit in my time but the best thing I ever done was be your Daddy. No matter what nobody ever tells you, including your Mama, don't ever doubt I love ya," Anthony said.

A park-and-ride lot came into view about five hundred feet up ahead. As they approached it, Anthony whipped the steering wheel to the right and the Duster skidded across the gravel until it came to a stop in front of a concrete parking bumper.

"Second: When it comes down to it, don't nobody care about you the way you care about yourself. Don't ever let nobody make you do for them something they wouldn't do for you. You hear me, boy?" Anthony asked.

Beauregard nodded. "I hear ya, Daddy," he said.

"People want you to put up with something for a lifetime they wouldn't put up with for five minutes. I'll be damned if I'm doing that. Hey, look, I know your grandma put her foot in them biscuits but I could use a shake. You want to go to the Tastee Freez?" Anthony asked.

Beauregard knew his Daddy didn't really want a milkshake. He was trying to be nice. He always tried to be nice whenever he did something that hurt him or his Mama.

"Yeah," Beauregard said.

"Alright then. We gonna get you the biggest strawberry shake they got," Anthony said. He put the Duster in gear and spun his tires as they sped out of the park-and-ride.

"Chocolate. My favorite is chocolate," Beauregard whispered.

TEN

Beauregard closed the shop early. He'd let Kelvin go around noon. The morning had been painfully slow. They'd passed the time playing checkers, listening to the radio and shooting the shit.

"You want me to call you tomorrow before I come in?" Kelvin had asked.

"Yeah."

"Just so you know, I told Jamal Paige I would help him out a few days next week. Driving his tow truck for him while he out of town. Just so you know," Kelvin had said.

"That's fine."

"Told him I might be available a few days a week. Until things pick up around here," Kelvin said.

"I understand. You gotta do what you gotta do. It's cool," Beauregard said.

Kelvin had stood there with his hands in the pockets of his coveralls. "I just don't want you to think I'm dipping on you."

"I know you ain't," Beauregard said. But he wouldn't blame Kelvin if he did.

After Kelvin had left, he had sat in his office watching the minute hand on the clock on the wall. It moved languidly. He held on for three more hours, then went over to see Boonie.

The yard was busy. Cars and trucks were moving across the weigh scale at a brisk clip. A cavalcade of rusted iron and crumpled steel was passing through the gates of Red Hill Metals. Beauregard wondered about where some of the items came from. A wrought iron bed frame sat on the back of a lime green pickup sitting in front of him, waiting its turn on the scale. The finials on the headboard were shaped like blackberries. Had children pretended they were real? Had a beautiful woman reached out and grabbed them as she sat astride her lover? Did an old gangster experience the death Boonie said was denied to men like him in that bed?

He got through the gate and went into the office. Boonie was sitting at his desk counting out money to a wide white man wearing a Confederate flag hat. Beauregard stood near the door.

"That's two-fifty, Howard," Boonie said after he had finished counting. He handed the wad of bills to the man, who seemed to hesitate before he grabbed them.

"That motor by itself is worth $200. It weighs damn dear a thousand pounds," the man grumbled.

"Howard, that's the motor out a Gremlin. Now if you want to try your luck somewhere else, go right ahead. But they gonna ask a lot more questions than I do," Boonie said.

Howard stood up and put the money in his pocket. He left without saying a word.

"You wanna bet he's calling me a nigger in his head?" Boonie asked.

Beauregard chuckled. "Hell, he was probably doing that before he sat down," he said.

Boonie swiveled in his chair and locked the safe that sat behind him. "Long as he don't say it out loud. You see that hat he was wearing? Them good ol' boys always telling us to get over slavery, but they can't get over having their ass handed to them by Sherman," Boonie said.

Beauregard sat in the chair Howard had just vacated. "I need a favor," he said.

"I haven't heard anything about any jobs yet," Boonie said.

Beauregard shook his head. "I need a car. I can't pay you up front, but I'll get you on the back end. Doesn't matter what condition the body is in, but the frame gotta be tight," he said.

Boonie leaned back in his chair. It wailed under his weight. "You got a line on something?" he asked.

Beauregard crossed his legs at the ankles. "Something like that," he said. He could feel tremors coming up from the floor as a dually drove by the window. Boonie rocked back and forth in the chair. It cried out for mercy.

"This wouldn't have anything to do with Ronnie Sessions, would it?" Boonie said. Beauregard held his face in check, but the shock registered in his hands. He squeezed them into fists so tight his knuckles popped. They sounded like pieces of glass thrown against a brick wall.

"Why you say that? Did he tell you that?" Beauregard said. His words came out in a slow monotone.

"Nah. But he came in here this morning talking a mile a minute with five rolls of copper that I know he fucking stole and five bags of mulch that I also know he stole, but I can't figure out why. I gave him four for the rolls. They were worth five, but I don't like that boy. He like to play dumb, but he as slick as two eels in a bucketful of snot. He told Samuel he had a job in the works and needed some money for tools. Told him it was a rocking chair job. He wouldn't never have to work again. And now you asking about a car," Boonie said.

He let the statement hang in the air between them. Beauregard didn't say anything. He kept his face placid.

"Well, shit. Just promise me you gonna be careful. Let's go out back. I think I got something for you," Boonie said.

They wandered through the maze-like back lot of Red Hill Metals. Dozens upon dozens of junk cars littered the landscape like the dead husks of some great forgotten creatures. The smell of stagnant rainwater mixed with oil and gas and grease filled the air. Dust devils chased at their feet as they crunched across the gravel. Finally, they came to a dark blue two-door sedan.

"Just got this the other day from Sean Tuttle's old house. '87 Buick Regal GNX. The motor's shot but I don't guess that gonna bother you much. The bones on this ol' boy are rock solid. Transmission was still good too. Sean didn't see himself doing anything with it, so we picked it up. I was gonna start selling parts off it, but I can let you have it for a grand."

Beauregard peered through the driver's window. The interior was torn and busted in multiple places. The headliner was drooping like a stroke victim's cheek. The front bumper had a hole in it the size of an offensive lineman's fist. Pockets of rust covered the hood like some oxidizing eczema. The side mirrors were barely holding on. A good stiff wind would send them flying. It saddened him to see a car in such a state of disrepair. It made his skin crawl to see a car deteriorate like this. There was a part of him that wanted to fix up every junked broke-down rambling wreck he saw. Kia told him he felt about cars the way most people felt about puppies.

"Can you bring it by the shop tomorrow?" Beauregard asked.

"Yeah, I can. Probably shouldn't, though. I know you pressed up against it, Bug, but I don't trust that boy. He so crooked they gonna have to screw him into the ground when he dies," Boonie said.

Beauregard knew Boonie meant well. He knew the old man cared. But Boonie had options. Beauregard didn't. "I'll get you straight after it's all done," he said.

"I know that. Just make sure you straight after it's done. And if that cracker come at you sideways, get at me and we'll make sure he meets Chompy Number One up close and personal like," Boonie said.

He better not come at me sideways, Beauregard thought.

"You know I used to drive too. Got hung up one time, almost didn't get away. Your Daddy said something to me that made me stop driving. Get into the other side of things."

Beauregard wiped his hands on his pants.

"What was that?"

"He told me that I had a wife who loved me. I had the yard. He said, 'Boonie, a man gotta be one thing or another. You either gonna run the yard or you gonna be running in the streets. Man can't be two types of beasts,'" Boonie said.

"Too bad he didn't take his own advice."

"Didn't he, though? Ant wasn't a mechanic who drove. He was a driver who sometimes worked as a mechanic. Love him or hate him, he knew who he was," Boonie said.

"You think I don't know who I am?"

"I think you know. You just don't like it," Boonie said.

He left the scrap yard and headed for his sister-in-law's place to pick up the boys. As Beauregard pulled into Jean's driveway, he wondered, not for the first time, how a single mom could afford such a nice house on a hairdresser's salary. He parked the truck but before he could get to the door of the two-story brick Colonial Darren was already running out the door.

"Daddy, look, Javon made me a tattoo!" Darren said. He rolled up the sleeve of his Captain America T-shirt to show Beauregard the drawing of Wolverine on his arm.

"It's just magic marker. It's not permanent," Javon said. He was walking out behind Darren.

"We should take a picture of it before your Mama makes him wash it off," Beauregard said. The detail in the drawing was uncanny. Javon had even added the iconic "Snikt!" in a thought bubble above Wolverine's head.

"No, I'm never washing it off," Darren wailed. Beauregard scooped him up with one arm and slung him over his shoulder.

"You gonna have to take a bath someday. You can't walk around with a shitty butthole," he said. Darren exploded with laughter. Javon walked past them carrying his backpack and Darren's bag of crayons, coloring books and action figures. He climbed in the truck and put in his ear buds.

"Hey Beau," Jean said. She had appeared at the door like a wraith.

"Hey Jean. How ya doing?" Beauregard said. His sister-in-law crossed her arms. She and Kia had similar features, but Jean had a video model's shape. Full in the hips and the chest with a figure like a Coke bottle.

"Oh, I'm doing alright. You are looking good, though. Being your own boss agrees with you."

"Well, you should know all about that."

"Yeah. I'm used to doing things my own way by myself. When you do it that way, you never get disappointed. At the end of the day, you're always satisfied," Jean said.

Beauregard felt his face get hot. "Well, I'm gonna get on down the road," he said. Jean smiled and faded back into the house. Beauregard carried a still giggling Darren to the truck and put him next to his brother. They backed out of the driveway and headed home.

"Is Aunt Jean lonely doing everything by herself?" Darren asked. He had his hand out the window waving it up and down in the wind.

"I think Aunt Jean is just fine," Beauregard said.

They pulled into their own driveway and Darren was out and running to the house before Beauregard had put the truck into gear. Javon didn't move. During the ride, Darren had fished his Iron Man action figure out of his bag. He was now pitting Iron Man against the geranium Kia kept on the porch.

"Are we gonna be okay?" Javon asked.

Beauregard sat back against the bench seat of the truck. "Why you asking me that?"

"I've heard you and Mama talking," Javon said. He had pulled his ear buds down around his neck.

"We gonna be fine. We might have hit a rough patch, but you ain't gotta worry about that. All you need to do is get ready for the eighth grade," Beauregard said.

"Mama was on the phone the other night saying she might have to get another job because that Precision place opened up," Javon said.

"Listen. Don't you worry about Precision or your mom getting another job. All you gotta worry about is hitting them books and getting through high school," Beauregard said.

"I wish I could just go to work too. I could get a job helping Uncle Boonie. I hate school. It's boring. The only thing I like is art class and I can do that on my own," Javon said. Beauregard drummed his fingers on the steering wheel. He knew Javon was struggling in math. Beauregard had tried to help him. He tried his best to unravel the Pythagorean theorem or scientific notation for Javon but he knew he was a piss-poor teacher. He couldn't seem to explain angles and variables to Javon in a way that made sense to his son. Beauregard just seemed to get it and it was hard to articulate how he got it to someone else. He figured Javon felt the same way about drawing. His son was smart and talented, just in a different way. His Daddy used to say you didn't call a fish dumb because it couldn't climb a tree.

Beauregard held his hand up in front of his son's face.

"You see this grease on my hands? I've washed them five times today and it still won't come all the way off. Don't get me wrong, there is no shame working with your hands for a living. But for me, it was the only choice I had. It don't have to be that way for you. You wanna go to Auto and Diesel school and get a job working on race cars, that's fine. You wanna go to VCU, take art classes and be a graphic designer, hey that's fine too. You wanna be a lawyer or a doctor or a writer, ain't nothing wrong with that either. Education gives you those choices."

Beauregard sat back against the driver's seat.

"Listen, when you're a black man in America you live with the weight of people's low expectations on your back every day. They can crush you right down to the goddamn ground. Think about it like it's a race. Everybody else has a head start and you dragging those low expectations behind you. Choices give you freedom from those expectations. Allows you to cut 'em loose. Because that's what freedom is. Being able to let things go. And nothing is more important than freedom. Nothing. You hear me, boy?" Beauregard said.

Javon nodded his head.

"Alright then. All I want you to worry about is keeping your head in them books. I'll take care of everything else. Now help me get your brother in the house. We don't watch him he'll be out here all night fighting with that damn plant," Beauregard said.

Beauregard got the boys inside and made them their favorite daddy dinner. Cheeseburger casserole with a pitcher of lemon-lime Kool-Aid. Later, after he had put them to bed, he waited up for Kia to get home. A little after eleven, she came stumbling into the house.

"What did you feed the boys?"

"Their favorite," he said.

She collapsed next to him on the couch. In less than five minutes she was asleep. Beauregard got up and carried her to bed. Her lithe body wrapped around him like a snake. He laid her down in the bed and went back out to the living room to cut off the lights. He pulled his key ring out of his pocket. As he was hanging it on the key hook the key to the Duster slipped from the ring. The 8-ball at the end of the chain clattered across the floor. He bent over and picked it up. The letters ATM were scratched into the surface of the plastic resin on the miniature 8-ball. Tomorrow he would start working on the Buick. He'd have to go back up to Cutter County and check the route a few more times. He needed to go over the plan with Ronnie and that Quan character again and again. Boonie was right about Ronnie. He was playing some angle that only he could see. That was his way. It was like he was addicted to being duplicitous. Quan was a wannabe gangsta playing with a grown man's gun. He didn't trust either one of them, not even a little bit. His father had trusted his partners and they had tried to kill him in front of his only son. He had no intention of letting that happen to him.

Beauregard knew there was no honor among thieves. Boys in the game only respected you in direct proportion to how much they needed you divided by how much they feared you. There was no doubt they needed his skill.

And if they weren't a little bit afraid of him then that was their mistake.

ELEVEN

Ronnie and Reggie sat in Reggie's car with the engine idling so hard the doors were rattling like maracas. They were parked on a lonely county service road. A cell phone tower rose out of the woods behind them like the arm of a titanic robot. Beauregard's truck came rumbling down the gravel road, throwing up a hazy cloud of dust. Beauregard pulled up to Reggie's car so that their driver's side windows were parallel to each other. He grabbed a cooler from the passenger seat and passed it to Reggie through the window. Reggie handed the cooler to Ronnie.

"We been out here for almost an hour. I hope you got some beers in here too," Ronnie said. Beauregard ignored him.

"The guy I got 'em from don't live around here. And he stay nervous. Takes a little time to do business with him," Beauregard said. Ronnie grabbed the lid of the cooler.

"Don't open it here," Beauregard said.

"Well can you at least tell us what you got?"

"Six-shot revolvers. Made from pieces of a .38 but with an extended barrel. No serial numbers and no ballistics history. Madness makes them clean. Ghost pieces," Beauregard said.

"'Madness makes them clean.' Where you get that from, some fucked-up fortune cookie?" Ronnie asked.

"Madness is the guy who makes them," Beauregard said.

"Oh. Six-shooters huh? Quan ain't gonna like that," Ronnie said.

"Quan ain't gotta like it. Revolvers don't leave behind shell cas-ings. And if you need more than six shots you in the wrong line of work," Beauregard said. He put the truck in reverse, turned around and flew down the service road.

He didn't really like leaving Ronnie with the guns but he didn't need to get caught with unregistered weapons. Beauregard didn't think Ronnie was dumb enough to use the guns before the job. At least he hoped he wasn't.

When he got to the shop, Kelvin was changing the oil on Esther Mae Burke's ancient Chevy Caprice. He had it up on the lift while Mrs. Burke sat on the bench seat near the door.

"How you doing, Mrs. Burke?" Beauregard asked as he passed her on his way to his office.

"I'm well, Beauregard. Things a little slow around here today?" Mrs. Burke asked. She was a trim, neat little white woman with a helmet of bluish white hair propped up on her head like a rooster comb.

"Things will pick up eventually," Beauregard said.

"My neighbor Louise Keating says them fellas at Precision Auto only charge $19.99 for an oil change. And they top off all your fluids and will even rotate the tires. All for $19.99. I told her if it's that cheap, they probably ain't doing it correctly. I'd rather come here where I know it's done right," Mrs. Burke said.

"Well, we appreciate your business," Beauregard said. He continued to his office.

"I'll keep coming here until you close down, Beauregard," Mrs. Burke yelled. Beauregard didn't break his stride. He went into the office and closed the door behind him. The mountain of bills on the desk had gotten higher. It was like financial plate tectonics. He sat down and began going through them. He divided them into two different piles. Thirty days past due and final notice. He had a credit card with about $200 left on it. He could use that to pay the light bill. But that would burn up his budget for supplies. He wasn't robbing Peter to pay Paul. They had both ganged up on him and were mugging him.

An hour later there was a knock on the door.

"Yeah," Beauregard said. Kelvin came in and shut the door behind him.

"Mrs. Burke told me to tell you if you're here in three months, she will get us to change her brakes," Kelvin said.

"I should thank her for the vote of confidence," Beauregard said.

"So you gonna show me?" Kelvin asked.

"Show you what?"

"Don't play with me, man. Come on, show me what you been working on under that big-ass tarp in the corner," Kelvin said.

Beauregard leaned back in his chair. "It's just a little personal project," he said.

Kelvin laughed. "Bug, I know it's for a job. I just wanna see it. You been working on it day and night for a week and a half. The other night I drove by around three A.M. and the lights were still on. Come on, let me see this masterpiece, then we can lock up and go over to Danny's for some liquid lunch. It's been a pretty slow day," he said.

Beauregard sighed. "Alright, come on," he said.

They went back out into the shop area and walked over to the far corner near the used oil container. He pulled the tarp off the car with a flourish. The body had been painted a dark navy blue. Nothing extravagant, just serviceable. Kelvin noticed the windows and the windshield were slightly opaque.

"You put homemade bulletproof glass in the windows," Kelvin said. It was more a statement than a question.

"Yeah. Fixed up some run-flat tires too," Beauregard said. He opened the driver door and popped the hood. The motor was pristine. Kelvin let out a low whistle.

"V6?" he asked.

"Yeah. I rebuilt it from the top down. Got some extras in there too," Beauregard said.

"Ha, I bet you do. Shit, man, I wish I was driving it. She looks legit. I bet she get up," Kelvin said.

"Yeah. She got some legs. I burnt up all my credit with Bivins Auto Supply getting her straight," Beauregard said. He slammed the hood down and took a step back from the car.

"Feel good, don't it? Getting ready for a job," Kelvin said.

"No," Beauregard lied. It felt better than good. It felt right. It was like he had found a comfortable pair of old shoes that he had thought were lost forever. Intrinsically he knew that was a problem. It shouldn't feel good or right. The list of things that should bring him joy should begin with his wife and children and end with something benign like an upcoming fishing trip or going to a see a legal drag race. But what should be and what was rarely aligned.

"Let's get that beer," he said.

The music in Danny's was as dark as the décor. "Hey Joe" by Jimi Hendrix was pumping through the surround sound. Danny's had a fancy new LED illuminated jukebox, but someone had decided Jimi's old tale of murder and woe was apropos for some day drinking. Beauregard ordered a Bud Light and Kelvin got a rum and Coke.

"You sure you don't need some help on this?" Kelvin asked.

Beauregard sipped his beer. "I'm sure," he said.

Kelvin threw back his drink. The ice cubes clinked together. "Alright. Just saying you keep me in mind," he said.

Beauregard sipped his beer again. "Yeah. I think this is gonna be a one-time thing. Everything goes right we can make some improvements to the shop. Add an auto body department. Compete with Precision for the next round of county contracts," he said.

"Yeah, I hear you. Don't mean we can't do a little something on the side," Kelvin said.

"Actually, that's exactly what it means," Beauregard said. He finished his beer and slid off the bar stool.

"Hey, man, I didn't . . ." Kelvin's voice trailed off.

"I know you didn't," Beauregard said. He leaned forward and put his mouth close to Kelvin's ear. "If anyone asks, I was at the shop all day this coming Monday and Tuesday."

"You didn't even have to tell me that. I already know what time it is," Kelvin said.

Beauregard patted him on the back and headed for the exit. As he approached the door a tall gangly white man stepped through. A mop of unruly brown hair sat on his head like a designer dog. His wide brown eyes were rheumy and bloodshot. The man gave Beauregard a brief glance before sidling up to the bar. As he passed, Beauregard noticed a red birthmark on his neck that bore a passing resemblance to a map of the United States. The birthmark ran in the man's family. His father and his two uncles had sported the exact same birthmark in the exact same place. That was how they had acquired their nicknames. Melvin's father had been Red, and Melvin's uncles were White and Blue. The Navelys had been what passed for bad around Red Hill back in the day.

Melvin Navely sat two seats down from Kelvin at the bar. Beauregard heard him order a gin on the rocks. When he raised the glass to his lips he noticed Melvin's hand was trembling. Beauregard wondered if it was the d.t.'s or seeing him as he entered the bar that made Melvin's hand shake. Despite Red Hill being such a small town, they didn't run into each other all that often. He could count on one hand the number of times he had seen Melvin Navely in the last fifteen years. Did Melvin consciously avoid him? Beauregard thought it was possible. He didn't blame the man.

He wouldn't want to see the person who ran his father down walking around free either.

TWELVE

Monday morning, Beauregard woke up at six. He put on a pair of blue jeans and a black T-shirt. He dug an old pair of sunglasses out of the nightstand. He left his wallet on the nightstand. Kia was lying on her side with her legs tucked up to her chest. He leaned over and kissed her on the cheek. She turned and kissed him back.

"Hey," she said.

He stroked her hair. "I'm heading out," he said.

Kia opened her eyes. "It's today, ain't it?" she asked.

"Yeah. I might not be home till late," Beauregard said.

She sat up and kissed him on the mouth. "You just make sure your ass comes home," she said.

"I will," he said.

They stared at each other and spoke with their eyes.

Don't get killed. Don't get caught.

I won't. I'm built for this. It's all I've ever been good at.

That's not true. You're a good father. A good husband. I love you.

I love you too.

He went in and kissed his boys too. Then he headed for the shop.

Beauregard slipped into the Buick and fired her up. It didn't sound as impressive as the Duster, but it was almost as fast. He had taken it out last night for a test drive. It handled smooth, taking the curves like a tango dancer executing a *balanceo*. He eased her out of the garage, got out and pulled down the roll door, and headed for Reggie's trailer.

Ronnie and Quan came out on the second honk of the horn. They were dressed identically in blue coveralls. They both carried plastic grocery bags with the IGA logo prominently displayed. Ronnie got in the passenger's seat and Quan climbed into the back seat. Ronnie was uncharacteristically quiet. Quan was humming a tune Beauregard recognized as "Regulate" by Warren G and Nate Dogg. He backed up next to Quan's car, then headed down Reggie and Ronnie's driveway. The Buick had tags from another old Buick in Boonie's yard and a counterfeit inspection sticker. Beauregard kept it well under the speed limit as they drove out to Cutter County. They would be fine unless some overeager Johnny Law decided to racially profile them and run the plates.

"Did you get everything I told you to?" Beauregard said.

Ronnie flinched like he had been kicked in the nuts.

"Huh?"

"The ski mask and the grease paint and the surgical gloves," Beauregard said.

"Oh yeah. We paid cash like you said. Got the mask at different stores than the grease paint, on different days."

"Good. You guys both straight?" Beauregard asked

"Yeah. I didn't even have a beer this morning," Ronnie said.

Quan didn't respond.

"Quan?" Beauregard said.

"I'm straight, nigga," Quan said. He spoke clearly and distinctly. His voice was even and clear. He pronounced each syllable with articulation so sharp you could have sliced bread on it.

"This thing got a radio?" Ronnie asked. Beauregard pulled on to Town Bridge Road and headed for the interstate. He had on a pair of black driving gloves with holes over the knuckles. He flexed his right hand and pushed a button on the radio in the center of the console. "Ante Up" by M.O.P. started to fill the car.

"Well, that's appropriate," Ronnie said.

The AC in the car did not work. Beauregard cracked his window and a torrent of wind barreled into the Buick. He felt his heart begin to pound. It felt like a dogfish flopping on a pier. The sky was so dark it looked like dusk. A blanket of clouds obscured the early morning sun. Another old hip-hop song came on the radio and Beauregard felt himself nodding his head before he realized the title of the song. "Mind Playing Tricks on Me" by Houston trio the Geto Boys. He remembered when that song first came out how Kelvin wanted a copy of the tape so bad he convinced Beauregard to hitchhike with him to the mall in Richmond and try and steal one. Beauregard had gone to the arcade and hustled some white college kids on *Pit-Fighter* and earned enough money to buy the tape. Kelvin had asked him why they didn't just take it.

"My Daddy says a risk always gotta be worth the reward. That tape ain't worth getting caught at the door," he had said.

"He told you that?" Kelvin had asked.

"Nah, but I heard him talking to Uncle Boonie."

He knew why that memory had come to him. He didn't need six years of overpriced psychoanalysis to understand his own mind. The diamonds were worth the risk. Even if Ronnie was shady and Quan was shaky. The reward outweighed the risk by a metric ton. Beauregard merged onto the interstate and hit the gas.

The parking lot of the shopping center was nearly empty when they arrived. There were two cars in front of a Chinese restaurant two doors down from the jewelry store. There were five cars in front of the jewelry store itself. The rest of the parking lot was bare. The clouds had cleared, revealing a cerulean sky. Beauregard thought it looked like someone had spilled watercolors across the heavens. He drove past the store and parked so that he was facing the exit. He took a deep breath. "Time to fly," he said as he expelled the breath.

"Huh?" Quan asked.

"Nothing. Check your guns. Make sure they loaded. Put on the makeup. One minute to make sure no heroes get in the mix. Two minutes to open the safe and grab the diamonds and some other pieces out of the display case. One minute to get back here to the car. Four minutes. At five minutes, I'm leaving the parking lot. You hear me?" Beauregard said.

Ronnie and Quan opened their bags and took out cans of white grease paint. They pulled on their latex gloves and light camo hunting masks. They both pulled out their pieces.

"I hear you, man. We'll be back quicker than a hiccup," Ronnie said.

"Quan, you hear me?" Beauregard asked. He studied Quan's reflection in the rearview mirror. A backwoods Grim Reaper was sitting in his car.

"I hear you, man," Quan said, over-enunciating each word.

"Are you fucked up?" Beauregard asked.

Quan shoved the .38 in his pocket.

"Nope."

Beauregard turned around and leaned over the seat. "Look at me."

Quan raised his head. "Nigga, I said I'm straight. Damn, let's just do this," Quan said.

Beauregard rubbed the thumb on his left hand against his forefinger.

"Four minutes. Two hundred and forty seconds. That will give us a two-minute head start on the cops that are three streets over. Get in, get out, get gone," he said. An old Irish bank robber he had worked with on three separate occasions had coined that phrase, but Beauregard never forgot it. That Irishman had been a professional. These boys were not in his league. They weren't even playing the same game.

"I got it," Quan said.

Ronnie adjusted his mask. "Let's shake, rattle and roll," he said. He opened the car door and hopped out. Quan climbed over the seat and followed him after slamming the door shut.

Beauregard watched them hurry across the parking lot. Fifteen steps to the door from where he was parked. He had come back up here a few days ago and counted the steps from the door to the closest parking space. He checked his watch. It was 8:15.

He gripped the steering wheel.

"Time to fly," he whispered.

THIRTEEN

Ronnie felt like he was in a movie. Everything around him seemed electric. Shimmering like scenes coming out of a projector. He had scored a tiny miniscule amount of coke the night before. This morning he had done two lines. Just enough to sharpen his senses. He realized now that had been a mistake. He felt overwhelmed by all the stimuli around him. He thought he could hear his eyelids click when he blinked. His skin felt raw and exposed as a nerve in a broken tooth.

Fuck it. Get this money. Blue suede shoes, motherfuckers, he thought.

Ronnie pushed through the door of the jewelry store with his shoulder. He had his gun in his right hand and his plastic bag in his left. The overhead recessed lights bathed the sales floor in a sepia tone. The display cases were laid out in an upside-down U shape. A long case at the rear of the store served as a sales desk. The cash register sat on the far left side. Two long cases ran the length of the store on both sides. A huge picture window took up most of the front of the store. Jenny was standing behind the desk with a stocky woman in a shaggy crew cut. They were talking to an older white woman in a rainbow-colored sundress. Her long white hair was plaited into two long pigtails. To his right a young black man was leaning over one of the display cases, obviously deep in thought.

"You know what time it is! Get on the floor and shut your god-damn mouths!" Ronnie screamed.

"Get on the ground or they gonna be cleaning your brains off the fucking ceiling tiles!" Quan screamed. At first no one moved. The young black guy didn't even raise his head.

"NOW!" Ronnie screamed. The young man dropped to the floor so quickly he might have stepped through a trap door. The older white woman took longer but she too got down on the floor. Jenny and the heavyset lady, who had to be the manager, also got down on the floor. Ronnie rushed over to the desk. The two of them were on all fours about to lie flat on the floor.

"Come on, Red, you and me going in the back," Ronnie said. The manager hopped up faster than her size would have suggested.

"Don't you touch her!" she said. She put herself between Ronnie and Jenny. Ronnie nearly took a step back. The ferociousness in her voice was palatable. Her eyes were bugging from their sockets and a vein was pulsating in her forehead. As a rule, Ronnie didn't believe in hitting women. He had enough Southern hospitality instilled in him as a kid that he found the idea distasteful. Under normal circumstances he would never put his hands on a lady. However, these were not normal circumstances. Not by a long shot.

Ronnie struck the manager just above her right eye with the butt of the .38. A divot the width of a popsicle stick appeared above her eye. Blood spewed from the wound like water from a broken faucet. The manager fell forward, grabbed at the counter, and fell to the floor. Ronnie grabbed Jenny by the arm and pulled her up to her feet.

"Keep an eye on them!" Ronnie barked.

Quan nodded his head vigorously. Ronnie dragged Jenny into the back room.

Once they were through the door that said EMPLOYEES ONLY, Ronnie pulled Jenny close.

"Did you deactivate the alarm?" he asked.

"I couldn't. Lou Ellen was here when I got here. She was supposed to be off, but she traded with Lisa."

"Fuck. Does the alarm run through the safe?" Ronnie asked.

"How the fuck am I supposed to know?" Jenny said.

Ronnie almost hit a woman for the second time in his life. "Just open the damn thing," he said. Jenny wrenched her arm free and navigated her way through three wide metal worktables and past a large metal desk. She stopped at a large gunmetal gray safe nearly as tall as Ronnie. She punched a few buttons on a keypad on the front of the safe. A green light started flashing on an LED screen on the door. Jenny pulled on the handle.

Nothing happened.

"Try it again!" Ronnie hissed. Jenny punched in the combination again. The green light flashed. She pulled the handle.

Nothing.

"Get out the way," Ronnie said. He pulled on the handle. At first it didn't seem like it was moving. He pulled harder. The door started to open, painfully slow. It was heavy as hell. He put his gun in the pocket of his coveralls, dropped his plastic bag and used both hands to open the door. Inside the safe were six shelves lined in black fabric. On the first shelf were three bundles of cash. Ronnie picked up his bag and threw all three bundles into the former grocery sack. He didn't know the money was going to be in the safe, but he wasn't going to look a gift horse in the mouth. On the next three shelves were ledgers, files and random papers. On the sixth shelf was a nondescript brown box the size of a pencil box. He grabbed it and ripped open the stiff cardboard lid. It flew up and Ronnie was greeted by the prettiest sight his eyes had ever had the pleasure of viewing. The box was full of uncut diamonds. Each one was as big as a good-sized raisin.

"Hello, ladies," Ronnie said. He snapped the lid back down and shoved the box in his bag. "Come on, you gotta lay down beside Indigo Girl out there." He grabbed Jenny by the arm and headed back out to the sales floor. His heart was a hornet in his chest. He tried to will it to calm down, but it was futile. That was alright, the job was almost done. He had done it. He had seen the opportunity and he had grabbed it. Like the King said, ambition was just a dream with a V8 engine. He was gonna ride that V8 all the way to a place with sand by the ton and water so clear you could see a mermaid coming up to give you a kiss.

Ronnie knew something was wrong as soon as he opened the door, but he didn't know what it was until he saw the dyke's reflection in the polarized glass in the door of the shop. She had a handheld howitzer pointed at Quan from the other side of the office door.

Ronnie reached into his right pocket and gripped his gun. He fired through his pocket into the door. Lou Ellen fired her gun as she lost her balance. As she fell she let out a jagged wail. While she was falling she continued to pull the trigger on her gun.

Glass rained down on Quan. One of the shots from the woman behind the counter had whizzed by his head and punched a hole in the picture window in the front of the store. Ronnie saw the brother on the floor pop up and run toward the door. Quan's hand raised reflexively.

The young brother's head snapped back like it was tied to an invisible rope that had been pulled taut. A red mist filled the space between him and Quan. The brother dropped like a wet sheet falling off a clothesline. Quan was blinking frantically. There was something in his eyes.

Ronnie stepped over the brother with half his head missing and grabbed Quan by the arm. He shoved him toward the door. He could hear Jenny screaming. Her sugar mama was howling like a banshee. The old woman on the floor was crying. Ronnie pushed Quan through the door. They hit the sidewalk in a dead sprint. The picture window in the front of the shop exploded. Ronnie didn't look back but he knew the dyke was still shooting at them. He ran toward the Buick with Quan in tow. It wasn't until he got to the car that he realized he was screaming too.

———

Beauregard opened the passenger door when he saw them run out of the jewelry store. Quan climbed into the back seat and Ronnie jumped into the front. Ronnie had barely closed the door all the way when Beauregard took off, tires squealing and leaving a cloud of gray smoke in his wake. The Buick sailed out of the parking lot doing 40. Beauregard slammed on the brakes and the gas as he twisted the steering wheel to the right. There were only a few cars on the street this time of morning. Beauregard careened around them going up on the sidewalk then back to the street. He ran a red light and Ronnie screamed as he threaded the needle between a jacked-up good ol' boy truck and a short-body delivery van.

Beauregard gripped the steering wheel like it was a life preserver. He could feel the vibrations of the engine radiating through the wheel and up his arms. His heart wasn't pounding. He guessed it wasn't doing more than 70 beats per minute. This was where he belonged. Where he excelled. Some people were meant to pound the keys on a piano or strum the strings of a guitar. A car was his instrument and he was performing a symphony. A coldness filled him. It started in his stomach and spread to his extremities. He knew no matter what happened he would never feel more alive, more present than he felt at this moment. There was truth in that idea and sadness too.

Quan pulled his mask off and tossed it to the floor of the car. He wiped at his eyes while simultaneously spitting repeatedly. There was a hot coppery taste in his mouth. Sirens erupted behind them. He turned and looked out the back window. Two blue and white police cruisers had materialized out of nowhere. The lights were nearly lost in the glare from the sun. Quan wiped his eyes with his sleeve again. He looked at it and noticed the grease paint had a pinkish hue. Blood. It was blood. The guy's blood. He had killed the guy. He had killed someone. Quan dropped his gun to the floor like it was on fire.

The vomit was coming out of his mouth before he even realized he was nauseous.

Beauregard cut his eyes to the left and appraised the cruisers rapidly approaching in his side mirror. During his second recon trip he had driven by the police station once again. It had been near dark and he had counted four cruisers sitting in the parking lot next to the station. Counting the one he had seen parked near the exit made five. A place the size of Cutter County didn't need more than five police cruisers. The two that were chasing them and the one that was likely on patrol were Dodge Charger Pursuit Special Editions. A 340 hp Hemi engine under the hood meant the car could accelerate from 0 to 60 in six seconds. They came equipped with advanced steering and suspension options. A powerful rear suspension camber linkage and wider-than-normal disk brakes gave the car near supernatural handling capabilities.

As his Daddy would have said, them dogs could hunt.

Beauregard had calculated they would have at least two minutes before the cops even knew the store had been robbed once they had left if everything went smooth. Conversely, he had figured they would only have thirty seconds if shit went south. He had heard gunshots as he sat in the Buick. That was a good indicator things had gone pretty far south. The cops showing up in his rearview mirror was not a shock.

A sign near the on-ramp indicated sensible drivers should slow down to 35 mph to access the ramp and merge into traffic.

Beauregard took it doing 60. He held the gas down with his right foot and the brakes with his left. The car drifted in a semicircle before emerging onto the interstate.

"Shit shit shit!" Ronnie howled.

Beauregard let up off the brake and held the gas pedal down to the floor. The Buick leaped forward as the five-speed transmission he had installed engaged. Beauregard merged and cut off a tractor trailer as he slid into the second of the interstate's three lanes. The trucker laid on his horn, but Beauregard only heard it as a faint trumpeting in the distance. The sirens soon overwhelmed the horn. Beauregard glanced in the rearview mirror without moving his head. Drivers were pulling over for the cruisers as they closed in on him. They would be close enough to ram him with their bullbars before he knew it. Beauregard cranked up the radio. "WHAM!" by Stevie Ray Vaughan was on the radio. He must have hit the PBS station. Regular radio didn't play instrumental tunes anymore.

A blue toggle switch was just below the radio. Beauregard pushed it and the engine roared like a cave bear. Nitrous oxide. N_2O. He had installed a plate delivery system on the engine. He'd also adjusted the piston rings so that when the engine heated up from the introduction of the nitro the rings wouldn't fuse shut and crack the pistons.

A lot of work but it would be worth it. The needle on the speedometer was lying all the way to the right. It trembled just above 135. An SUV with a plethora of stickers on the rear window that told the story of a stick figure family and several honor roll students loomed in front of him. Beauregard slammed the steering wheel to the right again and drove on the wide shoulder of the interstate to get around the SUV.

"OH JESUS!" Ronnie screamed.

Orange triangle-shaped road signs warned of construction ahead. Beauregard hazarded a look in the rearview again. The cruisers were still back there but he had at least six car lengths between the Buick and their Chargers. The overpass that carried the interstate over a two-lane intersection rose up in front of him like a pale white whale's back breaching out of the ocean depths. The interstate had narrowed from three lanes to two. When the construction was completed the lanes would widen to four. Two additional lanes were being added to the overpass. The new construction stopped well short of its older cousin. A gap sixty feet wide stretched beyond the end of the concrete and the exposed rebars. Twenty-five feet below this chasm, a mound of reddish clay-infused soil rose ten feet into the air. Orange traffic barrels and neatly stacked steel struts and angle iron occupied the space to the right of the pile of dirt. To its left was the intersection and a single-lane highway that had been closed off by traffic cones.

"Shit, tell me you ain't trying to jump this motherfucker!" Ronnie said over the last notes of Stevie Ray's Stratocaster.

"Put on your neck pillows," Beauregard said. He grabbed his own from his lap with one hand and slipped it around his neck.

Ronnie grabbed the pillows from the floor. He put one on then tossed one to Quan.

"Why we gotta wear these, Bug?" Ronnie asked. Instead of putting on his pillow Quan fell over and lay down in the fetal position.

Beauregard ignored Ronnie's question. He slammed on the brakes and yanked the steering wheel to the left. The Buick did a 180 as a gray cloud of smoke engulfed them. Without a second of hesitation he slammed the car in reverse and stomped on the gas. The wooden pickets that had surrounded the median had been replaced with orange snow fencing.

Ronnie was screaming in his ear. No words, just one long nonsensical wail. They were doing 60, hurtling toward an unfinished section of road.

Backwards.

The police were closing in like wolves chasing a deer.

Then the deer sprouted wings.

Beauregard didn't say hold on. He didn't say watch out. But in his mind, he heard his father's voice.

"She flying now, Bug!"

The Buick sailed off the overpass. It plummeted twenty-five feet like a stone. The trunk slammed into the pile of dirt, but the dirt helped to cushion their fall. The edge of the overpass rapidly receded from Beauregard's vision as they fell. He braced himself by gripping the steering wheel and leaning back in his seat as hard as he could.

The rear bumper took some of the force. The load-leveling shocks he had installed took the rest. He could feel every inch of the steel plating he welded to the chassis stretch to its tensile limit.

The cop car that had been closest to them had slammed on the brakes. The cop car behind hadn't. It crashed into the first one and sent it careening off the edge. It landed nose first into the asphalt. Steam and engine coolant burst from the crumpled hood even as the car fell forward on its roof. Beauregard jerked on the gearshift, dropped the car into drive and extricated himself from the dry dirt pile. Red clay flew fifty feet into the air as the rear tires strained for purchase. Finally, after what seemed like ten years Beauregard felt the rubber meet the road. He slipped by the upside-down cop car and crashed through the traffic cones. He took the road back to Route 314 and turned right.

"I think I done shit my pants," Ronnie mumbled.

The Buick streaked down the single-lane blacktop road. They passed one decrepit work van and then the road was empty. Two miles later Beauregard turned off the blacktop onto an old dirt lane with mud holes deep enough for spelunking. He did his best to navigate the Buick around the holes. The trees lining the lane cast awkward shadows as the sun seemed to rise higher in the sky.

The road ended twenty feet from a wide body of standing water. Beauregard had found the place on his second recon trip. The lane was overgrown now but once it had led to a quarry. Over the years, rainwater had filled it and created a man-made lake. There were no fish in the water but sometimes the local kids would ride down the road to go swimming. Sometimes young lovers would come down the road to engage in awkward couplings as they fumbled their way to ecstasy. Boonie's wrecker sat near the edge of the lake.

Beauregard stopped the Buick. Ronnie and Quan got out and stripped out of their coveralls. Ronnie was wearing his usual attire and Quan had on sweat pants and a baggy blue T-shirt. They tossed the coveralls in the car but not before using them to wipe the grease paint off their faces. Ronnie and Quan ran over to the truck. Beauregard got out and retrieved a short two-by-four from the back seat. One end was covered in what appeared to be ground beef and tomato sauce. He put that end against the gas pedal and wedged the other end into the steering wheel. Beauregard wound down the window and closed the door. Then he reached through the open window and shifted the car into drive. Beauregard jumped back as the car began to rocket forward.

The Buick hit the edge of the lake and for a moment it took flight again. Gravity reached out and snatched it out of the air and pulled it into the water. A spray of stagnant water rained down on Beauregard, but he didn't move. He watched the car sink until it was fully submerged. How long would the engine run underwater? The question popped into his head and he made a mental note to research it later.

"Come on, man, let's go!" Ronnie said.

Beauregard got into the truck and eased it back to the main road. He had borrowed it from Boonie. One of Boonie's guys had followed him to Cutter County last night. The guy had parked at the convenience store two miles down the road. Beauregard had hidden the truck then hoofed it back to the store.

They turned left onto Route 314 and headed for Route 249. Beauregard wanted to avoid the interstate. The old state roads would get them back to Red Hill. It would just take a while.

A state police cruiser shot past them doing at least 100 headed back toward Cutter County. Ronnie put his hand in his pocket as if reaching for the gun that he'd thrown in the lake.

"They're looking for a primer blue Buick. Not a tow truck," Beauregard said.

It took them nearly three hours to get back to Red Hill. Beauregard drove Ronnie and Quan back to Reggie's trailer. He stopped the truck and put it in park. The three of them climbed out of the truck. Ronnie had the box tucked under his arm like a high school textbook. He walked around the front of the truck to the driver side and playfully punched Beauregard in the shoulder.

"Now that was what I call some driving! That's why I needed the Bug! Goddamn, I thought I saw Jesus trying to take the wheel, but you were like nah, Hoss, I got this!" he said. He held up his hand for a high five. Beauregard put his hands in his pockets. Ronnie held his hand up for a few more moments then put it down by his side. Beauregard looked at Ronnie.

"I heard shots. Other people heard them too. That's why the cops got called. What happened in there?" Beauregard asked.

Ronnie shrugged. "That dyke pulled a gun."

"You kill her?"

"Well, I didn't stop and take her pulse."

"What about him? He kill anybody?"

"Man, it got crazy in there. Couldn't be helped."

"How she get the drop on you? I thought he was supposed to be crowd control while you went in the back," Beauregard said. Ronnie had been wondering the same thing but now that they were out and back home he wasn't that concerned about it.

Beauregard walked around him and went over to Quan. He stood well inside the other man's personal space.

"How about it, gangster? What happened in there?"

"Man, what difference it make. We made it," he said. He slurred the words "made it."

"What you say?" Beauregard asked.

"I said—"

Beauregard slapped him so hard it sounded like a rifle shot. Quan did a 180 and slid against the hood of the wrecker. His blue T-shirt got caught on the wire cage over the headlight. Beauregard squatted beside him.

"You fucked-up, ain't ya? I can see it in your eyes. Let me tell you what difference it makes. It's the difference between an armed robbery that they might chase for a few months and first-degree murder that they won't never let go. I told you not to get fucked-up. But you did it anyway. Let me guess. That lady got the drop on you when you zoned out while Ronnie was in the back. You stupid ass." Beauregard stood.

"Don't come back to Red Hill. You're persona non grata now. I don't ever wanna see you again. And you," he said as he turned to face Ronnie.

"I don't wanna see you until you got my money. Then we meet somewhere outside of town. Toss your phones," he said. He squatted down again. He grabbed Quan by his braids.

"I don't think I gotta tell you, don't say nothing to nobody about today. I heard you vomit in the back of the car. I know this gonna be hard for you to live with. But you gonna learn to live with it or you gonna die because of it. You hear me?" he said. Quan nodded. Beauregard got to his feet.

"Last time, Ronnie. After you pay me, don't ever come around me or mines again." Beauregard climbed in the truck and fired it up. Quan extricated himself from the grill and got to his feet. Beauregard backed all the way out of Reggie's driveway.

"I hate that motherfucker," Quan said.

"I don't think he too fond of your ass either. Come on, let's get a beer. In a week, you gonna be eighty grand richer. Then you can hire a boxing trainer," Ronnie said.

"Fuck you, Ronnie," Quan said. He rubbed his face.

"Yeah, yeah. Let's get that beer before Bug come back and give you a matching set," Ronnie said. He headed for the trailer. A few seconds later, Quan followed him.

"I hate that motherfucker," Quan murmured under his breath.

Beauregard drove out to Boonie's, traded the wrecker for his truck and headed to the shop. The sign on the door had been turned to CLOSED. Kelvin must have been at lunch. He unlocked the door, went inside and turned on the lights. The Duster sat in the corner mute as the Sphinx, yet it still spoke to him inside his head.

"We are who we were meant to be."

The voice in his head sounded like his Daddy. That rough, whiskey-soaked melodic voice that haunted his daydreams. But the words belonged to someone far more eloquent that he couldn't recall. He ran his finger over the hood of the Duster. People had been shot. They might even be dead. There was going to be major heat coming down after such a brazen robbery in broad daylight. He had a feeling Ronnie was going to try and fuck him over for his cut. Quan was a fucking train wreck.

But they had gotten away. He still had it. Whatever "it" was.

"We are who we were meant to be," he said.

His words echoed through the garage.

FOURTEEN

"Ms. Lovell, we just want you to know we are sorry about what you have been through," the first cop, whose name was LaPlata, said. He was tall and thin but had big veiny hands that looked strong enough to crack a coconut.

"Just so you know, the Commonwealth Attorney is not inclined to press charges against you for discharging your weapon," the other cop, Billups, said. "Mrs. Turner is going to be fine and she doesn't want to pursue any criminal action. Since the gun was registered, you're in the clear as far as that is concerned." He was built like a fire hydrant and had a hairline that was retreating like Lee at Gettysburg. They sat across from her on a narrow love seat covered in a fading floral pattern. Lou Ellen sat in her recliner with her legs elevated on the foot rest. Her crutches lay on the floor next to the chair.

"Well, that's good to know. I mean since I was trying to save her life," Lou Ellen said. She shifted in the recliner and felt a bolt of pain shoot through her entire left side. She grimaced and let out a long guttural moan.

"Can we get you something?" Billups asked.

Lou Ellen shook her head. "Docs already got me on the highest legal dosage of Oxy. They say the bullet bounced around in my thigh, bounced off my femur, and came out near my ass. It's been two weeks and it still feels fresh. I think I'm going to be in pain for a long time. Might as well get used to it," Lou Ellen said.

"Ms. Lovell, can you tell us anything about the people who robbed the store?" Billups asked.

Lou Ellen shook her head again. "They were both men, I think. They both wore masks. And gloves. They had gloves on."

"You're positive they didn't get away with anything? The safe was wide open when the deputies got there," LaPlata asked.

"Just a few hundred dollars in petty cash," Lou Ellen lied.

LaPlata stared at her. His almond-shaped eyes seemed to be studying her like a child studies an ant right before he holds a magnifying glass over it.

"It's just strange. There were pieces in the display cabinets worth a few thousand dollars. But they didn't go for them. This wasn't a smash-and-grab. They specifically went for the safe and safe alone," LaPlata said. His eyes never left Lou Ellen.

"I guess they thought we had the good stuff in the back, I don't know. Look, I don't mean to be rude but I'm really not feeling too great. Can we finish this later?" she asked.

LaPlata turned his gaze toward Billups. After a few seconds, the big man nodded. Both detectives stood.

"Well, Ms. Lovell, if you think of anything, please give us a call. We will get to the bottom of this, I promise you that," LaPlata said. He handed her a business card with his name printed on it in small neat letters. She took the card but didn't meet his questioning eyes. She could feel them boring into her skull.

"Get some rest, Ms. Lovell. We will be in touch," Billups said. The detectives stalked out of her apartment.

When she heard the door shut behind them, she closed her eyes and sighed. She dug in the pocket of her lounge pants and pulled out a brown plastic pill bottle. She dry-swallowed two more Oxy-Contin. The bitter taste soon gave way to a languid turgidity that moved through her body with a stealthy determination. She leaned the recliner all the way back and tried not to think about the cops or the store or the pain in her leg.

Twenty minutes passed before her cell phone rang. Lou Ellen sat straight up, feeling her heart pounding like a pile driver in her chest. She pulled it out of her pocket and looked at the screen.

The caller ID said John Elevonone. John 11:1. The first mention of Lazarus in the Bible. Getting a phone call from Lazarus "Lazy" Mothersbaugh was never a good thing. Getting a call from him after you had let one of his fronts get robbed was terrifying.

She could ignore it, but he would just call right back and that would make things worse. As if they could get any worse. She pressed her finger against the screen then held the phone against her ear.

"Hello?"

"Well, well, well, if it ain't Annie Oakley herself," a reedy, high-pitched voice said. You could hear the mountains of Lynchburg and Roanoke in his speech. Some people would make assumptions based on that thick accent. Those people were foolish.

"Hey, Lazy," she said.

"Hey, Lou. How ya feeling? I hear tell you got a bullet that took a tour of your nether regions," he said. He laughed softly.

"Nah. Got hit in the hip and it came out near my ass." She heard him take a deep breath. Phlegm rattled through the phone.

"This a mess, Lou. A big ol' greasy killing hog of a mess," Lazy said. Lou didn't respond. "You done good by me, Lou. That's why I let you work that store."

"I don't know what happened, Lazy. Those guys they just came busting in and . . . I just don't know," she said. She didn't really know. She had her suspicions, but she didn't know anything for sure.

There was silence on the other end of the phone. A loud banging came from her front door. It sounded like someone was trying to hammer through the door frame.

"Yeah, ya do. Horace and Burning Man gonna ask you about it and you gonna tell them. I tell you, Lou, I wish it didn't have to come down like this. But if wishes were horses, beggars would ride," he said. The line went dead.

Lou Ellen turned her head in the direction of the door. They were still pounding on it. Lou closed her eyes. "It's open!" she yelled. Fuck them. If they were coming to kill her, they could open the goddamn door themselves. She heard heavy steps and then she saw them come around the partial partition in the hallway.

Horace was grinning with a smile that made him look like a jack-o'-lantern that had been carved by a Parkinson's victim. His salt-and-pepper hair was piled up on top of his head in a bedraggled, greasy mop. He wore an old Texaco T-shirt and denim jeans. His arms were covered in Nordic tattoos. Vikings and battle axes and skulls. Billy "Burning Man" Mills stood next to him. He was a foot taller than Horace and half a foot wider. He wore a white button-down shirt open at the throat and a pair of wrinkled khakis. He had lank black hair with wisps of gray that was parted down the middle. His Van-dyke goatee was still more black than white. His green eyes were flinty flecks of jade. If not for the scar on the left side of his face he would be considered a ruggedly handsome man. A burn mark stretched from his chin over his cheek up to his eye and around what was left of his ear. Lou knew he wore his hair long to obscure the scar as much as he could.

"Hey, Lou Ellen. How ya doing?" Billy asked.

"I'm alright, considering," she said. She realized Lazy had only called to make sure she was home and not in the hospital. Lou dropped her hand to her right side. The cops had her gun, but she had a switchblade that she carried with her nearly all the time.

"Yeah. Getting shot hurts like a sonofabitch. Feel like somebody sticking you with a hot poker all the way down to the bone," Billy said. He sat in one of the chairs the cops had retrieved from the kitchen. He leaned forward and let his hands hang loosely between his legs.

"Makes you think it's the most pain you ever gonna feel," he said. Horace tittered.

"Yeah," Lou Ellen said. Her mouth was desert dry.

"It ain't, though. There's always more pain," Billy said. He ran his hand through his hair and she saw the rest of his scar.

"Billy . . ."

"Shh. I just gotta ask you two things, Lou. Just two questions. Then we gonna be gone," he said.

"The cops were just here. I didn't say anything. You know I didn't," she said. She felt tears building up in her eyes and hated herself for it.

Billy smiled. "Aw, I know that, Sis. We watched them leave. They long gone now. But thank you for answering my first question," he said. The smile seemed to make his scarification more disturbing. It was as if the ghost of his old face was rising from the grave. Billy scooted his chair closer to her recliner.

"Now my second question is the humdinger. Who'd you tell about them diamonds? You know, the ones Lazy was using to pay for them girls?" he asked. He smiled again and the skin around his eye crinkled like crepe paper.

Lou Ellen felt her tongue squirming in her mouth. She could tell the truth. Just let it all out and hope for the best. Or she could lie. Just pretend she had no idea how those guys knew there was almost two million dollars' worth of diamonds in the safe. Or she could try and find some middle ground.

"I didn't tell nobody. But there's this girl that work there," she said.

Billy leaned forward. "Aw Sis. Not another girl with a pussy that taste like cotton candy and dreams," Billy said.

"I didn't tell her nothing. Not really. We just kinda hung around each other. She might have picked up on some things," Lou Ellen said.

Billy nodded sagely. He ran his right hand along Lou's left thigh. "Lazy got a friend in the hospital. She says a little to the left they could have hit your femoral artery." His hand stopped at her wound.

"Yeah," Lou Ellen said.

He squeezed her thigh. His hand closed on her like a bear trap as his thumb dug into the wound. The pain was a living thing that grabbed at her throat and choked off her breath. She instinctively pulled out her knife. Billy's left arm shot out and caught her wrist as she came up with it.

"Come on now, Lou," he said. He gave her wrist a hard twist and the knife fell into her lap. "What's her name? The girl who must have a pussy that taste like magic and star-shine?"

"Lisa," she wheezed.

Billy let go of her leg. He plucked the knife out of her lap.

"Lisa's the blonde, right?" Billy asked.

Lou Ellen nodded.

"That means it was the other one. The redhead. Jenny," he said as he sat back in the chair. The biscuits that held it together creaked. Lou breathed heavily through her mouth. "I didn't think you'd give the real one up. You a bad liar, Lou Ellen. You always had a soft spot for a fat ass. Lisa too skinny for you." Billy stood.

"No, Billy, don't hurt her. Please."

"If it was just a jewelry store, this could go another way. But them cops gonna start poking around. They gonna be looking at the books and seeing the math don't add up right," Billy said.

"I ain't gonna say shit," Lou Ellen said.

Billy frowned. "I know you good people, Lou. But them boys gonna lean on you hard. If it makes any difference, I told Lazy it should be me. Seeing as I done known you the longest," he said. He walked around to the back of the recliner.

"Billy, just tell Lazy I can explain. I can make this right," Lou Ellen said. She twisted in her chair, so she could see what he was doing behind her. It hurt like hell, but she contorted her torso and tried to look over the top of the chair. Her eyeballs bulged from their sockets as she strained to see. Billy pulled a rolled-up black plastic bag out of his back pocket.

"Nah, ya can't, Lou. Some things when they get broke, you can't put them back together."

He slapped the bag over her head and pulled it tight around her neck. Lou Ellen bucked up out of the chair and tried to stand as she clawed the bag.

"Can you get her fucking hands, please?" Billy asked. Horace ran over and straddled her hips and grabbed her arms. Horace thought he could see the outline of her nose in the dark plastic. A bubble rose and fell where he thought her mouth was. Lou screamed but the sound was dampened by the bag. Her screams became a desperate squealing. The squealing devolved into animalistic grunts that became increasingly desperate. Her gesticulations slowly became less frantic. Her grunts slowed and became nearly imperceptible gasps. A few minutes passed, and her legs stopped kicking.

A few more minutes passed, and she stopped moving completely.

A pungent stench filled the apartment. Neither Billy or Horace were too perturbed by this. It wasn't the first time someone had voided their bowels in their presence. Billy removed the bag, rolled it up and shoved it back in his pocket. Lou's head lolled to the right. Her tongue protruded from her mouth like a turtle's head from its shell.

Billy reached into his pocket and pulled out a handkerchief. He wiped his forehead and put the cloth back in his pocket. From his other pocket he pulled a flat silver flask, a pack of cigarettes and a book of matches. He lit one of the cigarettes with one of the matches and dropped it on the floor between Lou's feet. He hadn't put it in his mouth. He'd just held the match to the tip until a small cherry appeared. He poured the contents of the flask on the floor and the curtains. He poured some of it directly on Lou Ellen's body. The acrid smell of moonshine overtook the scent of shit that had filled the air.

Billy let out a sigh and gently stroked Lou Ellen's cheek.

"Dammit, Sis," he mumbled.

He tossed another lit match onto her body. The flame started slowly, shyly. Then it spread quickly up her leg. He tossed another match near the curtains. They went up like paraffin. Billy watched the flames dance across the fabric like zealots full of the holy ghost.

The flames reminded him of the snake handlers at his grandfather's church. Gyrating across the rough-hewn wooden floor boogying for the Lord.

"I guess we better get going," Horace said. Billy blinked his eyes.

"Yeah. You go see the redhead. I'm gonna talk to Lisa."

"I thought Jenny was the one."

"Yeah, but it doesn't hurt to cover your ass. Come on, let's get the fuck out of here. I don't want to watch her burn," Billy said. He pulled his sleeve down over his hand and opened the front door. He and Horace strolled to the Cadillac. By the time they left the parking lot and turned onto the street, the first plumes of smoke were just beginning to pour from under Lou's front door.

FIFTEEN

Beauregard sat in the Duster and tapped his fingers on the steering wheel. The skies were overcast, threatening to release a deluge of much needed rain. In the distance a water tower emblazoned with the name CARYTOWN stared down at him like an iron giant. An abandoned train trestle bisected the horizon to his left. All around him the remains of an old factory were scattered like the bones of dinosaurs made of brick and steel.

He checked his watch. It was five minutes after four. Ronnie was supposed to meet him at two on the dot. He wasn't surprised he was late for the meeting. He had been a week late getting the money from his "guy" in DC. The delay had made Beauregard's already desperate situation worse. His suppliers were blowing up his phone like a spurned lover. The mortgage on the garage was due in three days. Not to mention the deadline for Ariel's college registration was approaching quick, fast, and in a hurry. The nursing home staff was gleefully packing his mother's bags, anticipating her imminent removal.

"God, Ronnie, don't fuck me on this. I think I just might have to make you into a paperweight if you do," Beauregard said to no one. He checked his watch again. It was ten minutes after four. He closed his eyes and rubbed his forehead. He heard the rumble of a big-block engine. He opened his eyes and saw a black Mustang rolling across the pavement. The driver navigated the vehicle around cracks and potholes with the gentle ease of a new car owner.

The Mustang pulled up alongside the Duster. Ronnie Sessions grinned at Beauregard from behind the wheel. Beauregard lowered his window as Ronnie did the same.

"What the fuck is this?" Beauregard asked.

"What? It's a car, man. A BOSS car. 2004 Mustang."

Beauregard leaned out the window. "Have you been watching the news? All they been talking about is that someone died, and two other people were shot in a brazen jewelry store robbery. The police are on this like stink on shit and you go buy a new car," he said. He said each word slowly and distinctly like he was biting them out of the air and spitting them at Ronnie.

"It's not new. I got it used from Wayne Whitman."

"What you pay for it?"

"I got a deal. $7,000. He even threw in a set of rims."

"And you don't think broke-ass Ronnie Sessions throwing around money ain't gonna attract some attention?"

Ronnie rolled his eyes. "Bug, will you get that six-foot-long stick out ya ass? We did it! The cops ain't releasing any information cuz they ain't got no information. They chasing their fucking tails. So, relax."

Ronnie leaned over and grabbed two cereal boxes out of the passenger's seat. He handed them to Beauregard.

"Go buy yourself something nice. Take your wife over to Barrett's. Go have some nice quiet married people's sex at the Omni Hotel."

"Don't talk about my wife, Ronnie."

"Hey, I ain't mean no harm. I'm just saying Captain Crunch and Toucan Sam are holding $80,000 that belongs to you. Enjoy that shit."

"$87,133.33. It's supposed to be $87,133.33."

"It is, Bug. Jesus, I was just talking."

Beauregard put the two boxes in the back seat.

"Hey, man, maybe down the road we can talk about working together again. We make a good team. I can get somebody to replace Quan. I know how you feel about him. To be honest—"

Beauregard cut him off. "No. We done. And keep my name out ya mouth, Ronnie." He wound the window up and started the Duster. He hit the gas and tore out of the lot. The sky began to cry as he passed the water tower and turned onto Naibor Street. As he merged onto the interstate a sign to his left thanked him for visiting Cary-town, Va. He turned on the radio and settled in for the two-hour ride back to Red Hill County. Felt like the bear crushing his heart began to relax a bit. No one had seen him in the store. Only Ronnie, Reggie and Quan knew he had driven for the job. If his name ever came up, he knew who he had to go see.

And who would have to disappear.

Ronnie passed a box truck on his way down 64. He had Jenny's cut in the back seat and an overnight bag in the trunk. He didn't know about Bug, but he planned on partying like Tony Montana all weekend. Ronnie steered around a ramshackle SUV while taking a sip from a pint of Jack Daniel's. He put the bottle back in the cup holder and popped in an Elvis CD. The King's deep baritone rumbled through the speakers.

"That's what I'm talking about," Ronnie said. He took another sip.

Bug was giving him a hard time, but he had a point. The Sessionses were not known for their immense wealth. People would start talking if he spent too much money around town. Good thing he didn't plan on being in town much longer. He realized he had meant what he had said to Jenny. They were going to leave the coal mines and cornfields and crab pots of Virginia behind. He was going to go somewhere and spend his days drinking piña coladas and his nights getting his dick sucked by Jenny until the cash ran out or it was time to trade up. He didn't understand why Bug couldn't take one minute to celebrate. True, he had held out on him and Quan a little, but they were still rolling in enough dough to make it rain in strip clubs for the next three years. That black motherfucker wasn't even grateful Ronnie had let him in on the deal.

He put the bottle in the cup holder and pulled out his new smart-phone.

"Call Jenny," he said into the phone. He had picked it up the same day he got the car. The hands-free feature was like science fiction. Fuck a flying car.

He'd gotten back from DC three days ago after spending some time in the nation's capital with Reggie. They'd met Brandon Yang in Chinatown and gone to see his boss at a bar that catered to Chinese diplomats and immigrants. Ronnie had met Brandon inside just like Quan and Winston. Brandon was doing a year for mail fraud. He'd told Ronnie that the mail fraud beef was nothing. He worked for a guy that moved so much money as a fence for high-end merchandise, he stored it in coffins stacked six high in a warehouse he owned in Maryland. Brandon said he would be taken care of for keeping his mouth shut and doing his time.

He hadn't been lying. No one hassled him inside. He had a cell to himself. He had a cushy job in the prison laundry. Guards let him have two conjugal visits a month. It was like he was on a vacation instead of doing a bid. The only thing he didn't have was someone to play chess with. He was absolutely obsessed with the game. Ronnie approached him one day and offered to play him for some cigarettes. He'd lost, but he made Brandon work for it. They'd hit it off and when Brandon left Coldwater he told Ronnie to look him up if he ever came across something that might interest his boss.

He had done just that. When they went to see Brandon's boss, he had learned two things. First thing he learned was that Chinese guys liked to smoke a LOT. Second thing he had learned was that he didn't know shit about diamonds and neither did Jenny.

"I give you $700,000," Brandon's boss had said. Or more accurately, Brandon had said after translating for the old guy, who looked like a villain in a kung fu movie.

Ronnie had held on to the sides of his chair. Seven hundred

thousand. You could add up all the money everyone he had ever known had made and it wouldn't come close to that. If they were offering seven there must have been three or four million worth of diamonds in the box. He couldn't speak. His tongue refused to work.

They thought he was negotiating.

"Seven-fifty. Final offer," Brandon said after some more gibberish from his boss. Ronnie found his voice.

"Yeah. Yeah, that's fine," he said. For a fraction of a second, he wondered why such a small store would have that much in diamonds sitting in a safe. The bag of money they handed him forced that idea to flee like a startled rabbit. It didn't matter. With what they were giving him, he could pay Chuly, give everybody their cut, and still have enough to shit on a gold-plated toilet.

After the meeting, they hit the town. Drinking up and down the alphabet streets. Going to rooftop clubs where the waitresses walked around opening champagne bottles with swords. They'd eaten in restaurants with names Ronnie couldn't pronounce. They had even picked up some women who had turned out to be working girls. He and Reggie and Brandon had taken turns with all three girls. Ronnie had lived out one of his fantasies and snorted coke off the sexiest hooker's ass. They had partied like rock stars. And why not? He was in high fucking cotton now. No more counting loose change for gas. He wasn't Bill Gates rich, but he was far from poor. Even though the AC was on, he lowered the window. He let out a loud whooping rebel yell.

"Hello?" Jenny said.

Ronnie raised the window. "Hey, sugar bottom. I'm on my way to you right now. I feel like Santa Claus. Can I put something in your stocking?"

"You got the money?" Jenny asked.

Ronnie frowned at the phone. She sounded . . . strange. Like a kid who had dropped his ice cream cone, lost his puppy, and seen his dad get beat up all on the same day.

"Yeah, I sure do. I'll be there in like forty-five minutes. Maybe sooner. This Mustang got some kick."

"Okay." She hung up. She didn't even ask about the car.

"What the fuck is wrong with you?" he said, staring at the phone.

SIXTEEN

Beauregard got back to Red Hill a little after six. He got to the bank just before the drive-thru window closed. He deposited three thousand for the mortgage payment and another five for all the other bills. He left the bank and headed for the nursing home. He pulled in and headed straight for the administrator's office.

Mrs. Talbot was putting her laptop in a leather valise.

"Mr. Montage, how are you? I'm just about to leave for the day. Perhaps you can come back in the morning? I can help you arrange transportation for your mother. And I'll be more than happy to organize her oxygen deliveries at your home," she said. Beauregard could count every one of her capped teeth as she smiled at him.

"That won't be necessary," he said. He had already counted out $30,000 in the car. He put six bundles of $100 bills on Mrs. Talbot's desk. Each bundle consisted of fifty $100 bills. The smile on Mrs. Talbot's face melted away like the wax from a cheap candle.

"Mr. Montage, this is highly unusual."

"No, it's not. I've paid y'all in cash before. I've specifically paid YOU in cash before when my Mama has shown her ass up in here. So, could you please give me a receipt? I'll have the remainder of the money later this week. I don't have any change right now," he said.

Mrs. Talbot sat down and pulled out her laptop.

His mother was lying back against a pillow that was engulfing her head. A few cardboard boxes were stacked in the far corner of the room. A talking head chattered on from the television about the weather. The rain that had blessed Carytown was not headed to Red Hill. She was so still he almost thought she was dead. Her thin chest barely rose as she took a breath. He turned to leave.

"You gonna make me sleep on the porch?" she asked. She sounded weaker than the last time he had visited her. He went to her bedside.

"No."

"Oh joy, I get to be in the big house, Massa," she said.

"I paid the bill. Well, most of it."

Her eyes widened. "That was you?"

Beauregard frowned. "What was me?"

"That shit on the news. The jewelry store. When they said the robbers got away in a Buick Regal that jumped an overpass under construction, I knew it. I just knew it. Sounded like something your Daddy would have done." She started to cough ferociously. Beauregard grabbed the pitcher off her nightstand and poured her a glass of water.

"Don't you worry about that."

"You would do anything not to have me at your house, wouldn't you?"

"Mama, please. It's not that. I'm just trying to do what's best for you."

"Right. Right." She coughed again, and he gave her another sip. She did not say thank you. Beauregard smoothed her head scarf.

"They gonna find you."

"I told you don't worry about that."

"They gonna find you, and you gonna have to run just like he did. Leave your kids and your wife behind. Let them fend for themselves like your Daddy did to me."

"To us," Beauregard said.

She ignored his correction. "You thought you was saving him that day at the Tastee Freez. All you did was postpone the inevitable."

Beauregard flinched. "Mama, don't," he said.

His mother turned her head. The low fluorescent lights gave her a cadaverous appearance.

"'I'll save you, Daddy. I'll stop the bad men from hurting you.' And what did he do? Left town while they tossed you in a cage. Lord knows I didn't have no money for a good lawyer. You did all that for him and he just ran."

Beauregard's head began to throb. "You think he ran from me or the cops? He ran from you. He couldn't stand to hear your mouth one more minute," he said. The words left a foul taste in his mouth, but he couldn't help himself. No one knew how to push his buttons like his mother. If anyone else had talked to him like that, they would be counting their teeth in the palm of their hand. All he could do to his mother was try and strike her where she was softest.

"That's how you talk to your mother?"

"That's how you talk to me."

"When I die, don't sit up in church pretending you miss me. Just burn me up and toss me in the trash like you doing now."

Beauregard rolled his eyes. This was her fighting style. Attack you from the front, then pivot and spring a surprise attack on your flank.

"Good night, Mama." He turned and walked to the door. Before he could leave, Ella had another coughing fit. He went back and gave her some more water, but it didn't seem to help. He slipped his hand under her back and was shocked by how insubstantial she felt. He pulled her up and lightly tapped her between her shoulder blades. She nodded, and he let her lie back on the bed.

"I . . . should have picked a better father for you. But Anthony had the cutest smile I'd ever seen," she said. She was wheezing, and a thin line of saliva was hanging from her stoma.

"You want the nurse?"

She shook her head. She wrapped her bony fingers around his wrist.

"You could have been better than you are, but you spent too much time looking up to a ghost."

Beauregard felt a hitch in his chest.

"Not anymore."

"Liar."

Beauregard got in the Duster and pulled out of the nursing home spinning tires. He had one more stop to make, and he was dreading it.

Beauregard brought the Duster to a stop in front of a two-story white farmhouse that was quickly going to seed. The black shutters had faded to a washed-out greenish color. The porch was beginning to lean on the everlasting. Beauregard got out of the car and tramped across the yard. His feet kicked up dust devils as he walked. There was no grass or shrubs near the house. An El Camino sat up on blocks near the front door. An old brown couch covered by a tarp sat on the right corner of the house. Empty beer cans and cigarette butts littered the yard.

Beauregard knocked on the screen door. He didn't hit it as hard as he could because he was afraid it was going to fall off the hinges. He could hear Fox News blaring from somewhere inside the house. Shuffling footsteps brought Ariel's grandmother Emma to the door. A short stocky woman with jowls on top of her jowls. An unfiltered Pall Mall was hanging on to the corner of her lip for dear life.

"Yeah?"

"Can you get Ariel for me? I called her phone, but she didn't answer."

Emma took a drag on her cigarette. The tip glowed red like a piece of ferrous metal being melted. "Phone's off. You'd know that if you called her more."

"Just get her for me," Beauregard said.

"What you want with her?"

"I want to talk to her. I'm her daddy. No matter how hard you try to pretend she has the world's best perm."

"You coming around here every once in a while with your drug money don't make you a father."

Beauregard leaned forward and lowered his voice. "Go get my daughter. Now. I'm not in the mood to play this fucking game with you. Not today."

Emma blew a cloud of smoke out through her nostrils before turning away from the door. He heard her whisper "asshole" as she walked down the hall. He went back to the Duster and sat on the hood. Ariel came out a few minutes later. She was wearing a tank top and shorts so tight they would become a thong if she sneezed.

"Hey."

"Hey. Where's your car?"

"Rip needed it for work. And since my phone is off, he can't call me to pick him up, so I let him take it."

"He got a license?"

"Yeah, he just ain't got a car."

"Come here."

She joined him on the hood of the car. "You gonna give some static about that?"

"Nah. There are more important things than Lil Rip driving your car."

He reached into his back pocket and pulled out a bulky rolled-up brown envelope like the one you used to mail documents.

"One year of tuition at VCU is $24,000."

"Yeah. Plus, textbooks."

He handed her the envelope.

"What is this?"

"Twenty-four thousand dollars. I guess colleges don't take cash so open some bank accounts. Don't deposit more than $10,000 in each. The government will come asking questions if you do."

Ariel's mouth was agape.

"Where the fuck did you get this money?"

"Watch your mouth, girl."

"Sorry. Where the hell did you get this money?"

Beauregard laughed.

"Look, don't worry about that. Just don't let your Mama or your grandmother know you got it. I can't promise you I'll be able to do more anytime soon, but this is a start."

Ariel twisted the envelope in her hands. She frowned.

"Am I gonna get in trouble taking this money?"

"Why would you say that?"

She pushed an errant curl behind her ear. The breeze came up and knocked it loose.

"Mama says that you do things. Illegal things."

"Does she."

"Yeah."

Beauregard crossed his arms and looked straight ahead.

"You take that money and you get the fuck out of this house. Out of this county. You ain't gonna get in any trouble. Go and don't look back. Don't ever come back. There's nothing here for you. Not Lil Rip. Not your Mama. Not me. Your star is too bright for a place like this," he said.

"I don't know what to say."

"You ain't gotta say nothing. You my daughter."

He didn't say he loved her. He wanted to, but it felt wrong to say it now. She might feel obligated to say it back and he didn't want that. Just because he had given her this money didn't mean he had earned an "I love you" just yet.

Ariel let out a long sigh.

"And you my daddy," she said. She hadn't called him that since she had learned how to tie her shoes.

There didn't seem much to say after that so they both stared straight ahead with their feet on the front bumper of the Duster. They stayed like that for a while, neither one of them saying a word. They just watched the sunset and listened to Emma yell at the television. At some point, Beauregard felt Ariel's hand in his own. He squeezed it and sat there for a little while longer.

Once he had left Ariel, Beauregard decided to go out to the Walmart and pick up some Delmonico steaks, potatoes and some ice cream for dessert. He wasn't going to buy a car, but Ronnie had a point. He should enjoy some of the money. He usually avoided going by the Walmart because it meant passing Precision and he didn't have any desire to see all the cars that should have been at his shop behind their black-powdered aluminum fence. Kia did most of the shopping by herself. On the days he did accompany her he took her over to the Food Lion in Tillerson two counties to the north.

He turned onto Market Drive and dropped his speed down to 35 miles per hour. A mile from the Walmart he heard the shrill whine of sirens. He clenched the steering wheel and got ready to punch it. He looked up in the rearview mirror and saw a fire engine bearing down on him. He pulled over and let it pass. Two more followed the first one, sirens and lights blasting at full power. Beauregard pulled back onto the highway and continued to the store. He wondered if the trucks were headed to the Walmart. Had some bored high school kids called in a bomb threat?

"Goddamn," he said.

Precision Auto was engulfed in flames. Plumes of fire shot fifty feet into the air, setting the sky ablaze. The volunteer firefighters were valiantly battling the inferno, but it didn't look like they were making much headway. The Precision Auto Repair sign was melting on its fifteen-foot-tall pole. Beauregard studied his rearview mirror as he passed by the scene. The flames glowing behind him made it seem he was driving straight out of Hell.

When he got home from the store, Kia was sitting on the couch with Darren.

"Hey, where's Javon?" he asked.

"He asked could he stay over at Tre Cook's house. I didn't think you would mind."

"I don't. I was just asking."

"What you got there?"

"Got some steaks. Gonna make some potatoes au rotten," Beauregard said as he brushed Darren's head with the shopping bag.

"Eww."

"What, you don't want no rotten potatoes?"

"No, Daddy, that's nasty."

"Well, more for me," he said as he walked into the kitchen. Kia got up and followed him into the kitchen.

"You got paid?" she asked.

Beauregard put the steaks on the counter. "Yeah."

"No more, right?" Kia asked.

Beauregard went to her and enveloped her in his arms.

"No more." He kissed her forehead before releasing her. He cut open the packages of steaks and placed the meat in a bowl. He poured some seasonings in the bowl and filled it with water for a quick marinade.

"Precision Auto Repair was on fire when I went to Walmart."

"What? When did this happen?"

"I just told you. About an hour ago."

"Well, fuck."

Darren collapsed into giggles.

"What?"

"You know they gonna think you had something to do with it, right?"

The thought had crossed his mind, but he hadn't so he didn't expend any energy worrying about it.

"Yeah, but I didn't."

"I know you didn't, but they still gonna say it."

He walked back into the living room.

"So? You gonna peel these potatoes?"

———

They had dinner then sat on the couch watching a movie until Darren fell asleep. Kia picked him up and he snuggled against her neck.

"I'm going to put him down. Then I'm gonna be right behind him. You coming to bed?"

"In a few. Gonna check out the news." Kia cradled Darren to her chest. Beauregard thought she was going to ask him a question. He waited for it, but the moment passed. "Tell your daddy goodnight," she whispered to Darren.

In response to her request Darren gave him a lazy goodbye wave.

"Night, Stink."

The two of them went down the hall and left Beauregard alone in the living room. The news was the usual collection of local political stories blown up to Watergate proportions. Human interest stories that weren't all that interesting. A report about a fire at an apartment complex in Newport News. Beauregard was just about to cut off the television and head to bed when the talking head mentioned Cutter County.

"And new at eleven, authorities have released the name of the man killed in last Monday's attempted jewelry store robbery. Eric Gay, nineteen, of Cutter County was killed in the botched robbery. He leaves behind a wife and a young son. Our Ellen Williams spoke with Mr. Gay's widow Caitlin as she struggles to find the words to one day explain to her son what happened to his father," the talking head said. The screen jumped from the studio to a cramped trailer. A young white woman was holding a picture in one arm and a baby with an ecru complexion in the other.

"Attempted?" Beauregard said out loud.

As the camera zoomed in on the picture, it showed a young man smiling in his high school basketball uniform. He was kneeling with one hand on a basketball and the other hand on the floor. He hadn't had the time or the money to take any new photos that could be used on the air. When you were that age, you thought you had plenty of time for everything. There would be time later for a professional portrait with your wife and your new baby. Except later had been stopped in its tracks by a bullet.

"That's right, Frank. Caitlin cried as she told me how she is struggling with the idea of explaining to her son Anthony how his father died."

The segment went on for another five minutes, but Beauregard didn't pay attention. He gripped the arm of the couch so tight his hand began to ache. All he could see was Eric Gay's smiling face. The same face that had stared at him pleading for help on the side of the road.

He got up and went into the kitchen. He grabbed one of the beers he had bought earlier. He checked the sink for a bottle opener. When he didn't find it, he started looking through the drawers.

Why had the news reported the robbery as an attempt? He'd seen the box. Seen the way Ronnie held on to it like it was a life preserver in the middle of the North Atlantic. He might be running game about the amount of the cut, but he had gotten paid. So why was somebody lying to the cops?

Beauregard rifled through the forks and spoons. Nothing.

Why had Eric Gay been in the store? He had told him he was broke. Maybe someone had given them some money. Slipped $500 in a card for the baby. Maybe Eric had gone to get his wife a gift. A thank you for bringing his son into the world. He had wanted to do that for Janice when she had Ariel. He'd thought about doing it for Kia when she had given birth to Javon. By the time Darren entered the picture, other things seemed more important.

He opened the catch-all drawer. There were rolls of duct tape, a ruler, a device to open jars, and other miscellaneous items that tend to accumulate during the life of a household. A bottle opener was not among their number.

Eric and Caitlin had named their baby Anthony. In the book of baby names Janice had dog-eared while carrying Ariel, it said Anthony meant praiseworthy. When they found out it was a girl, they settled on Ariel because Janice liked a cartoon character with the same name. When he and Kia had the boys, she picked the names. He had suggested "Anthony" both times. A subtle tribute to his Daddy's memory. Kia had shot him down both times.

Now there was a boy who would never have memories of his daddy. He would grow up without a father just like Beauregard.

He hadn't really thought they would actually do it. Why the fuck had they named the baby Anthony?

Beauregard hurled the bottle to the floor. It shattered. Shards of glass flew across the kitchen. The beer followed the uneven curve of the floor and pooled under the table.

SEVENTEEN

Ronnie pulled into Jenny's apartment complex with the radio blaring and an empty pint bottle of Jack on the floor. The smile on his face became wider the closer he got to her door. He knocked three times, paused, and then knocked twice more. She opened the door a crack. Ronnie saw she hadn't unlatched the chain.

"You got the money?"

He could barely see her face through the opening in the door. "Well, hello to you too. You gonna let me in?"

"Can't you just pass it to me?"

"No, not really. I got it in these boxes," he said, taking the cereal boxes from under his arm.

"Cereal boxes?"

Ronnie grinned again. "If the cops stop me with nearly a hundred grand in cash, they gonna ask questions. If they see a back seat full of cereal boxes, they just gonna think I'm a big fan of breakfast."

"Whatever. Just slide the box through the door."

A scowl rippled across Ronnie's face.

"You got somebody in there?"

"Ronnie, just give me my money."

"Hey, it ain't like we married or nothing, I'm just asking. I mean, I was hoping I could spend the night, but if you got some dude in there, I'll go on down the road. Can't say I ain't disappointed."

He handed her one box then the other. Jenny snatched them out of his hand with startling quickness.

"You alright? You don't seem like yourself."

"I just got a lot going on right now. I'll talk to you later."

"If I was you, I'd keep an eye on them. You don't need to let your new friend know you holding something magically delicious."

She shut the door and locked it.

"Ain't that bout a bitch," he said under his breath. He whistled a low short tune and headed back to his car. Maybe the time to upgrade was now. Jenny was beginning to look rode hard and hung up wet anyway.

Jenny opened the boxes. They were both stuffed to the gills with cash. She sat them on the couch and went to the bedroom. She grabbed a few shirts and pants and threw them in an overnight bag. She went back into the kitchen and took her sugar bowl out of the cabinet. She'd hidden twenty or so Percocets in the bowl. A gift from Ronnie. She shook all the Percs into her hand and put them in a pocket on the side of the overnight bag. A wet lock of hair fell into her face, but she didn't bother moving it. The wail of an electric guitar made her jump like a long-tailed cat in a room full of rocking chairs. She looked down at the kitchen floor.

The man had finally stopped bleeding. The handle of an eight-inch butcher knife stuck out of his neck like the crank on a jack in the box. The guitar sound was accompanied by a low vibration coming from the pocket of his jeans. That was the tenth or fifteenth time his phone had gone off since 3:00. Jenny stepped over him, careful to avoid the puddle of blood that was surrounding his body, and opened her freezer. She pulled out the ice tray and placed three cubes of ice in a small freezer bag. The ice felt good against her right eye.

Her daddy had been a mean son of a bitch but the one good thing he had done was teach her how to fight. That bastard never pulled any punches with his mouth or his fists. Those hard lessons had proved lucky for her but bad news for the guy lying on the floor. She stepped over him again and went back to the living room. It took some elbow grease, but she got both boxes in the overnight bag.

Jenny went to the window and peeped through the drapes. She didn't see Ronnie anywhere. She grabbed her keys from the hook by the door. She went back to the window. Her apartment complex was laid out like a motel. A series of units with one big front window and a front door that faced the parking lot. She only saw one strange car and that was parked right next to hers. The car looked empty. Still, she decided to wait a few more minutes. She didn't want to pass Ronnie on the road. He'd follow her and pretend he didn't care if she had a guy at her place, then he'd try sweet-talking her. She couldn't have that. She might just tell him everything. No, she had to run. Running might make her look guilty to the cops but staying would get her killed. She'd seen the news. Lou Ellen was lying. Whoever owned the shop didn't want the police in their business. They were sending guys like the dead guy on the floor of her apartment with a mouthful of rotten teeth to handle it for them. Once she got down south, she'd call Ronnie and warn him. She did owe him that.

Jenny checked her phone. The guy had knocked on her door around noon. He'd punched her in the face at 12:15. He was dead by 12:30. It was now nearly 7:00. Six hours of sitting with his rapidly cooling corpse waiting to see who would show up first. Ronnie or Yuckmouth's buddies.

Almost as if on cue, his phone rang again.

"Fuck this," she said. She grabbed her overnight bag and left the apartment. She hopped in her car and started the engine.

"Breathe. Just breathe and drive. That's all you gotta do," she said out loud to herself. She tossed the bag in the passenger seat.

Checked the rearview mirror. Nothing. As she backed out of her parking spot the fuel light started to blink. That was fine. She had more than enough gas money. She'd stop somewhere in North Carolina and score some Adderall or something. Drive all night to Florida. Getting to the Bahamas shouldn't be hard after that. Money talks and everything else walks. She pulled out of the parking lot and turned onto Bethel Road. A fine mist of rain began to fall. Jenny thought that was symbolic. It was like the rain was baptizing her. She'd come out of this a new creature. She didn't have any AC in the car, so she was going to leave the window down until it started raining harder.

A black Cadillac Seville passed her on the two-lane highway as she headed for the nearest gas station. It was the only car on the road. No cops. No gangsters with butter yellow teeth. No Ronnie. Just the old Jenny on her way to a new life.

She was almost to the interstate when she noticed the Cadillac had turned around and was following her.

EIGHTEEN

"Wake up, sleepy head," Kia said. Beauregard opened his eyes. "Can you pick Darren and Javon up this evening? I'm gonna pick up another office job tonight."

"Yeah. Where does that Cook boy live?"

"On Falmouth Road."

Beauregard sat up in the bed.

"Falmouth?"

"Yeah. They in that subdivision," Kia said. She clipped on some earrings and closed her Rottweiler-shaped jewelry box. Beauregard thought that box was one of the ugliest things in existence. You had to lift the head to open it at the throat. You basically had to decapitate it every time you wanted an adornment.

"Okay," he said.

"We gonna be alright, ain't we?" she asked.

Beauregard spun until he felt his feet hit the floor. He grabbed her hand and brought it to his lips. He gave it a brief peck. "Yeah."

She turned and hugged him against her belly. He felt her hand on the back of his neck. He breathed her in and smelled the scent of her body mixed with her perfume and the remnants of the dryer sheets she used in the laundry. Even if they weren't going to be alright, he would never let her know.

Kelvin was already at the shop when Beauregard arrived. There were two vehicles in the air on the lifts. Kelvin was under one, a black pickup truck, working on the oil filter.

"Hey."

"Hey. You just in time. Doing an oil change on this one and the car keeps making a funny noise that's not a rattle or a clank or a clang or a ping," Kelvin said.

"Then ain't a funny noise, it's just the engine," Beauregard said.

Kelvin laughed. "I'm just telling you what the lady said. And we got a call from the Cedars Septic Service. Wanted to know if we could look at one of their trucks today. I told them we didn't take no crap."

Beauregard frowned.

"Fuck you, that was funny. I suspect we gonna be real busy this week," Kelvin said.

"Yeah. Precision caught on fire last night," Beauregard said.

"Oh, I didn't know if you knew. Sucks for them, but good for us."

"I guess," Beauregard said.

They did twelve oil changes, replaced eight sets of brake pads and started on the septic truck. By four, they were both soaking wet with sweat and loving every minute of it.

"Nice being busy, huh?" Kelvin asked. He had just driven a two-seat sports car into the back lot after adjusting its fuel injector. Beauregard was using an impact wrench to take off the back tire of an old Caprice. Before he could answer, they heard two vehicles pull up and the sounds of multiple car doors slamming shut. Beauregard stopped trying to remove the tire's lug nuts and turned to face whoever was coming into the shop. It wasn't the cops. If they had come for him, they would have announced themselves as soon as they got out.

Patrick Thompson and his father Butch entered the shop through the first roll-up door. Patrick was a thin wiry figure with a shock of bright blond hair cut into a shaggy surfer-boy style. Butch was a square block of a man. All hard angles and broad shoulders. He was bald but had a prodigious blond and gray beard.

"Pat," Beauregard said. He had known Pat Thompson before he'd become the competition. He'd seen him at Danny's a few times. Pat had a '69 Camaro that he liked to run on the back roads sometimes. They had never gone head to head, but Beauregard knew the Camaro had legs. His daddy used to be a truck driver for a long-haul company out of Richmond. A year and a half ago, Butch Thompson had stopped at a gas station to fill up his rig. While he was in line to pay for his fuel, he'd purchased a one-dollar scratch-off ticket. He'd done the same thing a hundred times in the past. The most he'd ever won was $700. That day he received a huge return on his investment. He hit for $400,000. He called up his boss and told him to send someone to pick up his load because he had just quit. He and Patrick had opened their garage a few months later.

"Beau. You heard about my place?" Patrick asked. His blue eyes bore a hole into Beauregard.

"Yeah."

"That's all you got to say? Yeah?" Butch asked. He was clenching and unclenching his hands. They looked like bear traps.

"What you want me to say, Butch?"

"Somebody say they saw a black guy running from the scene, Beau. I thought maybe you might know something about that," Patrick said.

Kelvin picked up a torque wrench.

"Why would you think I'd know something about that?" Beauregard said.

"Cuz you the only black guy who owns a garage that's been getting its ass kicked," Butch said. He took a step forward.

"You think I set fire to your place? Really?" Beauregard asked.

"I think you might know who did. The cops say it was deliberate. My dad told them to come talk to you, but I guess they didn't take us serious," Patrick said.

"Pat, I didn't have nothing to do with what happened to your place. I'm sorry for you, but I don't know nothing about it."

"You a lying black bastard," Butch said. His face was mottled with splotches of red just above his beard.

"What you say?" Beauregard asked. He let the impact wrench slip from his hand and held it by the air hose. It hung loosely by his side.

"You heard me. You know who did it. You sent them. Couldn't compete with us anymore. Then we got that contract. In three months there was gonna be a CLOSED sign on your door and we all know it," Butch said.

"The cops say they need proof to arrest you. I just wanted to ask you to your face," Patrick said. His eyes were red. He'd probably been up all night. Beauregard knew he would have been.

"I told him it was a waste of time. All you people do is lie and steal. And make babies you can't take care of. Bunch of fucking nig—"

Beauregard whipped the impact wrench up and out by its air hose. It flew through the air and smashed into Butch's mouth. The bigger man stumbled backwards, his hands covering the lower half of his face. His blond and gray beard was stained with streaks of red.

Beauregard snapped the wrench back and caught it in midair. He ran at Butch and clocked him in the forehead with the wrench. Butch fell onto his ass. He raised his hands and grabbed at Beauregard's shirt. Beauregard hit him on the top of the head. The impact wrench split Butch's scalp open like an orange peel. Beauregard raised the impact wrench above his head.

Patrick tackled him. They tumbled to the floor. A thin arm snaked around his neck and gripped him like a python. Kelvin came running over. He swung the four-foot-long torque wrench like a golf club. The head struck Patrick in the small of the back. Beauregard heard him cry out like a wounded fox. Beauregard shrugged him off and got to his feet. He kicked Patrick in the gut. Then he kicked him again.

"Please . . . ," Patrick gasped.

Beauregard got down on one knee and shoved the socket of the impact wrench in Patrick's mouth.

"I should break all your teeth. Make you eat soup for a year. Give you time to think. If I had wanted to put you out of business, I would have just caught you outside of Danny's one night and broken both your hands. Not burn down your shop," he said.

Patrick's eyes were wild. Saliva dripped down his chin. Beauregard took the wrench out of his mouth and stood.

"Get the fuck out of here," he said. Patrick rolled into a kneeling position. He held his stomach with one arm and crawled to his father. Butch was flat on his back and mewling. Patrick struggled to his feet. He grabbed his father by the arm and helped the older man off the floor. The laceration on his scalp was bleeding freely, making his face a crimson mask. His beard was nearly soaked through. The two of them limped out the door. Kelvin tossed the torque wrench to the ground. It sent an echo reverberating through the garage. He was breathing hard.

"Well, that went well. How much bail money you think we gonna need?" Kelvin said.

"They ain't gonna tell nobody. At least not the cops."

"You don't think so?"

Beauregard set the impact wrench on top of the tool chest. The socket was smeared with blood and spit.

"They were here trespassing. They said the cops told them to let them handle it. They won't feel too much sympathy for them. Besides, guys like that only talk about the fights they win."

Beauregard turned into the cul-de-sac off Falmouth Road. It was called, not surprisingly, Falmouth Acres. He drove past the lawns manicured to within an inch of their lives and the only sidewalks outside of the courthouse area. This was where money lived in Red Hill County. His old pickup stood out among the luxury cars and SUVs.

The Cook house sat at the end of the cul-de-sac under the shade from an enormous elm tree. Beauregard would not have built his house there. A strong storm could send a branch crashing through the bedroom like an arboreal missile. Money made you value aesthetics over safety, he guessed. He parked on the curb and walked past a brick column with a plaque that proclaimed the House of Cook was established in 2005.

The doorbell was a white button in the center of an arabesque series of swirls. He pushed it once and heard the theme from every old horror movie he had ever seen ring through the house. The door opened, and a slim, pale white woman greeted him. A sharp bob with razor-cut bangs framed her narrow face. She wore a long black sleeved shirt and black tights despite the heat. Beauregard felt a cool rush of air when she opened the door. A central air unit was working hard to keep the whole house at a comfortable temperature.

"You must be Javon's father. I'm Miranda."

"Yes. Nice to meet you."

"Well, come on in." Beauregard didn't move.

"Actually, I'm kinda in a hurry. Could you just get Javon for me? Please."

Miranda smiled.

"Of course. I must say my husband and I were so impressed with your son. He is a perfect young gentleman," she said. She went back into the house through an expansive foyer. A few minutes later, Javon came down the stairs.

"Thank you for letting me spend the night, Mrs. Cook," he said as she slipped on his backpack.

"Well, you're welcome. Tre sure appreciated you hanging out with him. He was glad to have someone to talk to about Claude Monet," she said with a smile.

"Well, you take care now," Beauregard said. He put his hand on Javon's shoulder and half guided, half pulled Javon through the doorway. They walked to the truck in silence. Beauregard pulled out of Falmouth Acres. He turned right and headed deeper into the county.

"Where we going?" Javon asked. Beauregard didn't respond. He turned down Chain Ferry Road then down Ivy Lane. The lane ended at the old public landing for the Blackwater River. Once they reached the boat ramp Beauregard stopped the truck and killed the engine.

"We need to talk," he said.

"About what?"

Beauregard gripped the steering wheel. Then he relaxed his grip and turned to Javon. "I'm gonna ask you a question and I want the truth. Do you understand me?"

"Yeah."

"Don't just say that because you think that's what I want to hear. I want you to tell me the honest truth."

"Okay," Javon said. He had his head down with his chin nearly touching his chest.

Beauregard closed his eyes and ran a hand across his face. He left his hand over his eyes. "Did you set fire to Precision Auto?"

Javon didn't respond. Beauregard opened his eyes and caught a glimpse of the river. The sun was skipping across its surface like stones. The window was down so he could hear the water gently lapping against the riverbank. His grandfather used to take him here to fish for catfish and carp. He wasn't that good at fishing, but it didn't really matter. His Granddaddy James, his mother's father, was a patient teacher. If he hadn't gotten sent to juvie, then he might have gotten good at it. By the time he got out, his grandfather was dead.

"I ain't never heard you talk about this boy Tre Cook before. But his house is within walking distance of Precision Auto. So, I'm gonna ask you again. Did you do it?"

Javon ran his hands over his face the same way his father had a few moments earlier. He turned and glared out the window. When he spoke, his voice didn't crack or waver.

"I was just trying to help. Mama told Aunt Jean we might lose the shop."

Beauregard punched the dashboard. The old leather split just like Butch Thompson's scalp. Javon flinched and pressed himself against the door of the truck. Beauregard grabbed him by his arm and shook him.

"What did I tell you? Didn't I tell you that you didn't have to worry about that? Jesus Christ, Javon, do you even know how much trouble you could get into? They could send you to juvie, and trust and believe you don't want that! What if somebody had been in there working? Goddamn it, boy, what was you thinking?"

Beauregard had never hit his boys. For that matter, he had never hit Ariel. His mother had slapped him around a few times and his father had gone ballistic. He didn't let his kids walk all over him, though. He demanded their respect, and when he didn't get it, he let them know accordingly. The desire to strike one of them for some transgression had never been stronger than his desire to assure them that they were loved.

Until today. A part of him (the part that loved the thrill of driving, perhaps?) wanted to slap Javon right in the mouth.

"I just wanted Mama to stop crying!" Javon yelled.

"What?"

"You don't know because you always gone. She don't cry in front of you. But whenever you ain't home, by the time she puts us to bed she cries. She was telling Aunt Jean on the phone that every time you leave, she scared the next time she sees you it gonna be in a casket. She always talking to her about she don't want you to do stuff that gonna get you in trouble!" Javon said. He was weeping now. Tears and words flowing freely in equal measure.

Beauregard let go of his arm.

"I thought if the other place was gone, you wouldn't have to do the bad stuff. I thought things would get better. I don't want you to die, Daddy," he said. He grabbed the tail of his T-shirt and wiped his nose.

Beauregard clenched his jaw. He moved his head around in a circle like he was taking in his surroundings for the first time. A nasty bubble of acid was trying to work its way up his esophagus.

"Javon, I ain't gonna die. Not no time soon. And even if I do, that still don't mean you gotta try and take over. You ain't the man of the house. You just a twelve-year-old boy. That's all you need to be. That man of the house shit will get you hurt. Trust me," he said finally.

"Mama said you did when your Daddy left. She said you did what you had to do," Javon said. His tears had slowed to a trickle. He sniffed, then let out a wet cough.

"Don't do what I did, Javon. I ain't nobody you should be trying to be like. I made a lot of mistakes. Terrible mistakes. The only good things I've done is marrying your Mama and having you and Darren and your sister. The things I had to do hurt a lot more people than they helped. I was trying to be something I wasn't ready to be. Just like you did," Beauregard said.

He could see himself in the driver's seat of the Duster. Thirteen years old. His foot on the gas. The horrified faces of the three men that had been talking to his Daddy.

"Are you going to tell on me?" Javon asked.

Beauregard snapped his head to the right. "No. No, I'm not going to tell on you. Was that Tre boy with you?"

"No, I . . . I snuck out by myself. I told him I was meeting a girl."

"The only people that know is me and you. And that's the way it's gonna stay. But you gotta promise me something, and I mean you gotta swear to me, boy."

"Okay."

Beauregard studied the horn in the center of the steering wheel.

"I ain't gonna tell you it's wrong, because you know it's wrong. You gotta promise no matter how bad you think things are, you won't never do anything like this again. You start down a road like this and before you know it you can't find your way back. You lose yourself. One day you wake up and you're just this thing that does shit and don't feel nothing. And that's the worst thing you can be. I can't let that happen to you. I'm your Daddy and it's my job to protect you.

Even if that means protecting you from yourself. Promise me you won't ever do anything like this again," Beauregard said.

"I promise."

Beauregard put his arm around Javon and pulled him close.

"I love you, boy. As long as I got breath in my body, I'm gonna be there for you. My Daddy wasn't always there for me. I ain't gonna do that to you." He hugged him tight then released him.

"I love you too," Javon said.

Beauregard started the truck, but before he could put it in gear, Javon asked him a question that stopped him cold. It was a question he had expected him to ask one day. In some respects, it made sense he would ask the question now, after his Montage blood had made itself known in spectacular fashion.

"What happened to your Daddy?" Javon asked.

Beauregard sat back in the truck and let out a mirthless chuckle.

"My Daddy? My Daddy was like a thunderstorm in a world of gentle breezes. That's the way he tore through life. That's the way he raised me," Beauregard said.

Javon opened his mouth like he was going to ask another question, but then he shut it and turned to the window.

Later that night, Beauregard sat on the porch drinking a beer. The crickets and the katydids were having a battle of the bands. The moonless sky was black as pitch. The temperature had dropped approximately one degree from a high of 97 earlier in the morning. Moths danced around the yellow porch light. Drawn to their death by the same thing that fascinated them.

Kia came out and sat next to him in the other plastic Adirondack chair.

"Javon is quieter than usual. He fell asleep with those ear phones on. He ain't come out of his room since we finished eating."

"Uh huh," Beauregard said as he took a sip of his beer.

"Anything going on I should know about?" she asked. She touched his arm and he handed her the bottle. She took a long sip, then handed it back. Beauregard answered her question with a question.

"You tell Jean I was doing a job?" he asked.

Kia crinkled her brow. "No, why you ask that?"

"Javon said he overheard you telling her I might have to do something bad to save the shop."

Kia bit her bottom lip. "I might have said something like that, but I didn't say it was a job. Now I've answered your question. You gonna answer mine?"

Beauregard took another sip. "Pat Thompson came by today. Accused me of burning his place down just like you said he would. We got into it."

"Did you hurt him?"

"Nothing some iodine and bandages can't fix."

Kia leaned back in the chair.

"You think they gonna press charges?"

"Nah. They was in the wrong. I know this ain't the end of it, though."

"What's that got to do with Javon? You know why he's so quiet, don't you?"

Beauregard peered into the darkness. The light from the highway danced down the road like ball lightning.

"Javon set fire to the Precision Auto," he said.

Kia shot up and headed for the door. Beauregard reached out and grabbed her wrist. He pulled her back down as gently as he could.

"He thought he was helping. He's heard us talking about how tight things are. Burning down the competition seemed like a solution," he said.

"Jesus, Bug, what are we gonna do?"

"We gonna protect him, that's what we gonna do. You know, I used to think I was a better man than my Daddy. I tried hard to be a better father. But it's like I gave my boys a sickness. The counselor in juvie called it a 'propensity for violent conflict resolution.' That's one way to put it," Beauregard said.

He finished his beer in one long gulp. He stood up and hurled the bottle into the woods. He heard it land somewhere in the brush.

"It's a fucking curse, is what it is," he said. "Money can't fix it and love can't tame it. Push it down deep and it rots you from the inside out. Give in to it and you end up doing five years in some hellhole. I once saw my Daddy beat a man half to death with a bar stool over the man's wife. What Javon did ain't really his fault. Violence is a Montage family tradition."

Red Hill County

August 1991

"It's gonna storm, Bug. See them clouds over there? It's coming hard and fast. Can't you smell it in the air?" Anthony said.

Bug leaned out the car window and let the wind slap him in the face. His Daddy was right, he could smell the rain in the air. It was a high sweet scent that suffused the atmosphere. In the distance a mass of dark clouds were gathering. They were full like overripe plums ready to burst.

"After we get the shakes, maybe I should go get some neck bones. Take you home and make some soup for you and your Mama," Anthony said.

Bug knew what that meant. His Daddy was planning on spending the night. That meant an hour of laughing and two hours of arguing followed by two hours of hushed talking in his Mama's bedroom. It also meant he got to spend more time with his Daddy.

They pulled into the Tastee Freez and his Daddy put the car in neutral. He set the parking brake and hopped out with a deft agility that belied his size. He closed the door, then leaned through the open window.

"Two shakes and a couple of greasy cheeseburgers. You want anything else?"

"No. Can I get a chocolate shake instead of strawberry?"

"Sure. You changing up on me," Anthony said with a laugh. He jogged over to the sliding window to place his order. A few other customers were parked to the right of the building. Carhops made trips back and forth, ferrying food and drinks to families in minivans and the odd station wagon. Bug heard the high-pitched laughter of the girl taking the orders. He saw his Daddy trying to poke his head through the window and the girl giggling like a maniac. A few raindrops began to hit the windshield.

He wished it could always be like this. Him and his Daddy riding the roads on a rocket with wheels. Watching the rolling hills blur as they flew past. The smell of gasoline and burning rubber soaking into their clothes. Just him and his Daddy surfing the blacktop. No destination in mind, just enjoying the drive. But he knew that was a daydream. Things would never be that way and he was learning to accept that. The truth was his Daddy was always a better father in his daydreams than he was in real life. That didn't stop him from loving him so completely it felt as inherent as the color of his skin.

Screeching tires made him turn around. A white IROC-Z skidded into the parking lot and stopped just inches from the Duster's rear bumper. Bug saw three white men get out and start stalking toward his Daddy as he came over to the Duster carrying the shakes and the burgers. The men walked past the window and Bug caught a whiff of liquor. It was bitter and mean like the green rubbing alcohol his grandmother used on her knees. Bug sat straight up in the passenger seat as the men surrounded his father. The biggest man was wearing a light blue tank top that showed off his multiple tattoos. The blurry edges and the pale black-gone-green ink made the tats look like the scribblings of a child. A bright, wine-colored birthmark stood out against the pale skin on the man's neck. His black hair was slick backed and thinning.

"Ant," the man said.

Bug watched his Daddy give the man a once-over.

"Red," he said finally.

"Get in the car, Ant," Red said.

"What this about Red? Huh? We done. We quits," Anthony said. There was a tone to his Daddy's voice that disturbed Bug. He sounded like a different person. He spoke in a flat, robotic way that seemed in direct contrast to his usual jovialness.

"We ain't done, you motherfucker. We ain't done by a long shot. My brother got picked up Tuesday," Red said. He spoke with a restrained ferocity that was frightening. Bug thought he sounded like a rabid dog growling through a fence.

"And what that got to do with me? White went out and got a Corvette and dropping c-notes at Danny's Bar a week after we did what we did. Sheriff ain't gotta be Matlock to figure that out," Anthony said.

"You the only one that could put any of us at the scene. He called me last night saying the cops told him they got a witness that put him at the payroll robbery. Now I know it ain't me. And it ain't Blue. So, who the fuck you think that leaves? Now get in the goddamn car," Red said.

Bug saw him pull up his tank top. He caught a glimpse of a wooden handle. He had a gun. The man had a gun and was telling his Daddy to go with him.

"Red. We can talk about this but not now. Not in front my boy," Anthony said. Bug watched as his eyes narrowed to slits. He knew what that meant too. That was the same way his father had looked last night in the bar. A man had told his Daddy to stay away from the man's wife or he was gonna catch a bullet. His Daddy had finished his beer, then picked up the bar stool and beat the man half to death with it. They'd left Sharkey's shortly thereafter. His Daddy had made him promise not to tell his Mama they had been in a bar and Bug had agreed that was something his Mama definitely did not need to know.

Thunder boomed from the east. The rain began to fall faster.

"Why not? He need to see what happens to snitches. Now I ain't gonna say this again, Ant. Get in the goddamn car."

Bug was lifting his leg over the gearshift before he fully understood what he was doing.

"I'm not leaving my boy here, Red. You gonna shoot me in front all these people?" Anthony asked.

"Try me, Ant. My brother staring down twenty-five years. Just try me."

Bug slipped into the driver's seat.

"I ain't no fucking snitch, Red. You want me to go with you, okay. But you follow me and let me drop my boy off."

Bug gripped the 8-ball shifter.

"You must think I'm a fool. I ain't letting you get behind the wheel of no car. The last thing I ever see of you will be your fucking tail lights."

Bug eased the clutch in and slipped the Duster into first. The engine idled like a quiet man clearing his throat.

"Red. Please. Not here," Anthony said.

Bug stared at his father. His father caught his gaze and stared back. His nod was so subtle it had to be an unconscious gesture. Bug released the parking brake.

"Get your black ass in the car. I'm not telling you again. Last time, Ant," Red growled. His face was emblematic of his nickname. Anthony cut his eyes toward the Duster.

"Whatever you say, Red," Anthony said.

Bug took his left foot off the clutch and slammed his right against the gas pedal. The leather steering wheel cover was slathered in his sweat. He gripped it as the Duster leaped forward. Anthony threw the cardboard drink carrier into Red's face and jumped to the left. Smoke from the rear tires enveloped the Duster as the engine howled.

The space between the Duster and the three men who had confronted his father was less than twenty feet. The Duster went from

0 to 50 as it covered that distance. Bug could hear screams through the open windows. The screams sounded womanish, but they came from two of the three men in front of him.

The impact was horrific. The whole car shuddered when he plowed into them. One of the men was launched skyward. Red and the other one disappeared under the front bumper of the Duster. Bug kept the pedal to the floor and rolled over them. He heard their bodies bounce off the undercarriage. It reminded him of the time his mother hit a raccoon in her old LTD. A hollow knocking that traveled the length of the car. He passed by the order window doing 60. He saw that the young white girl's mouth was a huge O as he flew past her. He hit the clutch and the brake while twisting the steering wheel to the left. The Duster violently stalled and skidded to a stop.

Anthony got up off the concrete and ran over to the three bodies sprawled across the ground. They seemed to be bleeding from every orifice. Blue had tire tracks across his forearms and chest. His head was twisted at an odd angle in direct opposition to the position of his pelvis. Timmy Clovis had flown straight up in the air and landed directly on his head. A red and pink fibrous mass was leaking out the back of his skull. Beauregard realized that was his brain.

Red Navely groaned.

Anthony knelt beside him. Both his legs were bent backwards at the knee like a bird. Red's chest was crushed into a concave on the right side. Blood bubbled out of his ears and his mouth. A swath of skin had been sloughed off the side of his head, exposing an angry red wound. Every breath he took expelled more blood that then splashed across his chin. There were tire tracks across his thighs.

"I told you not in front of my boy," Anthony said. He placed his wide hand over Red's nose and mouth.

"Is . . . . is he okay?" a tiny voice squeaked. The girl from the register had come from behind the counter. Anthony bent over Red's body.

"Go call 911! Go!" he screamed without turning around. He

heard the girl's feet pounding against the pavement as she ran. Red tried to move his hand toward his gun, but it didn't seem to be working correctly. He trembled once, then twice, then was still. The life drained out of his eyes like a light bulb slowly going dim.

Beauregard squeezed the steering wheel so hard his forearms ached. He could see a willowy plume of white steam pouring from under the hood. The hood itself was dented in the middle. His chest felt like an elephant was standing on it.

"Get out the car, Bug. No need to give the cops a reason to pop a cap in you when they get here," Anthony said. He opened the door and helped Beauregard out of the car. Beauregard bent over and placed his hands on his knees. He waited for a stream of vomit that never came. Anthony rubbed his back with his huge soup bone of a hand.

"It's alright, Bug. You go on and be sick if you need to. You ain't meant for this life. That's a good thing," Anthony said.

"They were gonna kill you," Beauregard said between dry heaves.

"Yeah, I think they had that in mind, Bug. Don't you worry, I'm gonna tell the cops it was an accident. Everything gonna be alright."

Four weeks later, Bug was sentenced to five years in juvie for involuntary manslaughter.

By then his Daddy was long gone.

NINETEEN

"Wake up, Ronnie."

"Lemme alone, Reggie. My head aching like a gnome digging his way out with a spoon," Ronnie said. His mouth tasted like the bottom of an oil barrel. If his memory served him correctly, they had drunk three bottles of Jameson last night. He and Reggie had consumed most of it, but the two Mexican girls had their share too. What were their names again? Guadalupe and Esmerelda. That sounded right. Maybe.

"Ronnie, please wake up."

They'd picked them up at Laredo's Saloon in Richmond. Brought them back to Reggie's trailer for a night of debauchery so uninhibited it would have made Hugh Hefner blush. The last thing Ronnie remembered was one of the girls sucking his dick like she had been poisoned and the antidote was in his nuts.

"Ronnie, wake the fuck up!"

It had been two weeks since the job and he wasn't slowing up one iota. For all his talk about white sandy beaches and blue skies, he wasn't in such a hurry to leave Virginia anymore. Jenny had bailed on him but that wasn't such a bad thing. The same day she dipped, they found the dyke chick burnt crispier than grandma's fried chicken. The way the news was telling it, the cops figured she and Jenny had been in on the robbery. There was no mention of any of their possible accomplices. The heat wasn't off, but it was turned down from broil to simmer.

"You should listen to your brother."

Ronnie's eyes snapped open as he reached for his piece under his pillow. He had given Reggie the money to purchase it legally. A Beretta 9 mm.

"Ah, it ain't there, brother. You might want to sit up for this."

Ronnie turned over so slow he might as well have been demonstrating plate tectonics.

Two men were standing on either side of Reggie at the foot of his bed. One of them had a nasty scar on the side of his face. He wore a white dress shirt open at the collar with the tail untucked. The other man was as wide as a refrigerator. He wore a blue blazer over a black T-shirt. The T-shirt barely contained his belly. He was the one pressing the barrel of a .357 into Reggie's ribs.

"Morning, Sunshine," the man with the scar and the Colonel Sanders facial hair said.

"You from Chuly? Because I gave Skunk the money. I paid in full, with interest," Ronnie said. The man with the scar shivered and laughed.

"Nah, we ain't from Chuly. And we ain't nearly as bad as Skunk Mitchell. Not really," the man with the scar said.

Ronnie sat up and let the blanket fall and cover his waist. Reggie's eyes were as big as dinner plates. Ronnie wracked his brain. Was there someone he had pissed off in the last few weeks that would send some boys to rough him up? He drew a blank.

"Look, I don't know what this all about, so why don't you enlighten me a little bit, Hoss," Ronnie said. He spoke to the man with the scar. He seemed to be the brains of the operation. The man with the scar smiled.

"Well, let me see how I can put this. You done fucked up, Ronnie. You done fucked up so bad you might wanna find your mama and crawl back in her snatch and try again. But since that ain't gonna happen, you need to get up, put your clothes on, and come with us. Be quick now. I'm trying to catch breakfast. You boys ain't got nothing in the cabinet but a cereal box full of money. Can't eat that, now can I?" the man with the scar said.

Ronnie had heard the phrase "His blood ran cold" before, but it had never carried much weight with him. He always thought it sounded like something some Hollywood scriptwriter had convinced himself was cool. Now as a chill settled in his veins, he understood the time-tested phrase. They knew about the money. That could mean one of two things. A: This was just some random home invasion that got lucky. That didn't seem likely. A rust-covered single-wide trailer was not usually the target of a crew of home invaders. These boys didn't look like hopped-up meth heads looking for an easy score. So that led to Option B. They were pros who had come specifically looking for him and the money. That was the option that chilled him to his bones. That option led to all kinds of bad conclusions. He decided to play dumb and see if these boys would let him in on what kind of game they were playing.

"Hold on now, I mean, what's going on, man? I don't get what's happening. You gotta give me something. Y'all rolling up in here like Wyatt Earp and shit," Ronnie said. He spoke in low soft tones and let honey drip over his words.

The man with the scar frowned.

"You just ain't listening." He pulled out a gun of his own and shot Reggie in the right foot. The tiny bedroom was filled with the ear-splitting cacophony of the gunshot. Ronnie jumped back and covered his ears. Reggie fell to the floor clutching at his right leg. The light breaking through the window highlighted his pale sweaty face.

"Shit, man!" Ronnie squealed. Reggie had fallen over and was lying in the fetal position. His moans were wet and reedy. The man with the scar pointed his gun at Ronnie. It was a .38 with a wood grip. It looked like a toy in his wide hand.

"You wanna get your clothes on? I was serious about that breakfast."

TWENTY

Beauregard hadn't been dancing in years. Not because he didn't enjoy it, but there never seemed to be enough time. Between dealing with the garage and the boys and Ariel and his Mama, spare time was scarcer than hen's teeth. When he had been double-deep in the Life, he and Kia would drive up to Richmond at the drop of a hat. They'd get dressed up, hit the clubs, and dance until the ugly lights came on. They would leave having spent more on spilled liquor than most people made in a week.

It had been so long Beauregard worried he wouldn't be able to find the beat. Yet here he was in the middle of Danny's, dipping and gyrating in rhythm with Kia. One arm around her waist, the other on her firm hip. The music thumping from wall-mounted speakers filled the bar with a tribalistic carnality. Beauregard felt it working its way through his body as Kia pressed herself against his crotch. Even after all these years, she still captivated the savage that lived between his legs. She was a caramel-dipped Aphrodite to his chocolate-covered Pan.

The song ended but the spell remained unbroken. He pulled her close and nuzzled her neck. The scent of her skin beneath her perfume was more intoxicating than the $500 fragrance she had bought that morning. She had also purchased a new outfit and gotten her hair done.

"Now, Mr. Montage, you gonna take me out and we are gonna dance and drink, and if you're lucky, you gonna get some A1 pussy tonight," she had said after her shopping spree. He hadn't needed much convincing. The money from the jewelry store job had given them some breathing room. Might as well enjoy it. Ronnie was a weasel, but he had been right about that.

Eric, Caitlin and little Anthony aren't enjoying much these days though, are they? Beauregard thought.

He'd given serious consideration to sending Caitlin some money. Not a lot but enough to help with the bills or buy a toy for the baby. He'd ruminated on it long and hard before finally pushing the idea away. Things were still too hot right now. No way he could go anywhere near Caitlin and Anthony. That didn't stop him from thinking about them though. Especially that baby boy. He'd grow up belonging to the same fraternity as Beauregard. The brotherhood of fatherless sons.

But he wouldn't be a member if you hadn't done your part to induct him, now, would he, he thought.

Kia rubbed his thigh.

"The way you was dancing up on me I think you want this," Kia whispered in his ear. Beauregard forced a smile.

"All the time and twice on Sunday," Beauregard whispered back. She giggled and kissed him. The taste of whiskey and bubble gum–flavored lip gloss filled his mouth.

"Yo, let's get some shots!" Kelvin said. He had his arm around the waist of a woman Beauregard had never seen before and didn't expect to see again. Kelvin had some disposable income as well. The garage was busy as a one-legged man in an ass-kicking contest. Beauregard would never admit it, but Javon had been right. Burning down Precision had helped. That saddened him something fierce.

"Okay, what y'all want?" he asked.

"Nothing too strong. I'm feeling those Blue Motorcycles," Kelvin's friend said. She was a tall drink of water with long brown hair highlighted with blond and a hard-earned natural tan. A few of the regulars glanced at them when they came in but not with any serious intent. They just regarded her as another white woman lost to the other side.

"How about Red Headed Sluts?" Kia offered.

"I know a few of those," Kelvin said. His friend jabbed him with her elbow.

"I'll get some Royal Flushes," Beauregard said. He headed for the bar while everyone else went back to the table. Beauregard leaned against the scarred railing that surrounded the top of the bar and raised his hand.

"What can I get you?" the bartender asked.

"Four Royal Flushes."

"Coming right up."

"A Royal Flush is the hardest hand to get in poker. Almost never happens," a man sitting to Beauregard's right said. Beauregard turned and gave him a nod.

"Yeah, that's what they say," he remarked. He wasn't sure that was what they said or not, he was just making conversation.

"Yeah, the Dead Man's Hand is more common," the man said. He moved his hair out of his face. Beauregard saw he was scarred worse than the bar top.

"What?"

The man smiled at Beauregard.

"Aces and eights. The Dead Man's Hand. Wild Bill Hickok was holding that when somebody snuck up behind him and blew his head off," the man said.

"Oh yeah, that's right," Beauregard said. The bartender returned with the shots. He placed them in front of Beauregard and slipped away. Beauregard gathered up the four shot glasses and started to leave.

"Personally, I wouldn't never sneak up behind a fella. If I was going to kill you, I'd just pull up and put two in your face. That's how they taught us in Iraq. Double tap," the man said.

Beauregard stopped and studied the man's ruined face. The man was still smiling. "Uh huh. Well, you have a nice night," Beauregard said. He gathered the shots and returned to the table. A new song came on the jukebox and some couples made their way back to the dance floor. Beauregard handed everyone their shots.

"Woohoo. I felt that in my toes," Kelvin said. His friend laughed and leaned into him.

"Damn, you trying to get me drunk and take advantage of me, Bug?" Kia asked. Her skin shimmered under a patina of sweat and glitter makeup. Beauregard tickled her chin.

"It ain't taking advantage, if you want it," he said. Kelvin burst out in high peals of laughter.

"Smart-ass," Kia said but then she leaned in and kissed him again. Beauregard kissed her back, then surreptitiously peered over her shoulder. The man with the scarred face was staring at him.

Beauregard dropped his eyes. He hugged his wife, then gave the bar a quick once-over. He recognized most of the patrons or had an idea who they were save for the man at the bar and two men sitting at a table near the far-right wall. They were both Beauregard's height but considerably wider. They were wearing blue blazers and black T-shirts. They both had a mug of beer in front of them, but they had barely touched them.

Beauregard studied their faces. They were exceptionally unre-markable. Flat doughy visages with a narrow slash for a mouth. The only thing that stood out about them were their eyes. Dead brown eyes like pennies that had been buried in the dirt.

Red Hill County was not a place that strangers visited often. It wasn't at the crossroads of any major highways. The interstate on-ramp was mainly an escape route for the locals. Unfamiliar faces were a rarity. Beauregard watched the two men at the table. They stared straight ahead or occasionally up at the ceiling. They never once turned their heads toward the bar. They never looked in the direction of the scarred man.

"Listen to your gut. The day you don't, it's going to be a shitty situation."

He'd overheard his father say that dozens of times. A crude saying but also an accurate one. His gut was talking to him now. Whispering to him that there was something up with the three unfamiliar faces.

Beauregard pulled out his phone and sent Kelvin a text.

Take the girls outside.

Kelvin picked up his phone. He read the message and typed a response.

What's up?

Beauregard's fingers flew over the screen.

Guys at the table and the bar. I need to check them out.

Kelvin sent back a long response.

You want me to send them home?

Not going to leave you.

3 on 2 is better than 3 on 1.

"Who you texting?" Kia asked. She reached for his phone. Beauregard grabbed her wrist and pulled her hand to his mouth and kissed it. She rolled her eyes and pulled her hand away. "Everybody you know is here," she said. She was grinning like a mad clown.

"Jamal bringing a car to the shop. I gotta go down there and open up."

Kia slipped out of her chair and into Beauregard's lap. She threw her arms around his neck.

"Noooo, you can't leave. We just getting started." She kissed Beauregard on the neck, but he thought she was aiming for his cheek.

"You drunk, boo. I'm gonna get Kelvin to take y'all home. It's midnight and we gotta get the boys. K, you mind taking them home and picking up Darren and Javon?" Beauregard asked.

"You sure?" Kelvin asked. The jocularity that had been in his voice earlier had evaporated.

"Yeah, I'm sure. I'll call you tomorrow."

"Bug, I'll ride with you," Kia said.

"Baby, you need to go home. You gotta work tomorrow. Go with Kelvin and them. I'll be home after a while," he said.

"What's wrong?" Kia asked.

"Nothing. Just gotta go open up for Jamal. One day I'm gonna get my own wrecker truck and we won't have this problem," he said. He tickled her chin again, but her face was slack.

"NO, something's wrong." she slurred. The last shot was hitting her. It had also apparently improved her lie-detecting skills.

"Nah, baby, it's okay. I'll be home soon," Beauregard said. He slipped her off his lap and stood. Kia rose and wobbled but Beauregard gripped her left elbow and steadied her. Kelvin and his friend rose as well. Beauregard kissed Kia on her cheek.

"See you in a few, boo," he whispered.

"You sure?" Kelvin asked.

"I'm sure. I'll see you at the shop tomorrow," Beauregard said.

"Bring me a doughnut when you come home," Kia said.

"Alright, baby. I love ya."

"You better," she said. She headed for the door with Kelvin and his friend in tow. Kelvin looked back over his shoulder. Beauregard didn't say anything. Kelvin followed the ladies out the door.

Beauregard turned around and went back toward the bar. As he passed the table with the two hillbilly hoodlums, he gave them a closer look. The one on the left had a bulge in his waistband on the right side. Beauregard wasn't shocked they were able to get a gun into Danny's. The bar didn't have a bouncer. The sign on the door prohibiting weapons was taken as a suggestion by most of the patrons. Beauregard walked past the scarred man sitting at the bar. He had a bulge in the small of his back under his white shirt.

Beauregard went to the bathroom in the rear of the building. He ran some water in the sink and rinsed his face. Three armed men he had never seen before were in a bar in his hometown. Had the Thompsons hired some out-of-town hitters? That didn't seem likely. Patrick and his dad were hands-on type of boys. If there was going to be any blowback, they would do it themselves. Beauregard dried his face with a paper towel.

He'd been watching the news off and on since he'd seen the report about Eric. The jewelry store manager had been found burned to a crisp in her apartment. Ronnie's girl had skipped town but she'd left a dead body behind. The police said that arrests in the robbery were imminent but Beauregard thought that was some high-grade horseshit.

"Someone's tying up loose ends," he said to his reflection.

That was the risk you took being in the Life. No matter how smart you were or how well you planned there was always the possibility that some shitkicker would show up at your favorite bar looking to double tap your ass. It was the Sword of Damocles you willingly placed above your head every time you pulled a job.

He took a deep breath and exited the bathroom. He grabbed an empty chair from one of the tables in the bar and pulled it up to the table of the two gunmen in cheap blazers. He sat down next to the one on the left.

"Can I help you?" Lefty said.

"That depends," Beauregard said. Quick as a cat he grabbed Lefty's gun with his left hand while grabbing Lefty's left wrist with his right. Boonie always said he had his father's hands. He pressed the barrel of the gun into the hard slab of Lefty's belly.

"Maybe you can tell me why you and your buddy at the bar been eyeballing me all night." Righty reached under the table, but Beauregard shook his head. "No. Put your hands back on the table, palms down. Do it now or I'm gonna start pulling the trigger and I ain't gonna stop until it goes click."

Righty's face bloomed as red as a circus balloon, but he did as he was told.

Beauregard's neck tingled. Someone was coming up behind him. He didn't take his eyes off the two gunmen. The scarred man pulled up a chair and sat down. He had a glass filled with some dark liquid.

"You a slick one, ain't ya? Although to be honest, a one-armed monkey could get the drop on Carl here. No offense, Carl," the scarred man said. Carl didn't seem like he took too much offense to anything. Even a gun in his stomach.

"Who sent y'all?" Beauregard asked. He didn't turn and face the scarred man. He kept the gun pressed against Carl's belly. Someone had played a bluesy love song on the jukebox. Couples were slow dancing on the old parquet floor. Bodies gently twirling in small elliptical orbits in time with the mournful notes coming from the speakers.

"Right to the point. But this ain't the part where you ask questions. This the part where you use your eyes and your ears," the scarred man said. He reached into his pocket. Beauregard pressed the gun deeper into Carl's flesh.

"Burning Man . . . ," Carl said in a low rumble of a voice.

"Don't worry, Carl, Beauregard here is a smart boy. He ain't gonna ruin your guts here for no good reason. I just got something on my phone he needs to see," Billy said. He placed his phone on the table and touched the screen. Beauregard cut his eyes downward.

There was a cell phone on the table. A short video was playing. The video showed the tail lights of a car leaving Danny's parking lot. Beauregard narrowed his eyes. The tail lights belonged to a Nova. Kelvin's Nova.

"We was gonna pinch you when you left, but you made us. We had five guys. The three of us in one car and two more boys in another. Word has it you a real wild boy with a mean streak. But when you made Carl here, I says to myself, well, now we gonna dance. So, I told my boys in the other car to follow your little friends there. Now I seen how fast you is. And goddamn if you ain't as fast as a knife fight in a phone booth. So you probably thinking you might be able to shoot me, Carl and Jim Bob," Billy said.

Carl winced.

"But," he continued, "if my boys don't hear from me in say, oh I don't know, five minutes, they gonna light up that car like the goddamn White House Christmas tree."

Beauregard pulled back the hammer on Carl's gun.

"What if I don't believe you? What if I just shoot the three of you and call my friend and tell him to punch it? That Nova has some get-up-and-go."

Billy smiled.

"I bet it does. But that's an awful lot of what ifs, ain't it, Beauregard? Come on now, like I said, you a smart boy. Give Carl back his gun and let's go on up the road. Got somebody that needs to talk to you, and he ain't the type that likes to be kept waiting."

Beauregard leaned into the gun and it dug deeper into Carl's flesh. He could shoot Carl, that much was a given. Could he get the one on the right and the one Carl called Burning Man too? Even if he got all of them, could Kelvin outrun the car tailing him? Like Burning Man said, that was an awful lot of what ifs.

"Tick tock tick tock," Billy said.

Beauregard thought about what Boonie had said. About the way men like him died. He didn't want to take Kia with him. That honor was reserved for men like the three seated at the table with him. Along with whoever was their boss. Beauregard shoved the gun back in Carl's waistband.

"Let's go," he said.

Billy tossed back his drink. He grimaced, then put his glass on the table. He picked up his phone and let his fingers slide across the screen. He put the phone back in his pocket.

"See, now Christmas don't have to come early."

TWENTY-ONE

They didn't blindfold him. That was a bad sign. It meant they didn't care if he saw where they were going. Which most likely meant he wasn't ever leaving once they got to where they were going. They didn't tie his hands up either. No need really. They had their insurance policy, after all.

Beauregard sat between Jim Bob and Burning Man. They were riding in a 2010 Cadillac CTS. A nice midsized sedan with a powerful 3-liter engine. The interior of the car was bathed in a ghostly pale light. LED lighting ran along the inside of the doors and along the floor. Just a subtle accent lighting, nothing too overbearing. Beauregard noticed the child locks were engaged. He had thought about hitting Jim Bob with an elbow, opening the door and pushing him out after he had relieved him of his gun. Shove the barrel into Burning Man's eye and suggest he contact his boys and call them off completely. He could see that plan was going to be foiled by well-meaning consumer advocates.

They jumped on the interstate and headed west. The Caddy sliced through the night. Beauregard felt his ears pop as they began to climb into the Blue Ridge Mountains that bisected Virginia at odd intervals.

Finally, they took an exit near Lynchburg. The off-ramp deposited them onto the oak tree–lined main street of some quaint hamlet tucked away near Peaks of Otter mountain. Dark green streetlamps played peekaboo with the wisteria trees up and down the street. A banner stretched across the front of an imposing granite building lined with columns proclaimed that the Kimball Town Fair was one week away. The car turned off Main Street and down an equally well-lit side street. The car stopped in front of a tobacco shop at the end of the sidewalk. It was the last shop in a short row of stores. A brick facade was interrupted by a huge picture window. A glowing sign above the front door said it was THE HOT SHOP. The neon sign in the window of the shop said it was closed. Jim Bob pushed the barrel of his gun into Beauregard's ribs.

"Try something. I want you to. Then I can pull the trigger until the gun goes click," Jim Bob said. He leered at Beauregard, showing his crooked teeth.

"Alright now, Jim Bob, you know Lazy wants to talk to this boy," Billy said as he opened his door. Jim Bob pushed Beauregard toward the same door. They all exited the car on the same side. Carl got out and before Beauregard could react, he punched him in the right kidney. Beauregard stumbled and fell against the car. He took a deep breath, coughed, and then stood up straight.

"Goddamn, you boys got two-inch peckers or something? Stop that shit. Lazy wants to talk with him. He can't talk if he throwing up and pissing blood," Billy said. Beauregard didn't detect any real concern for his well-being. Burning Man's only concern seemed to be not disappointing Lazy. Whoever that was.

"Sorry, Billy," Carl mumbled. Beauregard figured Burning Man must be this Billy's nickname. That struck him as oddly cruel, but then again you didn't get to choose your nickname. If you did, no one would refer to him as Bug.

Billy aka Burning Man knocked on the door of the smoke shop. A thin white boy with lank blond hair and a sleepy face opened the door.

"Y'all came back quick," the boy said.

"He didn't put up much of a fight. He here?" Billy asked.

The boy shook his head. "Not yet."

"Okay," Billy said. He gestured toward the interior of the store. "After you," he said to Beauregard.

Beauregard entered the store. The overhead lights were off but there were enough novelty neon signs and clocks on the walls to light his way. The signs and clocks all depicted scenes from old movies. Some Beauregard recognized, some he didn't. There was Rick and Sam at a piano from *Casablanca* against a red backdrop. A clock on the far wall above a shelf full of cigars was adorned with the maniacal grinning face of Richard Widmark as Tommy Udo from the original *Kiss of Death*, outlined with a cool blue chemical fire.

The kid who opened the door sprinted past Beauregard and knocked on a door behind the counter. A huge beast of a man opened that door. Jim Bob pushed Beauregard on through. The room was sparsely decorated. There was a cheap oak desk with a rotary phone sitting anachronistically near the edge. The walls were blank slabs of gray concrete. There was a wooden chair behind the desk. Three metal chairs sat in front of the desk. The spartan confines of the room stood in stark contrast to the garishness of the rest of the shop.

"Have a seat," Billy said. There was only one empty seat among the three chairs. Ronnie was sitting in the first chair and Quan was sitting in the second. Beauregard sat next to Quan.

"Bug, I'm—" Ronnie started to say but Beauregard cut him off.

"Shut your mouth," he said. Ronnie dropped his head. Beauregard crossed his arms. Quan had his head in his hands. His breathing was hard and labored. He was tapping his right foot like he was keeping time with the world's fastest rhythm section. A box fan sat in the corner moving the stifling air around. A single light bulb encased by a wire mesh cage shone down from the ceiling. A few empty plastic milk crates were stacked in the far-left corner of the room. Beauregard figured it had been a storeroom at one time. Now it was a shabby torture chamber masquerading as an office.

Both Quan and Ronnie had been smacked around. Quan's mouth was bleeding profusely. His white basketball jersey was covered with red splotches. Ronnie had a mouse under his left eye. His nose was swollen and crooked. Neither of them had been restrained either. There was obviously no need. There was no fight in them. Beauregard could see that as soon as he entered the room. Their stooped shoulders and downcast eyes told the story of their submission. If it came down to it, they wouldn't be any help.

Beauregard heard the hinges on the door creak.

"Well now, the gang's all here," a high, tremulous voice said. Beauregard felt Quan flinch.

A tall, thin man entered the room. He wore a neatly pressed pair of khakis and a black button-down shirt under a black corduroy vest. He was narrow in the hips with jagged angles for arms. His ruddy face was narrow and ended in a wickedly sharp chin. A dark pile of brown hair tinged with gray stood up on his head like he had stuck his finger in a light socket while wearing a bad toupee. He stood in the center of the room directly under the lone light. He grinned at them. A rakish smile that spread across his face like spilled milk. Huge teeth too white to be real filled his mouth.

"This here the Apple Dumpling Gang, huh?" the man said. He laughed at his own joke. After a half a beat, all of his men laughed as well. He motioned toward the chair behind the desk. Carl grabbed it and the man parked himself in front of Quan. He crossed his legs. A smirk had replaced his grin.

"I love movies. Don't matter what kind. Horror movies, crime movies, old movies, new movies. Hell, I even like romantic comedies. Love me some John Hughes. And Molly Ringwald? Whew whee," the man said.

"We so sorry—" Ronnie tried to say but the walking wall who had opened the office door smacked him in the back of the head. Ronnie pitched forward and landed on the floor in a heap. Jim Bob and Carl grabbed him by his arms and sat him back in his chair.

"But some of my favorite movies are heist movies. I love that shit, man. Something about a heist that goes down smoother than a twenty-dollar hooker gets me every time," the man said. He stood and turned his chair around. He sat back down and rested his arms on the backrest before laying his chin on his hands.

"You gotta tell me. How'd y'all do it? Did y'all sew stop watches in your gloves? What kind of engine was in that car? Who came up with driving off the damn overpass? That was some brass balls shit there, I tell ya," the man said.

No one spoke.

"Come on now, it's alright. Y'all can talk now," the man said.

Still no one spoke.

"It was a modified V8 with a nitro kit," Beauregard said finally.

The man winked at him. "Nice, nice. See, that's what I'm talking about. Heist movie shit," he said.

"Are you Lazy?" Beauregard asked. He heard footsteps behind him. He braced himself for the blow but the man in front of him held up his hand.

"Hold on, Wilbert. This fella here just reminded me I forgot my manners. My mama named me Lazarus Mothersbaugh on account of how I died during delivery and then came back to life once they got the cord from round my neck. But everyone else round here calls me Lazy. I think cuz they was too lazy to say my whole name," Lazy said. All his men tittered except for Billy. He was staring off into space.

"Now back to the matter at hand. If you boys had robbed any other jewelry store anywhere else, you would be sitting pretty as you please. But you robbed one that belonged to me. So that means you in some deep doo-doo," Lazy said.

He smiled but this time it seemed forced. Beauregard thought it was an actor's smile. Just another part of a performance.

"Any of you ever heard of me?" Lazy asked. Quan raised his hand. "Goddamn, boy, you ain't in English class," Lazy said. Carl laughed.

"You boys really screwed me over at that store. I was using it as a pay window of sorts. I got hold of some diamonds in a deal that we don't have to go into right now. Let's just say I'm a silent partner in some very interesting developments. But son, them diamonds better than cash. Easier to carry and impossible to trace. That comes in handy when you paying for two or three of them Mexican fillies from out West. Yessir, I had a nice lil setup out there. And you boys fucked it up good. Now the cops snooping around. And some of my transactions have gone south," Lazy said. He sucked his teeth and nodded his head. "But goddamn, the way you pulled it off, well I just gotta tip my hat to you. Now that girl, what's her name, Burning Man?"

"Jenny."

"Yeah, Jenny. She said you was the brains, Ronnie. You the one that put it all together," Lazy said. He pointed one long narrow finger at Ronnie. Ronnie's face was ashen. "But Beauregard, you was the one behind the wheel. Goddamn, that was some high-test driving there, boy." Lazy kept pointing at Ronnie, but he turned his head to look at Beauregard. "That wasn't your first time at the rodeo, was it?" he asked.

Beauregard didn't say a word.

"Answer him," Burning Man said.

"No," he said.

Lazy got up and walked around behind Beauregard. He bent down and put his mouth near his ear.

"I asked around about you, boy. They say you could outrun the devil on the highway to Hell," Lazy said. He straightened up. "But no matter how much I like your style, boys, and God knows y'all get points for style, I can't let something like that slide. I mean, you stole from me and now I must be compensated," Lazy said in a sing-song cadence. He sounded like a Baptist preacher during a tent revival.

He pointed at Wilbert. The big man left the room. He returned a few minutes later with five cereal boxes. He dumped the contents of the boxes onto the desk. Bundles of cash spilled across the desk like the bounty from a fall harvest.

"You boys must have had a good fence. Take your cuts and add them to what ol' Ronnie had left, you must've gotten something like $700,000 on three million. That's a good return," Lazy said.

Beauregard and Quan glared at Ronnie. Lazy burst out laughing.

"Lawd, he shorted y'all? That's a damn shame," he said. He walked around to face them. "Now we got Ronnie and Jenny's cut. Quan didn't have enough to really bother with, but we took it anyway. Beauregard, you lucked out. I ain't gonna have my boys roust your house looking for your slice. I suspect you ain't dumb enough to keep it on you. And at this point it don't really matter. Even if we had it all, y'all still be behind. Now if this was any day, y'all asses would be dead as the bacon I had for breakfast," Lazy said.

He sat back down in his chair. Beauregard felt this was all building to a "but." If he was gonna kill them, he wouldn't have gathered them all together for a staff meeting. Lazy wanted something. He wanted it bad.

"However, God has smiled on you today. Yessir, you fellas done crossed my path at a time I have need of some boys with a special set of skills," Lazy said. Beauregard recognized the line from some stupid action movie a few years back. "I know it seems impossible cuz I'm such a charming fella, but I'm having some problems with a boy from North Carolina. We having a disagreement about who runs what round these parts. And I got to give it to him, that boy been giving me all I can handle down there. But I'm gonna win. Cuz all he got is soldiers. I got family," Lazy said. He nodded to his men. They nodded back.

"One of his soldiers got himself a nasty meth habit. Now as fate would have it, the boy he owes is one of mine. In exchange for his debt, the soldier told me a lil secret. His boss got a shipment coming through the Carolinas. A truckload of platinum that ain't even supposed to be on this side of the country," Lazy said. He held his hands out in supplication.

"This where you fellas come in. You gonna get that shipment for me. Now it ain't gonna be easy. This ol' boy got lots of firepower and he don't give two tight fucks about showing it off. And if that soldier is right, this here shipment is a big deal for him. Losing it would hurt him something fierce. So, you know he gonna fight for it like a dog on a bone. But if you get it, well then, I'll call us even," Lazy said.

That's a lie, Beauregard thought.

"How's that sound, fellas? I guess y'all a part of the family now," Lazy said.

"You got the route and the time? Do you know how many cars he got riding with the truck? You say he got firepower, so I'm gonna assume he got cars riding shotgun," Beauregard said. He braced for the blow and this time it did come. A short rabbit punch right between his shoulder blades. He gripped the sides of the chair. A bolt of lightning ran down his back to his left thigh, but he didn't fall.

"Honestly, that's a good question, Beauregard. Really it is. But our family works like a real family. I'm your Daddy now. And you don't speak unless I tell you to," Lazy said.

He pulled on the backrest of the chair and leaned back until two of the legs came off the floor. He balanced there for a second before putting all four legs back on the ground.

"The other thing we don't do in this family is run our mouths. We ride together, and we die together. And we never ever snitch on members of the family. Ever," Lazy said. He ran a hand through his wild rat's nest.

"Beauregard, you wanna guess which one of your partners gave you up? Jenny told us all about Ronnie and Quan, but she didn't know shit about you. We wouldn't have never found you if one of them hadn't ran they mouth. I'll give you a hint. It's the same boy who been running his mouth at the strip club about how he had to drop some fool during a robbery," Lazy said.

Beauregard didn't respond. He didn't need the hint. Ronnie might have been a cheat, but he wasn't a snitch.

"Oh Jesus," Quan moaned.

"I doubt you gonna see him," Lazy said.

Billy pulled out his gun. A small black .38. He shot Quan in the face three times. Each report sounded like a cannon inside the small room. Beauregard felt warm droplets rain against the right side of his face. Quan slid out of the chair and collapsed onto his side. His head landed at Beauregard's feet. Quan's whole body shuddered. He let out one wet gasp, then was still.

"Goddamn, man!" Ronnie screamed. A ham-sized fist slammed into the side of his head. He went flying and landed against the desk. No one moved to pick him up this time.

"That boy was like a broke icebox. Couldn't keep shit. Fellas like that ain't good for nothing except target practice," Lazy said.

Beauregard didn't look down at Quan's body or at Ronnie's prone form on the floor. He stared at a spot on the wall behind the desk.

"Pick him up, will you?" Lazy said. Carl grabbed Ronnie and sat him in the chair again. Lazy scooted his chair forward until the legs were pressed against Quan's thighs.

"Here's the thing, boys. You owe me. So, you gonna get this done. Cuz if you don't, I'll kill everyone you love. I'll do it front of you and I'll do it slow. Maybe I'll have Burning Man light 'em up. Maybe I'll have the boys beat 'em to death with hammers. It don't really matter how, just know they gonna end up dead. And you'll join them. I promise you that. My word is my bond," Lazy said. He got up and put his hands on his knees. He locked eyes with Bug then turned his attention to Ronnie then back to Bug.

"I can see the hate in your eyes, boys. That's fine. Hate me all you want. If you wracking your brains for a way to get at me, let that shit go. If God couldn't kill me when I was born, you two ain't gonna do it now. You try anything funny and I'll make you choose which one of your loved ones get they throat cut first," he whispered. He stepped back and clapped Billy on the shoulder.

"Burning Man here is gonna give you the info on the route and the day and time. You gonna get a throwaway phone with one number on it. When it's done, and I mean as soon as it's done, you call that number. Other than that, I think we finished here," Lazy said.

"Get up," Billy said. Beauregard and Ronnie rose. Jim Bob pushed them toward the door.

"Get to walking, Rock and Roll," Billy said.

Ronnie blinked. His eyes began to water but at last he began to walk. Beauregard looked over his shoulder at Lazy then followed Ronnie out the door.

When they were gone, Wilbert and the kid got a tarp from behind the crates and wrapped up Quan's body. Carl helped them. After they had the body wrapped up, Wilbert turned to the kid. "Go get the van."

The kid jogged out the front door. Wilbert started gathering the rolls of cash. Carl moved the three chairs back to the corner near the crates.

"We could take that truck," Carl said.

"Yeah, we could, but then Shade would know we got a man on the inside. Let them boys try and get it. He sees a mixed-race crew he won't put it on us. He thinks all we are is a bunch of backwoods racist rednecks," Lazy said.

"Ain't we?" Carl said.

Lazy smiled. "That's beside the point."

The kid came back into the store. He and Wilbert carried Quan's body out to the van. Lazy crossed his legs. Carl leaned against the wall. He knew Lazy was about to pontificate.

"That truck gonna have more than a thousand pounds of platinum coils on it. We killing a bunch of birds with one stone. We keep our man on the inside. We put a dent in Shade's pocket. We gonna get back triple what them boys pinched. And when they bring us the truck, I'm gonna let Burning Man turn them into fucking candles," Lazy said.

"You always got a plan, don't you," Carl said.

Lazy smoothed his vest with his wide hands. "It's like my Daddy used to say. While they picking apples, I'm planting seeds."

TWENTY-TWO

The car dropped them off just off the exit.

"Here's the phone and the time and the route. You got a week," Billy said. He handed Ronnie a flip phone and a scrap of paper through the window. Jim Bob spun his tires as he pulled away. Gravel flew up and nearly hit them. It was late. Beauregard checked his watch. Nearly five in the morning. The sky was still dark, but sunrise was just around the corner.

"Bug, I didn't know," Ronnie said. Beauregard started walking. Ronnie trotted behind him. "I swear I didn't fucking know. How could I? Bug, what are we gonna do?"

He caught up with Beauregard and put his hand on his shoulder. Beauregard spun around and clamped both hands on Ronnie's throat. He dragged him off the shoulder of the road and down into a ditch bed. Ronnie grabbed at Beauregard's arms. He might as well have been trying to bend steel with his bare hands. Beauregard's biceps stood out in sharp relief under the sleeves of his shirt. He put his full weight on top of Ronnie as he squeezed the life out of him. Ronnie tried to scratch at his eyes, but Beauregard's arms were too long.

"You ... need ... me ... ," Ronnie squealed. It came out in a garbled mishmash, but Beauregard caught it. Ronnie's eyes began to flutter in their sockets. Beauregard let him go and fell back against the ditch bank. Ronnie propped himself up on his left elbow. Rubbing his throat with his right hand, he coughed up a wad of phlegm and spit it on the ground. "It's just you and me, Bug. We need each other if we gonna get out of this."

"Shut up. Just shut your mouth and listen for a minute. You know he ain't gonna let us go, right? Even if we pull it off, he's gonna kill us anyway. Just like he killed Quan. Just like he killed Jenny. Just like he killed that lady that was the manager. You heard what he said about the cops. He cleaning this shit up. The only reason we still alive now is because he wants that truck. And he's scared of that guy he was talking about. That's our ace in the hole. The truck and his fear," Beauregard said.

"You got a plan already?" Ronnie asked.

"I been making a plan since he shot Quan," Beauregard said.

He climbed up the ditch bank and resumed walking down the road. Ronnie waited a few minutes before he fell in behind him. A tractor trailer passed them heading out of town at the same time Ronnie tried to ask Beauregard a question.

"What?" Beauregard asked.

"I said do you really think Jenny is dead?" Ronnie said.

Beauregard kept walking. "Yeah," he said.

"I was supposed to go to the prom with her when we was in school. I got expelled the week before the dance. I waited for her out in the parking lot after it was over. When she came out of the school, the light from the hallway lit her up from behind. She looked like a redheaded angel. I guess she a real angel now," Ronnie said.

Beauregard didn't respond. The sound of their footsteps on the gravel that lined the shoulder filled the space between them.

"This plan you got, do it include killing these motherfuckers?" Ronnie asked.

Beauregard put his hands in his pockets. "Yeah."

"They bad, ain't they, Bug? They some bad motherfuckers, ain't they?" Ronnie asked.

"They think they are. But they bleed like everybody else."

They got back to Danny's by eight. Beauregard gave Ronnie a ride back to his trailer.

"Give me the route information," Beauregard said.

He had parked his truck behind Reggie's car. Ronnie rooted around in his pocket and pulled out the scrap of paper.

"I'm going to call you tomorrow. We gonna need at least two other people. Can Reggie roll with us?" Beauregard asked. Ronnie shrugged, then slid his fingers through his hair.

"I dunno. He can drive. He ain't no good with a gun, though. And he wouldn't bust a grape in a food fight," he said.

"If it goes the way I figure, all he gonna have to do is drive. I'll call you tomorrow," Beauregard said.

Ronnie got out of the truck. He leaned on the car door. The passenger's window had been lowered all the way. "Bug, I swear if I had known that store belonged to somebody like this I would have never got y'all involved," he said.

The look Beauregard gave him made Ronnie shut his mouth with an audible plop. He stood up straight and backed away from the truck. He watched as Beauregard backed out of the driveway doing 35. When he hit the road, he whipped the truck around. He spun his tires as he drove off toward the horizon.

Ronnie went into the trailer. Reggie was lying on the couch with his foot on the armrest. It was wrapped in duct tape and what appeared to be an old T-shirt. Ronnie slammed the door. Reggie sat up straight. He was holding Ronnie's gun in his right hand. He swung the barrel around and aimed at the door.

"Jesus H. Christ, butt munch, put the gun down," Ronnie wailed.

Reggie blinked his eyes a few times. "Ronnie! Holy shit, I'm sorry. I thought it was those guys coming back," he said.

Ronnie held out his hand to Reggie. Reggie didn't move for a few seconds.

"Oh yeah. Here, I don't even know what to do with this thing," he said as he gave Ronnie the gun.

"Pull the trigger, dingbat," Ronnie said.

Reggie swung around and struggled to his feet. He hobbled over to his brother with unsteady steps. He threw his arms around him and squeezed him with unexpected strength.

"I thought you won't never coming back," he whimpered in his ear.

"What, and leave all this?" Ronnie said.

Reggie released him, and Ronnie helped him back to the couch. Reggie plopped down, and Ronnie plopped right next to him. They both leaned their heads back against the backrest in eerily similar motions.

"Ronnie, who were those guys?" Reggie said.

"Trouble with a capital T," Ronnie said. He closed his eyes tight. Sleep was creeping up on him like an assassin.

"How's your foot?" Ronnie asked.

"The bullet went straight through. It must have missed the nerves and stuff because I can still wiggle my toes. I cleaned it out with some peroxide and tied it up with the tape."

"I know it hurt like a son of a bitch," Ronnie said.

"I had some Oxy left. So, ya know. It's okay right now," Reggie said.

Ronnie rubbed his forehead. "Reggie."

"Yeah."

"How did they know the money was in the cereal boxes?"

"They came in waving guns, Ronnie. I . . . just blurted it out. I'm sorry. Is that what they wanted, though? The money?"

Ronnie snorted.

"Nah. They want everything, Reggie. They want everything we fucking got."

Beauregard parked next to Kia's car. The sun was up, and the grass glistened with dew. He got out of the truck and walked into the house. It was deathly quiet. He headed for the bedroom.

He slipped into the room without turning on the light. He was stripping off his shirt when the lamp on the nightstand came on.

"Where the fuck you been?" Kia asked. She was wearing one of his T-shirts and nothing else.

"Something came up," he said.

"And you couldn't call?"

"No," he said.

She knitted her brow as she appraised him.

"Bug, there's blood on your face," she said. She sounded far away, like she was speaking through tin cans tied with a string.

"It's not mine," he said. He pulled his shirt off and stepped out of his pants. He slipped out of the room and went to the shower. He took off his underwear and socks and let the shower run so the water could warm up. He stepped over the edge of the tub and let the water hit him full on in the face.

He was just starting to lather up when the shower curtain was pulled back so hard a few of the rings popped loose.

"Bug, what the fuck is going on?" Kia said. The water splashed over her face and chest, soaking the T-shirt.

"Nothing you need to worry about."

"It's got to do with that job, don't it? I told you! I fucking told you to leave it alone. Sell that goddamn car, but no, you wouldn't listen. Now you come in here after being gone all night with somebody's blood on your face," she hissed.

The hiss became a sob. Beauregard grabbed her and pulled her into a tight embrace.

"I'm going to handle it. I promise," he said. She pushed him away. He studied her face. She was still crying, but the tears were lost in the water that was raining down on them both.

"You always say you going to handle it. But I was here last night waiting for a call saying you was dead. You ain't handling it if I end up a widow," she said. "I know you was pissed at me for talking to Jean but it was true. Do you know how many times I've planned your funeral in my head? You gonna handle it. How can you stand there and say that to me with a straight face?"

Beauregard turned off the water. He stepped out of the shower. Kia took a step backwards. He reached around her and grabbed a towel. He wiped his face and chest, then hung the towel back on the rack.

"Because I always do," he said finally.

TWENTY-THREE

Kelvin raised his hand to get the waitress's attention. She came strutting over in her too-tight jeans and too-short T-shirt.

"What ya need, boo?" she asked.

"Two beers," Kelvin said.

"You got it, sugar."

She came back with two lukewarm bottles of beer. Kelvin grabbed his and took a long swig.

"You really think it will work?" Kelvin asked.

"I ain't got no choice," Beauregard said. He took a sip of his beer.

"Well, when we gotta be in North Carolina?" Kelvin asked.

"I can't ask you to do that, K," Beauregard said. The waitress played a blues song on the jukebox. Danny's sound system struggled to accommodate the deep bass coming through its speakers. There were only two other patrons in the bar sitting in the corner. He and Kelvin had just closed the shop for the day. Kelvin had suggested they get a beer. Once they got seated, Beauregard just let all the events of the last thirty-six hours spill out. He couldn't tell Kia and he didn't want to tell Boonie. Kelvin was the only person he could talk to. He hadn't been asking for his help. He just needed to vent.

"Nah, fuck that. If you think I'm gonna let you go on another job with low-rent Jesse James and his retarded brother, you done lost your mind. He the reason you in this mess," Kelvin said.

"It's my mess and I gotta clean it up."

"Beauregard, don't make me say it."

"Say what?"

Kelvin dropped his voice.

"I owe you. Not just for giving me a job. I owe you for Kaden. Let me help. I need to help you," he said.

"You don't owe me shit for that," Beauregard said.

"That's not how I feel. Let me do this," Kelvin said.

Beauregard finished his beer. He held two fingers up and the waitress winked at him from across the bar. A few more people trickled in just as a sugary doo-wop song filled the air.

"We got six days to get ready."

"What kind of resistance we liable to get?" Kelvin asked.

The waitress dropped off the beers. Beauregard waited until she walked away to continue.

"A lot, I think. I asked around about this fella. Seems like him and Lazy been butting heads for a while. You remember Curt Macklin? Got a chop shop in Raleigh? He said that most of the OGs and crews in the Carolinas and Virginia done fell in line with this guy. Lazy the only one taking a stand, and it ain't going so well for him. Curt told me Lazy sent some boys to a spot this fella was using to cook some meth. He sent them boys back to Lazy in a five-gallon bucket," Beauregard said.

Kelvin made a face. "What they call him?"

"Curt said all he ever heard them call him was Shade. I asked Curt was he really that bad. Curt said he was worse," Beauregard said.

"Why we ain't never heard of him before? Or this Lazy dude?" Kelvin asked.

Beauregard shrugged. "I guess the kind of shit they into don't really require wheelmen," he said.

"Like what?" Kelvin asked.

"I talked to a doughboy from Newport News I know. Did a run for him to Atlanta. He told me Lazy basically runs everything west of the Roanoke Valley. He owns a bunch of smoke shops out there. Some payday loan places too," Beauregard said.

"Legal loan sharking," Kelvin said. Beauregard nodded.

"The boy I know told me his real money comes from running girls up the DC-Maryland corridor. Services a whole bunch of them government and military types up that way. Said he supposed to be a college boy. Got a degree in chemistry or some shit. Controls the meth, heroin and pills coming in from West Virginia. Said he runs moonshine too," Beauregard said.

Kelvin laughed. "He must do that for old times' sake. Damn. So you caught between a wannabe Pablo Escobar chopping mother-fuckers up and putting them in grease buckets and a redneck Walter White. When you fuck up you do it right."

Beauregard rolled his eyes. "If you don't want to get in this . . ."

"I didn't say that. I'm down. Besides, both of my girlfriends are gonna be out of town this weekend so I ain't got nothing to do," Kelvin said. He took a long sip off his beer. "You really gonna try and play them against each other like a chess game, huh?"

"It ain't chess. It's more like playing with a train set. We gonna put them on the same track and let them run into each other," Beauregard said.

"You think ol' boy gonna go for it?"

"I think this Shade is eating him alive. He wants to hurt him, but he also needs what's in that truck. He already had his back against the wall before we came along and robbed his drop bank."

"And how you plan on not getting caught in the cross fire?"

"I'm gonna get in touch with Shade and tell him when and where I plan on meeting Lazy with his truck. Then I'll drop it off an hour earlier. They'll both show up at the same time."

"Well, it sounds simple. That means something is gonna go to shit," Kelvin said. "Wait, what if Lazy gets the drop on Mr. Shade?"

"I got a rifle with a scope," Beauregard said.

"Well, damn. It's like that, I guess," Kelvin said.

Beauregard took another sip of beer. "Yeah, it's just like that. But first things first. We gotta get that truck."

"Yeah, that's gonna be the fun part," Kelvin said.

Ronnie sat on the couch with the door open. The AC had finally died a horrible death. Spitting out water and Freon like it had mechanical tuberculosis. Reggie was lying down in his room with his foot elevated. Ronnie could see the sun setting through the open door. Orange and red streaks sliced through the sky. Sunlight danced across the waxed surface of his Mustang. He hadn't driven the car since he got back from seeing Quan get his face blown off. The car only had a quarter of a tank of gas left. It was enough to get down to Danny's, but then what? He didn't have enough to pay for a drink, let alone get back to the house.

"Oh, how the mighty have fallen," he said. He sipped the last beer from the fridge, which didn't sound so healthy either. A week ago, he was snorting coke off some hipster chick's titty, now he was rationing his beer. The vibrating of his cell phone interrupted his sad requiem for the life he had just lost. Ronnie pulled it out of his pocket and checked the display.

"Hey, Bug."

"We on. Your brother okay to drive?"

"Well, kinda. They shot him in his foot when they came and scooped me up. He patched it up with some gauze and duct tape. He hopping around here like Peg Leg Bates, but it should hold," Ronnie said.

There was a heavy silence on the line.

"We'll just have to work with it. We leave for North Carolina Friday night," Beauregard said.

"Bug, you still ain't tell me what this plan of yours is. How we getting our money back?" Ronnie said.

More silence.

"Ronnie, there ain't no getting your money back. If this goes the way I think, we are getting our lives. You should have put some of your money somewhere safe. Not cereal boxes," Beauregard said.

The line went dead.

"Fuck you, Bug. That was a good idea," Ronnie said to the mute line.

TWENTY-FOUR

Beauregard adjusted the bandana around his nose and mouth. It had the image of a skull and crossbones printed on it. He'd seen the characters in some of the video games Darren and Javon played wearing a similar type of mask. He pulled the baseball cap down tight on his head. He'd adjusted his disguise at least a half a dozen times since Kelvin had texted him and told him he was in place.

It dawned on him that he was actually nervous. The sensation was so foreign to him that the realization was jarring. Usually when he was about to do a job a sense of tranquility came over him. The knowledge that he had calculated all the possible outcomes and prepared for any eventuality gave him a sense of peace.

He didn't feel any of that peace tonight. Tonight, he felt like an amateur. A virgin fumbling and tumbling his way to either ecstasy or agony. Six days. Six goddamn days to plan, get the necessary pieces in place and get down to North Carolina to execute the goddamn job. Beauregard adjusted the knapsack digging into his shoulders. He took a deep breath. A few mosquitoes buzzed around his face, apparently attracted to his warm breath and the promise of a big heaping gulp of his rich delicious blood. He waved them away and checked his watch. The hands glowed softly in the darkness. It was ten o'clock. Lazy's man swore the caravan would be coming through Pine Tar Road between ten and ten thirty. Swore on a stack of Bibles they were coming that way to avoid the interstate and overzealous deputies manning obscure speed traps. Although Beauregard wasn't sure how much anyone could trust the word of a hophead.

Locusts bleated in the marshy woods behind him. A rivulet of sweat ran down from his forehead and dropped into his right eye. He rubbed his eye with the back of his gloved hand, then crab walked across the dry, shallow ditch and edged up closer to the road. The sun had set two hours before but heat still radiated from the asphalt. Beauregard checked his watch again.

"Come on. Come on," he whispered.

Beauregard touched the butt of his .45. It was tucked into the small of his back. He knew it was there but touching it was reassuring. There hadn't been time to get any pieces from Madness. Just another example of how far he had let his standards slip when it came to this particular pinch. But this wasn't a normal score, was it? His desperation and Ronnie's greed had landed them all in a hornet's nest surrounded by vipers. Yet despite the startling lack of preparation and the sharp vicissitudes he had experienced in his fortunes since they'd knocked over the jewelry store he still planned on getting out of this alive. Lazy had made the same mistake a lot of people made about him. People like his own mother. Or the boys at Precision. The folks at the bank. Ariel's mama's people. Even sometimes his own wife. They all underestimated him.

His Daddy used to say when Bug set his mind to something he was like a boulder rolling down the side of a mountain. And God help anyone who got in his way.

The throwaway phone in his pocket vibrated.

Beauregard pulled it out and checked the screen. It was a text from Kelvin.

Here they come. Five minutes away.

Beauregard stood up straight and slipped the knapsack off his shoulder. He unzipped it and pulled out a road flare. He ignited the flare and trotted over to a shabby, rust-flecked gray 1974 Lincoln Continental. Once he'd explained the situation to Boonie the old man had insisted on helping to get the vehicle Beauregard needed for his plan. This was after he'd unleashed a ten-minute profanity-laden diatribe about Ronnie Sessions and the circumstances of his birth. He'd tried to keep Boonie out of this, but like many things lately, that hadn't worked out like he'd planned.

The pungent scent of gasoline emanated from the Lincoln in nauseating waves. Beauregard tossed the flare through the Lincoln's open driver-side window and jumped backwards. The car burst into flame with a loud WHOMP. Beauregard had diluted the gas just a bit so the car wouldn't explode but instead burn with a nice and steady flame. He slipped back into the woods, pulled a pair of night vision binoculars out of his pack, and resumed his crouch. He'd parked the Lincoln horizontally across the narrow back road. A standard non-interstate dual-lane road varied between ten to twelve feet wide. A Lincoln from bow to stern was roughly nineteen feet long. Cars bar-reling down Pine Tar Road would not be able to maneuver around it in the best of conditions. Now that it was engulfed in flames and blocking the road they'd have to stop.

At least that was what Beauregard hoped would happen. He texted Ronnie and Reggie.

Get in place. Ten minutes.

He put the phone back in his pocket. The light from the flames engulfing the Lincoln cast odd shadows across the blacktop. The burning leather and plastic sent black plumes of smoke up toward the quarter-full moon and the bluish black sky that served as its backdrop. Beauregard could see why they had picked this route. He hadn't seen a car in over an hour. Pine Tar sliced through several counties whose total population was less than one borough in Man-hattan. It was a route he would have picked.

The sound of two vehicles approaching broke him out of his rev-erie. A pair of powerful LED headlights chased away the darkness. A white Econoline van crested the hill followed by a black four-door SUV. The driver in the van probably didn't expect to see a car on fire

in the middle of the road at ten o'clock on a Thursday night. Beauregard watched as he stood up on the brake pedal and the van started
to fishtail. The weight of its payload was throwing off the handling.
Beauregard filed that away for later. The black SUV slammed on the
brakes as well. For a second Beauregard thought the SUV was going
to rear-end the van but the driver of the SUV had the advantage of
better brakes and superior handling and stopped the vehicle three
inches shy of the van's rear doors.

That was the one thing Lazy's man had definitely gotten wrong.
It wasn't a truck that was transporting contraband for Shade, it was
a van. Burning Man had called them the day after they had watched
him ventilate Quan with that little tidbit of information. Their inside
man had called them in a panic. Beauregard wondered what he
was more afraid of, Shade or a lost hookup. When Beauregard had
asked for the make and model of the van Burning Man had been
incredulous.

"What difference does that make?" Burning Man had asked.

"I need the license plate number too," Bug had said, ignoring the
scarred redneck's question.

"I kinda wish I could see what you planning, boy," Burning Man
said with a chuckle. Beauregard made himself not crush the cheap
flip phone into a thousand pieces. Lazy's inside man got them the
info but it wasn't until this precise moment that Beauregard truly
believed he'd gotten it right. The van was just as he had described
it. A 2005 Ford Econoline with only driver and passenger windows.
The type of vehicle you saw on the road every day and hardly noticed
because it was so ubiquitous.

The driver of the SUV turned off his headlights but kept on his
parking lights. Beauregard peered through the binoculars.

Three men exited the vehicle. They walked around to the front
of the van, which still had its headlights on full blast. Even though
it was in the high 70s two of them were wearing light, loose-fitting
hoodies. Between the illumination from the headlights and the glow

of the fire Beauregard could clearly see the bulges in their waistbands under their hoodies. The third man, the driver, made no attempt to hide his weapon. He carried an AR-15 in his wide mahogany hands. The triumvirate stared at the immolating car, then glanced at each other, then turned back to the fiery mess of melting steel and shattering glass that blocked their way. Staring through the binoculars gave everything an emerald sheen. Even the flames from the car seemed to give off a chartreuse radiance.

"Should we call somebody?" one of the hoodie-wearing brothers asked.

"Who the fuck we gonna call? Smokey the goddamn Bear?" the driver asked. He was wearing a Washington Wizards jersey. He had long dreadlocks that fell down his back in serpentine coils. Before the first hoodie-wearing brother who had asked the pertinent-if-somewhat-naive question could respond, a pickup truck crested the hill and stopped behind the SUV. All three men spun around and faced the pickup. The driver held his AR-15 down by his side and stepped into the shadows. The driver of the pickup cut the ignition and killed his lights. The driver's door of the truck creaked open and Kelvin hopped out. He was wearing one of his work shirts with the name patch removed.

"Hey, what the hell is going on?" he asked as he walked toward the men and the car, which was now completely engulfed in flames. The driver, Mr. Dreadlocks, stepped from the shadows brandishing the AR-15. He didn't point it at Kelvin but he wasn't letting it dangle at his side either. He held it at an angle across his midsection. Beauregard took a deep breath. He'd told Kelvin he had to really sell it. Make sure he sounded irritated and confused. However, it was a precarious balancing act. If he came off too calm they might get suspicious. If he came on too strong they might just shoot him on general principles.

"Who the fuck are you, man?" Dreadlocks asked. Kelvin made a show of noticing the gun. He backed up and raised his hands.

"Hey man, I don't want no trouble. I'm just trying to get home,"

Kelvin said. He let the bravado and annoyance slip from his voice and replaced it with wariness and fear. Beauregard thought he could earn an Oscar with this performance.

"Turn around and go another way, cuz," Dreadlocks said. Now he was pointing the gun at Kelvin.

Fuck, Beauregard thought.

He put his binoculars down and grabbed the .45. He aimed it at Dreadlocks. No one said a word. Beauregard could hear the crackling of the fire as it consumed the former luxury car, the hooting of a lonesome owl, the idling engines of the van and the SUV and the beating of his own fluttering heart. The locusts had lowered the pitch and volume of their serenade to nearly imperceptible levels.

Beauregard felt his stomach tighten like a boa constrictor was in his guts. He had two extra clips in his backpack if things popped off. He put his left hand on his right wrist and steadied his gun hand. He should take out Dreadlocks right now. Then take out the Hoodie Brothers. The flames were giving off enough light that he thought he could nail Dreadlocks for sure. The Hoodie Brothers might be more problematic. They were standing in the shadows.

The longer he waited the more likely it was that Kelvin was going to eat a bullet. He squinted but he couldn't see how much pull Dreadlocks had on the trigger. He was pulling about three pounds of pressure on the five-pound trigger of the .45 himself.

"Look, man, this is the only road that I can take. I don't know what's going on and I got no interest in finding out, but I got a fire extinguisher in my truck. If we can put the fire out we can push the car out of the way and we can all go on about our business. And my business got nothing to do with your business," Kelvin said.

Silence.

"We gotta get down to Winston-Salem by two," one of the Hoodie Brothers said. Kelvin shrugged his shoulders. The muscles in Dreadlock's forearms rippled like rigging ropes.

He ain't going for it, Beauregard thought. He started to rise out of the milkweed and heather on the side of the road.

"Look, my wife already gonna bite my head off because she thinks I'm cheating on her. Let's help each other out, man," Kelvin said.

"Are you?" one of the Hoodie Brothers asked.

"Am I what?" Kelvin asked.

"Cheating on her?"

Dreadlocks motioned with the AR-15.

"Get the fire extinguisher," he growled. Kelvin nodded and jogged back to the pickup.

He grabbed a slim red fire extinguisher from behind the bench seat. He went back to the car, pulled the pin and sprayed down the Lincoln. A whitish cloud of CO_2 enveloped the car, dampening the flames. Kelvin had to hit the car three more times before the fire went out completely.

"Let me see if I can put it in gear. Then we can push it. Be careful though, it's still fucking hot," Kelvin said. He gingerly reached his hand through the window, taking care to not let his arm touch the still smoking car door. Beauregard had left it in neutral but this was all a part of the act.

"Hey, it's already in neutral," he said. He stepped back and pulled his shirt over his head. He walked to the back of the car. By wrapping his shirt around his hands he made it into an ersatz oven mitt.

"We all gonna have to push it. It's a Lincoln. An old one. It's heavy as shit," Kelvin said. The Hoodie Brothers put their hands inside the pockets of their hood jackets and took a position on either side of Kelvin. Beauregard saw the door of the van open and watched as an amber-colored dome light came to life. A big beefy brother wearing a baseball cap with a broken bill started to get out.

"Get your ass back in that van," Dreadlocks said.

The van driver got back in but didn't shut the door all the way. Eventually the dome light blinked out.

"Hey man, it's gonna take all of us," Kelvin said.

"Y'all got it. I got faith in you," Dreadlocks said. He was still pointing the rifle at Kelvin. He stood between the van and the Lincoln.

"Tyree, this car heavy as fuck. Come on, man, let's just move it and get on," one of the Hoodie Brothers said to Dreadlocks. Beauregard inched closer to the road.

Tyree set the rifle down on the road. He took a position next to the Hoodie Brother on Kelvin's left.

"I ain't messing up my jersey," Tyree said as he placed his Air Jordan on the trunk.

"Hey, I feel ya. Alright, on three," Kelvin said.

"One."

Beauregard put the binoculars back in his pack and crept over the dry ditch bank. He crouched down until he was crab walking again. He inched his way up to the driver's-side door of the van. His rubber-soled shoes slipped over the gravel and asphalt like a sigh.

"Two."

Beauregard pressed his back against the side of the van.

"THREE," Kelvin exclaimed. The four men pushed and kicked the Lincoln. The screech of metal against metal filled the night as the brakes ground against the rotors.

Beauregard stood up and aimed his .45 at the driver. The man had a wide face with a light, almost tan complexion. He stared at Beauregard's gun like a bird staring at a snake. The driver's hand hovered above the horn but Beauregard shook his head. He pulled a piece of white paper out of his pocket with his free hand. He pressed the paper against the glass.

"TURN OFF THE DOME LIGHT. DO NOT MAKE ANY NOISE. GET IN THE BACK AND LIE FACE DOWN. IF YOU DON'T I WILL KILL YOU" was written on the paper.

The driver hadn't shut the door completely so Beauregard grabbed the handle and opened it slowly. He motioned for the driver to get in the back. The man slid his considerable bulk over the center console and lay down in the back of the van. Beauregard balled up the paper, put it in his pocket and climbed in the van. He saw that the man had followed instructions as carefully as a dutiful child. He shut the door softly then slipped out of his pack while still holding his gun. Using his free hand he retrieved two sets of handcuffs from the knapsack. He handed both pairs of cuffs to the driver.

"Handcuff one end of one set of handcuffs to one of the straps holding down the pallet. Hook the other end to the chain in the middle of the other pair. Then put that pair on. Do it quickly," Beauregard whispered.

"Are you gonna shoot me?" the driver asked. His voice was a tremulous whistle.

"Not if you put on the handcuffs," Beauregard said. He checked his watch. Taking control of the van had taken a minute and a half. They were right on schedule.

"That should do it, fellas," Kelvin said. The smoldering Lincoln was at a lackadaisical diagonal angle in Pine Tar Road's northbound lane. They'd moved it just enough so they could all slip by.

"Yeah," Tyree said. He retrieved the AR-15 and aimed it at Kelvin again. Kelvin held his hands out in front of him. He dropped his work shirt and took a step back.

Beauregard watched the scene through the windshield. All the saliva in his mouth instantly evaporated. His breath came in ragged bursts.

"Don't you do it," he murmured.

"Hey man, come on," Kelvin said. Tyree walked up to him and placed the barrel against his cheek. He pushed forward until the barrel was making a dent in Kelvin's face.

Beauregard planted himself in the driver's seat. He had the .45 in his waist but shooting through the windshield would throw off his shot. The van was a 6,000-pound deadly weapon if it came to that. Beauregard watched as Tyree pressed the barrel of his gun even harder into Kelvin's cheek. His whole body flinched.

"No, no, no, you gotta talk this motherfucker down," Beauregard said, not caring if the driver heard him or not. He saw Kelvin's face in the bright bluish headlights. It was terribly animated. His eyes were big as dinner plates. Snippets of the conversation reached him in muffled chunks. The words were indistinct but the AR-15 made the nature of Dreadlock's threat perfectly clear.

Beauregard shifted the van into drive. He could close the distance between the van and Tyree in less than three seconds. Which wouldn't matter because if Tyree pulled the trigger Kelvin would be dead before he hit the ground.

Beauregard clutched the steering wheel in a death grip.

"If I was you I would forget all about tonight. I see you again, anywhere, your wife a widow. Ya feel me?" Tyree said.

"Forget about what?" Kelvin said.

"Come on, Tyree, we gotta go," one of the Hoodie Brothers said.

"Be gone, homes," Tyree said. Kelvin put his hands down and picked up his shirt. He grabbed the spent fire extinguisher and walked around the three men. He glanced at the van as he walked back to the truck. He climbed in and shut the door. Beauregard's bandana rustled as he exhaled deep from within his chest.

"Get in the car," Tyree said. The other two men hustled back to the SUV. As he made his way back to the vehicle he slapped the hood of the van. The windows and the windshield had a dark, smoke gray tint. In the faded gloom of the North Carolina night, with the blinding LED headlights blasting his retinas, Tyree failed to notice Beauregard sitting in the driver's seat.

"Let's get on, Ross," Tyree said after slapping the hood. He climbed into the SUV. Beauregard put the van into gear and hit the gas. The caravan was once again on its way. Kelvin counted to fifty before taking off as well. By the time he'd crested the next hill the tail lights of the SUV were just red pinpricks.

Beauregard kept the van near 60 as they navigated the serpentine road that twisted through the North Carolina hills. The SUV stayed about a car length behind him with its low beams bouncing off his side mirrors. He put the gun in the knapsack with his right hand while steering with his left. Switching hands, he grabbed the steering wheel with his right and slid his left hand under the dashboard near the door. His deft fingers found the van's fuse box. He visualized the fuse box's specs. He'd memorized them from the Chilton repair manual. He could see the square black box in his mind with the different colored two-bladed fuses in three short rows that ran the length of the box. Beauregard counted to himself as his fingers slipped across the hard plastic rectangles.

One, two, three, four down. One, two, three to the right, he thought. He pulled the fuse for the van's brake lights out of its socket. He let it fall from his fingers and buried the gas pedal in the floor. The van lurched forward as the engine screamed. A sharp curve was coming up but Beauregard didn't let up on the gas. He took the curve at 70. He felt the back wheels trying to slither to the right as he turned into the curve. He wrenched the steering wheel to the left and gave the brake a love tap. Glancing in the side mirror he saw the SUV was now about six car lengths behind them. He grimaced but his bandana hid his own visage from him as he flicked his eyes up toward the rearview mirror. Once again he stomped on the gas. The van's engine squealed in protest but Beauregard spared it no quarter. The speedometer topped out at 125 and he intended to get within shouting distance of that in the next two minutes. The road ahead careened into another hairpin turn that forced him to slam on the brake with his left foot while keeping his right foot firmly on the gas pedal. The van drifted through the turn like a big man who was surprisingly nimble on the dance floor. He checked the side mirror. The SUV's headlights appeared after a few seconds.

Beauregard heard the staccato rhythm of gunfire explode behind him. He took his foot off the brake and committed all his strength to pressing the gas pedal to the floor. He checked the side mirror again. Another burst of gunfire exploded even as the headlights of the SUV

receded. Soon they disappeared entirely. The crew in the SUV probably assumed the van driver had decided to double-cross them and
make off with their boss's loot.

That was exactly what Beauregard wanted them to think.

A long stretch of straight road unfurled in front of him like a
black ribbon. He checked the speedometer. 90 mph.

Beauregard fished his phone out of his pocket. Steering with his
left hand he scrolled through his contacts with a quick downward
glance. When he got to one that said R1 he pushed the green "call"
button. Returning his eyes to the road he saw a chestnut-colored doe
step daintily out into the middle of the road.

"Goddamn it!" he grunted. Beauregard whipped the steering
wheel to the right while letting up off the gas but not braking. He
heard the pallet in the back groan as gravity pulled at it with insistent
invisible hands. Beauregard drove the van onto the narrow shoulder
of the road and around the seemingly oblivious deer. The front right
tire tried to slip into the ditch but Beauregard refused to allow it to
escape. He'd come too far and had too far to go for that bullshit. He
hit the gas and slammed the wheel to the left. The van fishtailed,
shuddered, then the front right tire found the road again and dug
into the asphalt. Beauregard did all this with his left hand while still
holding the phone to his right ear.

"What is it?" Ronnie yelled.

"Nothing. Be ready. Two minutes," Beauregard said. He ended
the call and tossed the phone in the cup holder. Another series of
hills were coming up in one hundred feet. He had driven this road
twice since they had come down yesterday morning. He took notice
of every divot, pothole and twist and turn. The details were burned
into his mind like a cattle brand. He checked his side mirror. The
headlights of the SUV were nowhere to be seen. They had the faster
vehicle but he had the better skills.

At the top of the second hill Beauregard saw a white box truck
had pulled out in front of him from its resting place on the widest

part of the shoulder. He eased up on the gas and grabbed the phone. He called Ronnie again.

"You have to keep it at 60. I'm coming in hot," Beauregard said. His words came out in short clipped bursts.

"I got it. You want the door down now?"

"Yes." He tossed the phone aside again.

Boonie had gotten them the pickup truck and two other vehicles for Beauregard's plan. The box truck he had to steal. He and Kelvin had slipped down to Newport News and copped it from a plumbing supply store on Jefferson Avenue. The van they were going to steal was fifteen feet long, six feet wide and six feet seven inches tall. The Akers and Son box truck was just wide enough, deep enough and had barely enough headspace for the job. Originally it had a roll door that slid up and rolled onto two metal slats attached to the roof. Beauregard had gotten rid of the roll door in addition to making a few more adjustments.

Ronnie had wanted to go in guns blazing but Bug knew that was a fool's run. He'd figured, correctly, that the crew protecting the van would be strapped with some heavy artillery. They didn't have the time or the money to get into an arms race.

Beauregard inched closer to the box truck.

Instead of rolling upward the door of the box truck began to open outward like the lid of a coffin. Slowly, torturously it continued opening until it was nearly parallel with the road. After a breath-stopping pause it continued opening until the lip made contact with the road. The rubber weather stripping he'd installed at the top of the door began to smoke as friction began to devour it. He only had a few minutes before the rubber wore away and sparks began to dot the night. The door itself was made up of threaded rod welded together in a cross-hatch pattern like a sheet of rabbit wire. He'd sandwiched that between quarter-inch-thick steel plates. Two-inch-wide support struts ran from the bottom of the door to the top. They stopped just three inches before the weather stripping along the edge of the ramp began. Kelvin had helped him hook up the hydraulic system that opened and closed the door. A toggle switch dangling from the steering wheel of the truck controlled the entire apparatus.

Closed, it looked like any other door to any other box truck.

Opened, it became a ramp.

Beauregard focused on the ramp. They'd hit another flat stretch. This one went on for just under three miles. Ronnie was doing 60. He'd have to get the van up to at least 65 to get inside the truck and then stand up on the brakes to keep the van from crashing into the cab. This was their best shot. In about three minutes the road became a roller coaster and stayed that way for the next five miles until it passed a desolate gas station.

He pushed the van up to 65 and aimed it at the ramp. He felt it then. Felt it for the first time tonight. The high, the juice, the symbiotic relationship between man and machine. The thrumming vibrations that worked their way up from the blacktop through the wheels and suspension system like blood moving through veins until it reached his hands. The engine spoke to him in the language of horsepower and RPMs. It told him it yearned to run.

The thrill had finally arrived.

"Let's fly," Beauregard whispered.

He hit the ramp doing 70 mph. The van rocked like a skiff on the open sea. Beauregard heard the driver moan from the back. Grunting, he eased up on the gas infinitesimally. He'd adjusted the ramp so that the dip between it and the edge of the bed was minimal but if he came in too fast he'd pop the front tires. Without warning the truck shot forward, accelerating violently. Beauregard could feel the ramp slipping from beneath his wheels.

"Fuck!" Beauregard growled. He let up on the gas as the ramp disappeared completely from beneath the van. The front tires slammed onto the asphalt like Fat Man and Little Boy. The van careened from left to right as Beauregard struggled with the wheel. Once he had it under control he fumbled for the cell. He hit the "call" button with his right thumb as he steered with his left hand.

"What was that?" Beauregard said when Ronnie answered.

"I'm sorry, my foot slipped. Fuck it, Bug, I'm sorry I—"

Beauregard cut him off.

"Keep it at sixty. I'm coming in again," he said. They'd missed their best chance in the long straightaway. Now more steep hills loomed ahead of them. Beauregard gritted his teeth as the van struggled to drag itself up and over while carrying him, the driver and the pallet of platinum.

Ronnie was trying to keep the truck steady but it was jerking, faster on the downhills, slower as it struggled up. Impossible to time it right in these short valleys.

No headlights in the mirror. Not yet. He breathed deeply. They had one more shot. It wasn't ideal but they didn't really have a choice. After this last hill the road flattened out again. Only this time it was a matter of feet, not miles.

As Beauregard descended the hill he saw bright orange sparks erupt from the ramp. The rubber weather stripping had burned away and the metal was making contact with the asphalt. The sparks looked like fireflies from Hell. Two hundred feet. He only had two hundred feet left before the road ended and they were back on a main highway. Two hundred feet to make this work. The main high-way was forty miles of flat blacktop four lanes wide. Once they hit it the SUV would catch up with them. He couldn't outrun them on that stretch. Beauregard focused on the ramp. The van's powerful head-lights lit up the inside of the truck. The interior of the truck reflected the light back at him. Through a hail of sparks, he saw the four sand-bags he had attached to the wall to act as a backstop. A desolate gas station illuminated by flickering sodium arc lights zipped by his win-dow. The yellow lights left jaundiced streaks behind his eyes.

One hundred and sixty feet now.

Beauregard flicked his eyes toward the rearview mirror. He saw the ambient glow of headlights rising above the last hill they had gone over. The SUV hadn't crested that hill yet but it would in a matter of seconds. It was either going to be now or it was getting shot in the fucking face.

One hundred feet.

Beauregard grunted and hit the gas. The needle on the speedometer shot past 70 mph and leaned on 80. He passed a green rectangular sign that told him Pine Tar Road was coming to an end.

Drive it like you stole it, right? Beauregard thought.

He slammed the gas pedal to the floor. As the speedometer hit 90 mph, sparks washed over the van like a wave of falling stars.

"There! There it is, goddamn it!" Tyree yelled.

He whipped the SUV to the right and pulled into a desolate, dimly lit gas station. The gas station was about a mile from the end of Pine Tree Road. Tyree slammed on the brakes and jumped out of the vehicle with his AR-15 in one hand. The Hoodie Brothers followed him. They kept their weapons tucked under their shirts and kept their distance from Tyree.

Sitting under the sallow sodium arc lights that sat above the gas pumps was the van. Moths darted around and under the canopy above the pumps, casting strange, fluttering silhouettes that danced across the surface of the van. Tyree approached it from the rear with slow deliberate steps. He pressed the stock of his rifle against his right bicep while he grabbed the rear latch with his left. The doors swung open with a horrid creak.

"Motherfucker," Tyree said.

The van was empty. No driver, no platinum, no anything. Tyree seized the rear door and slammed it shut. He opened it again and slammed it shut. He did this five more times. The seventh and final time was too much for the rear window. It exploded into a million pieces. Chunks of tempered, smoke gray glass rained across the concrete.

Tyree threw his head back and howled.

"MOTHERFUCKER!"

Inside the store the cashier was putting a 40-ounce bottle of beer in a brown bag for his only customer. They both watched with mounting concern as the man in the parking lot slammed the door to the van again and again. He and his customer jumped when they heard the man in the parking lot baying at the sky as the glass in the rear door shattered. The cashier peered out the picture window at the front of the store.

"That don't sound good. Don't look good neither. I think that one boy there got a gun. You think I should call the cops?" the cashier asked as he handed the brown bag to his customer.

Reggie grabbed the bag and his change.

"None of my business, man," he said. His voice quavered a bit but since the cashier didn't know him from Adam he didn't notice. Reggie unscrewed the beer cap and took a big swig as he left the store. A warm wind rose up out of nowhere. It stirred the napkins and clear plastic lids and cigarette butts that dotted the parking lot. He headed for the highway, walking at a diagonal amble away from the van and the SUV. He tried to take another sip of his beer but his hands were trembling and he spilled it all over his T-shirt.

"Hey white boy, you see who was driving this van?" a voice asked from behind him. Reggie stopped. His throat felt like it was closing in on itself. He gripped his beer bottle tight. Exhaling rapidly, he turned to face the trio of men standing near the van.

"Nope," he said. Tyree stepped forward. Reggie stared at the gun in his hands. The beer in his guts started trying to climb out of his stomach.

"You didn't see nothing?" Tyree asked.

"Nope, sure didn't," Reggie said. His wounded foot began to

throb. He began to tap it like he was keeping time with a beat only he could hear. Tyree took another step forward. They were only a foot apart now.

"You sure about that?" he asked.

"Yep," Reggie said. His voice had dropped to a barely audible rasp. Tyree stared at him.

A cell phone rang. One of the Hoodie Brothers answered it.

"Hey Ty, it's Shade. He can't get in touch with Ross. He wants to talk to you."

Tyree clenched the grip on his gun. He started to step forward again but stopped. He held Reggie's gaze for a few seconds before swallowing hard and holding out his left hand.

"Give me the phone," Tyree said. His voice had lost some of its menace.

Reggie nodded abruptly and started hoofing it down the road. After he'd gone about about two hundred yards a pair of headlights appeared behind him and lit up his whole world. Reggie stopped, turned and used his free hand to shield his eyes.

A bedraggled pickup truck pulled over to the side of the road. The passenger door creaked open like a crypt. Reggie limped over to the truck and climbed inside.

"Everything go alright?" Kelvin asked.

"Yeah. I did just what Bug said. As soon as I saw the truck and the van go by I pulled out and drove to the gas station. Those guys pulled up like two seconds after I got in the store," Reggie said. He took another sip.

"You didn't get me a beer?" Kelvin said. Reggie clutched the bottle to his chest.

"I didn't know you wanted one."

Kelvin laughed.

"Calm down, Hee-Haw, I was just fucking with you," Kelvin said as they pulled back onto the road.

TWENTY-FIVE

Bug sat in the van in the dark and waited for Ronnie to make the turn. It would be a left turn onto an old dirt lane choked with weeds and grass, just past a shuttered feed and seed store. The dirt lane climbed up a steep hill and crested in a flat meadow. Beauregard guessed a house had stood in the meadow at one time, but it was long gone. Nature had not yet reclaimed the spot completely. He'd found the place the day before riding around in the Lincoln with Kelvin while Ronnie and Reggie had lounged at the motel. He didn't put too much stock in fate or luck but it had been fortuitous to find this spot. It was nearly a mile off the highway in the middle of nowhere with enough room for the truck, the van and the pickup Kelvin was driving to maneuver in. This time of night no one would notice them unless they came looking.

Beauregard hoped no one came looking. He didn't relish killing anyone. At the same time, it didn't fill him with tic-inducing anxiety. It was messy. Murder was always messy. If it had to be done, you had to expect to get dirty and clean up as best you could. When they had found those boys that had done Kaden, old Chompy had cleaned things up for them nicely.

The truck stopped. The hydraulic pump wheezed and shuddered as the ramp lowered once more. Beauregard started the van and backed down the ramp slowly. He hit the ground, turned the wheel to the right, shifted into drive and pulled up alongside the box truck. He killed the engine and climbed out and leaned against the

driver's-side door. The box truck's headlights gave the meadow an el-
dritch glow moments before they extinguished. A copse of pine trees
surrounded the meadow. Beauregard heard the door to the box truck
open, then slam shut. Ronnie ambled around the back of the van.

"We fucking did it!" he said. He held up his hand for a high five.
Beauregard glared at his hand until Ronnie lowered it and let it hang
down by his side.

"It's not done yet. We have to load the truck."

"So, what about . . . your passenger?"

"He ain't seen shit. We load up the truck and handcuff his ass to
a tree branch. If he's smart he'll wait till we gone and use the cuffs as
a rope saw to get loose," Beauregard said.

"You think that's a good idea? Leaving him like that?" Ronnie
asked. Beauregard pulled his bandana down past his mouth.

"I said he ain't seen shit. Besides, it ain't like he gonna go to the
cops."

Ronnie shrugged his shoulders. "Just asking. Shade's worse than
the cops," he said. He put his hands in his pocket. Beauregard noticed
the outline of a small pistol in the right-hand pocket. It sat there like
a sleeping scorpion. Deadly and inert all at the same time.

"Uh huh."

A pair of headlights climbed up the overgrown driveway.

Kelvin pulled into the meadow, then turned the truck around so
that the tailgate was facing the back of the van. He put the truck in
park with a loud clang. He and Reggie climbed out and met Ronnie
and Beauregard in the middle of the field.

"That transmission got about twenty more feet in it," Kelvin said.

"It'll be fine. Ronnie, get the flashlight out of the truck. Let's get
the old boy out of the van and find a tree to tie him to. Then we can
load up the pickup truck. It's eleven o'clock," Beauregard said. "I want
us on the road by midnight."

"You know, I've been thinking. How would Lazy know if we kept
a few spools for ourselves? I mean I know what you said but really,

you think that motherfucker gonna miss two rolls? Shit, two rolls is enough for the four of us. I know a guy can get us a real good price," Ronnie said. Beauregard put his hand on Ronnie's shoulder. He let his thumb lie on Ronnie's collarbone. Katydids began to call to each other from the undergrowth. Beauregard buried his thumb under Ronnie's collarbone and pressed against the brachial plexus.

"OW! Damn, Bug!" Ronnie squealed. He leaned over and put one hand on his knee while trying to remove Bug's hand from his shoulder with the other.

"You don't get to talk about keeping anything. You don't get to talk about what Lazy might know or not know. The only thing I want to hear you talking about is loading up this goddamn truck. Now get old boy out the van," Beauregard said. He released Ronnie, who then stumbled backwards into his brother. Beauregard untied the bandana and held it out to Ronnie.

"Make him put this on." Ronnie gave Beauregard a long hard look and for a second Beauregard thought he was going to make a move. Beauregard felt something akin to relief that they were finally going to get down to it, but then the fire faded out of Ronnie's eyes.

"Fuck, Bug. It's just a thought. Damn. You got the fucking key to the cuffs?" Ronnie said. Beauregard took the keys from his pocket. He placed the bandana in Ronnie's left hand and the keys in his right. Ronnie closed his hands tight and stalked over to the van. He opened the rear door and climbed inside.

"Listen up. I'm gonna put a blindfold on you. Then I'm gonna unlock the cuff from the strap. You ever want to see big titties and fat asses again you do exactly what we tell you. Cool?" Ronnie said.

"C-cool," the driver said. Ronnie straddled the man as he lay on his stomach and tried to tie the bandana around the driver's head. The two ends of the scarf barely met as Ronnie tried to tie a simple knot.

"Goddamn you got a big head. Like a damn pumpkin," Ronnie said under his breath. Groaning, he pulled hard on the fabric around the man's eyes and looped it into a harsh, tiny knot.

He unlocked the cuff from the metal banding strap that held the rolls of platinum in place on the pallet. He stood and grabbed Ross by the collar of his denim button-down shirt and helped him to his feet. They executed a slow backwards shuffle until they hit the bumper.

"Alright, step down. Easy. I ain't trying to pick your big ass up," Ronnie said. The driver's foot hovered in space as he tried to find the ground. Ronnie let go of his collar and grabbed him by the arm.

"Step down. Now your other foot."

The driver placed both feet on the ground. Ronnie held him at a somewhat perpendicular angle. He turned his head toward Beauregard.

"Where you wanna do this?" he asked.

"Poor choice of words," Kelvin said.

Before Ronnie could respond the tiny knot he had tied unraveled unceremoniously. The bandana fell from the driver's face and floated lazily to the ground. The driver looked over his right shoulder directly into Ronnie's face. They locked eyes for about half a second before he twisted from Ronnie's grasp and took off across the meadow.

"Fuck me!" Ronnie yelled. He pulled a .32 from his pocket and starting firing at the driver. The man began to run in a zigzagging pattern. He reached the tree line and began crashing through the woods.

"Get the flashlights!" Beauregard yelled. Kelvin ran to the truck and retrieved two heavy-duty Maglites. He tossed one to Beauregard.

"Come on. Reggie, you with me!" Beauregard said. He took off for the woods.

"You heard him, dipshit!" Ronnie yelled. Ronnie lit out for the woods. Kelvin passed him like he was standing still as they headed for the pines. Reggie limped after them but his loping gait didn't have much urgency.

Beauregard clicked on the flashlight. The pine trees and wild azaleas appeared ghastly in the harsh yellow light. He threaded through the woods, ducking under low-hanging branches and jumping over the rotted trunks of trees that were dead when he was still in juvie. He stopped for a second and listened. He tried to ignore the insects and the animals and just listened for the sounds a fat frightened man running for his life would make. A part of him wondered if Ronnie had intentionally tied the bandana with a slipknot or something. He'd been so intent on killing the driver, maybe he'd done it to force Beauregard's hand? Beauregard shook off that thought. That was a chess move. Ronnie was strictly a checkers kind of guy. Ronnie Fucking Sessions. That should be his nickname instead of Rock and Roll. The man was a congenital fuckup. Couldn't even tie a goddamn blindfold right.

A sharp embankment rose in front of him, dotted with dying pines and sickly cedars. The sound of his own breathing seemed unbelievably loud, like a bellows in an old steel plant. His .45 was heavy against the small of his back. He pulled it and brought it up in his right hand while holding the flashlight aloft with his left.

He heard a crashing and snapping behind him and to the left. That was Ronnie, Kelvin and Reggie. He eyed the embankment again. Could the driver, who was two cheeseburgers away from cardiac arrest, climb such a steep hill in less than two minutes? Normally Beauregard would have said no but fear gave men wings. He started climbing up the embankment. He pushed himself and reached the top of the ridgeline in less than five minutes. He paused and took a deep breath. It came out ragged.

The first few notes of "Born Under a Bad Sign" echoed through the night. They were harsh and sharp, nearly robotic. Someone liked the blues and had the song as a ringtone. Beauregard's head snapped to the right.

Too late he realized the forest was playing tricks on him. As he turned the driver slammed into him. They landed in a thunderous heap with Beauregard on the bottom. His right wrist cracked against a root or a rock. Pain sprinted up his right arm and he felt his gun slip away. The driver's bulk crushed him into the ground.

Every inhalation was agony. As he grasped blindly for his gun he felt warm metal biting into his throat. He couldn't breathe. Calmly, almost abstractly, he realized the driver was using his handcuffs to garrote him. Beauregard let go of the flashlight, stopped reaching for the gun and pushed himself and the driver up off the ground. The two of them pitched onto their sides but the driver still held on. Beauregard's hands scrambled across the driver's face like a pair of tarantulas. His thumbs found the man's eyes as his chest began to burn and black spots began to dance in front of his face.

Beauregard jammed both thumbs in the man's sockets. The driver cried out like a wounded bear. He released his hold on Beau's neck in an attempt to protect his eyes. Beauregard rolled away from the driver. Taking in huge gulps of air, he scuttled across the forest floor on all fours. He ran his hand over and through the detritus. His gun. He needed his gun.

The beam from his flashlight began to dance across a few trees that were a foot or so in front of him.

Beauregard flipped onto his back just in time to partially block a blow from the driver. He had gripped the flashlight with both hands and was wielding it like a club. Beauregard tucked his legs up to his chest and kicked at the man while using his hands to block his strikes. He had to get to his feet. Forget the gun. On his feet they were literally on a level playing field.

A corona illuminated the man from the back as a volley of shots resounded through the forest. A fine mist of blood and bone chips filled the air between him and the driver. The man started to fall forward. Blood leaked from two wounds in the center of his chest. Beauregard caught the body as it pitched forward, the flashlight falling from his hands. He shoved the driver's body off to the left and squirmed to the right. His face and neck were dotted with droplets of blood. Ronnie and Kelvin stepped up onto the ridgeline. They were both holding guns. Kelvin was also holding the other flashlight. He stepped over the driver and held out his free hand to Beauregard. Beauregard gripped it and Kelvin pulled him to his feet.

"You alright?" he said.

"Yeah. Most of this is his blood."

"Man, why did he take off running? Did he think there was a buffet up here?" Kelvin asked. Beauregard shook his head. He felt a smile trying to spread across his face.

"I owe you one," Beauregard said.

"Nah, we just even now. You owe Ronnie one though. I think he was the one that hit him," Kelvin said. Beauregard peered over Kelvin's shoulder. He saw Ronnie looking down at the driver's body. He was humming a tune that Beauregard didn't recognize. Beauregard turned his attention back to Kelvin.

"Let's get back to the van and get loaded up. I want to be back in Virginia by sunup," Beauregard said. The plan was for him and Kelvin to drive the pickup. Ronnie and Reggie, by virtue of Ronnie getting all of them into this, would have to take the risk of riding in the stolen box truck.

Kelvin was about to respond when his left cheek exploded. Warm fluid splashed across Beauregard's chest. A sharp pain ripped across his right deltoid as Kelvin crumpled to the ground. Beauregard jumped backwards. It was a move born of instinct more than anything else. He felt himself floating in midair for what seemed like minutes before his body crashed into the western slope of the embankment. He tumbled head over heels as shots rang out from the ridgeline and bullets ricocheted off the desiccated trunks of diseased pine trees. Dirt and twigs and dead leaves found their way down his shirt and into his pants and into his mouth as his body careened down the side of the hill. The world was a swirling kaleidoscope until he flipped one last time. The wide trunk of an old pine tree rushed toward his face then there was just blackness.

TWENTY-SIX

For a moment Beauregard thought he was blind. The world seemed dim and full of shadows. He blinked his eyes and felt something warm and wet running down his face. He sent his left hand on an exploratory mission and touched his face. It was blood. He had blood in his eyes. A wound above his left eye had clotted but his rough fingers opened it again.

He wasn't blind. It was still dark. Beauregard sat up and immediately regretted it. Vomit raced up his esophagus and out his mouth. He leaned on his left side and let it pour out across the ground. He felt like he was trapped on a merry-go-round.

Taking a deep breath, he tried sitting up again. He didn't vomit this time, but he sure wanted to. An owl hooted at him from somewhere. He listened for any other sounds. Like people walking or voices commiserating about him. But all he heard were the usual sounds of the forest at night. He hesitated then sent his left hand on an expedition. Up his right arm. When his fingers found the gash, he pressed his lips together tight and groaned. The gash was about two inches long but not deep. The bullet had grazed him. He flexed his right hand. His fingers moved, albeit begrudgingly. He touched his forehead. A knot the size of a chicken egg was sitting just above his left eyebrow and a little to right of the laceration that had bled into his eyes. He checked his watch. The pale glow of its face was not enough to draw anyone's attention. It was two thirty in the morning.

They had chased the guy into the woods around eleven. He'd been out for more than three hours.

Kelvin had been dead for three hours. His cousin, his best friend, had been dead for three hours.

Ronnie Fucking Sessions. He should have seen that coming. He should have been prepared. He'd seen Ronnie's face when Lazy had spilled that money across his desk. That lean and hungry look that said Ronnie did not want to give up his hard-earned loot. Beauregard had seen that look and dismissed it. Foolishly he had assumed Ronnie's desire to live would outweigh his greed. What he hadn't counted on was that for Ronnie, a life without money was no life at all. Now because of his avarice and Beauregard's hubris, Kelvin was dead.

Beauregard closed his eyes. He had to get up and he had to get moving. Kia and the boys were in the crosshairs of a movie-loving hillbilly psycho. A hillbilly who expected a van full of precious metal to be delivered to him no later than Sunday night. His inside man would tell him that the van never made it. Lazy would then sit and wait for a phone call that was never going to come. Lazy would surmise they had double-crossed him. He'd send shit-kicking Freddy Krueger after him. Ariel was safe because they didn't know about her. But Kia and the boys had to get out of town. Beauregard reached in his pocket. He pulled out the burner phone. It was broken. Probably crushed in the fall.

"Shit," he croaked.

He'd have to climb back up the hill. The van would be long gone. He'd left the keys in the ignition. Another mistake. The pickup and the box truck would still be there though. Ronnie probably had the keys to the box truck. That was okay. He could hot-wire the truck. Or he could get the keys out of Kelvin's pocket and drive the pickup truck.

Grief as strong as an earthquake hit him, sending tremors throughout his whole body. He felt his esophagus spasm but his stomach had nothing left to give so he just dry-heaved. Groaning, Beauregard smacked himself. Hard. After a few seconds he did it again. The tremors began to subside. He rotated onto his hands and knees. Taking a deep breath, he pushed himself to his feet. The world around him shimmered like he was walking through a wall of water. Beauregard closed his eyes and steadied himself. One more deep breath and he began climbing up the embankment. Each step was like walking through molasses. He stumbled, caught himself and kept going. The closer he got to the top the slower he climbed. He knew what was waiting for him up there. He knew what he would see once he scaled this nondescript North Carolina hill. But he had to see it. Not just because he needed a set of keys.

He deserved it. Deserved to be confronted with the blank emptiness that would be etched on what was left of Kelvin's face. So, he climbed. He pulled at saplings and clawed the moist earth and climbed. He marched toward his penance with a grim determination.

Kelvin's dead eyes greeted him as he reached the top of the hill. His head lolled to one side and his mouth was agape. The wound in his cheek was a raw red crater. Beauregard could see jagged remains of Kelvin's teeth through the hole.

Beauregard dropped to the ground next to Kelvin's body. Ants were crawling across his face. Some trundled in and out of his open mouth. Beauregard grabbed his hand. It was like touching a piece of hard cold wax. Kelvin's fingers were rigid as stone. Beauregard tried to brush the ants off his face but his hands started to shake. He shook his head and steadied himself. The ants he cleaned off climbed back on Kelvin's face with the pitiless proficiency of a hive mind. Beauregard tried to close his remaining good eye but the lid refused to stay down. He lowered his head until it was lying on Kelvin's chest. The fetid aroma of fresh death was so potent he could taste it. He swallowed it down and dared his stomach to rebel.

"Once I take care of all this I'm gonna come back and bury you right. I promise you that. You should've never been here. You never owed me a damn thing," Beauregard mumbled into Kelvin's chest. A few moments passed. Beauregard's mind played him scenes from the past like a home movie spliced together from old 8-millimeter reels. Kelvin and him as kids souping up their bicycles with playing cards stuck in the spokes to replicate the sound of a motorcycle. Kelvin daring him to drive without lights through Callis Road knowing damn well Bug would do it. Kelvin in a tuxedo handing him a ring. Those moments and a thousand more like them slit his soul like razors and flayed it open.

Finally, Beauregard raised his head. He touched his face. The blood, Kelvin's blood, the driver's blood, was still dry in the corners of his eyes. He hadn't cried. He hated himself a little for that but there would be time for tears later. He reached into Kelvin's front pocket for the keys. He moved over the ground on his hands and knees turning over the soil searching for his gun. He found it a foot from where he and the driver had tumbled to the ground. He put it back in his waistband and slid down the other side of the embankment. As soon as he reached the meadow he saw how the box truck and the pickup were both listing to one side. Both sets of tires on the driver's side had been slashed.

"You think you slick, don't you, Ronnie?" Beauregard said.

When they had scoped out the rendezvous spot Beauregard had noticed a few houses up the road a piece. A few trailers and some single-story ranchers. Most of the homes had cars sitting in the driveway. A few of them even had garages.

Red Hill was six hours away. Depending on what kind of vehicle he boosted and how much fuel was in it, he could make it and only have to stop once for gas. He had a little over $200 in cash on him. That had him hitting Red Hill around eight, give or take an hour. He could have Kia and the boys out of town by nine. Boonie could patch up his wounds. Then he could deal with Mr. Ronnie Sessions and Mr. Lazy Mothersbaugh.

Beauregard walked across the meadow. He slipped among the pines like a wraith and headed north.

There was a paucity of cars on the road as Ronnie crossed the state line into Virginia. Reggie had reclined the seat and drifted off to sleep. He hadn't spoken a word since they had come down off the hill.

"Hey, you hungry?" he asked Reggie.

"No," Reggie said.

"You gonna be like this all day?"

"Like what?"

"Sitting there like the goddamn Sphinx."

"I just keep thinking about that day we went by Bug's house when he pulled a gun on you. Put the barrel right up against your guts. He was willing to kill you in front of his wife and kids for coming by his house without calling. I keep wondering what he gonna do to us for killing his homeboy," Reggie said.

"First, if I had known you was gonna keep talking that shit, I wouldn't have said nothing to you. Second, Beauregard is dead," Ronnie said.

"You sure he dead? Did you go down that hill and make sure his neck was broke? Oh, wait, I know the answer to that," Reggie said.

"You know what? Shut up. Go back to sleep," Ronnie said.

Reggie shifted in the seat and turned his head to the door. Ronnie pushed a button on the radio, but nothing happened. He stared straight ahead trying to ignore what Reggie had said.

"I got him. I know I got him."

Reggie started laughing.

"Oh, you know you got him? Do you? I'll tell you what I know. I know that you double-crossing Bug and that Lazy guy done killed us. You know that, right? You've fucking killed us. Bug is gonna come for us. He'll come for us and he'll kill us like cockroaches. And if he don't, then Lazy and his boys will. We are so fucking fucked," Reggie said. He crossed his arms and stared out the window.

"Reggie, that's not going to happen. Trust me."

"Trust you? Quan trusted you. Kelvin trusted you. Bug trusted you. Shit, Jenny trusted you. How'd that turn out for them?" Reggie said. Ronnie put his hand on Reggie's knee.

"They weren't my brother. Look, even if I didn't get him he probably broke his neck rolling down that hill."

"You always say trust you but you always just making shit up as you go along," Reggie said in a voice as placid as a frozen lake.

"Did you want to go back to being poor white trash? Huh? This van is carrying twenty-eight rolls of platinum. Bug said every roll is ten pounds. Even if we get fifty cents on the dollar that's enough money to get us out of Virginia and set up somewhere where every road ends up at the beach," Ronnie said. Reggie didn't respond.

"He was going to give it all away, Reggie. All of it. Three million dollars' worth of second chances just gone," Ronnie said. Reggie moved Ronnie's hand off his knee.

"We always gonna be trash, Ronnie. Money ain't gonna change that," Reggie said. Ronnie opened his mouth to offer a rebuttal to Reggie's assertion but none was forthcoming. The truth had a strange way of ending an argument.

They drove in silence for a few miles. Ronnie opened his mouth to say something to get Reggie's mind off their current situation when the burner phone started vibrating in his pocket. Ronnie almost ran off the side of the road. Why were they calling so soon? He checked his watch. It was a little after five in the morning.

"That's them, ain't it?" Reggie asked.

"Nah, it's *Who Wants to Be a Millionaire*," Ronnie said. Sweat spilled across his forehead like an oil slick.

"You better answer it."

"Shut up, just let me think, okay?" Ronnie said. The phone continued to vibrate. Ronnie drummed his fingers on the steering wheel. The phone stopped vibrating. Then almost immediately it started again. Finally, Ronnie reached in his pocket and answered it.

"Hey."

"Rock and Roll. I thought you was ignoring me. You almost hurt my feelings. Where's the van? My man say Shade is pretty pissed it didn't make it to Winston-Salem. He asking the boys that was guarding it what happened but he don't much like they answers. He pulling they teeth out until he gets some answers he do like." Lazy chuckled. "Now I've gotta say, you boys keep impressing me, but weren't you supposed to call me when the deal was done? I thought we had an understanding," Lazy said. Ronnie let that last sentence hang in the air for a beat before he answered.

"Here's the thing. That fella Beauregard? He stole the van."

"I know that. That's what I told y'all to do," Lazy said.

"No, you don't understand. We had the van and then him and some fella he had with him turned on me and my brother. He shot at us and took off with the van," Ronnie said. There was a heavy quietness that carried a weight through the cellular network. It seemed to make the phone cumbersome.

"Where you at, boy?" Lazy said. He spoke with a deep deliberate articulation.

"Me? I'm about forty-five minutes from my place. He left one of the vehicles we used behind. I guess that was lucky for us," Ronnie said. A line of cars passed him like he was standing still. He checked the speedometer. He was doing 70. The van was rattling like a washing machine full of bricks.

"Alright. You get to your place, you stay put. We gonna come out there. See if we can figure out where this old boy done run off to," Lazy said.

The line went dead.

"Why'd you tell them we were going home?" Reggie said.

"To buy us some time."

"We gotta go home eventually."

"No, we don't. We going to see your girlfriend out at Wonderland. I got a guy who can sell this shit, I just can't run up on him without calling first. We just need a few more hours," Ronnie said.

"She don't particularly care for you," Reggie said.

"I don't give a fuck. As long as she don't eat me, we be alright," Ronnie said.

Lazy put the phone down on his desk. Billy finished with a customer in the front of the store, then walked into the back office.

"Rock and Roll says that boy Beauregard took off with the truck," Lazy said.

"How you want to handle this?" Billy asked.

Lazy pulled out a pipe and filled it with a pungent wad of apple-flavored tobacco. "Call the boys you got watching they places. When Ronnie and his brother show up, bring 'em back here. Get Beauregard's people too. If he did run off with the van, he gonna try to warn his wife. We get her back here, he'll bring us the van. If he got it," Lazy said.

"If he got it? "Billy said.

Lazy lit his pipe and took a deep drag. "He might done run off with it. But he struck me as smarter than that. He also might be lying face down in a ditch and that Sessions boy might have it. Either way, we gonna figure it out. We might have to roast a few marshmallows over them, but we'll figure it out," Lazy said as he exhaled a bluish plume of smoke.

TWENTY-SEVEN

Beauregard pulled into the rest stop with the Jeep hidden inside a cloud.

Steam was pouring from under the hood and enveloping the entire vehicle. He had just crossed the state line back into Virginia. The clock on the radio said it was nine in the morning. The needle on the temperature gauge was so far in the red, it needed to file for bankruptcy. Beauregard parked the Jeep and killed the engine. He checked the rearview mirror before he got out of the car. The cramped single-wide he'd broken into had a surprisingly well-stocked medicine cabinet. Large and small bandages, peroxide, rubbing alcohol and some aspirin. The long-sleeve black shirt he had taken was too big for him and the pants were too long, but they would do for now. The Jeep had been a gamble from the start. A rust-covered relic with a severe oil leak and two bald tires in the front. It looked like a leftover prop from some apocalyptic movie.

Still, it had made it all the way to Sussex before it started giving up the ghost. Beauregard got out and popped the hood. More steam swirled around his head. The sickeningly sweet smell of antifreeze filled his nose. Beauregard waved away the steam. On the side of the radiator, he saw a plume of steam coming from a pin-sized hole. Beauregard looked around the rest stop. It was one of the larger ones on the interstate. A line of picnic benches sat under some huge oak trees. A brick building housed the bathrooms, snack machines and an information desk. Beauregard headed for the picnic tables.

The first three were bare. Nothing on the tables and nothing on the ground under them. It was just his luck to pull up to a rest stop with a fastidious cleaning crew. The fourth table was occupied by an Asian family eating their breakfast. Beauregard tried to put on a smile when he approached them.

"Excuse me."

The father appraised him with a wary stare.

"I hate to bother you, but do you folks happen to have some pepper?"

The father conferred with the mother silently. The looks they exchanged seemed to acknowledge that pepper was not a deadly weapon that could be used against them. The two children, a boy and a girl, both under ten, reached into their fast food bags and pulled out several pepper packets. The mother gathered them up and handed them to Beauregard.

"Are you eating breakfast too?" the little girl asked.

Beauregard smiled. "No, my car is running hot because the radiator is leaking. Some pepper will fix the hole for a little while," he said. She nodded her head as if she discussed emergency car repair every day.

"What happened to your face?" the boy asked. His mother shushed him.

"An accident," Beauregard said. He stuffed the pepper packets in his pocket.

"Thank you," he said. He headed back to the Jeep. Halfway there he stopped and turned around. "Say, you folks don't have a phone, do you?"

Kia was pouring milk for Darren's cereal when she heard the knocking at the door. Javon was still in bed. He'd been up all night drawing while she and Darren had watched a marathon of animated movies. She finished pouring the milk and slid Darren his bowl.

"Eat your breakfast," she said. She got up and started for the door. As she went to answer the door, her cell phone started chirping. Kia stopped and turned toward the bedroom. Then she looked back toward the door. The cell phone stopped chirping. She continued to the door.

"Mama, you forgot the cereal," Darren said. She barely heard him. She peeked through the diamond-shaped window in the center of the door. There was a white man standing on the porch. Two more white men were standing next to a late model LTD. The one on the porch was as big as her refrigerator. The other two were considerably smaller. The man on the porch was wearing a white button-down shirt and jeans. The two by the car were both wearing T-shirts and jeans. One had on a faded CAT baseball hat.

She opened the door a crack.

"Can I help you?"

The big man wrenched the door from her grasp. She stood in the doorway wearing one of Beauregard's T-shirts and sweat shorts. She was painfully aware of how they clung to her ass.

"You married to a boy named Beauregard?" the big man asked.

"Why? What's going on?" she asked.

The big man gave her the once-over. "Get your boys, y'all gotta come with us," he said.

"I ain't going nowhere with you and neither are my boys. Now tell me what the hell is going on," Kia said.

The big man turned to the two leaning against the car and beckoned them. Without warning, he grabbed Kia's arm and started dragging her out of the house. He moved with such astonishing speed, she was on the first step before she started fighting back. She scratched at his eyes and kicked at his balls. She got one grunt for her trouble. The white boy in the CAT hat brushed by them. Her heart shattered when she heard Darren start to scream.

"Mommy! Mommy! Mommy!" he howled as the CAT-wearing man dragged him out of the house by his thin arm. The third man went into the house as Kia and Darren were being forcibly walked to the car. Kia twisted and fought with everything she had in her, but it was no use. It was like trying to wrestle a mountain.

The big man stopped dragging her. He pulled her close and put his forearm around her neck. She felt something cold and hard against her temple. No one was moving. Kia craned her eyes toward the house. The third man was backing out of the house with his hands up. When he got to the bottom step he stopped.

Javon was standing on the porch holding a gun. It was a Beretta 9 mm 92 series. One of his father's guns.

The big man gripped Kia tighter.

"Now you just wanna hold on a minute and put that gun down. You don't want nobody to get hurt now, do you?" he asked.

Javon didn't move. He held the gun straight with his free hand bracing his wrist. "No, I don't. So, let my mama and my brother go," he said. He didn't stutter or whisper. He spoke with a loud, clear voice that was on the verge of changing.

"Look, son, you don't know what to do with that," the man said.

Javon never took his eyes off the big man. He clicked the safety off.

"Let my mama and my brother go," he said.

The big man was still trying to make up his mind how to handle this situation when CAT Hat raised his gun and mumbled under his breath.

"Fuck this shit."

Javon pointed the gun in his direction and pulled the trigger. The pistol jumped in his hand like it was alive. The man in the CAT dropped to a crouch. The bullet zipped over his head and shattered the headlight of the LTD. Javon kept pulling the trigger. He moved from the man in the hat to the man standing right in front of him. A red flower bloomed on the man's chest as he fell like a marionette whose strings had been clipped. He never even reached for his gun.

The big man pulled his gun away from Kia's head and pointed it at Javon. As soon as he did a bullet slammed into his neck. He pulled the trigger reflexively but without aiming. CAT Hat dived to the ground and crawled back toward the driver's side of the LTD. He raised his gun and fired over the hood.

The big man staggered back to the LTD. His gun slipped from his grip and landed in the grass. He fell into the car with his legs still hanging out of the door. CAT Hat jumped in the driver's seat. He started the car and pulled at the big man's shirt, dragging him further into the car. Bullets cracked the windshield as he put the car in reverse. The big man's feet dragged across the ground as they backed out of the yard and tore down the lane.

Javon kept pulling the trigger even though no more bullets came out of the gun.

"Javon!" Kia screamed.

"Javon, call 911!"

Javon kept pulling the trigger.

"Javon, call 911!" she screamed. Her eyes were bugging from her head. Her face and chest were covered with streaks of red. She was clutching Darren in her arms. It was then that Javon finally understood. He ran inside the house and went to his mama's bedroom. Her cell phone was on the nightstand. He dropped the gun to the floor. He grabbed the phone and dialed 911. His mother's screams echoed throughout the house.

"911, what is your emergency," a robotic voice asked.

"Somebody shot my brother," Javon said. He dropped the gun and started screaming too.

Kia sat in the waiting room directly under a television that was showing an advertisement for the hospital on a loop. The light from the fluorescent fixtures reflected off the white floor tiles. It was giving her a headache. Her eyes were stinging. She had cried all the way from the house to the emergency room. They wouldn't let her sit in the back with Darren. She stared at him the whole way to the hospital through a small window in the cab of the ambulance. The driver had tried to get her to put on her seat belt, but she ignored him. She had to keep her eyes on him. If she kept looking at him, then he couldn't die. She told herself that as they careened down the road. As long as she could see him, he wouldn't die.

Kia put her head in her hands. Her chest was a nest of knots that were continually tightening. Jean rubbed her back as she stared at the floor through splayed fingers. He was only eight years old. Eight-year-olds aren't supposed to die. They're supposed to make stupid jokes and refuse to wash off a fake tattoo their brother gave them.

"Kia."

She raised her head. Beauregard was running through the waiting room. He was calling her name. Not screaming it but using the full force of his deep baritone voice. When he came around the corner, he stopped five feet away from her. He looked like Hell warmed over. The left side of his face was one huge angry bruise. He had on a long-sleeve black Lynyrd Skynyrd shirt two sizes too big. A pair of oversized pants hung from his frame.

"Kia. What did they say?" he asked.

She glared at him. "You not even gonna ask what happened?" Kia asked.

Beauregard dropped his eyes. "I went to the house. I saw the bullet holes. I went next door. Linda told me. The car broke down. I would have been there, but the car broke down," he said. She could barely hear him.

"Men came to our house. Men that were looking for you," Kia said. She rose from her seat.

"I know. I tried to call but you didn't answer," Beauregard said.

"Don't do that. Don't you do that. If you hadn't gone off with that white boy pulling some goddamn job, you wouldn't have had to call," Kia said. She spoke through bared teeth.

"Kia. Let's go outside and talk," Beauregard said.

"Talk about what, Beauregard? About how you fucked around with some gangsters and they came to our fucking house? You wanna talk about how I told you to sell that goddamned car? But you wouldn't do it, would you? Because you didn't want to get rid of your dear Daddy's car. My son is on an operating table fighting for his life because you care more about a dead snitch than you do your own children. My other son is down at the police station because he had to shoot two people to keep them from taking his mama and his little brother. Do you get that, motherfucker? My son had to kill somebody today. But I guess you think that's alright. It's a Montage family tradition, right?"

Beauregard knew she was trying to hurt him. The only person who knew your weak spots better than the woman who raised you was the woman who shared your bed. But he took it. Took it like he had never taken it before because she was right. He had brought this horror down upon his family. But that didn't mean he didn't love them.

"They my sons too, Kia," Beauregard said.

Kia stepped forward and slapped him. Her tiny hand caught him flush on his bruised cheek. Flashing lights appeared in front of his face. For a moment he felt something cold and alien bloom in his chest. He raised his right hand and curled it into a fist but only for a split second. He deserved that. That and so much more.

"Not today they ain't. Today they my sons and I've got to protect them. Protect them from people like you," Kia said. She pressed her body against his. Her limbs felt like steel wires. Her breath smelled of smoke and stomach acid.

"Kia, I'm not people. I'm their father."

"Go," she said.

"The car broke down. I would have been here, but the car broke down."

"GOOOOO!" she shrieked. She pounded on his chest with her

fists. When he tried to put his arms around her, she recoiled like he had the plague.

"GET THE FUCK OUT!"

"No, Kia please," he said as he reached for her. She shrieked again. A raw guttural howl with no discernible words but in a language that was clearly understood.

Jean got up and pulled her into her bosom. Kia went limp in her sister's arms. Jean guided her back to her seat.

"Beauregard, just go. I'll call you when we hear something," Jean said.

He turned around in a near perfect 360-degree circle. The intake clerks, the nurses, the janitors, other patients, they were all gawking at them.

"The car broke down. I would have been here, but the car broke down. I fixed it and I came straight to the house. I fixed it," he said under his breath. He said it again as he headed for the sliding glass doors. And again, as he walked toward the rust-covered Jeep sitting in the parking lot with a screwdriver jammed in the ignition. Beauregard got in and slammed the door. He began to scream and pounded his palms against the steering wheel. Every muscle in his body worked in concert with his diaphragm. His chest began to ache as he arched his back and howled. People walking across the parking lot lowered their heads and looked away as they hurried past the Jeep. The sound coming from that battered vehicle needed no explanation or translation.

It was the pure and unmistakable sound of despair.

TWENTY-EIGHT

Boonie unlocked the door to his house with one hand while balancing a six pack in the crook of his free arm. The sky was filled with streaks of magenta as the sun dipped below the horizon. As he stepped across the threshold, his guts jumped up into his mouth.

Beauregard was sitting in his leather recliner.

"Jesus, boy, you scared the shit out of me. What the hell are you doing in here?" Boonie asked.

Beauregard raised his head. "I fucked up, Boonie," he said.

Boonie closed the door and got a good look at him.

"What the hell happened to your face?"

"You was right. About Ronnie, about everything," Beauregard said.

Boonie sat down on the couch that was perpendicular to the recliner. "Talk to me," he said.

Beauregard gingerly ran his hand over his forehead. He told Boonie everything. The jewelry store, Lazy, the van, Kelvin, everything right up to what happened to Darren. Boonie listened quietly, never once interrupting or asking any questions. When Beauregard was done, Boonie got up, went into the kitchen and returned with a mason jar. He unscrewed the top, took a sip, and sat it on the coffee table between them.

"I'm so sorry, Bug. What you want us to do?" Boonie asked.

Beauregard turned his head and leaned his good cheek against the side of the chair. The surface was cool. Boonie's central air unit was working overtime.

"You know, I used to think of myself as two people. Sometimes I was Bug and sometimes I was Beauregard. Beauregard had a wife and children. He ran a business and went to school plays. Bug . . . well, Bug, he robbed banks and armored cars. He drove 100 miles per hour on hairpin curves. Bug threw the people who killed his cousin in a car crusher. I tried to keep them apart, Beauregard and Bug. But my Daddy was right. You can't be two types of beasts. Eventually one of the beasts gets loose and wrecks shop. Rips shit all to Hell," he said.

He grabbed the mason jar and tossed it back. When he sat it down, nearly half of its contents were gone. Tears leaked from the corners of his eyes.

"They shot my boy, Boonie. They shot my boy because Bug fucked up and Beauregard wasn't there to fix it."

"We gonna fix it, Bug. You just tell me what you want us to do," Boonie said.

Beauregard sat forward. "I'm gonna fix it. I might need a few favors."

"Anything," Boonie said.

"I parked up the road back down by that old house on Carver's Lane. I need to get that car to the yard and get rid of it. Then I'm needing to borrow a vehicle. Can't make no moves in my truck."

"Okay, no problem. But what we gonna do about this Ronnie and Lazy situation?" Boonie asked, his voice full of malice.

Beauregard smiled. It didn't go much farther than the edge of his mouth. "We ain't gonna do nothing. I'm gonna find Ronnie and get that van back. There's only two places he could be. He can't just roll up on somebody to move that much swag. The way he moved them diamonds, I know he got a connection, but it'll take a couple of days to set up a deal. I don't think he's dumb enough to be at his house.

So that leaves Wonderland. Once I get the van back, I'm gonna call up Mr. Lazy."

Boonie grunted.

"You can't go up against these boys by yourself. Them fools up at Wonderland ain't shit, but this Lazy fella is bad news."

"I already got Kelvin killed."

"And I ain't gonna let you get killed. Anthony was like a brother to me, but you done become like a son. I can't just let you go out here all alone like you some fucking cowboy. Your family needs you. Hell, I need ya, you stubborn son of a bitch," Boonie said.

Beauregard leaned forward and stared in Boonie's eyes.

"I'm already gone, Boonie. I know what you think my family needs, but I'm gonna tell you what I need. I need for you to do for my sons what you did for me. Be there. I think I understand why Daddy left now. Beauregard and Bug are the same person. And that person ain't no good for a family."

Boonie snatched off his cap and slapped it against his knee. "Stop talking that crazy shit. You they father. You're Kia's husband. They need you. You leave, and you make the same mistake Anthony made," Boonie said. Spittle flew from his lips.

Beauregard stood. Boonie stood as well although it took him a bit longer to get to his feet. He jammed his stained cap back on his head.

"You don't want to help me then I'll go," he said.

Boonie crossed his arms. "I would do anything for you. You know that. But I saw what Anthony leaving did to your Mama. What it did to you. I know he thought he was making the right decision, just like you do. But you were both wrong. Bug, look around. You the closest thing I got to family these days. Don't do this," Boonie said.

"This thing inside us. This thing in me. The thing that was in my Daddy. It's like cancer. It gotta end with me, Boonie. Kia ain't like my Mama. They won't grow up fucked-up like I did. Javon ain't going to juvie. He'll get off with self-defense. And if Darren pulls through . . ." Beauregard swallowed hard. "When Darren pulls through, he and his brother and his sister are going to grow up and get out of Red Hill. They are going to go to college and fall in love. Have kids of their own. But the only way any of that happens is if I get ahold of Ronnie and Lazy. Now if you can help, I appreciate it. If you can't, then get out the way. I'd appreciate that too," Beauregard said.

Boonie breathed deeply through his mouth. His eyes moved past Beauregard to the wall behind the recliner. There were old photos in cheap frames on the wall. Boonie and his wife. The first day at the scrap yard. Him and Anthony posing next to Boonie's '67 Mercury Comet. His eyes moved back to Beauregard.

"Let's go move the car. Then we can get straight on everything else," Boonie said.

"Hey, Mama," Beauregard said.

His mother trembled as her eyelids quivered. They rose slowly and Beauregard could see her mind working as she struggled to focus.

"You look like hell," she said finally.

Beauregard chuckled. "I know."

"What time is it?"

"A little after nine."

"They let you in after visiting hours?"

"I didn't give them much of a choice."

Ella gave him a long sideways glance.

"What's wrong? Did they tell you I only had a week left?"

"No. Hey Mama, you remember that time we picked all them blackberries out back of the trailer? We must have picked a gallon. Daddy came by later, brought me that knockoff G.I. Joe action figure. I think it was called Action Man or something? He stopped by with that and he helped us pick some of the blackberries. Then we went inside, and you made that cobbler. Remember that?"

"They must have told you I'm gonna die in an hour," Ella said. Beauregard threw his head back and laughed. Ella shivered.

"God, you sound like your Daddy," Ella said. Beauregard stopped laughing.

"Nah. I was just thinking. It wasn't always bad. You know with you and me and Daddy. That day was nice. Wasn't often we got to act like that."

"Like what?"

"A family," Beauregard said.

Ella stared straight ahead.

"You running, ain't ya?" she said.

"Now why you say that?"

"Mothers know their children."

"I'm not running. I just gotta take care of some things."

"Huh. That's what he used to say. Then one day something took care of him."

Beauregard got out of his chair. He went to his mother's bedside. He leaned over the railing and kissed her on her forehead.

"You can be as mean as a rattlesnake dipped in arsenic sometimes, but you're my Mama and I love you," he said into her ear. "I don't expect you to say it back." He gently ran his hand over her brow before heading for the door. Ella watched him walk out and turn down the hall. She licked her dry lips.

"Goodbye, Bug," she whispered.

TWENTY-NINE

Reggie took another hit. He hadn't done coke in a long time. He preferred the languid honey-drip high a taste of heroin provided. However, beggars couldn't be choosers. Ann had coke, so he did coke. As soon as it hit his bloodstream, he remembered why he didn't like it. Every inch of his skin increased in tactility by a thousand percent. Even the strands of his hair seemed to be receiving sensory input. Ann took the vial from him and poured out a thin line on the back of her hand. She snorted and immediately started rubbing her nose vigorously.

"Goddamn Almighty! That shit is potent," she said.

"Uh huh," Reggie said. His heart was Irish clog hopping in his chest.

"Come on. Let's do something. Coke makes me horny."

"What, you hungry?" Reggie asked.

Ann crinkled her nose and grabbed his crotch.

"No, I'm HORNY. We can eat after," she cooed.

Reggie let her pull him on top of her. As he was letting her slide his pants down, he heard a commotion out front. That wasn't unusual. Wonderland was nothing but one long commotion with momentary respites of peace and quiet.

Whenever Beauregard came up to Wonderland, he marveled at how the name had stuck. He couldn't believe any of the inbred zombie tweakers that hung out up here understood the concept of sarcasm. To them, it really was a Wonderland. Beauregard thought a better name would be "Lost All Hope Land" or "Crabs and Syphilis Land." Secreted deep in the rolling hills of Caroline County at the end of an oddly scenic drive, Wonderland was an oasis of sorts. A collection of four double-wide trailers connected to form a two-legged T near a picturesque lake. Wonderland's pastoral location was at odds with the entertainment it provided. You could indulge a wide variety of vices at Wonderland. The ones that were the most popular were the old favorites. Sex and drugs with a splash of white lightning thrown in for good measure. He hadn't bothered going to Reggie and Ronnie's place. Ronnie was a lying, double-crossing piece of shit but even he wasn't that stupid. He might have thought he'd gotten rid of Bug, but he knew he still had Lazy to contend with. There was no way he'd go back to their trailer. He'd want to go somewhere he felt safe. Somewhere he could relax while he tried to unload the platinum. Somewhere he could celebrate outsmarting both Bug and Lazy.

Wonderland definitely fit the bill.

A menagerie of cars and jacked-up trucks were parked off to the right near the base of the mountain. Reggie's car was parked next to a truck with a Dixie flag in the back window. A honky-tonk standard was blasting out of one of the windows of the mobile home monstrosity. Back in the day, a place like this might be called a shot house. Nowadays, shoot-up house was a more apt description. Beauregard tucked his .45 into his waist and stomped over the moss and grass to the foot of the T where someone had fashioned a crude front door.

A thin man sat on a stool near the door sipping from a flask. He gave Beauregard a long hard look.

"What's up, Hoss?" he asked.

"What up, Skeet," Beauregard said.

Skeet sipped from his flask. "Long time, no see. If you looking for Jimmy, you out of luck. He got picked up. Doing two years in Coldwater for possession with intent," Skeet said.

"Nah, I'm not looking for Jimmy," he said.

A short wide man with a Dixie flag baseball cap and a face like a gravel road ambled over to the door. He was holding a red plastic cup full of liquor. Beauregard took in the scene. The first trailer served as a bar and lounge. A raven-haired beauty named Sam was standing behind a bar made from an old sheet of plywood and some milk crates. Near the bar were five or six ragged beanbag chairs. A few people were splayed across them like dolls. The rest of the denizens were sitting around two different plastic patio tables. A long-haired hipster in khaki shorts and sandals was chatting up Sam near the bar. No one was really paying attention to the naked girl dancing on the stage made from an old high school cafeteria table. A neon Coors sign hung on the wall behind her. It gave her skin a devilish red glow. The rest of the lights were turned down just low enough so that you could still find your crystal meth if you dropped it. A pungent scent filled the air. It was a witch's brew of weed, whiskey and body odor.

"Sam running things now?"

"Might could say that. I mean she is his sister."

"How's that working out?"

Skeet shrugged. "Alright. Most people just go on like Jimmy still here."

"Uh huh. Look, Skeet, where Ronnie and Reggie at? I saw Reggie's car outside."

Skeet's watery brown eyes flicked left to right. He hesitated before answering. "Well, Ronnie left a while ago. Reggie in the back," he said.

"Thanks."

"What you want, boy?" the man in the Dixie hat said. His words came out sideways.

"Nothing," Beauregard said. He moved past the man. Dixie Cap reached out and grabbed his arm. Beauregard looked at the hand on his arm then at the hand's owner.

"Can't we have one place without you poking your head in it? Goddamn, y'all done took over the White House," Dixie Cap said.

"If you don't get your hand off me, I'm gonna feed it to you," Beauregard said.

"Bobby, get on now," Skeet said. He hopped off the stool and removed Bobby's hand from Beauregard's arm. Bobby mumbled something, but Beauregard ignored him. He threaded through the first trailer until he came to the intersection of the T.

Left, or right? Beauregard decided it didn't matter. He had to be in one of the rooms back here. Jimmy Spruill rented rooms at the top of the T an hour at a time. Just in case you wanted to get high in private with your soul mate for the night. Back here Wonderland gave up any pretense of civility. The four trailers attached end-to-end were a smoked-filled Tartarus awash in dying embers and used needles. No one looked up from the belts they were tying off to acknowledge him as he passed. The layout of the bedrooms changed as you moved from one trailer to the next. Sometimes they were on your right, then they were on the left. None of them had doors. Instead they sported beaded curtains or sheets draped over a compression shower rod. When Beauregard peeped in, he wasn't admonished. A few times he even received an invitation to join the festivities.

Reggie was in the last room in the last trailer. His pale white ass was pistoning up and down on top of the big girl that had been at his trailer a few weeks ago. His pants were bunched around his ankles. The woman opened her eyes and stared at Beauregard over Reggie's shoulder.

"Baby," she squeaked.

"So . . . close," Reggie panted.

"Baby, somebody here!" she squealed. Reggie froze in midstroke. Beauregard stepped in the room and grabbed Reggie by the hair. He pulled him off the big girl and slammed him face first into the wall. When he pulled his head back blood was pouring out Reggie's nose and chin. He slammed his face into the wall again. It left a bloody Jackson Pollock painting on the wall.

"Hey, Reggie, pull up your pants, we gotta talk," Beauregard said.

Reggie pulled up his pants as Beauregard held a wad of his hair. After he had covered his narrow ass Beauregard dragged him out of the room. The large woman was struggling to get out of the bed. Her prodigious breasts spilled across her belly like an avalanche.

"You let him go!" she screamed. Beauregard ignored her and dragged Reggie down the hallway. Reggie tried to claw at the walls, but he could find no purchase. Ann finally got up and tossed on a T-shirt. She waddled after Beauregard and Reggie as fast as she could. When Beauregard reached the front lounge area, Skeet hopped off his bar stool.

"Yo Bug, what the hell?" he asked. Bobby jumped up from his beanbag and launched himself at Beauregard and Ronnie. Beauregard figured he'd been spoiling for a fight ever since he'd seen a brown face walk through the door. As Bobby hurtled toward them, Beauregard pulled the .45 out of his waist. He flipped it so that he was holding it by the barrel and slammed the butt into Bobby's mouth and jaw. His Dixie flag baseball cap flew off as his head snapped back. Beauregard herded Reggie to the side as Bobby fell into one of the patio tables. Drinks went flying as the table collapsed under his weight. Beauregard wheeled around with the .45. He panned across the room with the business end.

"Get him!" Ann screamed.

"I'm taking him out of here. Anybody got a problem with that, say something," Beauregard asked. No one spoke. Beauregard backed out the door with Reggie, shirtless and crying, in tow.

"Y'all just gonna sit there? Some friends you are!" Ann screeched.

Sam poured some moonshine out of a large plastic jug into a mason jar and handed it to the hipster. "Can't argue with a .45," she said in her throaty voice.

The men who had been sitting at the demolished table floated over to the bar. Conversations that had been muted returned to their normal volume. The girl onstage stepped down and another skinnier girl took her place. Skeet and a few other guys helped Bobby up and gave him some paper towels for his bloody mouth. After a few minutes, it was like nothing had happened. And for all intents and purposes, nothing had.

Beauregard turned off of Route 301 and navigated the narrow back roads that led out of Caroline County and back to Red Hill. He hugged the white line as he drove down the single-lane road masquerading as a double-lane highway. Reggie lay in the passenger seat with his face pressed against the glass. Neither he nor Beauregard spoke. There was nothing they needed to say.

Beauregard turned onto a gravel-covered road. They passed a cell tower surrounded with bright new chain-link fencing that shimmered in the truck's headlights. Beauregard turned off the gravel road onto a narrow driveway covered in cracked asphalt. The driveway led to a clearing where the remnants of an old factory held court like an ersatz Stonehenge.

"Get out. Don't run. I'll shoot you in the back," Beauregard said.

Reggie climbed out of the truck. He took off running as soon as his feet hit the ground. He headed for the woods surrounding the clearing. Beauregard shot up in the air. Reggie dropped to the ground. Blades of grass scratched his chest. He felt a hand grab him by his hair and pull him to his feet. He let himself be dragged back to the truck. Beauregard pushed him against the passenger door. They locked eyes for a moment.

Beauregard punched him in the stomach. Reggie doubled over, then fell to his knees. He made a wet gagging sound. Beauregard thought Reggie might throw up but he didn't. He made some more gagging sounds then raised his head. Beauregard dropped to his haunches so that they were eye to eye.

"I'm only gonna ask you once. Where is Ronnie?"

"I didn't know. I didn't know about it. I would have never gone along with it," Reggie wheezed.

Beauregard put the .45 in his waistband near the small of his back. He grabbed Reggie's left hand with his own. Using his right hand, he opened the passenger door on the truck. By the time Reggie realized what he was doing it was too late to struggle.

Beauregard gripped Reggie's wrist and forced his hand against the door frame. He slammed the door shut on Reggie's hand.

Reggie's mouth filled with hot stinging bile and this time he did vomit. It dribbled over his loosened teeth and down his shin. He screamed. He kicked his feet. He swallowed some vomit, then threw it up again.

"Where is he, Reggie?" Beauregard asked. A slight breeze moved the grass in the clearing. The blades undulated like waves in a lagoon.

"I . . . don't . . . know," Reggie said.

Beauregard pulled the door back and slammed it on Reggie's hand again. Reggie threw his head back and howled. His eyes widened to the size of silver dollars.

"Don't . . . make me tell. He's my brother. Don't make me tell. You're gonna kill him if I tell," Reggie cried. Fat tears rolled down his cheeks, cutting tracks through the blood on his chin.

"I'm gonna kill you if you don't. They came to my house, Reggie. They shot my son. All because Ronnie couldn't stick to the plan. I don't want to hurt you any more, Reggie. But I will. And I won't stop until you tell me where he is. You pass out and I'll wake you up. Once this hand goes numb, we'll start with the other one. Then we move to your feet. Then your dick. I'll feed you to this truck piece by piece," Beauregard said.

"I'm so sorry. I didn't know what he was gonna do."

'I know you are, Reggie. I know. Where's Ronnie?"

Reggie's Adam's apple bobbed up and down like a fishing lure.

Beauregard pulled the door back.

"Wait!" Reggie begged.

"I don't have time to wait, Reggie."

"Please. He's my brother."

"And Darren is my son."

Neither man said anything. As the seconds ticked by, a dog bayed in the distance.

Reggie hung his head. "He went over to Curran County. Other side of the hills here. Crashed with some girl named Amber Butler. I think she lives off Durant Road. I don't know what he did with the van."

Beauregard stood.

"Alright. Alright," he said. His tone was robotic.

Reggie looked up at him. His eyes were red and rimmed with tears.

"I'm scared, Bug."

Beauregard pulled out the .45.

"Nothing to be scared of, Reggie. Just close your eyes."

Beauregard got back to the salvage yard just before sunrise. A man-sized blue tarp was on the back of the tow truck. The office was locked, but he knew Boonie kept a spare key in an old Pontiac next to the main building. Once he had retrieved the key, he went inside and grabbed another key from the rack to the left of Boonie's desk. He went back outside and grabbed the man-sized tarp off the back of the truck. Beauregard hoisted it up on his shoulders with a deep groan. He stomped around the back of the office and headed for a dilapidated Chevy Cavalier. He used one hand to unlock the trunk with the key he grabbed from the rack. He dropped the blue tarp into the trunk and slammed it shut. Once that was done he went back inside the office and locked the door behind him. He scooped his phone off Boonie's desk as he headed for the couch. He had one text message. It was from Jean, not Kia.

Darren came out of surgery. They got the bullet. Still touch and go.

Beauregard flopped onto the couch. He pressed the phone against his forehead. Darren was finally out of surgery. Darren, who loved to giggle at the absurdity of curse words. They had pulled a bullet out of his baby boy. Beauregard's eyes began to burn. He buried his face in his hands. Sadness and guilt hovered around his heart like buzzards. He wiped his eyes and pushed those feelings away.

They could have his heart when this was over.

THIRTY

Ronnie bent over and lit his cigarette on the burner of Amber's stove. He inhaled deeply and let the smoke fill his lungs. Cancer never tasted so good. He went to the window, pulled the vanes of the blinds down. Nothing. Just darkness. He let the smoke in his lungs billow out of his nostrils. Amber had just left for her shift at the hospital. He'd asked her to cop him a few Percs, but she had blanched at the request.

"Ronnie, I ain't into that no more. I got my RN now. Can't fuck that up."

"Hell, get me the extra-strength aspirin then. I need something," he'd said. He'd take whatever he could get. His nerves were as raw as a bedsore. He'd tried Reggie all day and couldn't get him. His phone wasn't even going to voice mail. Just rang a few times and disconnected. He took another drag on the smoke and let the smoke flow from his nostrils and mouth. Lazy had been blowing up the burner phone so much that it finally ran out of minutes.

Ronnie knocked some ash off his cigarette into the sink. Amber had her own trailer at the end of a long driveway, just like Reggie. The driveway was bordered by a cornfield on one side and a thin grove of walnut trees on the other. Hard for anyone to sneak up on him. Not that anyone should know where he was. Unless they got to Reggie. But Lazy didn't know anything about Wonderland. At least Ronnie didn't think he did. Ronnie inhaled again. He might need to ride up to Wonderland. Grab Reggie and make for the West Coast.

There was nothing in Virginia for them. Not anymore. He couldn't even—

An engine was revving outside in the dark. Ronnie went to the window again. He didn't see any headlights. He ran to his bag and grabbed his gun. He stubbed out the cigarette on the linoleum and cut off all the lights. Breathing hard, he peeped through the blinds. The engine was close. He could almost feel the vibrations as it revved again and again. Ronnie sucked his teeth. Could he make it to his Mustang? It was at least ten steps from the front door to the car. He licked his lips. The engine stopped revving. Now it was a high metallic whine. Ronnie opened the blinds a crack.

"Oh fuck!" he yelled. He ran for the back door.

A wrecker truck was racing toward the trailer with the headlights off. As Ronnie ran through the kitchen, the truck rammed into the trailer. The front wall imploded, showering the interior of the mobile home in glass, metal and wood. The roar of the engine filled the structure. The impact threw Ronnie into the fridge. The door handle caught him in his right side like a kidney punch. He bounced off the fridge and headed for the back door.

Ronnie kicked open the back door and took the rickety wood steps two at a time. He was almost on the ground when someone grabbed the door and slammed it into him. He lost his balance and fell to the ground. The gun leaped from his hand and disappeared into the darkness under the trailer. Ronnie rolled on his back and used both his feet to kick the door back toward whoever had grabbed it.

The door rocketed back into Beauregard's face. He felt something in his nose give way. Blood and snot poured from his nostrils and down his face. A piece of his incisor tumbled down his throat. He stumbled backwards and landed against the back wall of the mobile home. He pushed off and stepped from around the swinging door with the .45 leading the way. He caught a glimpse of Ronnie's form running into the cornfield next to the trailer. Beauregard ran back around to the front of the trailer. When he reached the truck, he removed the crowbar he had wedged against the dash and the gas pedal. He hopped in and jammed the truck into reverse. Backing up, he flicked on the headlights and the running lights. There was only one beam of light on the passenger side illuminating the dark. One of the headlights must have been damaged in the crash. One would have to be good enough. He shifted into first and floored the gas pedal.

Ronnie was leaving a trail in the dry cornstalks a blind man could have followed. The headlight cast animated shadows as the truck bounced over row after row. Ronnie was running straight ahead, leaving broken stalks in his wake. Beauregard shifted into second and closed the gap. Ronnie must have realized the futility of trying to outrun the truck by sticking to a linear route. He slashed to his right. Beauregard figured he was heading back to the main road. Maybe get across the highway into the woods. Or maybe he was just running with no idea where he was going. Terror had a way of making smart men stupid.

Instead of wrenching the steering wheel to the right, Beauregard stood up on the brakes and wrenched it to the left. The back end of the truck skipped across the rows like a stone across the water. Ronnie saw a wave of dirt and cornstalks flying toward him a second before the back of the truck crashed into him and sent him flying like a softball.

Beauregard felt the truck make contact with Ronnie's body. It was like hitting a good-sized buck. He put the truck in neutral and shut off the engine. He grabbed his gun and climbed out. Standing by the truck he heard moaning coming from the west. Beauregard walked through the brittle stalks dried almost to dust from weeks without rain.

Ronnie was lying on his back with his legs twisted into odd angles. Even in the dark, Beauregard could see his jeans were stained. Fluids were leaking out of Ronnie Sessions at an alarming rate. He was trying to scuttle backwards but his arms failed him. Beauregard let the gun dangle at his side. He wiped his nose with the back of his free hand. His own blood looked like oil on his skin.

"Ah Jesus, Bug, I fucked up. I know it. I'm sorry. I think I done broke my legs," Ronnie said. His salt-and-pepper goatee was stained burgundy by the blood bubbling out of his mouth.

"No, you didn't. I broke your legs. And you're not sorry. You just sorry I caught up with you," Beauregard said.

Ronnie took several deep breaths. "I am, Bug. About the job, Kelvin, everything."

Beauregard stepped on Ronnie's shin and let his full weight press down on the shattered bone. A strange sound came out of Ronnie. It was half scream, half strangled groan.

"You don't get to say his name. Are you sorry about my son too? They came to my house, Ronnie. My little boy is laying in a hospital bed fighting for his life. You sorry about that too?" Beauregard said. Ronnie's eyes rolled back in their sockets then focused on Beauregard. Beauregard dropped to his knees beside Ronnie's body. "You just couldn't stick to the fucking plan, could you?"

"I couldn't go back to being poor white trash, Bug. I could take being trash. I just couldn't stand being poor again," Ronnie said.

Beauregard shook his head slowly.

"Where's the van, Ronnie?"

A thought sliced through the fog of pain clouding Ronnie's brain.

"You found Reggie, huh? Did you kill him, Bug? He didn't know what I was gonna do. Did you kill my brother, Bug?" Ronnie asked.

Beauregard didn't say anything. All Ronnie could hear was his own labored breathing. Ronnie blinked his eyes hard three or four times. Tears ran away from the corners of his eyes and sluiced through his crow's feet.

"The van, Ronnie."

"Hey, Bug? Fuck you."

Beauregard shot Ronnie in the left knee. Ronnie opened his mouth wide in a rictus of agony. Beauregard got to his feet.

"That was for Kelvin."

Beauregard shot Ronnie in the other kneecap. Ronnie vomited, choked on it and vomited again. Beauregard pushed Ronnie's head to the left with his foot to clear his airway. He didn't want him to pass out.

"That was for Darren," Beauregard said. "I'm gonna ask you again. Where's the van, Ronnie?"

Ronnie craned his neck to meet Beauregard's gaze. "Why should I tell you, Bug? Ain't ya gonna kill me?" he rasped.

"I can hurt you a lot more before that happens," Beauregard said.

Ronnie closed his eyes. Beauregard could see movement behind his lids like he had entered a REM state. Moments ticked by as Beauregard waited for him to answer.

"I don't have time for this, Ronnie," Beauregard said. He stepped on Ronnie's right knee and ground his heel into the bullet wound just above his patella. Ronnie screeched and sat straight up at the waist like a vampire in a coffin. He pawed at Beauregard's thighs. Beauregard kneed him in the face. Ronnie fell back onto the dirt with his arms outstretched. His fingertips brushed against a few downed cornstalks. When his eyes opened Beauregard could see there was no more fight left in him.

"It's down at my granddad's old place. Crab Thicket Road. Bank owns it, but nobody wants to live out there in the middle of no-fucking-where," Ronnie wheezed. "Jesus, it's a fucked-up world, ain't it, Bug?" he croaked. Blood was flowing freely from his mouth now.

Beauregard turned his head and spit out a globule of blood and saliva. He put his foot on Ronnie's chest and aimed at his head.

"The world's fine, Ronnie. It's us that's fucked up," he said.

Beauregard got back to the salvage yard around midnight. Boonie's truck was still there when he pulled up to the office. Boonie met him as he climbed out of the wrecker. He stood in front of the office door with his hands on his hips as Beauregard pulled a green tarp out of the truck. It tumbled to the ground with an audible thump.

"You find out where the van is?" Boonie asked.

"Yeah," Beauregard said.

Boonie sighed and tugged at his hat.

"We can put him in the Cavalier with his brother. In an hour, they won't be nothing but a big-ass paperweight," Boonie said. He squinted and studied Beauregard's face. He gestured to the busted headlight and the cornstalks stuck in the grill.

"Looks like he didn't give it up easy."

Beauregard caught a glimpse of himself in the driver's-side window.

"I'm glad he didn't," he said.

THIRTY-ONE

"That'll be $87.50, ma'am," Lazy said. He slid two cartons of Marlboro Reds across the counter. The old woman set the bag with her oxygen tank in it on the counter. She pulled a hundred out of the pocket of her yellow polyester pants and handed it to Lazy. As he was counting out her change, he heard a shrill whistle echoing from his office. He handed Mrs. Jackson her change and went into the back office.

The burner phone was ringing and vibrating on his desk.

"Hello?"

"You want the platinum? I got it. You come on down here. Just you and the boy with the scars and somebody to drive the van. It's a little after two. I figure y'all can make it down here by five. After five, I drive the whole fucking thing into a lake," a voice said.

"Is this the missing Mr. Beauregard? I thought Ronnie had this phone."

"He don't need it no more. I'll text you the address," Beauregard said.

Lazy chuckled. "Beau, I don't think you get how this works. You don't give me orders. You don't tell me where to go or what to do. I do the telling, son. If I say bring me the van, you bring me the goddamn van. If I tell you to eat a shit sandwich, you eat the goddamn shit sandwich and ask for a glass of piss to wash it down. That's how things work around here," he said. He heard Beauregard breathing on the other end of the line.

"I don't think you understand. You need this more than I do. And trust me, Lazy, you don't want me coming up that way. You sent men to my house. Threatened my wife. They shot my baby boy. We meeting someplace neutral so we can be quits with this. I come there and I'm likely to kill everything I see. You want the address or not?" Beauregard said.

Lazy squeezed the phone. "Fine. Send it on, boy. We'll have a little conversation when I see you," he said.

"Five o'clock," Beauregard said. The line went dead.

Lazy watched a narrow crack slither across the screen on his phone as he gripped it tight.

Beauregard closed the flip phone and set it on Boonie's desk.

"He going for it?" Boonie asked.

"He ain't got no choice. Shade is kicking his ass. He lost the jewelry store. He needs this," Beauregard said.

"You think this gonna work?" Boonie asked. Beauregard rubbed his wide hands on his thighs. His legs were still sore from the fall. The pain made him wince but it also made him feel sharp.

"I gotta make it work," Beauregard said.

He got up out of his chair. Boonie rose as well. He slipped from behind his desk and stood in front of Beauregard. A second passed, then another and another. The moment stretched on and on until it collapsed under the weight of its own tension. Boonie threw his arms around the bigger man and squeezed him tight. Beauregard squeezed him right back.

"It's alright. Everything's gonna be alright," Boonie said.

"No matter what happens you make sure Kia and Ariel and the boys get what I left 'em," Beauregard murmured against Boonie's cheek.

"Don't you worry about that. Go handle your business, boy," Boonie said.

He let go of Beauregard, stepped back and rubbed his eyes.

Beauregard nodded then headed for the door. He opened it and paused for a moment. The afternoon sun carved an elongated shadow around him.

"I loved my Daddy. But you was a better father to me than he ever could have been," he said. He stepped through the open door and closed it behind him.

Beauregard went to the hospital after he left Boonie's. He headed straight for the ICU department. A tall, gaunt nurse with her chestnut brown hair pulled back into a severe bun was standing at the nurses' station.

"Excuse me, what room is Darren Montage in?" he asked.

The nurse looked up from her clipboard. Her light green eyes were hard. "Only immediate family can see him, sir."

"I'm . . . I'm his father."

"Oh, I see. He's in room 245. He can only have visitors for fifteen minutes," she said. She returned to her clipboard.

Beauregard entered the room like the floor was made of lava. The pungent, antiseptic odor of the hospital was even more concentrated in the ICU. It was like the whole area was dipped in Lysol.

Darren was lying on his back in the middle of the bed. The head of the bed was slightly elevated, letting the overhead lights illuminate his face. It gave him an otherworldly countenance. Beauregard knew he was small. The last time they had taken him to the doctor for a checkup they said he was a bit undersized for his age. In the middle of the hospital bed, hooked up to tubes and machines, he looked positively miniscule. Like one of his action figures. Beauregard approached the bed. He took his son's impossibly tiny hand. It was cool to the touch. The machines beeped and hissed like some Rube Goldberg contraption.

"I never wanted any of this for you. Or your brother or your sister. But I brought it to you. Somebody else might have pulled the trigger, but I did this. I gotta own that. I hope someday you'll know how sorry I am. No matter how things go today, I don't think I'm ever going to see you again, Stink. So, I wanna tell you I love you. A father who really loves his children doesn't do anything to hurt them. He doesn't put them in harm's way. Not on purpose. He ain't an outlaw or a gangsta. It done took me a long time to realize that," Beauregard said.

He leaned over the railing and kissed Darren on his forehead.

"I'm never gonna hurt y'all again," he said.

Ariel was trying on sunglasses when her phone rang. She checked it, didn't recognize the number and hit end. It rang again a few seconds later. It was the same number. She groaned and answered it this time.

"Hello?"

"Hey," Beauregard said.

"Hey. You get a new phone?" she asked.

"Yeah. What you doing?"

"Me and Rip at the mall. What's up?"

"Uh, nothing really. You ain't spending that money, are you?" Beauregard asked.

"No. Me and Rip just hanging out. We both off."

"Oh. Well, I just wanted to tell you something."

"Tell me what?"

Beauregard waved a fly out of his face. The van didn't have any AC anymore, so he had both windows open.

"I love you."

Beauregard heard the indiscernible din of disembodied voices on the phone. The aural flotsam and jetsam of a large American mall. The cacophony of hundreds of footsteps. Everything but his daughter's voice.

"I . . . I love you too, Daddy," she said finally.

"I gotta go, baby," Beauregard said.

"Okay," Ariel said.

The line went dead.

Beauregard put the phone in his pocket. He climbed out of the van cradling the double-barrel shotgun in the crook of his arm. Fluffy cumulus clouds rolled across the sky, obscuring the late afternoon sun. He walked to the front of the van and leaned against the hood as he watched a long black car wind its way down Crab Thicket Road.

THIRTY-TWO

The Caddy came to a stop fifteen feet in front of Beauregard. It idled under the setting sun like some predatory beast growling at its prey. The passenger door opened, and Billy climbed out. Both rear doors opened next. Lazy and a man Beauregard didn't recognize got out and stood beside the car. Lazy was wearing a light tan golf shirt and white pants. His wild hair looked like a woodland creature had made a nest in it. He was grinning at Beauregard. He started to walk forward but Beauregard pointed a shotgun at him.

"That's far enough," he said.

"Well here we are, Bug. This supposed to be a showdown? Like in—"

Beauregard cut him off. "No. No, it's not. It's just me giving you what's yours and you leaving me and mine alone."

Lazy let his tongue slide over his lips.

"Where's Ronnie and Reggie, Beauregard?" Lazy asked.

"Nowhere you gotta worry about," Beauregard said.

"Now see, if that's how you treat your partners, how can I trust you? How do I know you ain't replaced all the platinum with aluminum foil?" Lazy asked.

"Come take a look. Just move slow," Beauregard said.

"Check it out, Burning Man. See if we all gonna go home happy," Lazy said. Beauregard kept the shotgun trained on Billy as he walked backwards. Billy followed him at a relatively safe distance until they reached the back door of the van. Beauregard gestured toward the door with the shotgun. Billy gripped the handle, then looked back at Beauregard, whose slick brown face was unreadable. Billy opened the door while simultaneously jumping backwards.

"You can't blame me for being jumpy," he said. Beauregard didn't acknowledge him. He poked his head around the swinging door. There in the back of the van was a pallet of metal coils five or six levels high. Billy closed the door and walked back to the Caddy. Beauregard followed him, listening to their feet crunch on the dry dead grass. Sweat was pouring down his face but he didn't dare wipe his eyes.

"Well, what you say, Burning Man?" Lazy asked.

"It's in there," he said.

"The keys are in the van," Beauregard said as he began to back away.

"Hold on. I can't just put a member of my family in that van on your word," Lazy said.

"What you saying?" Beauregard asked.

"I'm saying why don't you start the van up for us? Make sure this ain't like the beginning of *Casino*," Lazy said.

Beauregard didn't move.

"Or do you have a little surprise fixed up for us in there, Beauregard?" Lazy asked. A few crows cawed as they flew overhead. The clouds had parted and now the full fury of the sun was bearing down on them.

"Fine," he said. He used one hand to reach through the driver's window and cranked the motor. It came to life with a cough and a sputter, but it finally caught and turned over. It idled as rough as a rock polisher.

"Shit, is it gonna make it down the lane?" Billy asked.

"It'll make it just fine," Beauregard said.

"Alright then. Sal, go on get in and follow us back home," Lazy said.

Beauregard stepped back and to the left. The man Beauregard didn't recognize was wearing a white wife beater and blue jeans at least one size too small. He climbed in the van. "This got AC?" he asked in a squeaky tin whistle voice.

"No," Beauregard said.

Lazy appraised him with his hands on his hips.

"You know this ain't over, right? We gonna see you soon, son," Lazy said. He winked at Beauregard.

"You wanna come for me, then come on. This . . ." He nodded at the van. "Is so that you leave my family out of it. What we got going on is between you and me. Don't worry, I'll be around. But I think you gonna have your hands full with Mr. Shade and his folks for a while," Beauregard said.

"I just might. Don't worry, though, we ain't gonna forget about you," Lazy said. He got back in the car. Billy used his thumb and forefinger to make a shooting motion toward Beauregard as he climbed back in the passenger seat. The driver put the car in gear. He backed up into a clutch of honeysuckle, then turned around and headed down the driveway. Sal followed them. They crept through the brush and over the potholes at a snail's pace.

Lazy pulled out his cell phone.

"When he leaves, follow him. Then grab him and bring him and his family to the store. We gonna make this last over a three-day weekend. Don't fuck around with this boy. Go in there with guns blazing. Don't let him get the drop on you," Lazy said. He ended the call and put the phone back in his pocket.

"You want us to give them some backup?" Billy asked.

"No. We need to get this van back. I got some bills I gotta pay and I want you with me," Lazy said.

"You sure they can handle it?" Billy asked.

"They better," Lazy said. He sat back and gazed at the cedar trees that lined the driveway. Billy turned on the radio. He kept spinning the dial until he found a country song. Not that slick Nashville shit but a real country song with some steel guitars and a whiskey-soaked melody.

Beauregard watched them ease their way down the lane. The setting sun bathed the vehicles in a soft magenta hue. He pulled out a cell phone and brought up the number to the burner Lazy had given Ronnie. He was a practical man not overly enamored with irony. That being said, he thought it was kind of fitting he'd used that phone as the trigger for the bomb.

He'd never made a bomb before, but it wasn't that difficult. In a way, it was like the ignition system in a car. He'd called Madness and received an over-the-phone tutorial. After a quick ride to the hardware store and some experimentation, it was ready. The convoy reached the end of the driveway and paused.

Beauregard pressed send.

The explosion didn't look like a mushroom cloud, but it was still impressive nonetheless. One minute the van was there, the next it was an exponentially expanding ball of fire. Despite the van being a good eighty feet away, the concussive force hit Beauregard like a sledgehammer. His ear popped so hard he thought he might have ruptured his eardrums. He saw the van explode a split second before he heard it. The shotgun was knocked from his hands as he landed on his ass. Luckily it didn't discharge. The world was a twisting piñata that made him nauseous. He closed his eyes and tried to find his equilibrium. Transitioning from his behind to his hands and knees, he heard the sounds of suffering over the roaring of the fire.

They weren't dead. They might be fucked up, but they weren't dead.

An overabundance of saliva was filling his mouth, but he didn't throw up. He took a deep breath and pushed himself off the ground. He shielded his eyes with his hand as he peered through the fire. The back window of the Caddy was gone. The lid of the trunk was bouncing up and down like a stripper on the pole. The bumper was missing in action. It was a testament to American engineering that the car was still moving. It paused for a moment as the driver's door opened and a body was pushed out onto the ground. The door closed and seconds later Beauregard watched as the back wheels kicked up clods of dirt and dead grass as the Caddy sped down Crab Thicket Road.

"Shit," he mumbled. For his first foray into bomb building, the complete annihilation of the van was impressive. However, the van was only half the equation. He'd intended to get the Caddy too. Whatever his intentions had been didn't matter now. He couldn't let them get away.

He scooped up the shotgun and headed to the barn. It sat in the middle of the heather and goldenrod like it had dropped out of the stratosphere. The paint on the doors had faded long ago. There was only the suggestion of crimson on their surface now. Beauregard wrenched the doors apart.

The Duster sat in the shadows of the old barn like a dire wolf in the recesses of a cave. Beauregard tossed the shotgun in the passenger seat. He climbed in and fired up the engine. It roared to life, stirring up the decades of dust in the barn. The duals played a concerto as he shifted it into gear and burst out of the barn. He skirted around the remains of the van, rolled over the body in the grass and hit the blacktop doing 40 mph.

"Get us the fuck out of here!" Lazy screamed. Glass and blood littered the back seat. The lid of the trunk bounced up and down like the mouth of a huge puppet. The car swerved from one side of the road to the other but it never slowed down.

"He can't catch us!" Billy screamed back.

Lazy took a look out what was left of the back window.

The Duster was bearing down on them like 2,000 pounds of thunder and steel.

———

Beauregard closed in on the Caddy, a shark zeroing in on a seal. He shifted into fourth. The front bumper of the Duster kissed the empty space where the bumper used to reside. The Caddy lurched out of his reach. The Caddy's one remaining tail light glowed like the eye of a demon as it braked for an upcoming hairpin curve. Beauregard crushed the brake and the clutch and drifted through the curve right behind the Caddy. As he drifted, he leaned to his left.

The rear window of the Duster shattered. Shards of glass rained down on his back and shoulders. He held onto the steering wheel, but the Duster tried to get away from him. The rear end fishtailed like it was salsa dancing. Beauregard downshifted, regained control, then hit the gas again. He gave the rearview mirror a quick glance. There was a baby blue Mazda chasing him. A man was leaning out the passenger window with a pistol. The three-vehicle car chase turned onto Route 603. An eight-mile straight stretch that bisected Red Hill County. The man in the blue car fired at the Duster again. The passenger-side mirror disappeared.

Beauregard slammed the clutch, hit the brake and shifted into reverse. He then immediately released the clutch, hit the brake again with his left foot, and floored the gas pedal with his right while twisting the steering wheel to the left. All this fancy footwork resulted in the Duster spinning 180 degrees. He was now going backwards at 50 miles per hour facing the Mazda. The driver of the Mazda hit his brakes as he braced for an imminent collision. The passenger was thrown forward, then he fell backwards.

Beauregard grabbed the shotgun with his right hand, transferred it to his left, and wedged the barrels between the side mirror and the door frame. He adjusted his aim to the left and fired both barrels at the blue car. The recoil made the gun jump from his hand. It fell out the window and clattered onto the road.

He'd aimed for the driver, but his shot had gone low and punched a hole in the grill. Steam began to billow from beneath the hood. Moments later the hood popped up like a jack in the box. Beauregard repeated his previous machinations and spun the Duster another 180 degrees. As he was completing his revolution, a trash truck blew past him in the opposite lane, nearly clipping the front of his car. The trash truck swerved to its right just as the blue car drifted into its lane.

Beauregard barely heard the crash in the rapidly receding distance. The ringing in his ears was relentless. He shifted into fifth gear. The Duster's tires clawed at the asphalt. He pulled into the passing lane and pulled alongside the Caddy. He caught a brief glance of Burning Man's ruined face before a minivan forced him to slow down and drift back into the northbound lane. Burning Man's reflexes must have been dulled by the explosion. He fired his gun out the window of the Caddy, missing the Duster entirely and shattering the window of the minivan. The van ran off the side of the road and into the ditch. The landscape changed from dense undeveloped woodlands to wide open fields. Beauregard shifted back up into fifth. He pulled alongside the rear quarter panel. He swung the Duster into the Caddy at over 90 mph.

Billy saw him coming in the rearview mirror. When the Duster slammed into them, it felt as inevitable as the setting of the sun.

That motherfucker sure can drive, he thought.

Beauregard watched as the Caddy fishtailed across the highway. Burning Man tried to maintain but he wasn't a wheelman. He overcorrected, and the Caddy ran off the road, hit the ditch and somersaulted through the air. The Caddy crashed into a fence surrounding a pasture. It rolled a few more times, sending a few cows scampering for cover. It came to rest upside down with the wheels still spinning. Oil and gas were pouring from the hood and spilling across the ground. Beauregard skidded to a stop, backed up and drove down the service driveway next to the pasture. He guided the Duster through the ruined fence.

He stopped a few feet away from the Caddy. He didn't shut it off, just put it in neutral and hit the parking brake. He pulled his .45 from the glove compartment and got out of the car. The cloying scent of engine coolant mixed with the raw, mean aroma that surrounded bovines in the middle of summer. Beauregard trained his .45 on the upside-down driver's door. He took quick shallow breaths as he inched his way to the door. A tanned arm stretched out the window. The hand was lying on top of a cow patty. Beauregard kicked the arm. The rest of the body slipped out of the driver's seat and collapsed in a loose tangle of limbs against the headliner. Burning Man was extinguished.

Beauregard moved to the back seat.

A fusillade of bullets ripped through the rear door. Beauregard felt two sharp scorching pains to his forearm and the lower section of his thigh. It felt like someone had hit him with an incredibly hard, incredibly tiny hammer. A red-hot hammer that burned him to his bones. He stumbled and fell to the ground. He landed on his side. His head and neck were slathered in cow shit. Where was his gun? He must have dropped it. The rear door started to creak open. Beauregard pushed himself off the ground and dragged himself back to the Duster.

Lazy fell out of the back seat. His left arm was twisted like a bread tie. He scrambled to his feet and leaned against the Caddy. He raised a Desert Eagle .380 and scanned the field.

"Where you at, boy? You hiding behind that car? I got you, I think. I heard you squeal, boy. Give me a minute, I'm coming to finish you off. I told you God himself couldn't kill me, how the fuck you thought you was gonna do it?" Lazy screamed. He blinked his eyes. Lights were flashing around his head like fireworks. The .380 was so heavy in his hand. If he wasn't leaning against the car, he felt he might topple over. His adrenaline was beginning to wear off. Pain gnawed at the edge of his perception. Racing up his arm and across his back. That was alright. He could handle pain. Just like he'd handled Beauregard.

He heard the engine of the red car rev up like God screaming at Moses on Mount Sinai. His damaged ears felt like they were bleeding. He saw Bug pop up in the driver's seat. Lazy brought his gun up and started pulling the trigger.

Beauregard ducked down until his chin was on the steering wheel. One bullet punched a hole in his windshield and sailed over his head.

Beauregard slammed the gas pedeal to the floor.

The Duster plowed into Lazy, trapping him between its grill and the rear of the Caddy. The Caddy spun like a merry-go-round as the Duster rammed into it. Lazy disappeared under the front tires. Beauregard felt the car bounce once, then twice. He moved his foot off the gas. He pushed in the clutch, put the car in reverse and backed up. The car bounced once, then twice. Beauregard hit the brake and the Duster stalled.

Beauregard fell back against the headrest. There was numbness in his right leg that was now spreading to his right side. His left forearm was missing a chunk of flesh the size of a quarter. Blood raced down his arm and entwined his fingers. There was a hole in the right leg of his jeans that was weeping red tears. He took a deep breath. The world seemed to be contracting and expanding at the same time. He closed his eyes. He let his hands run over the polished wood grain steering wheel. Along the leather seats. He caressed the 8-ball shifter.

"You ready, Bug?"

Beauregard rolled his head to the right. His father was sitting in the passenger seat. He was wearing the exact same clothes he had been wearing the last time Beauregard saw him. White ribbed tank top under a short-sleeved black button-up shirt. A pack of cigarettes in the breast pocket. He grinned at him.

"Come on, boy. You ready to fly?" his father asked.

"You're not real."

His father blanched. "Boy, what the hell you talking about? Shut up that fool mess and let's go."

Beauregard turned his head and looked straight ahead. He heard sirens coming from the northern end of the county.

"You're not real. You're dead. Probably been that way for a while now. I never stopped loving you, though," he croaked. He closed his eyes again and started the Duster. When he put the car in gear, he opened his eyes and glanced toward his right. The passenger seat was empty. Pushing the gas pedal was agony, but he bore it. Beauregard drove across the pasture. A few cows stared at him as he passed. The Duster turned left onto a dirt lane at the back end of the field. The lane went from red clay to gravel. Beauregard got to the end and turned left onto a narrow blacktop back road. Soon the sirens were just faint horns playing a mournful tune to an audience of beasts.

THIRTY-THREE

Kia entered Darren's room carrying a teddy bear with a GET WELL balloon tied to its arm. The machines that monitored his vitals beeped and hummed as she sat down in the chair near his bed. She placed the teddy bear next to his slight form and took his tiny hand in hers.

"He's gonna make it," Beauregard said.

Kia didn't turn her head to look at him. She didn't even acknowledge him. Beauregard was standing in the far corner of the room. The glare from the fluorescent light over Darren's bed gave his son a ghostly countenance. He moved from the shadows and pulled up a chair to the opposite side of Darren's bed. The steady pulse of the EKG was comforting to him. It meant his son's heart was still beating. Seconds turned to minutes and neither of them made a sound.

"You were right. I should have sold the car," Beauregard said finally. Kia swallowed hard and wiped her eyes.

"You ain't never gonna sell that car," she said.

"You're right. I told Boonie to crush it," he said. Kia looked at him then.

"What do you mean, 'crush it'?"

"I told him to get rid of it," Beauregard said. Darren's eyes were closed but his lids twitched. Quick spasmodic movements that teased Beauregard's heart with the possibility of seeing his son open his eyes.

"I don't believe that," Kia said.

"You don't have to. It's getting done though. Probably happening right now," Beauregard said.

"Why would you do that to the Duster? You love that car," Kia said. Beauregard interlaced his fingers and stared at the dull lino-leum floor.

"The men that came by the house, they won't be coming back," Beauregard said.

"You don't know that."

"Yes, I do."

Kia looked at him then. She made a noise that was halfway be-tween a sob and a laugh.

"So, you took care of it," she said. Beauregard rose from the chair. He went to the window and stared out across the hospital parking lot. The setting sun was an orange beacon in the hazy sky.

"A man can't be two types of beast," Beauregard said.

"What the hell do that mean, Bug?" Kia asked. Beauregard let his head hang.

"When my Daddy ran off, I felt like somebody had put my heart in a vise and kept tightening that motherfucker till they arm got tired. It ruined me. And my Mama, she couldn't help because she felt like him leaving her was worse than him leaving us. I can't say I blame her really. My Daddy was the kind of man who left a big hole behind. It was easy for her to fill that hole with hurt," Beauregard said. He turned and faced Kia. She saw his eyes were rimmed in red.

"I couldn't do that. I just couldn't let myself hate him. So, I made him into my hero. I pretended that he wasn't a gangsta or a drunk or a bad husband or a bad father. I got out and I fixed that Duster up. I'd ride around and I'd tell myself that even if he was all those things it didn't matter because he loved me. But it does matter. It matters a lot. If your Daddy is the kind of man that can run people down with a car or shoot 'em in the face, it matters a whole hell of a lot. And there's not enough love in the world to change that," Beauregard said.

"Bug, you ain't your Daddy," Kia said. Tears danced on the edges of her eyes.

"You're right. I'm worse. My Daddy never lied about who or what he was. He owned it. I was the one who put him on a pedestal. He never climbed up there. But me? I lied all the time. I lied to you. I lied to myself. I thought I could be an outlaw part of the time and the rest of the time be a daddy and a husband. That was the lie. Truth is I'm an outlaw all the time. I was playing at being a good man," Beauregard said.

"What am I supposed to do with that, Bug, huh? You want to me to make you feel better? Tell you never mind what's happened, you are a good father and a good husband? Because I can't do that," Kia said. She squeezed Darren's hand. Beauregard moved to Darren's bedside and touched his other hand.

"No. No more lies. All I gotta do is look around and see what kind of man I really am. Ariel is dating some fucked-up gangster wannabe. Javon had to kill a man on his own front step. Darren laying here fighting for his life. You've had to watch it all go down. Kelvin is . . ." Beauregard's voice cracked.

"What about Kelvin?" Kia asked. Beauregard didn't answer.

"I can't keep doing this to y'all," he said. He walked over to Kia's chair and put his hands on the backrest. He watched the muscles in her back roil under her shirt. He could feel her body stiffen even though he wasn't touching her.

"Boonie's sitting on ten rolls of platinum for you. He gonna sell them and split it between you and Ariel. He gonna take over the note on the garage too. When I get settled I'll send you some more money," Beauregard said.

He moved to the door. His hand had fallen on the handle when he heard Kia's voice.

"So, you just running, is that it?"

Beauregard stopped in his tracks. The handle in his hand felt as heavy as a bag of bricks. He licked his lips. He spoke to her without turning around.

"You told me to go."

"I know what I said. You ain't gotta tell me what I said."

"What do you want from me, then? Tell me what you want, Kia."

"It ain't just about me or you, Bug," Kia said.

Beauregard laid his head against the door. Its polished wood surface was cool against his skin. He turned the handle a quarter inch. The door opened a crack.

"I know you telling yourself what you doing is for the best, but is it? Or are you just taking the easy way out?" Kia asked.

"You think this is easy for me? You think walking away from you and the boys is easy for me?" Beauregard asked.

"Look, I can't make no promises about you and me. But if you stopped doing gangsta shit I'd never keep you from the boys. You walk out that door and I won't have to. They'll hate you all on their own. I can promise you that," Kia said.

"I can live with them hating me if I know they're safe. If they around me they won't be," Beauregard said.

"You really believe that? Then do what your Daddy couldn't. Stay. Change," Kia said. Beauregard opened the door. The hallway was full of doctors and nurses hovering around all kinds of equipment. A few patients tethered to IVs were moving past the staff like forlorn zombies.

"I love you, Kia," Beauregard said. He stepped out into the hallway.

"Bug!" Kia shouted. He whirled around, afraid something had happened to Darren. Kia was standing near the bed with her arms crossed across her chest.

"If you're gonna go . . . do you have to go right now? Like, right this minute? Jean's bringing Javon up here in a little while. They let him go. I don't think they gonna charge him. He's been asking for you," she said. Beauregard stepped back into the room. Kia stared at him hard. Her eyes shined with a light born of fury and despair. He didn't know what to say. He waited for his father's voice to share some pithy words of wisdom but that wraith no longer spoke to him. He was on his own.

"You sure?" Beauregard asked.

"No. But I don't want to be here alone anymore," Kia said.

Beauregard went back to his chair. He sat down and enveloped Darren's small hand in his own. Kia sat down and did the same thing on the other side of the bed.

The dying light of day cast their shadows against the far wall. Their silhouettes overlapped, entwined like lovers. Silence filled the spaces between them. Kia lowered the railing and lay across the foot of Darren's bed. Beauregard studied the back of her head. The gentle slope of her neck.

After a while she let out a sigh.

"You're never really gonna change, are you, Bug," she said. The statement came out flat and listless. Some might say hopeless.

Beauregard closed his eyes. Faces rushed at him out of the darkness.

Red Navely and his brothers.

Ronnie and Reggie.

Lazy.

Burning Man.

Eric.

Kelvin.

A dozen other faces floated up from the river of his memories, their mouths slack, their eyes glazed over. Their last words wasted on pleas of mercy. Their last breaths becoming a death rattle in their throats. Other faces joined them, accompanied by the squeal of tires and the shriek of bullets.

Wives he had made widows. Mothers who waited in vain for their sons to come home. Sons who would never see their fathers again. All those faces, all those lives, nothing more than earth, ashes and rust now.

Finally, he whispered, "I don't know if I can."

ACKNOWLEDGMENTS

It is said that writing is a lonely endeavor. This is only partly true. I have been blessed to be surrounded by an incredible group of friends and family and fellow writers who have supported me, cajoled me and when needed given me a swift kick in the rear during this journey.

First and foremost I'd like to thank my agent, Josh Getzler, and all the great folks at HG Literary. Josh was the first person to believe in *Blacktop Wasteland,* and he has always been its fiercest champion. I'm forever grateful I stopped and talked to you in that hotel hallway in St. Petersburg.

I'd like to thank my editor, Christine Kopprasch, and everyone at Flatiron Books. You have been my own personal Virgil through this Divine Comedy. Always supportive, always insightful and always, always trying to make me a better writer.

I'd like to thank some of the people who gave me invaluable advice as *Blacktop Wasteland* moved from an idea I rambled on about to an actual book: Eryk Pruitt, Nikki Dolson, Kellye Garrett, Rob Pierce, you are all talented writers who were generous with your time and your wisdom.

Finally I'd like to thank Kim.

She knows why. She always has.